Relic

By Kathleen R. West

Copyright © 2008 by Kathleen R. West
www.kathleenRwest.com

ISBN: 978-0-9765337-3-3
Library of Congress Control Number: 2007942113

Printed in the United States of America

10 9 8 7 6 5 4 3 2 1

First Edition June, 2008

Cover Design by Brandon Roach

Published by
Bottom-Up Media • Dallas, Texas
www.bottomupmedia.com

RELIC

A Novel By

Kathleen R. West

Bottom-Up Media

Dallas, Texas, USA

Acknowledgments

Acknowledgments, like movie credits, very often are slipped past without notice, unless your name is among the ones mentioned. I sincerely hope you will take the time to read the following and get to know a little about the people nearest and dearest to me.

First, always, comes my family.

Michelle, my beautiful daughter never stopped believing and encouraging. She is gifted far beyond her own imagination, and loves traveling in Europe!

Gary, my son, was skeptical but proud of me for completing the project. He has the greatest personality of anyone I've ever known.

Julie, Christian, and Madison, Gary's wife and children, who have given me much to think about and mull over when writing, sometimes creating fodder for thought. They are beautiful.

My dog, and best buddy, Cody, who never left my side, because dogs never leave your side; and my precious rescue dog Sheba who passed away in 2006 but is always in my heart.

Anna Moore, who passed away before the book was completed, shared her love and knowledge of the saints and the True Cross. Anna and her husband Bob were volunteers at Good Samaritans way into their '70s.

John Lescroart, well known author of several novels, was always available with advice and encouragement.

Kim Frazier, true-life police officer, served beautifully as the model for the petite police officer in this book—also called Kim Frazier! Thanks, Kim!

My favorite uncle and aunt, Stan and Harriet Johnson, have encouraged me to write since I was in my teens. They were my summer family and I was their summer headache. They never lost faith in me and they are always in my heart.

No life would be complete without friends, and two of my "go-to" people throughout this endeavor have been Deanna Parker and Nan Tomlinson. I love you both and appreciate your comments, criticisms, and kudos. Not all blonds are dumb, are they Nan!

A very special thanks is extended to my good friend "Roberto" who told me to "just do it!" and wouldn't take no for an answer. Some days, his sense of humor was all that kept me going. That and black pepper!

My publisher, Steve Walker, whose patience and guidance have been priceless, and who has taught me more than I ever thought I would or could ever know.

Most importantly of all, my God.

Dedication

There are so many people who have been important to me in this lifetime, but I would like to dedicate this, my first book, to six very, very special people. First, my four brothers, three of whom passed away much too young:

Richard (Rich) Dalquist (1947-2006)
Donald Evjen (1950-2005)
Paul Evjen (1951-?)
William (Bill) Dalquist (1952-1998)

And to my daughter Michelle J. West and my son, Gary L. West, both of whom are far greater human beings than I could ever aspire to be.

Chapter 1

Life is ...

... full of surprises, some fun and others not so much. All are inevitable. Those inevitable woes encountered in life are not easily overcome by home remedies, the very least of which would be a nasty hangover.

Paul Grant came to this same conclusion the morning he awoke on the kitchen floor of his small house in Duluth, Minnesota. Even in his state of inebriation, the dream from his childhood had come back to haunt him one more time. His back was stiff, his legs cramped, his head throbbing and his tongue felt three times the size of a bale of cotton. In spite of all this suffering he was still alone. It was the dream that made him shiver with fear. He touched his right ear gingerly to make sure it was not bleeding. It wasn't.

Sarah, his wife of sixteen years, was gone. Her exact words had been, *I love you Paul, but I can't live like this anymore.* He had no idea what "this" was and what was so bad that she couldn't live with it anymore. Sarah was his soul mate, he thought. Was she with another man? Did she move back to California? In three days, he would be forty-six years old. And then another week and it would be Christmas. Forty-six, with no wife, no future, a vague past, and a psychology practice that, at this moment, made him want to vomit again. What would he do now?

He wanted to cuss, but found it unnatural—about as unnatural as the drinking and the hangover. Not a religious man, in fact an avowed agnostic, he made no pretense of being polite for ecumenical reasons. It just wasn't him.

The long trip up from the floor left him weary and shivering. Minnesota in December was critically bitter with its negative temperatures and Canadian winds. He made the obligatory excuse-call to his office on the yellow wall phone in the kitchen over the counter, and then took the long walk down the empty hallway to the bedroom. Sleeping in their bed just wouldn't work without her. For the past three days the couch had been his resting place, except for last night, of course, when he didn't get past the kitchen floor. He turned from the room and sought out the hall closet where Sarah kept the extra linens. Rummaging through the Downy scented sheets, towels, and variety of other cloth-type bundles, he found some blankets. He chose one of a forest green color. Green ... a dark color without emotion. With his selection, he stumbled to the guest room, relieved himself in the guest bath, and sought solace in the soft mattress and down pillow, a wedding present from his grandmother. He unplugged the phone beside the bed wondering why anyone would need a phone in the guest room. And then he slept.

My birthday began with the water —
Birds and the birds on the winged trees
flying my name

Dylan Thomas
Welsh Poet

Chapter 2

By Wednesday, Paul had returned to work offering no explanation for his absence other than feeling under the weather. Rob, his closest friend and associate, picked him up early in the morning and drove him over to the bar where his car still sat, frozen solid. It took a jump from Rob's car to get it running and they were both surprised that the block hadn't cracked. An ample dose of antifreeze must have been sufficient.

Paul's clients, as usual, didn't know or care about his problems and were totally absorbed in their own, some real, some imagined, all needing the undivided attention of someone who would just listen. For this they were willing to pay a considerable price. Paul often chuckled to himself about the progress of man. In this age, we had to pay for clean water when two-thirds of the earth was made up of water, we paid for air to fill up a flattening tire, and we willingly paid someone to listen when there were billions of people all around.

After work, Paul and Rob agreed to drive separately and meet at the Surly Cow, a steak house on the shores of Pike Lake, just north and west of Four Corners off Highway 53. The restaurant and bar had gotten its name from the owner who had a rather dry sense of humor, claiming no cow would go to slaughter willingly if it knew it would end up as steak-on-a-plate for carnivorous Homo Sapiens. A throw-back to the hippie era, Doobie, the owner, always dressed in flip flop shower shoes, tunic tops, and blue jeans with paintings on them. Living in two rooms in the back of the restaurant made life easier for the barefoot flower child. His long brown hair was held back with a hair net and a red ribbon. Red was for the Christmas season. Generally it was a leather strap. He shaved only because the health department required it, and he wore the small round tinted glasses made famous by the late Beatle John Lennon. Doobie believed in free love, peace, smoking dope, the spirituality of every soul, chakras, meditation, and evolution through reincarnation. He didn't, however, have any qualms about making the Surly Cow his personal Cash Cow by serving up the juiciest, most tender steaks in the state of Minnesota. He was certain the cows would return in a higher life form for having sacrificed their lives to the God of High Cholesterol, not to mention his own bank account.

Music played continually on the jukebox at the Surly Cow, mostly oldies from the sixties, featuring the Beatles, and other groups singing songs like *One Toke Over the Line* and *Don't Bogart That Joint*, songs that Doobie could sing along with since he'd memorized, or perhaps lived, each word.

Paul arrived at the restaurant first and ordered a couple of beers for himself and Rob, wondering how Doobie made a living out here in the middle of nowhere. When Rob joined him moments later, they scanned the short menu and ordered their steaks rare, with baked potato, salad, and rolls. Rob pulled two packages out of the pocket of his coat and handed them to Paul. One was a small gift-wrapped box containing an engraved money clip from Rob. The other was wrapped in brown paper with strange printing on the front. The return address was in Italy.

"That arrived for you at the office late this afternoon, so I figured it was probably a birthday present and saved it for tonight," shouted Rob over the juke box. "Hey Doob, can ya turn that thing down? We can't hear a word over here."

"Sure, man," crooned Doobie from behind the bar.

"Hurry up and open it. Curiosity is killing me." The raw pine benches and table, polished to a high sheen, added to the rustic décor of the Surly Cow. Featured above the huge stone fireplace was the stuffed head of a real cow with eyes crossed, a demonstration of Doobie's humor.

Paul looked at the strange package, just about half the size of a regular envelope but much thicker. It was wrapped in coarse, brown paper and tied with string. The writing was not familiar, but it was correctly addressed to him at the office. He had never heard of Giovanni's before, but the return was to a shop by that name in some undecipherable town in Italy. With furrowed brow he looked at Rob. "What is this?"

"I honestly don't know," Rob replied. "Like I said, it came in this afternoon, really late. You were with the Murdock woman and I didn't want to disturb you, so I just shoved it in my pocket and brought it along as I was leaving. You know anybody in Italy?"

"I don't even like pizza! Is this some kind of joke?" Paul hesitated for a moment watching Rob shrug his shoulders, and then tore open the package. Inside was another package, wrapped in more brown paper and taped shut. Inside that was a four inch piece of wood, very old wood, with a stain on one side. The texture of the wood was still visible, but by the feel Paul could tell it was nearly stone-like as if it had gone through a process of petrifaction over a very long period of time.

"What is it?" asked Rob leaning across the table for a better look. "Do you think Sarah sent it?"

"I doubt it, she just left on Friday. This is Wednesday. Hardly enough time to get to Italy, pick out a piece of old wood, and get it delivered here in time for my birthday. Besides, why would she?"

Rob picked up the paper wrapping and looked at the front again. "Do you know any Italian?"

"Besides pizza, calzone, and Mama Mia? No. Why?"

"Well, I'm no linguist, but it looks like this was maybe mailed in July. Isn't Luglio Italian for July? Took long enough to get here."

"Maybe they need to raise the price of stamps in Italy. It's sure worked wonders for mail service here, don't you think?" Paul looked at him with sardonic innocence.

"You know anyone who was in Italy in July?"

"Besides the Pope, a bunch of Catholics and a whole slew of Italians, uh ... no. Not a soul."

"You're awfully flippant about this. Aren't you even curious?" The jukebox had started blaring again, this time to Doobie's favorite song, by Jim Morrison and the Doors. "C'mon Doob, we're trying to have a serious talk over here and it's Paul's birthday. Play something nice, would ya?"

"Hey man, why didn't cha tell me it was old Paul's birthday? I woulda baked a cake or somethin' man. All I got's a few reefers and a rhubarb pie. Guess you'll have to settle for the pie. Want me to sing for ya, Paul? I don't sing so well, but after a couple of beers I start to sound pretty good. Let me know when you're ready. I'll go ahead and get started on the beers."

"Thanks just the same, Doob, but this is kind of a low key birthday, know what I mean? Save the pie, and no singing, please. I hate to be the center of attention. You know how it is? Don't you?" Paul realized one second too late he was talking to a man who loved being the center of attention at every possible opportunity.

"And back to you," he said looking at Rob, "this is just a piece of junk that someone thought would be a good joke, and they ..."

Paul's face went white, frozen in mid sentence. He glanced quickly up at Rob, and then back down at the package. A small, hand-written card had accompanied the piece, hidden in the wrapping. As Paul stared at it now, his whole body felt as if the blood was draining out of the bottoms of his feet. He felt dizzy. He was losing control. Again.

"Paul? What's wrong? You okay?" Rob stared, not knowing what had caused such a dramatic reaction in Paul. An eternity seemed to pass before Paul took the small card and handed it across the table. Rob took it without looking at it immediately, still staring at his friend's eyes which appeared to have dilated to an extraordinary dimension. Finally, he allowed himself to lower his own eyes to the card which bore several Italian words. Nothing seemed out of the ordinary to Rob, but he knew very little Italian and was certain Paul knew even less. "I still don't get it." He looked at Paul questioningly. "Is there something I'm supposed to see here?"

"Malchus," Paul whispered hoarsely. "The name Malchus is on there. Can't you see it?"

"I see it, but I still don't understand. What's Malchus got to do with you? Who's Malchus?"

"I think I am," croaked Paul, a cold sweat riming his entire body, his throat tight with fear as tangible as the semi-petrified piece of wood.

> The only aim of human existence is to kindle
> a light in the darkness of mere being.
>
> ———————
>
> Carl Gustav Jung
> Swiss psychiatrist

Chapter 3

Once again, Paul's mind wandered back to the first time he'd experienced the dream. It was that day on Nana's farm, the day he got to clean the fish. It was July then, too. But this was December, not July. Who could have sent this to him from Italy in July? Why? No one else knew about the dream, except maybe Sarah. Had he told Sarah? He couldn't remember. Instinctively his hand went to his ear. Even now when it got cold he could feel the ache in his right ear.

"Paul, are you alright?" Rob's voice sounded distant, remote. Paul could hear himself reply, though he didn't feel himself talking. He was at the far end of the tunnel again. Everything was happening without him, without his conscious participation. Willing himself back into control was impossible. Every other time he'd partially dissociated, only sleep had brought him back to himself. Although he was alert and aware, he had lost control and the best he could do was try to keep things on some kind of normal behavior level until he could get away from Rob and this restaurant. The sounds of the jukebox and the other patrons talking appeared to be miles away, echoing through a long, hollow tube. His vision narrowed and he tried to focus on one thing at a time.

"I'm fine," he heard himself say, "just kind of a shock. I can't explain it right now. Would you be upset if I went home? I don't feel so good. Just a headache, nothing to worry about."

"Not at all," said Rob, still looking worried. "You go on along and I'll take care of this. You want me to drive you? Let me just take care of the tab and I'll be right behind you."

"Uh, no, um … I just need some fresh air and I'll be all right. Eat your dinner. I'll see you to-morrow." Paul grabbed his coat and without even looking at Rob, headed for the door. His car keys were in his pants pocket, easy to retrieve, but in order to get to them, he had to transfer the piece of wood from his right hand to his left. In doing so, he realized the rough sensation of what had once been raw wood and shuddered at the last time he had seen that wood. The penetrating coldness of the air helped bring him back. He was never quite certain if his episodes of dissociation where actually attempts to split or just fugue states caused by the heat, stress, and a need for sleep. Whatever the case, they seldom lasted long and so far he had not been "away without memory" for any periods of time. He felt his left thumb and first two fingers rubbing the rough wood as his right hand reached in and retrieved his car keys. The coat he held over his arm was tossed into the back seat of his car. It took only seconds for the car to warm up and defrost. He maneuvered through the parking lot and out onto Highway 53 headed back into town. The drive was only twenty minutes and he kept the driver's side window partially down the whole time, not wanting to lose control again. The frigid air, flowing in through the car window, made his cheeks and mouth too numb to move. He didn't care as long as it kept him awake, aware.

At the house, he wasn't able to pull his car into the driveway because of the snow drifts, so he parked on the street in front of the house. Once inside, he realized it was barely eight o'clock. A walk through the park down the street would do him good. The jacket was retrieved from the back seat of his car. The walk in the fresh, bitingly cold air was invigorating. His lungs inhaled deeply, and felt the sharpness, like razor blades slicing through his lungs with each breath. The needles of icy air stung his cheeks as he walked. The snow glittered as if tiny jewels had been tossed about, giving the night a bright glow, almost like daylight. In the distance, he could hear the excited voices of young boys playing hockey. He walked in the direction of the park and trudged through the snow to sit on a bench beside the ice rink and watch. At first the boys eyed him suspiciously, but quickly ignored him and got back into the game. One boy, dressed in thin jeans and jacket with just a worn out stocking cap on his head, seemed much smaller than the others, and was getting pushed around more than was necessary. When Paul saw one of the older boys trip him and then shove him so his face smashed into the fence on the opposite side of the rink, Paul was on his feet in a matter of seconds, and running to the prone body of the boy.

"Holy cow, Corey, you killed my brother!" one boy yelled as he raced over to the boy on the ice.

"The little runt needs to stay out of my way," growled Corey. Glancing up he saw Paul speeding across the ice in their direction. "Who the ..."

"Don't even think it," snarled Paul through gritted teeth. "I'm a doctor and I saw what you did to this kid. You better pray he's okay." Kneeling beside the boy, Paul shook his hands free of his jacket pockets. It was only then that he realized he had removed the piece of wood from his pants pocket to the right hand pocket of his jacket. The roughness had felt good against his fingers, so he had been rubbing it unconsciously.

The child wasn't badly hurt. A lot of blood poured out of his forehead, but head wounds always bleed a lot. With his left arm, Paul cradled the child's upper body, and with his right hand he used snow to brush away the blood and dirt. There was no evidence of a cut anywhere, so it must have been very tiny indeed. Within minutes the child was fine and fighting mad, wanting to get up and take out his revenge on Corey. Paul advised the older brother to take the child home and make him rest.

When everyone had agreed it was time to call it a night, Paul began his short walk home again. The crunch, crunch, crunch of snow beneath his shoes with each step gave him a feeling of security. The night was wind-free and very still. The scent of freshness that goes with clean winter snow was all around. In spite of the shake-up in his marriage, Paul felt comfortable, almost happy. Get the blood pumping, he thought, and you feel better every time. Trees were bare of leaves, with the exception of a lone one here and there hanging on as if to cheat death itself. The skeletal fingers of their branches reached out to embrace, waiting for nothing, expecting nothing, receiving nothing. Bareness was all around him, while homes were lit with the brilliant hues of holiday lights. Gargantuan figures of Santa Claus, Frosty the Snowman, or even The Grinch obscenely desecrated many yards. The birth of their so-called Christ seemed to have faded like the hula hoop and pet rock, being replaced with larger-than-life storybook and movie figures. Where were all those people who claimed to be Christians?

He had gone less than two blocks when he heard someone running after him and yelling for him to stop. "Hey, mister," a boy's voice called from somewhere behind him. "Hey, wait up, mister. I gotta talk to ya!" The kid, running in heavy snow boots, caught up with Paul who was waiting to see what he wanted.

"You're the guy who fixed Billy, aren't ya," It was a statement, not a question. "I'm Bobby, his brother. What did ya do back there? Billy was hurt bad, man, and you made him better. What'd ya do?"

"I don't know," said Paul truthfully. "I'm not a medical doctor so I don't know what was wrong with your brother, but I would say he probably just got a little dazed from that last blow from your friend Corey and was already coming to his senses when I got there. I just happened to be there when he came around. Don't read more into it than it was, okay Bobby? As long as Billy's okay, everything's fine." Paul patted the young boy on his shoulder and turned to leave, believing that was the end of the story.

"There's one more thing," said Bobby softly. "Billy had a scar over his left eye from the day our dad … from when dad … from one day when he asked the old man for five dollars for school pictures. He had to have stitches, seven of 'em that left a scar. It don't look bad, but everyone teases Billy 'bout that scar 'cuz when he gets mad it turns red and it's kinda crooked. The scar's gone. You did something to my brother when you touched him. I don't know what it was, but thanks, okay?" Bobby removed the glove from his right hand, and stuck the small hand out to Paul. Paul took it in his own. They looked into each other's eyes for just

13

a few seconds, and Paul could see all the pain and maturity behind those of the young man. Then Bobby turned and walked away, slowly, but with his head held high. He could not have been more than eight years old and Paul wondered what horrors this young child had already experienced in his few years.

"Bobby," Paul shouted after the retreating figure, "My name's Dr. Paul Grant. I'm a psychologist at the Superior Clinic and I live right over here at number twenty-three-ten. If you need to talk, ever, you or Billy, come see me."

Bobby smiled. "Thanks, Doc. My last name's Landers, like the lady in the paper. Don't forget us, okay?"

"I won't," yelled Paul as he waved. He turned around and headed for home. There was a big smile on Paul's face and he didn't even know why. He felt connected to Bobby and his little brother, Billy. Maybe that was where he needed to be, helping people. He knew he had done no more than brush away the snow and blood from Billy's face, but as long as Bobby believed there was more, it was okay. Bobby needed something, someone in whom to believe. It might as well be him, a decent role model. Sounded as if their father wasn't the most reliable or safe person to be around. He wondered what their mother was like and how much abuse she had to endure. Surely the pain of seeing your children abused was difficult for a mom. Or, was she also an abuser? Paul made himself a mental note to look into the Landers family and see what the situation was.

At last, he reached his own front door and his mood plummeted once again. Home. Alone. No one here to say anything at all. It was his 46th birthday and the only one who had remembered was the friend he'd left sitting alone in a restaurant two hours ago. Stomping the snow off his feet, and removing his outer clothing, he went to the kitchen to call Rob and apologize.

"Hey," said Rob after Paul had said hello. "Where have you been? I've been trying to call. You okay?"

"Yeah. I'm fine. I went for a walk to clear my head. Saw some kids playing hockey down by the park. One of 'em got knocked over by a bigger kid, so I had to step in and referee the fight. It was really kinda cool. The kid that got knocked down was only about six or seven. He and his older brother apparently have an abusive father so it felt good to have someone appreciate me for being there."

"Sounds like you did more than break up a fight. You learned all this about the kids from standing between two boys saying 'knock it off?'"

"Not really. The older brother came after me, just to say thanks I guess, and kind of let it slip that dear old dad wasn't always so dear. Anyway, I wanted to call and say I'm sorry for running out on you like I did. How was your dinner?"

"Dinner was fine. How are you? That little gift still got you spooked?"

"Naw. It's somebody's idea of a joke and it's just a coincidence that the name Malchus was on that card. I had this weird dream when I was a kid, about a guy named Malchus." He shuddered even as he said it. Looking around the kitchen he saw signs of Sarah everywhere and this helped distract him from the birthday gift, but didn't help elevate his mood, which was slowly sinking.

"You wanna talk about it?" asked Rob with genuine concern.

Paul chuckled as if everything was right with his life. He knew where Rob was headed, but showing weakness, even to your best friend, sometimes didn't feel right for a man. "Dr. Scott, I don't need a shrink, thank you. I can psychoanalyze myself if I need a doctor. Besides, I'm free. You cost too much."

"Okay," laughed Rob. "Guess I'll go to bed and see you in the office tomorrow."

"Sure thing," said Paul. "And, thanks again for the money clip. I'm really sorry about dinner. See you tomorrow."

That night, Paul slept again in the guest room, in the bed Nana had given them, under the quilt that Nana had made. And that night, again, Paul had the dream. The same dream he'd had that July day on Nana's farm in New Jersey. When he awoke the next morning, there was blood on the pillow beneath his right ear.

In ancient shadows and twilights
Where childhood had strayed
The world's great sorrows were born
And its heroes were made
In the lost boyhood of Judas
Christ was betrayed

George William Russell
Irish Poet

Chapter 4

Bobby Landers walked back home very slowly. It didn't seem like that doctor guy was too impressed by what happened to Billy. The boys had only been to Sunday School a few times when the social worker lady took them. She was nice. His knowledge of people in the Bible was minimal, but, if he wasn't mistaken, the doctor was really that Jesus guy who healed people. The lady with the funny hair and crooked teeth, the teacher at Sunday School, said this guy, this Jesus, had died but then came back to life. She made it sound like such a big deal. He'd seen a dead person before, and she just looked like she was asleep, so why wouldn't she wake up? Billy said a cemetery was where dead people went to get better, and this guy, the doc, was headed in the same direction as the cemetery. He was going there to make people better. It had to be him.

What did he say his name was? Paul something. That's it! The Sunday School lady talked about a guy named Paul too. That could be his alias. I don't like it when that funny lady hugs me, he thought, but I gotta go to Sunday School and find out if there's two guys or just one.

His thoughts continued to carry him through one possible explanation after another. It was easier to stay out here in the cold and think about this than to go home. He should have been home an hour ago, but, it was payday, dad would be drinking. He shuffled his feet and stopped to inspect the bark on a tree. The knot in his stomach got bigger and bigger and probably looked like the knot in the big tree. It was getting pretty dark so he knew he was already in trouble. Thoughts of running away filled his young head, but he had no place to run and he couldn't leave Billy alone to take the old man's crap. He should have asked Jesus Paul more questions. JP, that's what he'd call him around the guys because going to church and stuff was for sissies, at least that's what Corey said. Maybe dad would leave and mom could marry JP and then they'd have a nice dad. JP wasn't drunk, even on payday.

Bobby stopped by the park to pick up his hockey stick and skates before he walked the last few blocks home. The night was briskly cold, but refreshing. There was enough sharpness in the air to give Bobby the strength to go home and face whatever was waiting. Winter was his favorite time of year. The clean snow, the icicles hanging down from everywhere. And then there was the ice on the rink, perfect for skating and hockey. Sometimes he played hockey so long and breathed in so much cold air, he got dizzy and had to put his head between his knees. That's what the lady from social services told him to do. Just one more slide across the rink in his boots, and then he'd go home.

Home. Not a place either Billy or Bobby looked forward to each day. Their dad had been drinking every day they could remember, except for that time when he had to leave for awhile. That was right after he hurt Billy and left the scar. It was a night just about like this one when Billy and Bobby returned to their house after a quick game of hockey. Dad was drunk and mom was cowering in a corner, sewing a button on his shirt. Whenever dad was home she tried to make herself as small as possible hoping he wouldn't notice her. She smiled briefly at her sons as they came in with their rosy cheeks and twinkling eyes. They were the only reason she stayed, and as much as she was able, she did her best to protect them. Ralph had done a little drinking when they were dating, but after they got married and he couldn't keep a decent job because of his temper, the drinking became worse and worse. She didn't mind the beatings so much because when he was beating on her he was leaving the boys alone. The second year of their marriage she had suffered two miscarriages because he beat her too hard, but that was the past. Now she had two beautiful boys who made everything worthwhile.

Slipping off their coats, the boys stood near the heater to get warm. Little Billy, her baby boy, was all excited about school pictures. The teacher had announced that afternoon that school pictures would be taken the next day so everyone should dress their best. The cost of individual pictures was $2.50 for what Billy claimed was a whole bunch. A group picture could be purchased for $1.75. Billy thought this was a pretty good deal. For less than five dollars he could have a whole bunch of pictures to share with his friends and one of him with all his classmates. Unfortunately, it was payday and Ralph was drinking again. In his excitement about the pictures, Billy ignored his father's intoxication and asked for five dollars for school pictures.

The request threw Ralph into a rage. "What makes you think you deserve five dollars, kid? You think you old man's made of money, huh? C'mere, let me show you what five dollars is worth to a snot nosed brat."

It always started out with just words, words that no child should be subjected to at such a young age. Words became actions, and soon the actions escalated to bodily injury.

Billy Wayne Landers, a tiny child not quite six years old, in kindergarten at school, felt the full force of his father's hand as he was swatted across his small face, a swat that lifted his fragile body off the floor and sent him flying, face first, into an open grate on the floor. When Billy turned and tried to get up, there was a large gaping gash over his left eye producing a lot of blood. Then he lay back down, not moving. Mary Esther's face had gone white. She didn't know if she should move to help her child or sit still and wait to see what Ralph would do. Neither choice was the right one. Billy lay on the floor, not moving, while Ralph yelled at him to get up, along with a few other choice words which sent chills down Mary Esther's spine. Gathering all the courage she could, she got down on her knees and crept across the floor to her little boy who lay motionless. Her greatest fear was that Ralph had finally killed the boy, but as she grew nearer she could see he was breathing, and a slow whimper came from his lips.

"Get off your knees woman, there ain't nothin' wrong with that boy. He's just a big sissy thinks his old man's made a' money or something. He wants to lay there and cry like a girl, let him."

"Not this time Ralph," Mary Esther heard her voice say, although she had no idea where the courage to speak had come from. "Billy's hurt. He's hurt bad and needs a doctor. He's bleedin' real bad Ralph. I won't tell 'em you hit him, I'll just say he fell. Please, let me take him to the doctor. Please Ralph, he's hurt bad."

"Shut up. You baby them boys too much. They ain't never gonna grow up to be nothin' but pansies if you keep wet nursin' em. I don't want no son of mine growin' up to be no titty baby. Now, get your ass up and get me another drink or I'll give you the same thing the boy got."

"No. I'm taking my boy to the doctor. Bobby, put your coat on, son. You can help me get him in the car." With shaking fingers Mary Esther wrapped her smallest child in a blanket and carried him to the car. Bobby, older than Billy by nearly two years, rushed to stay near her, afraid of what his dad would do next. He had never seen his mom stand up to the old man before and he was scared. But he was even more scared that Billy was going to die.

On the way to the hospital, Bobby sat in the back seat with Billy's head cradled in his lap. His mom drove the car slowly, not accustomed to spending much time driving at night on slippery streets. It seemed to take forever to get to the hospital. Mary Esther pulled the car into a vacant space near the emergency room entrance and turned it off. "I'm gonna take Billy inside and see if they can fix him up. You stay here, Bobby. I'll be right back. If you get too cold baby, wrap yourself up in that old blanket. If you can rest a bit, it's probably gonna be the only sleep you get tonight. Your dad didn't mean to hurt Billy, but you know how he is. He's mad at hisself so he's gotta lotta pain inside."

21

She wrapped Billy up again with the blanket and carried him into the hospital. Bobby waited for ten minutes or so before he started getting cold. The old blanket was thin and didn't provide much protection against the bitter Minnesota winter cold. When he could take it no more, he slipped quietly out of the car and into the hospital. Ma was sitting in the hallway, still holding Billy in her arms. She didn't even look up when he walked through the door and down the hall, taking the seat beside her.

"It's gonna get better Bobby, I promise," she said very softly. Bobby noticed for the first time that tears were slipping slowly down her thin cheeks. "I pray to God every night that He'll keep you both safe from harm and I believe He will Bobby. It just takes time for Him to get around to poor people, but He still loves you and He'll protect you. We've just gotta have faith Bob. Faith is the hardest part. My mother always used to say, Mary Esther, you were named after two women in the Bible and that makes you special. You may have to suffer a lot in this here world but in the next one, you'll be wearing jewels and crowns for your sacrifices. You just gotta keep the faith. That's true for you too Bobby, and Billy here. I didn't exactly name you after no one in the Bible, but you've suffered enough on this earth already, so when you get there, to heaven, you and me and Billy, we'll live in a mansion and wear fine clothes and be free of all pain and sorrow. That's God's promise Bob, and God don't break His promises."

"Is Pa gonna be there too?" asked Bobby without looking up at his mother again. His eyes were on the floor, the square tiles making a checkerboard pattern of cream and brown.

"I don't know honey," she sighed softly. "Sometimes I hope not, but maybe God loves him too."

"Maybe God can give Pa his own mansion so's he don't hafta live with us."

"That would be nice, wouldn't it?" She smiled down at him as though he had just said the most wonderful, thoughtful thing she had ever heard uttered. "That would be real nice. You and Billy could each have your own room with lots of toys and a color TV and a computer and the sun would shine into the windows and everything would be bright and warm and clean all the time. Ralph could live in a bar and never be allowed to leave."

Mary Esther started laughing and was joined by her son. "Yeah," he joined in, "he could have his own biffy right outside the door and it would always be cold and dark and whenever he ordered another drink the bartender would slap him across the head and tell him to shut up."

"Yeah," said Billy who had awakened in his mother's arms, "and for Christmas dinner he'd have to eat Spam sandwiches with sourkrap."

The three of them laughed out loud, "That's sauerkraut, you silly boy," Mary Esther teased. Besides, I like Spam."

"Hey, me too," added Bobby with a look of mock scorn. "You shouldn't talk bad about Spam."

"I like it too," laughed Billy, "but he don't!"

"Well then, Spam and sauerkraut he'll have for Christmas dinner when he gets to heaven," said Mary Esther, reveling in the free moments with her boys, and glad to see Billy conscious.

"With peanut butter and mustard and brown sugar and rhubarb," Billy added.

"All on one sandwich?" asked Mary Esther, pretending to be shocked by Billy's suggestion.

"Why not?" he smiled back at her, "he's gotta keep one hand free to hold his beer."

"William Landers?" The nurse in her crisp blue scrubs looked at Mary Esther and her boys. "Is this William?" she smiled at them kindly as she bent down to look at Billy's cut. "What happened here?"

"He fell and hit his head on the floor grate," Mary Esther spoke quickly, nervously. "It was an accident. You know how boys are." Even to herself, the smile on her face felt forced, unnatural.

"Well," smiled the pretty young nurse, "why don't I just take William in here and clean that off so Dr. Bailey can take a look at him. I'll bet you're his big brother, aren't you?" she said looking at Bobby. "Can you stay here and take care of your mom while we take care of Billy? I don't think it'll take too long. There's a pop machine just down the hall, and a coffee machine with hot chocolate too." She smiled, looking up at Mary Esther. "Why don't you two go down there and get something warm in your tummies?"

A look of sheer panic crossed Mary Esther's face. "Shouldn't I be with him, I mean, if the doctor has questions and all. I was there, I saw what happened. It was an accident. He just tripped and fell on the rug."

"Mrs. Landers, kids have a tendency to be less cooperative when parents are around. You know how it is, they want your attention, so they get a bit more dramatic. My own son fell off the jungle gym and had to have four stitches. His babysitter took him to the ER and he didn't shed a tear, until I walked in. Then all he could do was cry and want me to baby him. So, why don't you and your other son get something to drink and this won't take long at all. Okay?"

A look of sad resignation came across Mary Esther's face. With no money to buy soft drinks or coffee, she and Bobby sat in the hallway and waited. It seemed like hours before the doctor came out and asked her to come into a small cubicle area just off the exam room. Bobby looked up at them both expectantly, wanting to be there to help his mom and find out for sure that Billy was going to be okay. He hated his dad for putting them through this, again.

"Mrs. Landers, I'm Dr. David Bailey. Please have a seat."

The gentle tone of his voice was anything but comforting. "What's wrong? Is Billy okay? He just had a little accident, you know how boys his age are, always running and not looking where they're going. There's nothing wrong with him, is there?"

Dr. Bailey motioned her into a chair and took a seat facing her. "Mrs. Landers, Billy has quite a large file with us." He pulled a thick medical file off the table behind him and began leafing through. "Three years ago he was here with a dislocated shoulder. Six months after that, he had a cracked rib. Two years ago it was a broken arm." He closed the file and looked up at Mary Esther. "I don't need to go into detail with all his injuries," he said softly, placing the file back on the table. "You know every one of his injuries without having to look into a file. Why don't you tell me what's going on?"

"What do you mean? He had an accident." Mary Esther's hands were shaking behind the purse on her lap. She wanted to cry, wanted to tell the whole story, but she knew what the consequences would be for her and the children. It was too big a risk to take.

"Mrs. Landers," Dr. Bailey leaned forward, his knees on his elbows, hands clasped in front. "Billy didn't have an accident. He was hit. Again. The file, his X-rays, my exam, they all point to pretty regular physical abuse. Mrs. Landers, if you need help controlling your temper ..."

"No!" The word was out of her mouth before she realized she had spoken. "I would never, never touch my children. They're my life. No. You can't even think that. It was an accident, I swear!"

The doctor looked up as two women entered the cubicle behind Mary Esther. "Mrs. Landers, this is Angel of the Child Welfare department, and Officer Frazier of the Duluth Police Department. I had to call them. Whenever there is evidence of child abuse, and I sincerely believe we have conclusive evidence in this file, it is my responsibility to report it. I'm going to leave you alone to talk to these ladies for a few minutes. If you need me, I'll be right down the hall."

The doctor left the room and the two ladies who had come to take her boys from her sat down facing the distraught mother.

Never admit the pain,
Bury it deep;
Only the weak complain,
Complaint is cheap.

———————

Dame Mary Gilmore
Australian poet

Chapter 5

Bobby sat quietly on the bench in the long hallway. He could see Billy just briefly as the doctor went back behind the curtain. There was a big white thing over Billy's left eye. This made Bobby nervous. And now, two women, one was a cop, were in talking to mom. The lady that wasn't a cop looked familiar. He thought maybe she had been to the house before. When the door opened again and she came out, he was not sure what he should do, where he should look.

27

"Bobby," the welfare lady spoke very sweetly as she bent down in front of him. "Do you remember me? I'm Angel. Your brother's going to be fine. He needed a few stitches in his head and Dr. Bailey wants to keep him here until tomorrow just to make sure everything's okay." She hesitated for a moment, studying his face. "You understand that what happened at home tonight is not supposed to happen, don't you Bobby?"

"I guess." He couldn't look her in the eye because he was trying to look around her to see his mom. She seemed to sense his need to know mom was okay, so she took a seat beside him.

"Sometimes," she continued, "things happen that can hurt children. No one wants them to happen, but when they do, it's best if we can keep all the children away from danger."

"No!" he shouted, jumping up from the chair. "I'm not leaving my mom. You can't make me. She needs me or he'll kill her."

"Bobby, it's not your job to protect your mom. That's why we're here. She told us what happened at home, what's been going on for a long time. To-night she's going to the police station with Officer Frazier. There she'll fill out some papers so your dad can be removed from your home for hurting Billy. It's going to take a long time for all of that to get done, so I'd like you to come with me and I'll take you to my friend's home just for the night. I promise you, we won't let anything happen to your mom or your brother. In a day or two, all of you will be safe and free to go home."

Bobby looked up and saw his mom and the police officer approaching. Mom had red eyes from crying and streaks down her cheeks. He ran to her and grabbed her around the waist. "I'll stay with you mom, I won't let him hurt you no more. Please, just don't leave me. Please." His sobs could be heard muffled through her dress.

Mary Esther placed her arms around her son and kissed the top of his head. "It's going to be okay Bobby. It's not your job to take care of me. It's my job to take care of you and Billy. And to-night I'm going to do that. Go with Ms. Angel, honey. She'll see to it you get something warm to eat and a nice bed to sleep in. I made her promise to bring you home tomorrow. Billy will be there by then too, and we can all be together again, without your dad. We'll never have to worry again. It's over sweetheart. It's finally over."

"Mom," Bobby sobbed, "please don't make me go nowhere alone. You and Billy are all I've got. I don't wanna be alone. Can't I stay with you?"

Mary Esther looked into the eyes of the social worker, recognizing both the concern and the rules she would have to follow. Keeping Bobby with her most of the night at the police station would not be in the best interest of the child. If she made a fuss now, it could cost her, she feared, custody of her boys and that wasn't a gamble she was willing to take. As long as Ralph was gone, out of the house, unable to hurt them anymore, she could make it on her own. She'd get a job, support them somehow, and the boys could feel safe.

"Bobby, you have to understand how important this is. I promise you, you will be back at home with me and Billy as soon as it's safe."

"That's not what she said," Billy looked into his mother's face with anger. "She said I'd be back tomorrow. Now you're changing it. It ain't never gonna be safe." He turned his anger on Angel, "If I ain't brought back home tomorrow, I'm runnin' away and none of you will ever find me. Y'hear?"

Angel knelt down in front of Bobby and took hold of his hands. "Bobby, you have my word, my solemn oath. I'll personally pick you up from where you're staying tonight, and I will return you to your home where your mom and your brother will both be waiting. But I need you to go with me tonight so Billy can get some rest and your mom can do what she has to do to get your dad taken out of the house. This isn't easy for her and if she has to worry about you too, it will just make it harder and take longer. Think about your mom.

Let her do what she has to do and you will see her tomorrow."

Bobby walked slowly, head down, to his mother. Standing in front of her, hands at his sides, eyes cast at the floor, his voice trembled when he spoke. "Mom, I know Billy's always been your favorite, but I love you too and I can help you protect him. Please don't send me away. Please promise me I can come home tomorrow. I'll be good. I can get a job and help you ..." The sobs were coming hard and his thin shoulders shook. "And if Pa comes back, I'll beat him up so he can't hurt you or Billy again ..."

Mary Esther grabbed her oldest son and held him to her breast. The tightness in her throat wouldn't allow any words to come out, only tears. She kissed the top of his head and let his sobs sink into her, wanting to absorb his pain. She cringed at the thinness of her child, the bones of his ribs resting just under the skin of his frail frame. "Bob," she was finally able to whisper. "I have no favorite child, you are both my favorites. You are my favorite oldest son and Billy is my favorite youngest son. I can't love one more than the other. You're a child, Bobby, not a man who needs to protect us. That's why you have to go with Ms. Angel, so I can do what I have to do as your mom, to take care of you, both of you, so you won't ever be hurt again. I am sure tomorrow will be safe, and you can come home, but I won't let you come home until I know you're safe. If Ms. Angel says it will be tomorrow, then it will be tomorrow. Whenever it is, I will be waiting for you and so will Billy. And, if we can't go home tomorrow or the next day, we'll go somewhere else. I won't let him hurt you and Billy again. Please go now. Ms. Angel's going to take you someplace where you can get a good night's rest, have a warm breakfast, and tomorrow we start a whole new life. And no matter where you are, I have you in my heart. I love you very, very much Bobby Landers. Don't ever forget that."

Bobby clung to his mother a moment longer, then stood on his tiptoes to kiss her on the cheek once before he left with Angel. He felt as if his heart would break, but he was way too tired to care. Tomorrow, he promised himself, he would be a man. Tomorrow he would learn to fight and beat up his old man. Tomorrow.

Bobby slid across the skating rink one more time. He wished he had the time to put his skates back on, but he was going to be in trouble anyway. It was too late. Chasing after Jesus Paul had taken up a lot of time and now it was dark outside. Pa was going to be mad, but he didn't care anymore. They never should have let him back in the house after that last time. He'd tried to be such a great dad when he was having to live in his own place, but as soon as he was allowed to come back home the drinking started, and with it the bullying. Ma had promised. Ms. Angel had promised. Even Pa had promised, but it was all just words. None of them meant what they said. They thought he was just a stupid kid, but now he had a secret weapon. He had Jesus Paul who could heal people and maybe he could make Pa disappear.

When he stepped off the rink, Corey came running across the park from the opposite direction.

"Where you been Bob?" Corey gasped, "the whole town's looking for ya."

"Why? What'd I do this time?"

"Nothin. It's Billy ... your pa ..."

Bobby didn't wait to hear more. He dropped his gear and took off running, his heart racing ahead of him. As he turned the corner down his street, he stopped short, sliding on the icy sidewalk. His breath came in loud gasps, his heart pounding like a fist to get out of his small chest. The flashing lights of police cars, an ambulance, and a fire truck lit up the entire block ... and they were all parked in front of his house.

> I beseech you ...
> think it possible you may be mistaken.
>
> ───────────────────────────────
>
> Oliver Cromwell, English general and statesman

Chapter 6

The pounding of fists on the front door combined with the ringing of the doorbell brought Paul out of a fitful sleep before dawn. He lay in bed a moment or two trying to orient himself, thinking the noises had been part of his dream. Then they came again, banging, chiming, someone calling him JP and then Doc.

"This better not be some prank," he yelled as he pulled on some sweats and walked to the front door. Peeking through the hole he could see the top of a boy's head, not much more. He opened the door and saw the tortured face of Bobby Landers. Quickly he unlatched the storm door and Bobby rushed into the house.

"Bob, what's wrong," he asked, bending down to look into the child's face. Bobby plunged his head into Paul's abdomen, threw his arms around him and bawled like a baby. The small frame of the very thin boy shook with each sob. Paul had no experience with children, but he responded with instinct to the child's despair. He put his arms around the boy and let him cry it out. Whatever it was, he was shattered.

It took several minutes for Bobby to calm down and ease up on his grip. Paul led him into the kitchen, got a clean cloth and wet it with cool water to wash off Bobby's tear-smudged face. Then he got some pop out of the fridge. Before sitting down with Bob, he put on a pot of coffee for himself.

"Can you tell me what's going on?" he asked softly when the boy had taken a few drinks of the pop.

"Billy's dead. My old man killed him." The eyes remained downcast and dull, as if life had left them when Billy's soul had left his body. "I need you to bring him back. He's all I got."

Paul, not at first comprehending the full meaning of the child's words, looked at him in disbelief. "Bobby," he soothed, hoping for a more rational response, "what exactly happened? Tell me. Billy's your little brother, right? Did your dad hurt him again?"

"No!" Bobby screamed back, "you're not listening. The old man beat him up, he's dead. But you can bring him back, I know you can. You gotta do it. Please!"

"Bobby, son, I ... I don't know what you want me to say. If ..." the whole matter was too difficult. Paul couldn't find the words for this child who not only believed his brother was dead, but seemed to believe Paul could bring him back.

Bobby gasped, a deep, ragged breath, looking at Paul through puffy, red eyes. "You made him better last night. When Billy got home my old man was drunk. It was payday. He's always drunk on payday. Billy didn't know no better, so he showed the old man where you'd healed the scar. Then Pa went crazy 'cuz that scar put him in jail. The doctor who put the stitches in at the hospital reported Pa to the cops. So Pa got ticked off and said Billy had been faking it all this time, that there never was no cut and no scar and he went to jail for nothing. Billy tried to explain, but the old man just kept hitting him and hitting him and hitting him. Pa's in jail and I hope he never gets out! Never! The ambulance took Billy away and I don't even know where he is, but I bet you can find him. You gotta help us. I know who you are. I heard about you in Sunday School. You make people better and you can bring Billy back."

"Bobby, listen to me. I can't bring back someone who's really dead. Last night I just wiped away the blood. Small cuts in the head can bleed a lot, but I can't do more than…"

Bobby jumped up and knocked over the bottle of RC Cola. "You lied!" he choked. "Last night you said we could call you if we needed anything. You said we could, but you're just like all the rest! Some Jesus you are!"

With that he ran out of the house and down the street before Paul was able to get to him. Paul stood on the top step of the house's front porch and wondered why he hadn't handled that more tactfully, why he hadn't gotten an address of the Landers' home, and why Bobby called him 'Jesus.' That last thought brought back remnants of the dream.

Without stopping to put on a coat or even shoes over his socks, Paul tore down the steps and ran after Bobby, yelling his name as he did so. Bobby was faster and more agile than the 46 year old in sweats and socks, plus he had a rather good lead. Paul was finding it difficult to keep him in sight, but waited to follow him at least long enough to find out where he lived. The sound of a police siren didn't deter either of the runners until a bullhorn told Paul to halt! It was the police. He stopped and looked around, bewildered, not understanding what he might have done to incur the wrath of the peace officer. He glanced back one last time at the retreating figure of Bobby Landers before approaching the police cruiser. Once again, the bullhorn bellowed at him ...

"Stand back and put your hands behind your head." Paul did as he was told, realizing for the first time he was underdressed for the winter weather. The door to the police car opened and a petite female cop stepped out, holster unsnapped.

"What's going on here?" she demanded in the most officious voice she could muster. Her small frame, dainty face, and soft brown eyes would not strike fear in the hearts of small furry animals, much less hardened criminals.

"What do you mean?" asked Paul, trying hard to keep one eye on Bobby who had by now disappeared, and the other on the lady officer.

36 "Why are you chasing a kid down the street, half dressed, at this hour of the morning. Is that one of your victims fleeing?"

"Victims? Fleeing what?" The word "victims" kept reverberating in his head, bouncing around looking for a place to light and take hold. There was no place. Victims of what? It took him a couple of seconds to realize what she meant.

"How many more little boys you got locked up around here?" she asked, hand hovering over her gun, feet spread in a most manly staunch.

Accepting the full realization of what she was inferring, Paul nearly laughed until he considered how stupid that would be. "No ma'am," he said. "I'm a psychologist and that kid's brother was killed last night by his dad. He came to me because he thought I could help and ... it's really kind of a long story and I'm freezing."

"Got any I.D. on you?" The petite officer was trying very hard to appear tough, but it was a far stretch for such a dainty creature. Her one foot, spread wide from the other, began to slide on the icy edge of the road near her car. She jerked it back, nearly toppling over in the process, but maintaining her composure at the same time. If this had not been such a serious situation, Paul would have laughed.

He looked at her in amazement before under-standing she had already caught her own gaffe. "No," grinned Paul, looking down at his attire, "I forgot to grab my billfold, but I live just about a block and a half down there if you want to follow me home."

"What's your name, mister?" she barked at him, more like a Pekingese than a Rottweiler.

"Grant. Dr. Paul Grant. I'm a psychologist with the Superior ..."

"Get in the car." She barked the order.

Paul walked over to the vehicle, anxious to get out of the cold and get his feet off the snowy walk-way.

"Backseat," she yelled as he attempted to open the front passenger door.

Nestled into the back of the cruiser, Paul was glad for the warmth of the car's heater. "Are you taking me downtown or something?" he asked, still trying to keep the smirk off his face.

"Maybe," but she didn't put the car in gear and go anywhere. She picked up the car radio and was ready to ask someone to run a check on him when she realized she had no information to give. "What's your address?" she asked over her shoulder at Paul in the back seat, a steel screen between them.

Paul recited his address and she wrote it down on her pad. "Know your social and license numbers?" she asked, only slightly less briskly. Again Paul recited the numbers and again she wrote these down and called the information in on her radio. In a few minutes an all-clear response came through from somewhere in the air. The lady cop turned around in her seat, placing her arm on the back of it to look at Paul again. "Want to tell me what was going on back there?"

"I tried to," said Paul. "I'm no pedophile. That kid, Bobby Landers, came to me because ..."

"Did you say Landers?

"Yeah, why?"

"Is he Ralph Landers' son? The guy who beat the life out of his other kid last night?"

"Yeah, that sounds right. I don't know the old man, but Bobby told me his brother Billy had been ..."

"We're trying to figure out what happened over there. So far we're not getting much out of the old man or his old lady. How do you know Bobby?"

"I happened to be walking in the park for some fresh air last night when I saw the boys playing hockey, so I stopped and watched. Another kid pushed Billy down and ..."

"You aren't that healer guy, are you?" she started the car and pulled out onto the roadway. "I'm due for a break. Care to join me in a cup of coffee and tell me what you know?"

"Can I get dressed first?"

"How do I know you won't skip out on me?"

"Lady, this is Duluth, not exactly L.A. or New York. I live right there," he pointed to his house as she drove past. " ... okay, I live back there." He turned his head to the rear window of the cruiser, watching his house fade in the distance behind them. It seemed strange that she wouldn't let him get dressed, and he wondered who was going to pay for the coffee, but his options were few and he decided it was best to relax and cooperate with this little stick of dynamite who thought she was a cop.

The lady continued to drive through the tunnel of streets banked by gray and frozen clumps of snow and ice. Speaking into her radio, she gave some code which Paul surmised was to put herself on break, or something akin to a coffee break. Finally, they pulled into the parking lot of a Perkins Pancake House and she stepped out of the car. Paul looked for a handle on the back seat doors and found none. The lady cop hoisted her holstered uniform pants up and stretched to her awe-inspiring height of perhaps five-three or -four before opening the rear door of her car. Silently they walked into the coffee shop. Paul once again welcomed the warmth of the building after his short trek from the car to the front door still scantily clad in socks and sweat suit.

Mini-Cop lead him to a booth and when the waitress came over she ordered two coffees without asking Paul what he wanted. "Okay," she said, fiddling with the silverware while looking into his eyes. "Let's hear what you have to tell me about the Landers family."

He was not at all surprised to see the warmth in those eyes. Her muscles were taut, like she was straining to appear larger and stronger than she was. The uniform blouse was too big around the neck so it made her look even smaller, more child-like. "There's not much, really," he began, and then told her about the events of the evening before and the visit from Bobby this morning.

"So you *are* the guy everyone's been looking for all night." She said softly. The pitch of her voice had lowered considerably since the tense moments of apprehension on the street near his home. She actually had a very husky, melodious voice for someone so small. That voice and those bedroom eyes would be captivating to any red blooded male on earth.

"I don't get it. Why me?" Paul looked at her with caution in his eyes. He hadn't done anything illegal, so it must be that fantastic story Bobby made up about healing.

"The older kid, Bobby? He told us about you fixing his kid brother and the mother filled us in on what happened with the dad. 'Course, no one believed you were actually Jesus, as Bobby insisted, but we had to find you to find out what was going on. You really didn't heal that kid of anything, did you?"

"Jesus? He told you I was Jesus? Twenty minutes ago you thought I was a pedophile, now I'm the savior. By the way, what made you so sure I wasn't a father chasing after my own kid?"

"If you'd been the kid's father, when I pulled up you would have begged me to help you catch him. But you didn't. You kept watching him run, but you let him get away. Let's get back to the Landers family. Bobby said you were Jesus and you'd come back to life."

"And you thought … ?"

"To be honest with you, I don't know what to think. I do know that old man Landers beat up on those kids when he was drinking, and I was there the night the little one got the stitches that left the scar on his forehead. I haven't seen the body yet, so I don't know if there's still a scar there or not. But you can bet I'll be checking into it. In the meantime, I wouldn't tell anybody about last night if I was you."

"Why's that?"

"The headlines on today's paper will say something like ... 'Search on for Miracle Worker' — that's going to bring out every lunatic in the county, probably the state, claiming to be able to heal, and all that. I don't know if you want to be classified with them just yet. By the way, my name's Frazier. Officer Kim Frazier. Here's my card. Get back to me if you think of anything that can help us or if you hear any more from that older boy." Their coffee had arrived and Paul watched as Kim loaded hers with cream and sugar, just like a child. He preferred his black and strong, and was glad to find the coffee wasn't fresh enough to be weak and watery.

"I um ..." He looked down at his clothing, pulled at the sweatshirt. "I don't happen to have one of my cards on me at the moment. Hope you understand. What's going to happen to the old man?"

"I'd like to see him shot, but unless he comes up with bail money, if bail's even set, he'll sit in jail until trial. I don't imagine there'll be any plea bargain options, but you never know."

"What about Bobby and his mom?"

"They have an excellent social worker. In fact, I think she's with them right now, helping them make arrangements for Billy as soon as the M.E. releases the body."

"She can't be all that great if she left those kids in that home knowing the dad had a problem with alcohol and anger."

"Hey, her job's tough enough without outsiders who don't know the whole story criticizing what she's trying to do. Angel's one of the best we have."

"Angel?" Paul looked up surprised to hear the name.

"Yeah, Angel Scott. You heard of her?"

There are silent griefs which cut the heart-strings.

John Ford
English dramatist and poet

Chapter 7

When Paul was returned to his home, he was anxious to give Rob a call and tell him about the cycle of events. There was no answer at Rob's place, but Paul didn't sit around. He needed to find the Landers' residence. The phone book offered no assistance. Before leaving his home this time, he dressed in appropriate Minnesota winter attire.

The walk to the park was a short one. Rather than take out his car, he made the choice to get some exercise. None of the boys were playing hockey today, so Paul took a seat on the bench alongside the rink and waited, hoping someone would stop by. His wait wasn't a long one. Corey, the older boy who had beat up on Billy the day before, appeared from the far end of the rink, skates slung over his shoulder. Because of the evergreen and blue spruce foliage in the park, he didn't appear to notice Paul sitting on the bench.

Paul watched as the child put on his skates, laced them up tight, and slid onto the ice rink. His movements were smooth and graceful, surprisingly so for the tough guy image he presented. The smell of fresh, new snow tingled in Paul's nose and his eyes watered from the sharpness of the still, frigid air. Through that watery vision, he watched Corey glide, leap, land and spin. It finally dawned on him the child was practicing a dance routine when none of the other boys were around to see.

Paul was hesitant to make his presence known, but he desperately wanted to find the Landers' home. Taking off his gloves, he stood up and applauded Corey's performance. Screeching to a halt, Corey's skates gutted into the ice spewing a thin spray off to the side.

"What're you doing here?" he asked angrily.

"Watching you perform. You're quite good," said Paul, stepping onto the ice and walking carefully towards the lad. "Where'd you learn all those fancy moves?"

"My old lady makes me take lessons."

"You've got star quality, if you ask me," said Paul flirtatiously.

"Really? I don't like it or nothing. I just do it 'cuz my ma says if I don't she'll ... hey, ya really think I could be a star or something?"

"Well, I'm no expert, but you look like you know what you're doing."

"Thanks. Hey, aren't you that guy?"

"From yesterday? Yeah. That's why I'm here. I need to find out where they live."

"Did ya know the cops are lookin' for ya? Don't worry, I won't tell no one. If ya really wanna find them, I'll take ya there."

"That'd be great," said Paul. "I really appreciate your help."

"You won't tell no one I was ... ya know ... out there?" asked Corey sheepishly when they had left the rink and were walking away.

"Not a soul," replied Paul, smiling to himself.

The walk to the Landers' home was short, only about five blocks on the opposite side of the skating rink from where Paul had entered the park. The closer they came to the house, the more nervous Paul became. He wasn't sure what he was going to say once he arrived. He expected Angel to be there with the family, and that alone could be uncomfortable. About a half block away from the house, Corey stopped and pointed to the exact one, stating nonchalantly that he wasn't welcome there. Paul proceeded alone. He walked up to the house, and knocked on the door. Angel answered and stared at him in puzzled disbelief.

"Paul! What are you doing here?" she asked when she was finally able to speak.

"I came to talk to Bobby. It's important."

"How do you know Bobby?" She looked at him suspiciously and wasn't about to let anyone near this family without making sure it was for their good. Even though she'd known Paul for fourteen years, this family came first.

"I was in the park last night and saw the boys playing hockey, and ..."

"That was *you*?" She opened the door wider to allow him to enter. Paul glanced around the room casually as Angel looked up and down the street before closing the door again. The furniture was old, worn in many places, and stained in even more. Stale beer smells permeated the air and assaulted Paul's nose. The other smell, the smell of blood, was sickeningly pungent mixed with the sour smell of the beer, a combination no one would care to bottle and market. Not surprisingly, the room was dark, as if keeping the blinds and curtains closed could keep the world from seeing into the horrors of the household. None of the furniture was part of a matched set. Each piece stood alone in its ambiguity, never knowing exactly where it belonged or what it was supposed to represent. Together, the mish mash of colors, designs, textures, and the states-of-unseemliness were dizzying. A small woman sat hunched over in a wooden rocking chair. Paul looked at her, and then at Angel, questioningly.

"The grandmother," said Angel in a soft whisper, "paternal side. She's having a difficult time with this."

"Where are Bobby and his mother?" Paul kept his voice as low as hers.

"Asleep. After Bobby came back this morning he was very upset, so I gave him some Tylenol and asked him to lie down for awhile. Mary Esther hasn't had much sleep. I asked her to lie down with Bobby so he wouldn't be alone, and they both fell right to sleep. Please, sit down. I need to know what happened last night. Bobby told me you ..."

"I can imagine what Bobby told you, but I don't want you to believe it. It's not true." He told her his side of what had happened.

"Paul, I have known this family for several years. I was there when Billy was taken to the ER with his head split open above his left eye. I was there when the doctor released him into protective custody with about seven stitches in his head. I have seen the scars left on the child's forehead from those stitches. When I went with Mary Esther this morning to identify the body, there were no stitches on that child's face. Not one scar.

You tell me what happened because I can't understand it."

"I thought you were the Jesus freak. Why don't you tell me?"

Angel looked away in anger and frustration with a hint of embarrassment thrown in for good measure. When she spoke again, she tried to keep her voice from betraying her emotions. "I need to know what happened last night with Billy. It's really important. The press is having a field day with it and the cops are trying to find you for questioning. This is the weirdest case to hit Duluth in a long, long time."

"What about you? Do you believe I healed that child?"

"God works in mysterious ways. It doesn't sound logical, but I've seen Billy, like I said, and I know something happened. Bobby said it was you, but he could be looking for answers in the wrong places. Who knows what goes on in the mind of a child in a home like this?"

She led him to the kitchen where a pot of coffee was already made. Inviting him to sit at the table, she poured each of them a hot cup of coffee, and offered him a cinnamon roll from a box. He refused the roll, even though the smell was welcoming and warm. When Angel joined him at the table, a Formica-topped gray square with chrome legs and four mismatched chairs, she looked up at him expectantly. Paul noticed the redness about her eyes, the worry lines on her forehead. She had aged considerably and matured to become an even more beautiful woman than she had been when Rob met her. The fullness of maturity looked good on her.

"Before I tell you anything." Paul began, "I need some answers. Why did you, their case worker, allow the parents to get the kids back after what's-his-name beat Billy so badly he had to have stitches? I understand he went to jail for that. Shouldn't that tell you something?"

"Yes. It did. But there's more to the story. After that incident, the children were placed in foster care. Mary Esther was a basket case. She was allowed limited, supervised visitation, and Ralph was prohibited from seeing the kids until he met all the requirements of the court-ordered probation. That meant he had to go to AA, move out of the house, get counseling, and do all kinds of other stuff. I don't know if he did it for real or if he just did it to stay out of jail, but he followed through on every one of them. Mary Esther had to go to counseling too, and she had to attend Al-Anon meetings. After a few months, things looked good at home and the boys were anxious to be back with their own family. Ralph had his own place and was complying with the rules. Mary Esther had a job at the school so she could be home when the boys were home. Then, another couple of months and Ralph showed up begging for forgiveness and promising never to hurt any of them again. After a big pow-wow with all of us, and several days of investigating his record for the past year, we had no legal right to keep him away from his own home. So he moved back in. For about three weeks everything was fine. Then, the second payday after he returned, he came home drunk. He's been drinking ever since, but he hasn't done anything that we can stick him with. No slapping, no beating, no abuse of any kind ... until just recently. There's only so much we can do as long as he plays by the rules. I figured just his drinking again would be enough to remove him from the home, but the law disagrees with me. If he was living somewhere else and drinking, he could still have come over here and hurt the kids. But,

48

as long as he didn't get abusive, everything was fine."

Paul looked at her with sad eyes. "I understand a little. It's too bad the law isn't always on the side of the innocent victims like Bobby and Billy. It's got to be a tough job for you having to follow the legal rights of the families while trying to protect the kids. I'm sorry Angel, I didn't realize how really hard your job must be. I wish I could be of some help. Rob and I would gladly take on pro-bono cases occasionally to help your clients out."

Angel's eyes were moist. She reached over and touched Paul's hand. "I know you would, Paul, and I appreciate that so very much. You're really such a good guy. I can see why Sarah's so crazy about you." She hesitated for a moment, noticing the wince of pain that passed over Paul's face and was instantly gone again. "Do you want to tell me about last night now?"

Paul told Angel the whole story, beginning with Sarah's departure and ending with his meeting earlier in the day with Officer Frazier. For a long time Angel listened and then just looked at him, not sure how to react or what to say. At last, she asked to see the piece of wood he'd received in the mail. Paul reached into his jacket pocket and pulled it out, placing it into the palm of her delicate hand.

"It's warm," she said, not lifting her eyes. "It's almost as if it's generating its own heat. Has Rob ever told you about Father Michael, his friend in the Cities?"

"I don't think so. Why?" Somehow this conversation wasn't heading in the direction Paul had believed it would. Angel was taking this whole matter seriously, which was somewhat of a surprise to him.

"Father Mike is somewhat unorthodox in his beliefs and his teachings, but he's studied Christian history, and particularly the history of the True Cross. He might be able to tell you if this is an actual relic or just a piece of junk."

"You don't really think ..." Paul stopped, stunned at the implication of what she had just said. "Can you tell me who Malchus is?" He asked, nearly in a whisper.

"He's the servant whose ear was cut off by Peter when they came to arrest Christ. Why do you ask that?"

"Not much makes sense right now. That name was on a piece of paper that came with the wood. I'd heard the name before, but couldn't remember who it was." Paul couldn't meet her eyes, afraid she would see there was more to the story than he was revealing. He looked down at the worn yellow linoleum tile covering the floor. The incongruity of the ever-stylish Angel in this worn-out, battered and beaten old house, was startling.

Paul stood to leave, placing the relic back in his jacket pocket. "I'll come back to check on Bobby later. I don't know what I'll say to him, but ..."

"I understand," said Angel, touching his arm softly. She had risen from her place across from him at the table, and walked around to stand in front of him. "If this is real, I'm glad it was you. There's a reason, you know."

"So I've heard. I just don't know what it is." Together they walked to the front door. "Maybe Rob's friend can help me straighten it out. Any message you want me to give him?"

Angel looked into his eyes, tears brimming up in her own. After a few seconds, she turned away and looked at the grandmother grieving in the corner rocker. "No. No message." She whispered so softly Paul barely heard. "Mrs. Landers," she spoke gently to the old lady, "can I fix you a cup of tea?" She walked away from him then and approached the elderly lady, placing a comforting hand on her back.

Paul stared at her for a moment, watching her caress the shoulders of the woman, then he, too, turned and walked out the door, closing it very softly behind him.

Who can find a virtuous woman?
For her price is far above rubies.

———

Bible
Proverbs 31;10

Chapter 8

When Paul Grant had left the Landers home, Angel sat in a chair in front of the elderly woman and held her hand gently. Her own mind was racing back to a time long before she had even heard of the Landers family. To a time when all her dreams almost came true.

———

"How many cups of coffee do you plan to order?" asked Paul slyly looking at his good friend Rob. "That pretty young waitress has all but given you her phone number, so stop ordering coffee and ask for it."

"I can't just ask for it," whispered Rob, "she'll think I'm some kind of pervert or something."

"Well," laughed Sarah, Paul's wife, "you certainly look the part in your ivy league loafers, freshly pressed slacks, long-sleeve shirt, and v-neck sweater. You must be that Preppy Pervert I've heard so much about! I'd be scared of you too!"

"Okay, maybe I don't look like one, but that Ted Bundy guy wasn't exactly Dracula either.

Besides, it's her job to flirt, that's how she gets tips."

"Do they flirt with you like that, Paul?" Sarah asked nudging her husband of two years.

"Nope. I think that stamp on my forehead that says I'm married to the most beautiful girl in the world scares most of them off. Married men don't tip big unless they're looking for trouble."

"And what type of tipper are you, my darling husband?"

"Cheap. Very, very cheap. She'd be lucky to get a dime out of me."

"Good answer," she smiled up at him lovingly. "But the truth is, she knows you're cheap so she's not flirting with you. She doesn't care whether you're married or not. How about you Rob, are you a big tipper?"

"I can answer that," chimed in Paul, wrapping an arm around his wife. "He's been coming in here every day for the past two weeks, ordering only coffee and maybe, just maybe, a piece of pie, and leaves her a two dollar tip every time. Sarah thinks the girl wants you, and I say she's after your dough. I'd be real careful if I were you. Let's face it you're not all that good looking."

"That's twenty-eight dollars in two weeks. You are a big spender Rob! I think Paul and I should go on to this movie alone and you stay here and ... *Get! Her! Phone number!* I don't want you to leave here until you do. Do you understand? We'll show this miserly husband of mine who's right. That girl's so into you, Robert, don't you leave here without her number."

"But I wanted to see this movie too," Rob protested.

"Not as bad as you want ... and need ... that phone number. Sorry Rob, you're grounded. No movies for you until you get a girlfriend and this is the one, I guarantee it." Sarah winked at Rob as Paul helped her get into her coat. "Do you want me to drop any hints on my way out?"

Rob was nearly on his feet in protest. "No Sarah, please don't. I can handle this, just don't do anything to embarrass me. You guys go on to the movie and I'll get a phone number."

"*A* phone number or *her* phone number?"

"I'll get her phone number. Did either of you remember what she said her name was?"

"Rob, honey, it's on her name tag," whispered Sarah. "It's Angel. How much more perfect could it get? We're outta here. Go get 'er, Tiger!"

Paul and Sarah left the diner arm in arm after saying loud goodbyes to their friend and thanking Angel for the great service. When they had gone, Angel approached the table again and asked Rob if he'd like more coffee, even suggesting he might want to try the pie of the day, blueberry.

All Rob could do was stare at her. Whenever she was around he lost his ability to speak intelligently and this was not a time to make a fool of himself by stepping on his tongue. Taking note of his shyness, Angel placed the glass coffee pot on the table and sat down across from him.

"You come in here a lot," she said with a sweet voice and a smile. "You must like coffee a lot or need a lot of caffeine to keep you going. What kind of work do you do?"

'I'm a, uh, I'm a psychologist. I work at Superior Clinic. What do you do?"

"Well," she laughed looking around the diner, "I kind of waitress some."

"I'm sorry," Rob hung his head, embarrassed. "I knew that."

"That's okay," she smiled. "I get that a lot. So, are you going to ask for my phone number or are you going to disappoint your friends?"

"Oh! You heard that? Hey, I'm really sorry, they were just ..."

"They were just looking out for a friend, I'd say. So, here's my phone number. Try not to lose it, okay?" After sliding a small piece of paper across the table, she stood up, taking her coffee pot with her to wait on the other customer in the diner.

Rob picked it up and looked at it. Angelina Stone. Phone number 218-555-5656. Single. Half white, half black, originally from Texas. Working my way through school to be a social worker. My nights off are Sunday and Monday. Call me any time.

And he did. The very next day was Sunday. Angel had gone to early mass and at 10:30 in the morning her phone rang. It was Rob. Would she like to go for a ride on the lake? Yes. She would. She would pack a lunch basket. He would bring a bottle of wine. He also brought flowers. Yellow roses. It was years and years before she was able to ask him how he could find yellow roses on a Sunday morning in Minnesota.

From that day on, they were either together or talking on the phone every day. If either of them believed in soul mates, they knew they had found theirs in each other. Angel danced through her shifts at the coffee shop, studied hard, and completed her degree in social work. Within weeks she had a job with the county welfare department while continuing her studies towards a master's degree.

Rob was there to take her home after her shifts at the diner, coach her with her homework, and provide welcome breaks whenever they could get out for a movie or boat ride. They confided in each other and learned as much as they could about one another. He was a mulatto from Garland, Texas who sought solace from the prejudiced South in the quiet town of Duluth after completing his doctorate at the University of Minnesota. She was a mulatto from Garland, Texas who won a scholarship to the University of Minnesota and loved the cold climate and four seasons. He was the oldest of five brothers, the son of an alcoholic white man and a pious Baptist black woman. She was the oldest and only child of a beautiful white woman and handsome black man, both very successful and both devout Catholics. He didn't care if he never saw his family again. She visited her parents as much as possible on holidays and for two weeks every summer when they vacationed together in Europe. He sought to rise above the poverty of his childhood and blamed his parents for staying together while one was a drunk and the other too weak to leave. She sought to look beneath the privilege of her station and help those to whom the fancy, artificial life of wealth and status were no more than television stories. He dressed like a successful man, and now he was. She dressed simply and unpretentiously, because now she was. She, still a devout, nearly fanatic Catholic, he a back-sliding Baptist, they were the perfect complement to one another. They filled in for each other's inadequacies, they talked and shared everything, or nearly everything, and they agreed to disagree on many things. And, they fell very much in love.

It was nearly a full year before Rob felt it was time to pop the question. First he went to Paul and Sarah for advice. Having never dated seriously before meeting Angel, he had no idea how to go about proposing, buying a ring, and everything else. The three of them spent weeks planning the big night. As a trio they shopped for rings, rehearsed various scenarios on how and when to ask, and enjoyed a lot of laughs. The three best friends were about to become officially four best friends, and everyone was excited and happy. Life was perfect.

On a cool Saturday evening in September, over fifteen years ago now, Rob took Angel to dinner at the Surly Cow. He was nervous and she sensed something was terribly wrong. Her heart beat loudly in her chest believing he was about to break up with her.

"Angel," he began after they had placed their order. "I know this isn't the fanciest place in the world, but you are always saying you want common, not expensive."

Angel looked around. There was not another customer in the place, and Doobie and staff could not be seen anywhere. This was indeed a common place, but a place they both loved. "I love the Surly Cow," she said softly, "but it sure is empty tonight. I wonder ..."

Rob had gotten down on one knee next to her side of the booth and held a very small box, a ring box, in his hand. "Angelina Stone," he said, nearly choking from nervousness, "I am in love with you. Nothing in this world could make my life more complete than if you would marry me. It's what I dream of every day." He opened the small velvet box and inside sat a beautiful diamond and pearl engagement ring. Without her knowledge, Rob had taken a weekend trip to Texas to ask her parents' permission to marry her, and to consult her mother about rings. Angel had thought he was up North fishing with some guys from work. His first real lie to her. The ring was far more than he felt he could afford, but according to Margarita Stone, Angel's mother, this was the ring she had always wanted.

Angel sat in the booth at the Surly Cow staring not at the ring, but into Rob's eyes. Tears were streaming down her cheeks and her hands shook. Finally, when Rob was beginning to think he'd misunderstood her completely, she whispered "yes" so softly he could hardly hear it.

"Angel," he looked at her questioningly, "did you say something, did you say yes?"

She nodded her head, still unable to speak.

"Is that 'yes,' you said 'yes' or 'yes,' you said something?"

Again she nodded, hands over her cheeks, tears still flowing.

"Okay, Angel, I need a little more to go on here. Do you need medical attention? Are you having trouble breathing? Did you say yes you will marry me?"

This time Angel starting shaking her head no. And a frustrated Rob began to get up off he knees and close the ring box. He didn't know what to do and Sarah was nowhere around to advise. Before he could put the box back into his jacket pocket, Angel grabbed his arm, and at last, spoke.

"No, I don't need a doctor, no, I'm not having trouble breathing, yes, I love you more than anything on this earth, and yes, I will marry you. Now can I have that beautiful ring, please?" She was laughing and crying and trying to scramble out of the booth to hug him, but she was becoming tangled in her skirt and purse. Finally, in desperation, she pushed the table clear to the other side of the booth and jumped up and into his arms.

Rob hugged her and cried with her, then they both started laughing at the whole situation. "I never thought I'd have to rescue you from a killer booth to get you to marry me," he choked through the laughter.

"And I ... I never dreamed I'd get a marriage proposal under the supervision of a cross-eyed cow!" she howled, and they both looked up at the stuffed cow head above the fireplace.

The night was perfect for the two young people from Garland, Texas who believed God had planned for them to meet in Duluth, Minnesota. After a wonderful dinner at the Surly Cow, topped off with a warm rhubarb cobbler and ice cream, compliments of Doobie, the owner, they took a stroll around the lake to make plans. Angel insisted she would be a virgin when she married, and although Rob was disappointed in a physical sense, he accepted her chastity as another beautiful and wonderful part of who she was.

Later in the evening, they went by the Grant residence to show off the ring and ask Paul and Sarah to be their best man and maid of honor. A round of champagne was poured to celebrate the event, and calendars were brought out to start making plans. As soon as a tentative date had been set, the two guys headed for the television set to watch some guy show, and the girls went straight to the kitchen to talk dresses, flowers, and trousseaus.

On June 20th of the following Spring, the couple, along with Paul and Sarah, traveled to Garland, Texas for a week of festivities and a wedding.

They arrived on Saturday morning and were immediately swept up into the social calendar of the big event as planned by Angel's mother and relatives. The two couples had driven to Texas in a mini van so Paul and Sarah could drive back with all the gifts while Rob and Angel were on honeymoon. One bridal shower and one couple's shower later, not to mention the wedding gifts, the van was as full as it could possibly be. The rest would have to be shipped up North or brought back on another trip. Margarita Stone was in charge of everything except the honeymoon, and Rob would not allow anyone to know anything about that in advance, not even Angel.

As the big day neared, Rob grew more and more uncomfortable. His entire family had been invited. His greatest fear was that his four brothers, all losers, would attend, or even worse, his dad would show up and be drunk. Truth be told, Robert Scott was ashamed of his family. His mother had been invited to the bridal shower, but didn't attend. The couple's shower was limited to family and friends of the bride, and no mention of Rob's family was made. The day before the wedding was to take place, Rob made an early morning visit to his humble home.

"I was wondering if you were going to bother to come and see us," his mother scolded when he entered. "You got yourself a fancy woman and all these big wedding plans. Guess you just don't have time for us no more."

"Ma, you know that's not true." Even as he said it, Rob knew his mother was right.

"Yes it is, son, and it's okay. We didn't give you nothing fancy 'cause we didn't have nothing fancy to give. Your daddy's illness hasn't helped us ... "

"Illness my foot, Ma. When are you going to stop defending him and kick him out? He's nothing but a lousy drunk and his drinking has kept you poor all your life. He's been a no-good husband and a no-good father."

"You shut your mouth, young man. You may be educated and have lots of money, a fancy bunch of friends, and a new life way up there in the cold, but we're still your family and he's still your father. You don't speak disrespectful of that man in my presence, do you hear me? If you can't respect him as your father, at least show the respect for me because he is my husband and the only man I ever loved. The illness I was talking about wasn't the alcohol, though Lord knows that was always his biggest illness. The one I'm talking about now is the cancer. It's eatin' him alive and there ain't nothing we can do. Your daddy's dying, Robert."

Robert stood staring at his mother for some seconds before he was able to answer. Guilt and shame were savagely written across his face, marring the happy demeanor of a man about to marry. At this one single moment, he regretted everything he had said. For just a fleeting second he wanted to run into this tiny woman's arms, his mama's arms, and cry like a child.

"Ma, I'm sorry. I didn't ..."

"No, Robert, you ain't sorry. If you ever called to see how any of us was doing, you'd have known he was sick and you wouldn't have been all fired up to criticize him when you walked through that door today. The only reason you came here at all was to make sure none of us attended your fancy wedding tomorrow. Don't worry son. We won't embarrass you."

"You're right Ma. I was wrong. I didn't know daddy was sick because I've been selfish and now if you don't come to my wedding it'll be because you're ashamed of me, not the other way around. You have every reason to be ashamed of me Mama, and I am truly sorry for what I've thought, what I've said, and all the things I've never done. If you're not there it won't be my wedding, it'll be Angelina's. I want this to be *our* wedding. Please say you'll come, Mama. I need you there. We're having a rehearsal tonight at Good Shepherd Catholic Church and dinner afterwards at A Taste of Italy. Please say you'll come. You're the mother of the groom. You have to be there."

His mother's eyes were red and tired looking. "Son, why you getting married in a Catholic Church?"

"Angel's Catholic mama."

"You're not, are you son?"

"Mama, does it matter where I worship God as long as I worship?"

"It's not that Robby, but them Catholic weddings go on and on and on and I'm not sure my arthritis can take it. Now, what do you suppose I should wear to this shindig of yours? Do they know I'm black?"

Robert picked his tiny mama up and whirled her around. "They know you're black and so is Angel's daddy. You can wear anything you want and you'll still be the most beautiful woman in the room."

"What! You marrying an ugly woman?"

"Okay, you'll be the second most beautiful woman in the room!" They laughed together and Robert peeled off some bills from his wallet and insisted his mother buy herself something new to wear to his wedding. He also made her promise to call him if she needed a ride to the rehearsal, though she claimed she did not.

Mama Scott did indeed look very beautiful at the wedding. She was escorted by her other sons and their wives, all looking well-groomed and successful, a real surprise to Rob. Only Rob's father was missing and he was being attended to by a hospice care nurse while his oldest son took Angelina Stone to be his lawful wedded wife.

Angel smiled through her own tears at the memories of the beautiful wedding, how handsome Rob had been, and how delicate and sweet her mother-in-law was. A new bond had been formed between Rob and his family through his wife, a bond that would last all day, but no longer.

63

I do honour the flea of his very dog.

———————

Ben Jonson
English dramatist

Chapter 9

Shortly after Paul reached his own house again after visiting Angel and the Landers' household, he was watching TV in his sweat suit and slippers. He heard the thunk of the newspaper hitting the light post out front. Why can't that kid get it right? It's supposed to be here in the morning when I get up, and it's supposed to be on my doorstep, not next to the lamp post by the sidewalk. Without putting on his jacket, he slipped out the front door and ran to the post to get the paper. As he reached down to pick it up, a car pulled along side the curb, the driver honked. Paul looked up to see Officer Frazier smiling and waving for him to approach her car.

"Get in!" she barked with a grin when he opened the car door, the front passenger door this time.

"What'd I do now? Is it against Minnesota law to retrieve your newspaper after a certain hour?"

Kim laughed. "No, but I thought I'd take you down to the Salvation Army and get you a coat or something. You look cold."

"I have a coat," Paul retorted as he sat down. She was already pulling the car away from the curb when he reached out to close the door. "Where are we going now?"

"You'll see." She smiled with mischief in her eyes and Paul wondered if she really had a job to do or just drove around in her car all day looking for fun.

"I'm really kind of busy," he said. "I have things I need to do."

"Like what? Expecting five thousand for dinner or something? Got a few lepers coming by for a quick cleansing?"

"That's not funny!" said Paul.

"I know, but you're the one who's not taking this whole thing seriously. Do you even go to church? Do you have a pastor or priest you can talk to about this? And what are you doing home on a Thursday? Don't you ever work?"

Paul didn't answer. Sitting in the warm car, holding his newspaper in his lap, he tried to understand just exactly what was going on. There was nothing that he could see. A child making a mistake about something that he thought happened and the whole world was up in arms about it. The gift had been a joke, he was quite sure, and had no powers at all. The name Malchus was just a coincidence and had nothing whatsoever to do with his dreams from the past. Nothing was going on.

"Where are we going, by the way?" he asked Kim. "I'm not exactly dressed for anything too fancy."

"I don't think Elmer will mind much."

"Who's Elmer?"

"You'll see."

The police car swerved rapidly along various streets and through numerous intersections before coming to a halt in front of a dilapidated old house on the edge of the city. "Welcome to Elmer's house!" she smiled over at Paul. "Come on, I'll introduce you."

In spite of the freezing cold temperatures which had dipped far below the zero point, Paul exited the car and followed her around the side of the house to a large backyard surrounded by chain link fencing. Inside the yard were dozens of dogs of all sizes and breeds, romping and playing. In the center of the yard, an old man sat on a pillow placed on top of a galvanized bucket watching the many dogs, petting a few as they came near him. He was all wrapped up in coat, muffler, hat with ear flaps, and the old fashioned rubber winter boots men wore back in the first half of the twentieth century, the kind with metal fasteners down the front.

"Hey Elmer!" yelled Kim rather too loudly. "I brought you a new customer. This here's Dr. Paul Grant, a shrink from the clinic. He's wanting a good companion dog. What do you have for a lonely guy like him?"

"Heh? Who's Paula? She ain't been here." Elmer scrunched up his face, trying to decipher what Kim was saying.

"No, Elmer," Kim yelled back. "This is Paul and his last name is Grant."

Elmer got up from his stool and shuffled slowly over to the fence where Kim and Paul were standing. "What you say? His name's Paul? That's a dumb name. How about a dog, mister Paul? That there white lady over there's about as gentle as a dog can get. You don't look like you bin 'round too many animals. Let me see your hands." Paul held out his hands and let the old man feel them, flipping them over and back, over and back. "Yep, you got them sissy hands, so you need a gentle dog. That one's a good one fer ya. Name's Sheba, like the queen, but she don't put on no airs. She's just a good companion dog and a good guard dog, too, if you got prowlers. She been spayed so you don't need ta worry about neighborhood dogs sniffin' her out. You ever thought of wearing a coat? This here's Minnesota winter, y'know."

Paul looked at the white dog Elmer had pointed out. "What kind of dog is she?' he asked believing this was an intelligent question.

"Four legs and barks. What more ya need ta know? I ain't got no pedigrees here, just the homeless ones that's been abused or abandoned, or both. Sheba, she was a tough nut to crack when she first came here. Someone'd been beatin' her and then just tossed her outta the car on the highway. Lucky I was drivin' right behind when he done it, so I stopped and put her in my car and brought her home. She healed okay on the outside, but that inside takes a lot more time. Takes a lotta love and a lotta patience but they come around. They don't need none of them fancy shmancy head doctors. Just love and patience. That's it. You want her or don't ya?"

67

"How much?" asked Paul trying to figure out how he was going to pay for a dog when, once again, he was caught without his wallet.

"How much? Heck, I don't know. I don't weigh 'em or nothing, so I guess she's probably around 50, maybe 60 pounds. Why ya askin?"

"No," said Paul as loudly as he could without sounding rude, "How much do you want for her?"

"Nothing. Why you yellin? You hard a'hearin'?"

"Excuse me," Kim interrupted. "Elmer Jorgenson, this is Paul Grant. Paul, meet Elmer Jorgenson." The two men shook hands and Kim continued. "Paul, Elmer takes in strays and gives them away to good homes. If I wasn't with you he'd probably run a background check on you and make you wait three days before letting you know if you could adopt one of his dogs. But, he knows me and he knows Carson, my husband. We only bring people to him we know will take good care of a dog. If you let us down, you'll have Elmer to answer to, so don't let me down. He gives the dogs away and expects you to stop by every now and then, bring the dog by to visit. Not often, but a couple of times a year, especially on holidays. Elmer's alone, except for these dogs. His family's all gone, but he'd rather spend every holiday with this family than with anyone else. He is a little hard of hearing, but he doesn't know it or won't admit it."

"Speak up there missy, these dogs is barkin' too loud and I ain't hearin' what yer saying," said Elmer somewhat loudly.

"I was just explaining policy to Paul. He said he'll take Sheba and he'll stop by every once in a while to let her visit you."

"You gonna treat her like a lady, young man? You gonna give her a good home and make sure she got food and water and lots of love and attention? You gotta walk her every morning and every night, make sure she stays reg'ler. And, don't never give her table scraps unless it's really good home cookin' like your ma used to make. No fast food, no preservatives, and none o' that microwave crap. And no alcohol. Some people thinks its funny to see dogs drunk, but it ain't so funny when the vet tells you the dogs dying 'cuz o' bad liver. So no alcohol, y'hear? And Sheba likes to sleep on a cool floor. She's a big girl so she likes the coolness. If you got carpet in your bedroom, rip it out, it ain't no good for Sheba. She'll wanna sleep right there in the room with ya, but she won't be sleepin' on no bed. She likes that cool floor. Now you wait here a minute and I'll get her bowls and her leash and a bag of food that'll hold her over 'til you got time to get to the store. Get the same kinda food every time. Always use the brand I'm givin' ya. She likes it. Keeps her reg'ler." Elmer walked off towards the little house, talking all the way. Paul just looked at Kim who shrugged her shoulders and smiled.

"Looks like you got yourself a new roommate to fetch that paper for ya." She laughed, her brown eyes sparkling. It was obvious she was proud of herself for having thought of it. "Congratulations."

"Thanks, I think," said Paul. "Now, I'm a parent without an owner's manual. I don't know who to feel sorry for, me or Sheba."

After taking the next ten minutes letting Elmer show Paul how to handle the dog, how to pet her, where she liked to be scratched, and how much to feed her, they finally loaded Sheba into the back seat of the squad car. As they began to drive away and wave, Elmer ignored them and just looked at Sheba with tears in his eyes, waving only to her through the car window. When Elmer was no longer in sight, the big dog laid down on the back seat, her sad face between her front paws.

"What made you decide I needed a dog?" Paul asked as Kim drove back in the direction of his house. He was shivering cold and wished she would turn the heat up.

"Hey, your wife left, your neighbors think you're crazy running around in your underwear, your friends probably think you've gone off the deep end, and a ten-year-old kid thinks you're Jesus. At least a dog makes you look sort of normal, don't you think? Can't exactly introduce you to any of my friends when half the world thinks you're nuts."

"Your friends? Why would you want me to meet your friends?"

"Let's face it Paul, all this started when your wife left. What you need now is a good woman to help you forget the last one. I'll keep my eye out for one."

"I've got one," he turned around in his seat, "right back there. Her name is Sheba and it's my job to keep her reg'ler!"

70   "Sheba's a roommate, a companion, someone to talk to when you're alone and feel like no one cares. Trust me, dogs are the most loyal, loving creatures in the world. And if you train her right, she'll wake you up in time so you get to work, too."

"Rats ... I should be at work right now. Kind of a confusing day. It's Thursday, right?"

"That's what I said, Thursday. Angel called me, worried about you after you left the Landers' house, and then I find you out in the long johns ..."

"Sweats."

"Sweats, long johns, all the same to me. So, I thought I'd protect and serve, as they say, and keep an eye on you."

"Okay, you've done your job well. Now, can I just go home and play with my new dog, get some rest and go to work tomorrow so everyone gets off my back? Are you sure you're a real cop?"

"What makes you think I'm not?"

"You're just too cute and cuddly, those big, puppy-dog eyes and petite frame hardly scream 'stop or I'll shoot!'"

"Try breaking the law and you'll find out just how cute and cuddly I can be. This time of year crime's a bit slow. Drunks fall down on the ice before they can hurt anyone else, and the rest of the world stays in out of the bitter cold. Ride along next summer, you'll see some action. By the way, is your friend Robert related to Angel Scott?"

"Only by marriage. Why?"

"I don't know, just saw a reaction in Angel's face when I mentioned you and him."

"I didn't know you'd met Rob."

"I haven't exactly. I did some checking up on you after our first encounter. You're a shrink. He's a shrink. In case you're wondering, you have no criminal background."

"Kind of knew that since I've never been in trouble with the law, but thanks for putting my mind at ease. Now I can let my neighbors know you're not chasing me down with that bull-horn for any reason that could alarm them. See ya." He jumped out of the car and waited for Kim to unlock the back door to release Sheba and her supplies. There was a stranger standing on his front doorstep. A woman.

Thy touch has still its ancient power;
No word from thee can fruitless fall.

―――――――

Henry Twells
British canon and headmaster

Chapter 10

Paul approached the front porch of his home gingerly, not knowing exactly what to expect any more and hoping this was not some news reporter who'd found out who he was. The lady was fair-haired, had big blue eyes and a wonderful smile.

"Paul Grant?" She smiled at him as he moved closer.

"That's me. How can I help you?"

"May I come in and talk with you? It's about Sarah."

"Sarah! What about her? Is she okay? Where is she?"

"Please," said the stranger, "let's talk inside. We'll both be more comfortable."

Paul's hands trembled as he slid the key into his lock and fumbled to get the door open while holding onto Sheba's leash. He had put her gear on the step and would retrieve it in a few minutes. Once inside, Paul turned on some lights and invited his guest to sit down, even offering to make a pot of coffee. Meanwhile his heart was racing, pounding so hard he was sure it would break through the walls of his chest.

"First of all," said the fair-haired lady, "I want you to know that Sarah is just fine. She needs time to heal."

"From what?" asked Paul. "What is going on? She tells me she loves me but can't live like this any more, then you come in and tell me she needs time to heal. Has she had a breakdown? Was she hurt? Is there another man in her life? And you, who are you? How do you know my wife? I've never seen you before."

"I guess you could say I've known Sarah most of her life. You can call me Tina, and I'm just an old family friend who knows you're both having a hard time with things right now. There has been no other man, and she is not having a breakdown. Time to heal doesn't always mean from physical or even emotional injuries. Sometimes it involves the soul. Spiritual healing is needed. Give Sarah her time, Paul. Let God heal her soul ... and yours."

"This doesn't make any sense," He said in response. "Sarah's not a spiritual person and doesn't even believe in God. My soul, I believe is just fine. Maybe you need to be a little more specific. You're talking about my wife, my *wife*, and she's missing. If you know where she is, for gosh sakes, please tell me. I need to know where she is, how I can find her, how we can work this out. I need my wife here with me."

"Actually, Paul, your healing is about to begin too, so it's best that you not be together."

Her voice was so velvety soft, so calm and reassuring, Paul barely realized she had told him he was to begin a healing of his soul.

"Look lady, uh, Tina, I'll make us a pot of coffee and you can fill in the blanks for me, because I'm not getting whatever it is you're trying to say. Just give me a second."

Paul left the room, still shaking with disbelief and confusion, and even wondered to himself why he was so obsessed with making coffee at a time like this. He rushed to make it and get back to his guest, hoping to find out more about where Sarah was and what kind of spiritual healing she needed. He would go to her and they could work this out together. But when he returned to the living room, the stranger was nowhere in sight. He looked around the house and there was no sign of her. When he heard a soft knock on the front door, he imagined it would be her, but didn't know why. It wasn't her. The little lady cop, Frazier, was standing on his porch.

"Who was that?" she asked almost as if it was her business.

"I have no idea," Paul answered, still dazed and very much confused. "She says she's an old family friend. Says her name's Tina, but I've never seen her before."

"Must be a relative of yours. Did you notice she was wearing a pink blouse, white pants, white heels, and no coat?"

"I didn't really notice, but I'm not surprised. That's how Sarah would be dressed. She was raised mostly in California and it never left her blood. Her old man's a retired bird colonel from the Marine Corps. He just got married for the fourth time last year. I figure that's where Sarah went. California."

"Okay. That sounds logical, if her dad's there. Not to change the subject, but do you have that relic thing on you right now?"

"No, it's in my jacket pocket. Why?"

"I don't know. Just kind of wanted to see it, that's all."

"You're one weird cop, did you know that?"

"Please?"

Paul stared at Officer Frazier for a second or two before moving. There was something in her eyes, a pleading that made him want to protect her. It wasn't the kind of look Sarah would use to get her own way, this was more like a needy, little-sisterly look. Frazier was still standing in the doorway, half glancing out the picture window of the living room occasionally. Paul moved toward her, placed his hand on the upper part of her back to move her into the room so he could close the door and gain access to the coat closet behind it. He felt an overwhelming sense of tender protec-tiveness towards this fragile girl masquerading as a police officer. Reaching into the closet to get his jacket, the acrid smell of moth balls violated his nostrils and made his eyes water. He hated moth balls, but Sarah had always insisted on placing them in the closets where woolen garments were stored. The closet door was quickly shut and Paul put his hand in the pocket of the jacket, feeling to make sure the nearly-petrified wood was still there.

75

"Here it is," he said holding his hand out for her to see.

"That's it? Just a little piece of what? Wood? What's that over on that side?"

"It appears to be a stain of some kind. Do you think it's blood? Maybe we should have it tested for DNA. Hey, do you think you could get carbon dating done on this piece? "

"Now you're making fun of me." The officer looked at him with a wee bit of hurt in her eyes. Then she turned away and looked out the window once more.

"Hey, I'm sorry. I wasn't trying to be offensive or make fun of you. Actually, I was quite serious. I don't know where this came from, how old it is, why I got it. There are so many questions and no answers. Maybe carbon dating and DNA testing could fill in the blanks for me."

Kim turned to stare into his eyes with a look of deep knowledge and wisdom. "Some questions don't want to be answered easily."

"You make it sound like questions have a life of their own. This is just a piece of wood, nearly petrified, and rough, nothing special and certainly not a thing that has a choice of wanting or not wanting to be answered."

"I think you're wrong about that. This piece is very special and you got it for a reason. Look at what's happened since it fell into your hands. Some things you just don't want to question too much or you get the wrong answer. To be quite honest, it would be kind of hard to do DNA on a piece of petrified wood, I think, and my boss would certainly have a lot of questions if I requested carbon dating on it. That costs money, you know. I'm not trying to be rude and change the subject, again, but can I ask you a really stupid question?"

"Um, sure. Why not? What is it?"

"This is just a test you understand. I got this, um, sore or something on my foot and I thought we could test to see if that thing's for real."

"What? You want me to put it in your shoe?"

"I don't know. Maybe if you just gave me a hug ... no that sounds stupid, but I ... uh ..."

Officer Frazier looked back at him shyly, uncomfortably. "You know this isn't like a romantic thing or anything, don't you? I mean, it's just sort of a test to see if I get any reaction from that goofy thing in your pocket." She blushed when she realized how crassly that could have been taken.

"Hey, I understand completely. I don't find you attractive either, and besides, you're an old, married woman. In my profession I'm not allowed to hug my clients, so a freebie now and then is a welcome relief. Come here."

Kim Frazier stepped into his embrace, placed her own arms around his waist, and rested her head on his chest. It was such an inviting, comfortable hug she felt the urge to cry. No one had hugged her like this in years. Cops, after all, don't need hugs. All of the strains of her personal life melted away in his arms and she felt like a child being held in the arms of a loving father. The tears that came to her eyes were a release of so many difficult emotions. She wanted to stay in this hug forever, be protected and loved unconditionally like this forever. Somehow she knew the love and peace and warmth were not coming from the man hugging her, but from something deeper, something indefinable.

After a few seconds she felt the weight of Paul's cheek on the top of her head, and she sighed. So this is what it's like to have a brother. She thought. Someone who protects you when you're not out there protecting the whole world. For the first time in many, many years, she felt the power of undemanding love. And it frightened her at the same time as it comforted her. I don't deserve this kind of love. She thought. He's asking nothing of me and he's willing to give everything to me. Who is this man? What is this gift he's been given?

Some moments passed before Paul made the first move and, gently taking Kim by the shoulders, he held her out at arm's length. "Well," he said. "Did you feel anything?"

"Yeah," said Kim, wiping her eyes, "but certainly not what I expected."

"What exactly were you expecting?" Paul looked at her with a slightly lascivious glint in his eye.

"That's just it. I don't know. Maybe I was expecting nothing at all or maybe I expected this cut on my finger to go away. What I really felt was peace and love and security. Not sexual love, but ... I really can't explain it. I'll let you know tomorrow if it worked, though."

His gaze stayed on her for an extended second while the phone began its irritating ring. "I'll be right back," he whispered, not wanting to take his eyes off hers and wanting her to explain why tomorrow. Grabbing up the phone on the kitchen counter, he growled into it, "Yeah."

"Nice greeting," laughed Rob. Where've you been? You forget today was a work day?"

"Rob, hey, can I call you right back? This is really important."

Paul hung up the phone and hurried back into the living room just in time to see the police cruiser pulling away from the curb in front of his house. He stood at the picture window and watched the cruiser disappear down the street. The front door was still open and a chill from the outside air was causing the heater to kick in, vainly trying to heat the house. Paul stood next to the burgundy and cream drapes staring out the window for some minutes before moving over to close the front door. He went back into the kitchen to pick up the cordless phone he'd left sitting on the counter. Back in the living room he slid the heavy recliner to a position directly in front of the big window and sat down. Anything that passed this house tonight would not be missed by him. He loved to sit and watch the world go by, past this big picture window. It was like watching a movie. Slowly he dialed Rob's number. When the phone was picked up on the other end after two rings, Paul didn't bother with hello. "Rob," he said very softly, "I think I need to see your priest friend in the Cities. Can you take me to him?"

"Come into work tomorrow and we'll talk about it. You okay?"

"Yeah. I'm fine. See you tomorrow." He hung up the phone, pulled the afghan off the back of the recliner to cover himself, and settled in to watch the Minnesota winter day and night of December 18th pass by. His right hand rested in his pocket, holding on to the piece of wood. Sheba, his canine companion, settled down with a sigh on the floor next to his chair. He turned and looked at this new responsibility lying at his feet. She looked back up at him, tongue hanging out expectantly, big, brown eyes bright and loving. He dozed off for several hours and awoke to find her still at his feet, waiting.

"You really are a faithful friend, ole gal," he said patting her on the head. "How about you and I take a late night stroll around the block? I hear it keeps you reg'ler."

Sheba understood the words and was spinning in circles with excitement. Paul grabbed the leash off the inside of the back door and snapped it onto Sheba's collar. Once again he pulled on his jacket and gloves, hat and muffler, and the two companions headed out the front door for a brisk, late night walk. The air was crisp and refreshing. Sheba left her stains in the snow frequently and Paul enjoyed the crunching sound beneath his feet. His thoughts were quiet for a change. Everything, at this moment, felt pretty okay. The piece of wood he carried everywhere with him these days, was safely tucked inside his pocket. When he and Sheba turned the second corner of the block, he was surprised to see a group of boys out playing in the front yard of a house almost directly behind his own. He had never been one to socialize in the neighborhood, so he didn't know many of his neighbors. He hadn't realized young kids lived behind him. It puzzled him why they would be out so late playing in the snow. Maybe they didn't have parents who cared enough to keep them in on a school night, or any other night. These boys couldn't have been more than 11 or 12 years old.

Paul nodded at the boys as he passed, three of them standing in the snow staring at him. He was concerned about their welfare at this hour, but never contemplated the idea that they could be of danger to him. Suddenly one of them had pulled a knife and was approaching him with the blade glinting in the moonlight, held at chest level so Paul would not miss seeing it.

"How about some money, old man?" the boy snarled.

Paul stopped and looked at the child, unable to believe his ears. "You're what? 12, maybe 13, and you're trying to rob a man with a big dog?"

"There's three of us and only one of you," sneered the boy, less confident than at first.

"Yeah," said one of his buddies, "you may be older, but you sure ain't as strong or as fast. Now give us yer money!" This last was nearly shouted, like a whispered shout.

"Um, I'm afraid I'm gonna have to pass on this proposition, tempting as it sounds," said Paul making an effort to step around the boy with the knife.

"Hey, old man, I don't think ya heard us. We want your money. We're gonna take it whether you like it or not." The boy plunged forward with the knife, attempting to swipe it against Paul's chest. Paul was quick to twist out of the way, and as he did so he let go of Sheba's leash. She growled and took a threatening stance against the boy who swung again, this time trying to scare off the dog. Sheba kept up the constant growl as she leapt forward and knocked the kid off his feet. The second boy backed up, and the third ran between the houses and out of sight.

"Call your dog off, mister, or I'll stab it," demanded the boy in the snow. His voice was a whole lot less confident now.

"You hurt my dog and I'll have to hurt you. Now get off your stupid butt and get home. You look like a sissy lying there in the snow."

This was the wrong thing to say to a testosterone junkie feeling the first surges of manhood in every vein and corpuscle.

"I want your money, you sorry ..."

"Hey!" yelled Paul. "I will not tolerate that kind of talk in the presence of a lady."

"What the..."

"My dog is a female, and to me she's a lady. You back your scrawny little carcass out of here and leave us alone or I'll tear you apart piece by piece."

Paul was surprised at his own anger. He didn't like hard cussing, thought it showed a low mentality, and he was at a boiling point with this punk kid. If the kid made one more comment or move, he was afraid Sheba might have to tear him away. This kind of anger, this aching for physical release, was new to him.

The boy tried one more time, scooting in the snow to get away from Sheba and demanding money. Paul couldn't believe the stupidity and audacity of someone so young, but he took a quarter out of his pocket and flipped it at the boy. His friend started laughing, which only served to anger the boy more.

"What's so funny?" he snapped.

"Nothin', Rog."

"Rog? You're name's Rog? My name's Paul. Now, let's shake hands and forget this whole business. Shouldn't you be at home in bed on a school night?" Paul grabbed Sheba's leash and patted her head to calm her down. She had ceased the growl, but every muscle in her body was taut, ready to spring into action.

The boy refused the outstretched hand, but scrambled to get back on his feet and put the knife away. He ignored the quarter still lying in the snow near his foot. Paul dropped his hand and walked away, down the sidewalk in the same direction he had been heading when he had stopped. As he neared the next corner he looked back and saw the boys were following him. If he walked straight to his house, they would know where he lived and he feared reprisals for having embarrassed Rog. Nearing the fourth corner, he looked back again. They were still following. Paul knelt down next to Sheba and released her collar from the leash. He spoke softly to her and then stood again ... she turned and charged after the two remaining boys. Paul was surprised she'd understood, but she did exactly as he had commanded. The boys turned and tried to run from the powerful jaws of the Labrador Retriever. She was quicker and far more sure of herself than they. Paul chuckled as Sheba took a bite out of crime in the back of Rog's pants. Rog slid into the snow howling in pain. Not wanting the whole neighborhood to get in on the action, Paul ran over to the boy, pulled Sheba off his backside, and assessed the damage. There were definitely some bite marks and tears in the pants and the skin. It looked like a couple of stitches would be required. Rog was crying like the child he was, trying to cuss between sobs, threatening Paul with all kinds of legal action. The other boy approached cautiously from behind one of the bushes by the nearest house.

"Holy smoke!" he exclaimed looking down at Rog's painful posterior. "You're gonna be hurtin' tomorrow, Rog."

"I hurt now," wailed Rog, writhing in the snow. "Get that stupid dog away from me."

"Are you sure you don't want my money?" asked Paul enjoying the moment."

"Just get outta here, leave me alone."

"Can't do that," said Paul. "Officer Kim Frazier is my good friend and I believe she's going to want to have a word with you."

"I'm sorry!" seethed Rog through gritted teeth, trying to buck up to the pain. "I didn't mean nothin'. Okay? We was jist out havin' some fun. Didn't mean no harm to nobody. 'Specially me. My butt hurts, man! Your dog tried to kill me."

Paul knelt down beside the boy. "Look son," he said in a soothing voice, "I'm a doctor and if you promise you will never, ever try to rob anyone, anywhere again, I'll do something about that pain."

"I promise," said Rog. "Anything. Just make it stop hurting."

Paul reached into his pocket and felt the piece of wood with his left hand. He placed his right hand over the bites on Rog's back side and gently massaged. Within seconds the puncture wounds and bleeding were gone. Paul stood up and looked down at the boy who was staring up at him in total amazement.

"Holy ... !" said the boy's friend. "What kinda doctor are ya? Rog, your whole back end is healed, like new."

"He ain't no doctor!" snarled an embarrassed Rog trying to stand up again. "He's some pervert jist likes little boys. You sick jerk."

Paul walked up to Rog and got in his face, taking the boy's jacket front in his hands. "I just fixed your sore back end. I am no pervert. You wanna start running your mouth again we'll just let my dog put her bite back where you found it and maybe you'll remember your promise. Now get your scrawny butt home and don't you ever, *ever*, show your face in this neighborhood again. Do ... you ... understand?"

Rog nodded his head, pulled away from Paul, turned and ran across the street and behind the nearest house. His remaining friend stared at Paul for just a second longer, then turned and ran after Rog. When they had both disappeared, Paul knelt down at Sheba and patted her on the sides.

"You're a great dog, ole gal," he said. "No punk kid's going to be disrespectful in front of you. You're all lady."

Sheba lapped up the attention with her tongue all over Paul's face. For the remainder of their walk home he kept the leash in his pocket and let Sheba walk beside him unrestrained. She had proven her loyalty. When they got to the house, Paul dug out the dog treats and gave her one. They were both happy to be home.

No testimony is sufficient to
establish a miracle, unless
The testimony be of such a kind
that its falsehood would
Be more miraculous than the fact
which it endeavors to establish.

David Hume
Scottish empiricist philosopher

Chapter 11

Kim Frazier sat stiffly in the cold reception room of her doctor's clinic. Harry Feinberg had been their family physician since she was a child. She trusted him implicitly, but that didn't allay her fears. The magazines on the various tables were old and uninteresting. Only two other patients were in the room, waiting to be seen. One, an elderly man with a bulbous nose and a heavy wheezing sound emanating from his chest, stared at Kim without focusing on her. His hands shook where he held the top of a walking stick. The shiny pants he wore were much too large for his emaciated frame, and with his legs spread wide, the crotch hung down shapelessly. His canvas jacket had seen more than one rough winter and stains of nasal mucus starched the sleeves. A cap with ear flaps was still on his head, although the flaps had been pushed upward, away from his ears. Grayish colored skin sagged on his boney face, cavernous ridges under red-rimmed eyes. Eyebrows pointed in all directions in a variety of colors from white to pumice gray, and occasionally, black. Each looked to be lethally coarse.

The only other occupant of the waiting room was a middle-aged, plump woman with frizzy, permed red hair, red cheeks, red hands and a tiny red nose. She was hungrily devouring the contents of a movie gossip magazine as if the future of the world depended on who was sleeping with whom in Hollywood. Her plumpness didn't allow her to close her legs in a ladylike fashion, so she sat with them liberally separated under her long pleated, gray skirt. A wedding band dug savagely into the ring finger of her left hand where nails were bitten down to the quick. A home-crocheted scarf hung around her neck over the collar of a masculine looking thermal jacket of brightest, electric blue. The blue eyes, nestled into her chubby cheeks like robins' eggs, sparkled with good humor and joy. There, thought Kim, sits a woman with little who has everything she wants.

"Kim Frazier," the voice jolted Kim out of her reverie. "Come on back please."

Kim picked up her handbag, grabbed her coat, and walked through the door of mystery beyond the waiting room. She had dressed in loafers, warm socks, tweed slacks, T-shirt and a cashmere sweater for this visit. If it was bad news, at least she'd look good when she fell apart.

Irritatingly, the doctor's assistant insisted on the weight, height, temperature, and blood pressure routine even though Kim had been in less than a week ago. When finished, she was asked, in an excruciatingly cheerful voice, to relax, doctor would be with her shortly. It amazed Kim how they always said doctor, like speaking to a child. It wasn't 'the doctor,' it was simply 'doctor.'

Shortly, in doctor speak, is generally forty-five minutes to an hour. Today it was less than twenty minutes before Dr. Feinberg stepped through the door, closing it softly behind him. In his hand was the file he had been compiling on her for so many years. The look on his face told her what she didn't want to know.

"Kimmy," he said softly, settling in the chair next to the small built-in desk. "I don't want to frighten you dear, but something is definitely showing up on your X-rays. I'd like to schedule a lumpectomy for the —," he turned to the calendar on the wall as if he hadn't given it a thought before entering this room, "let's see, how about the 27th? That gives you a chance to enjoy Christmas and still be out of the hospital and ready to catch all the bad guys on New Year's Eve." His smile was genuine in spite of the news he had just imparted.

Kim looked back at him, her gaze steady, her resolve sure. "I want you to take another set of X-rays," she said.

"Kimmy, Kimmy, Kimmy," the doctor wheeled his chair closer and put his warm hand on her leg. "I know this is frightening, my dear, but another set of X-rays is only going to confirm what we already know. Take a couple of days to think this over, let it sink in, and then get back to me about the 27th. We don't know for certain that it's anything more than a little benign lump. Let's get it out of there so we can move on. Okay?"

"No," said Kim, more determined than ever. "I want to be checked again. I won't agree to surgery until you promise me you'll check again."

The doctor looked at her directly for a few seconds, and then sighed heavily. "I'll tell you what," he said with his most gracious, irritated smile,

"You get undressed, just to the waist. I'll do a breast exam and if I don't feel the lump, then we'll schedule more X-rays. But, if I can still feel a size-able mass with my fingers, I want you to agree to the lumpectomy. Is that fair? What I felt last week wasn't good, and these X-rays have confirmed it. There is a mass, maybe the size of a nickel, in your left breast. That's a pretty fair sized ... you're not listening to a word I'm saying. Kim, I've been your doctor since you were a child, I know what I'm doing and I really think you should trust my judgment by now." He waited a moment for her to change her mind and agree to the surgery, but that didn't happen. "Okay, young lady. Get un-dressed. I'll be right back."

Kim smiled slightly and the doctor left the room to give her time to disrobe. Nurse Nancy, or whatever her name was, came back in with a paper top for Kim to wear. When she had left, the sweater, T-shirt, and bra were removed, replaced by the cool paper gown. Kim was unsure whether to keep the opening in the front or in the back. This was, after all, a breast exam. It wouldn't do much good to have the opening in the back, so she opted for keeping it to the front and holding it together with her hands. The window in the small exam room had only Venetian blinds covering it, and these were open sufficiently to allow light into the room, so Kim began to shiver from the draft from that window. It seemed like an eternity be-fore Dr. Feinberg returned to the room. This time he was not wearing the same friendly smile. His demeanor was that of one who had been unneces-sarily inconvenienced, not to mention whose au-thority had been placed in question by the whim of a mere mortal who knew nothing of medicine.

"Okay, young lady," he began officiously, "I want you to lie down on your back and just re-lax."

Kim did as she was told. The cool, efficient hands of Dr. Feinberg massaged each side of her breast, around the circumference, up each side of the small hills, and down again. He manipulated the nipples and pressed with his fingers along the area from her breasts to her underarms. Then he started again, this time more slowly, more meticulously, a furrow of worry having creased his brow. After several more minutes, he turned away from his patient and picked up the phone. "Maxine," he said to his assistant in the outer office via the phone, "I want you to schedule another set of X-rays for Ms. Frazier. Make it for this afternoon or first thing Monday if you can."

He turned back to his patient who was now sitting up on the exam table, holding the paper garment close to her chest, and smiling. "I don't know what's happened here, Kim, but I don't find any evidence of a lump. Before you get all excited though, remember, these things can move around, hide behind things, even shrink and then grow larger. Don't go getting your hopes up just yet. Stop by the front desk and Max'll give you an appointment time for your X-rays. I'll give you a call as soon as I get the result."

With that, the doctor left the room. Kim smiled broadly, wondering why she was holding this stupid napkin of a blouse to her chest so tightly when that man had just put his hands all over her breasts and scrutinized them with his eyes. Suddenly she laughed out loud. This was what she had felt in Paul's arms. This was the warmth, the glow, the love that had encompassed her. This was what it was all about and she no longer feared the X-rays. In fact, she couldn't wait to see the doctor's face when ...

Chapter 12

Saturday morning, the drive with Rob down Interstate 35 from Duluth to the Twin Cities of Minneapolis and St. Paul was beautiful. Even at the pre-dawn hour of 4:30 AM, the clean, bright snow provided sufficient light to give the whole area a surreal effect.

Minnesota is not well known for huge metropolitan areas other than the Twin Cities, and there were none along this route. Small towns and farms dotted the landscape. There were lights in many farm homes where whole families were up early to milk cows and gather eggs. Life on the farm was often rugged and cruel, and few ever realized great financial rewards for their physical efforts. No member of a farm family was exempt from the chores that needed to be done daily, early in the morning and up until it was dark at night. America was built on the farmer and his family, and Minnesota is a prime example of what it took to build a great nation, one day at a time, rain or shine, sleet, snow, hail, and whatever else came along. Maybe one year out of three or four the grain farmers would have a good crop.

Other years there was too much rain, not enough rain, a tornado, early frost, heavy hail, or insects to wipe out an entire year's income. Low prices have caused many a farmer to lose everything after a year or two of bad crops, but still, those who remain, remain with faith. Six days a week the farmer toils, and on the seventh day he and his family attend church together. It's just the way life is.

Paul leaned back in the passenger seat of Rob's car. The old car had a heater that rattled and banged, but produced enough heat to keep their feet and legs warm. The miles slipped easily by with minimal traffic on the roads at this hour of a weekend morning. Stillness was all around, and the scenery, though somewhat monotonous, was glittering silver-white in the last vestiges of moonlight. There was no need for conversation, not yet. Each had his own thoughts to ponder and, unlike many women, men can be comfortable with each other without having to talk. Rob and Paul could spend hours together, neither one saying a word. Companionship and friendship said it all.

When they finally arrived in Minneapolis, the streets were slushy gray with snow packed along sides of streets. Paul gave directions as Rob drove through the angry-looking roadways to the alleyway diner called Al's. It was Rob's first visit to the infamous greasy spoon, and after the hearty meal he was as enamored of Al's Diner as Paul. Returning to the car with the sun peeking over the city's tall buildings, they steered through the streets once more to a seedier side of town where Rob was sure they would find Father O'Shea. They were not to be disappointed. A large tent with cords running every which-a-way to provide electricity for space heaters and a few kitchen appliances was set up to feed the homeless. Twenty wooden tables with benches filled the back three-fourths of the tent, with men, women, and even small children breakfasting on scrambled eggs, oatmeal, orange juice, and coffee. It was a meal fit for a king to those who had nothing. Paul was amazed to see the number of young families in the tent. He couldn't imagine life without a place to live, food to eat, a bed to sleep in every night. He wondered where these people and their children spent the remainder of their day.

The front quarter of the tent was filled with a steam serving table, paper plates and utensils, and a huge urn with coffee. Two women stood behind the serving table dishing out food to the breakfast guests. A third person, a young man in blue jeans, a sweatshirt, and thin boots ran back and forth between the serving area and the tables. He glanced up when Paul and Rob approached the front of the tent and was about to tell them what was on the menu when he recognized Rob.

93

"Well, I'll be a son of a gun," he said pumping Rob's hand enthusiastically. "I can't believe my Irish eyes are seeing what they're seeing. How have you been? Come by for breakfast or just to help out?"

"Father Francis Michael O'Shea! It's great to see you," Rob smiled in return. "Sorry I haven't been around for awhile, but business is good in the loony bin, too." Turning to Paul, he introduced the two men and accepted Father Mike's invitation to sit down and have a cup of coffee so they could talk as soon as Father Mike was free.

"That's your priest?" asked Paul. "I was expecting a more, um, I don't know, fatherly type person I guess. Are you sure he's a real priest? Are you sure he's Irish?"

"Trust me on this one. He may not be a conventional priest, but he is definitely a man of the cloth. Sometimes I wonder which cloth, but he's a great guy. If anyone can answer your questions, this one can. He's a genius on all kinds of historical stuff that has to do with the church."

"You said his name was Francis Michael O'Shea. So, why doesn't he look Irish? He looks more Jewish if you ask me. And why doesn't he use Francis, or Frank? Isn't that supposedly one of those solid Irish names and all?"

"I'm sure it is," said Rob, "and I asked him about that one time. He said, and I quote, 'a name like Francis is a sure way to get your butt kicked seven ways from Sunday in any school,' so he started calling himself Mike in the first grade."

"Where's his church?" asked Paul looking around again at the breakfast crowd. It was remarkably warm and cozy in the tent, and the guests who had come for breakfast seemed to feel right at home. Paul wondered if they were regular customers of the unorthodox shelter.

"You're probably lookin' at it," Rob replied, looking around the canvas enclosure filled with people eating breakfast. "Mike's not into fancy pulpits and big bucks. He wants to be down here in the streets helping people. He lives in one room over the liquor store down the street, and more often than not, you'll find homeless people seeking shelter for the night on his floor. He lets them in and never asks anything in return. He prays for them, hears their confessions, and administers the sacraments. He's a one man fight against homelessness and hunger in this part of town."

"What about those two women? Who are they?"

Rob looked at the serving table for a moment, before replying. "They're probably homeless people helping out."

"Doesn't the city kind of frown on running a homeless shelter out here like this?"

"Knowing Father Mike, he tells them he's holding revival whenever they come around. I'm sure there are those who know and turn a blind eye so they don't have to deal with the homeless problem themselves. You know how cities are. Most of them don't want to admit there is a problem, so if they can sweep it under a rug, or in this case a tent, they're just as happy to overlook any code violations or whatever."

The two men sat in silence for another minute or two, and then without saying another word, they both rose and went to the serving line to help. Rob poured coffee and dug orange juice cartons out of the plastic dairy case, while Paul dished out oatmeal and jovial greetings. Over an hour had passed before they realized all the work had been done. The cleaning was left to the guests who had enjoyed their meal and the three men were able to sit down and enjoy another cup of coffee and some rest from their labors.

"So, what brings you two to Minneapolis this fine Saturday morning?" queried Father Mike.

Rob opened the conversation. "Paul has a bit of a problem we'd like to ask you about. It's kind of a silly story when you think about it, but ..." and he continued to tell the whole story to Father Mike, ending with the question, "Is it possible this could be a real piece of the cross?"

"Sure," smiled Father Mike as he preferred to be called. "There are hundreds of pieces of the cross still unaccounted for. And just because it came to you so mysteriously doesn't mean it isn't real. Let me tell you a little bit about the cross, but before I do that, I want to fill you in on the history of crucifixions. What you have all been taught in your churches and catechism classes isn't the complete story. Crucifixion was the most cruel, barbaric form of punishment meted out for centuries before Christ was born. It was performed only on the most hardened criminals, albeit their idea of hardened criminals back then was far removed from what we see today. They considered as grave crimes things such as highway robbery, piracy, a slave publicly accusing his master, sedition, tumult, things like that. This was the Romans, of course. The Hebrews never practiced crucifixion as a form of capital punishment. They preferred stoning. Roman citizens, however, were immune from the crucifixion as punishment, so it was reserved for non-Romans and meted out by Romans. Are you with me so far?"

Paul and Rob both nodded, ready to hear more.

"Crucifixion was always preceded by scourging, sort of a cleansing by whip. And when you see pictures of Christ carrying his cross, those pictures may be incorrect. I say 'may be' because I really wasn't there. Generally, the transverse beam was the only portion the criminal was required to carry to his execution. The vertical portion was already there. When the entourage arrived at the execution site, the condemned was first tied to his cross with cords, and then four nails were hammered into his hands and feet to secure him. He was, of course, entirely naked. The executioners would place a placard called a titulus above the dying man's head giving his name and the charge against him. As in the case of Jesus, it supposedly read, 'Jesus of Nazareth, King of the Jews.' Frequently the condemned didn't die for three or four days. The body was left to the vultures, rodents enticed by the smell of blood, and other rapacious birds. In very special cases, family members were allowed to remove the bodies and give them a proper burial. The Jews didn't want their condemned spending days on the cross dying of starvation and dehydration, so they insisted that the men's legs be broken. That way they couldn't lift themselves up to get air into their lungs and would suffocate faster. This was a rare exception in most Roman executions, but the Jews insisted on it. In the case of our Lord, His legs were not broken because He had already died before they got around to it, thus fulfilling Old Testament prophecy that not a bone in His body should be broken. His scourging was a bit worse than most, as was His trial and everything else, so His body was too weakened to withstand the cross for very long. So, prophecy was fulfilled and He died without broken bones. And, of course, we know His family was allowed to remove His body for proper burial although I think people would have been more inclined to believe the resurrection story if He'd jumped down from the cross fully healed after three days. But, if you notice, God very often works His miracles so that they leave room for argument. That's why it takes years for the Catholic Church to check one out. Trust and faith are better to rely on if you believe in miracles, and I for one am all in favor of believing in them. Did you know doctors are even starting to believe in miracles? Yeah, they found out they weren't gods after all and are actually promoting the power of prayer. Pretty cool stuff, huh! Let's get back to the cross.

"Now, here's some interesting stuff. The cross and crucifixions did not originate with the Romans. In fact, the use of crosses probably goes back to the time of Cicero, the politician, orator, lawyer, philosopher, and all-around everyday pain in the butt, know-it-all-genius who lived from 106 to 43 B.C. Then he was murdered. Go figure! During Cicero's time it was called the 'arbor infelix,' or 'unhappy tree.' I would have to say that was a bit of an understatement. Can you imagine how different Christianity would be today if they still called it the unhappy tree? I can just about imagine that would have been the end of Christianity for all time. There would have been his little band of religious zealots going around talking about the man who died on the unhappy tree. And we'd have hymns like *The Old Rugged Unhappy Tree*. That just doesn't do it for me. What about you?"

Again, Rob and Paul shook their heads in agreement and waited for Father Mike to go on. Both were completely absorbed in his tales and opinions.

"Good. Anyway, back to history. The cross originally consisted of a single pole, sharpened at the top. The transverse bar was added in later years so the person to be executed could be tied or nailed, or both, to the cross until he died.

"Okay, now to the matter of relics. I see you're both still with me, so let's move along, shall we?" Another nod in unison from his audience. "Good. First of all, we know the cross that Christ died on was made of pine. I've heard other stories that it was made up of five different woods, but I doubt seriously that the Romans put that much craftsmanship into an instrument of execution. Two thieves, as you know, were crucified at the same time, and their crosses were most likely made of the same material, pine. A large part of the cross of the good thief, Dismas, is still preserved in Rome on the altar of the Chapel of the Relics at Santa Croce in Gerusalemme.

"The crosses were buried when Jerusalem was ruined in the Roman wars. After peace was restored under Constantine, a Bishop in Jerusalem by the name of Macarius ordered excavations to find the place where our Lord was crucified and buried. This was way later, like in 327 A.D. During these excavations, the cross was found and verified as the true cross by the titulus.

"This is all very interesting," said Paul, "but what does it have to do with me?"

"Not much, I just enjoy hearing myself talk. Don't exactly get to do a lot of intellectualizing around here. Anyway, now where was I? Oh yeah, we were about to get to Saint Helena, I know you've heard of her, right?"

Rob and Paul looked at one another, each hoping the other had a clue what Father Mike was talking about. Neither had.

"Excellent," smiled the young Father. "I can tell you what I think and you'll never know the difference. As you well know, I hope, there are lots and lots of saints to which Catholics pray and look to for guidance. Some have spent their entire lives dedicated to serving God in special ways. Most of these were accompanied by pious biographers following them around and writing down everything they said and did. No random acts of kindness ... everything was well scripted and documented. If not, who'd remember them before TV and radio? So we depend on the biographies to be factual. Then, there are those who have attained sainthood by one single act. It's in this category that we find the Dowager Empress, Saint Helena."

"Wait a second," said Rob. "I thought a dowager was an old lady who got rich when her old man died. What would she have to do with the cross?"

"Good question. And you're almost right about the dowager part. Helena was married to Constantius and he left her for a woman of royal blood, probably younger and better looking. Actually, when he became a Caesar and was given the Britain and Gaul territories, he was forced to get rid of his wife and marry Theodora, the step-daughter of Maximian.

"Max," the priest continued, "was actually Marcus Aurelius Valerius Maximianus Herculius, Roman Emperor from 286 to 305 A.D. He gave Constantius the Caesar position way up north there in Gaul and Britain, and for political reasons insisted he get rid of his wife and marry a local chick to impress the natives. Rumor has it he too was a Christian, but he pretended to be pagan to move up in the business. He left Helena rather well off though, it appears. She had one son, Constantine the Great. You've probably heard of *him*. She became a very devout Christian after her divorce, probably in Trier, which is in southwestern Germany, where she decided to settle. Supposedly, she lived her life being a very kind, very gentle, rich old lady. Nothing spectacular, but she did believe and trust in God for everything. This in itself was pretty amazing since it was still a bit dangerous to be a Christian in those days. She never did anything of import until God gave her the instructions about finding the true cross. She claims it was divine intervention, and most tend to believe her because she wasn't exactly an archeologist or anything and there really was no plan as to where to excavate. She was guided, she claims, by God."

"So, she found the cross?" asked Paul, totally enraptured by the story.

"Well, she may have, she and Bishop Macarius and the crew. Of course we can't be certain. There were rumors that she found some old pieces of wood and the titulus was added later to make it look authentic. But, according to legend, she was eighty years old when Constantine, her only son, decided to have the site excavated where the crucifixion had supposedly taken place. Even though she was old, she was determined to be there and was on hand when the three crosses were unearthed."

"What happened to the cross after that?" asked Paul. "Did she break it up and hand it out or what? I mean, this piece, if it's real, is just about four inches long and really just a splinter."

"Do you have it with you? I'd really like to see it."

Paul dug the piece of wood out of the pocket of his jeans and handed it to Father Mike. The priest turned it over in his hands several times, looking at it very closely.

"And you say some strange things have happened only when you had this with you, is that right?"

"That's it. A little boy who was hit with a hockey stick was healed instantly. That, I figured, was just a fluke. Y'know, he stopped bleeding and there was no sign of injury. But later his older brother came back and told me that a scar the kid had on his forehead was gone too. Apparently the scar was from an abusive father. And was probably a year to a year and a half old. The older brother thinks I'm Jesus come back to earth. Then, two nights ago a kid got a bite in his posterior by my dog, broken skin, blood, the whole nine yards. I placed my hand over his gluteus and rubbed just a little. Completely healed. I was sure the kid was going to need at least three or four stitches."

Father Mike looked at Paul reflectively. "I'm not sure I want to hear why your dog was biting this boy's posterior. I don't want you to tell me you're having your dog attack people so you can heal them with this thing. What's your spiritual background, Paul? Are you anything like the other Paul?"

"And who would that be?"

"I, uh ... I guess not. Have you any experience with the church at all?"

"To be honest, Father ... do I have to call you Father, it feels so weird when you're so much younger than I?"

Father Mike laughed. "You can call me anything you like, within reason. Mike is fine if you're more comfortable with that. That Father part is a title, like doctor to you, and if you don't insist I call you Doctor, I won't insist you call me Father. Is that fair?"

"That's very fair," agreed Paul with a little chuckle. "To be completely honest, Mike, my only experience with church was the summers I spent with my grandparents when I was real young. My grandma was Southern Baptist ... to the core. They lived in New Jersey, but Nana had been born and raised in the South, and you can't take the South out of a Baptist, no matter how hard you try. Anyway, she made me go to church and Sunday School at her church all summer. They had this awful preacher who scared the living daylights out of me, so I never got into the religion stuff much. My own folks never went to church and my wife — actually, estranged wife — claims to be agnostic. The only time I was ever in a Catholic church was when Rob here got married. To be quite honest with you, none of it's impressed me a whole lot."

"So you never got into it on a personal level, you know, one on one with God. Am I right?" asked Mike, getting very serious. "There's a great deal of difference between going to church and being the church. If this piece really is a relic of the true cross, and I'm not saying it is or it isn't, but if it is, then God has a message for you and has chosen you for some reason."

Paul glanced around the tent again, a look of puzzlement on his face. "Why me? Why not someone like you who knows what he's talking about?"

"That's a good question and I don't really have the answer. God only knows. I wonder sometimes if Jesus might have asked the same question ... why me? After all, He wasn't born a king and warrior like the Jews expected their Messiah to be. He was born in an abandoned cave that had been used to protect animals in harsh weather. His mom was no more than a mere child herself, and his earthly dad was a carpenter, not a king. He was born into a common family, a common child. Actually, he was less than common because there was some question of his parentage. Mary, as you know, was pregnant before she and Joseph married. Jesus was considered illegitimate. So, I'm sure He wondered many times, why me? What have I got to offer that's worth anything?"

"Yeah, but He was the son of God and all that," Paul argued. "He knew what His mission was."

"Did He? Did He know from birth why He was here? You're a son of God too, but you don't know what your mission is with regard to God's message for your life. Jesus was fortunate in that He was brought up in a family devout in their faith. I'd say He found His calling through His prayer life. If you read your Bible, you'll find out He spent a lot of time in prayer. Listening for God's voice to tell us where we need to be and what we should be doing is what prayer is all about. It's not always doing all the talking. Did your mom ever say, Paul, shut up and just listen?"

"You've met my mom?" Paul laughed. "You sound exactly like her when you say that."

Mike laughed too. "I don't know that I've met your mom, but mine sounds the same way. It's a mom thing they learn in mom school. But, God does the same thing, sometimes in more subtle ways. Then again, sometimes He's not so subtle. If this is a true relic and the things that have been happening are truly from God, then I'd say He's pretty much beaten you upside the head to get your attention. You might want to spend a little time just listening. But ... now it's time to start fixing lunch."

"We just got through with breakfast," protested Rob.

"Yeah, so? You're thinking maybe lunch fixes itself? These folks will be wandering back in here about ..."

"Hey, Father." A soft, shaky, desperate sounding voice came from behind where Rob and Paul were sitting. "It's bad, father. I can't make it!" Tears were welling up in the man's bloodshot eyes. His hands trembled visibly inside his coat pockets. Nearly collapsing onto the bench where they were sitting, he grabbed onto the table to support himself. A scraggly bearded face with patches of gray skin barely supported the haunted, frightened eyes.

Mike stood up and went to the man who was obviously going through withdrawal here on the streets, without the benefit of medical aid or even a decent place to lie down and rest.

"You can do this, Mick. You've gotta have faith, man. When you're jones'n just grab onto me and hold on. I'm here Mick. I'm always here." Turning to Rob he asked, "Can you get some O.J. out of the fridge back there, Rob? Mick here just needs a little sugar and some Vitamin C." Then, turning back to the man in his arms, "Mick, did I ever tell you about the time my old man took me to a whore house? I'd decided real young that I wanted to be a priest, so I didn't date any of the girls in my high school. Well, the old man thought I was gay, so he takes me ..."

Mike's voice trailed off as he half led, half carried Mick to a cot behind the stove, in a small room protected by canvas tent hangings. His voice could be heard in murmurs from where Paul and Rob sat. After giving the orange juice to Mike, Rob had rejoined Paul on the bench by the table. Neither one of them knew what to say. This was a new world, a world into which they had never ventured before, and it was a very rude awakening.

"Maybe we should go," whispered Rob. "I feel like a peeping tom just sitting here and watching, waiting."

"I'm staying." Paul replied. "You go ahead. I think I need to stay."

"What're you saying?"

Paul looked down at the piece of wood in his hand. It felt rough, and yet reassuring. After hearing the stories Mike had told, he wanted more. After a second's pause, he looked up at Rob. "I'm saying I need to stay."

"For how long? All day?"

"A few days."

"What?"

"I just need to do this Rob. I don't know why, but I really need to know more and I need to do more. We work with some weird ones, but nothing like this. Our clients generally are just people looking for someone to listen. These people have some serious problems and maybe I can do something. Go on back. I'll be fine. I'll call ya, okay?"

The worried expression that flickered briefly through Rob's eyes did not go unnoticed by Paul. Rob tried to think of an argument that would convince Paul to return home with him. "Paul, are you sure this is something you should do? Mike's done this for years. These people know him, trust him. You're a stranger in an expensive coat, shoes, nice shirt, sharp hair cut. They're not going to trust you."

"Flattery will get you nowhere, doc. You really like the hair cut?" Paul smirked as he patted his neatly combed hair. "Look Rob, I understand your concern, but it's time for me to take a risk ... show someone here I can be trusted. But they won't trust me if my own friends don't. Give me a chance Rob. This is something I've got to do. And, maybe it's me that needs to learn to trust them."

"You got any cash on you?"

"Yes, mother. I'm fine. I have my milk money in my pocket."

"I was going to say, if you do, put it in your shoe or you won't have it long. These people are sad, yes, but some of them haven't seen a dollar in a long time. And, like that Mick guy, they may be in need of a fix real quick. Don't play stupid here, Paul. It could be very dangerous."

Chuckling at this, Paul put out his hand and placed it on Rob's shoulder. "Thanks. I appreciate that, I really do. I'll stick close to Mike and he'll tell me what to do."

"What if he doesn't want you to stay?"

"He will."

"How can you be so sure?"

"He needs help here. You know that. Do you really think he'd turn away another hand? Besides, you heard him, he loves to hear himself talk. I'm a captive audience."

"You're right. Want me to stay with you?"

"No. This is something I have to do. If you find it's something you have to do, that's all up to you, but I need to do this for my own reasons. I don't want you to stay because of me."

"And your job?"

"Tell them I'm sick. Or better yet, I'll call in Monday and tell them myself. What're they going to do? Fire me? I'm part owner of the clinic and I've never really taken any personal time off. So, this is it. Just tell them I'm taking some personal days and I'll be back in a few."

"Our own clients need both of us, not one of us there and one of us working in a homeless camp."

"I'm just going to stay a few days, not a lifetime. Just give me 'til Wednesday, okay? I'll be back in the office Thursday morning. I promise. You can handle it 'til then. Get a couple of those cute interns to do the testing and scoring and all you have to do is sign off. If it comes to needing therapy, let them handle that, too. It's all so easy. You just work too hard at it."

"I like what I do and I'm darn good at it," returned Rob defensively.

"Don't get your feathers ruffled, Robbie, old boy. I'm not suggesting you're not good. I'm just saying make it easy on yourself. Act like the boss, like the guy in charge."

"How're you planning on getting back?"

"I heard the bus runs from here to there. Or, if I have to, I can rent a car."

Looking around in all directions, Rob nodded, "Uh, I hate to disillusion you buddy, but I don't see any Enterprise Rent-A-Car places anywhere in this neighborhood. Maybe you can roll a kid and take his bike."

Paul chuckled. "Get out of here before I start insulting your heritage."

He walked to the door of the tent and watched as Rob walked back to his car. He wasn't sure he was doing the right thing, but he was very sure it wasn't wrong. Looking around him, he wondered what he was going to do for the next four days, where he'd sleep. He hadn't given any thought to these matters before telling Rob to hit the road and leave him here. He reached around and made sure his wallet was in his back pocket. It was. Then he remembered what Rob had said and took the wallet out, extracted his cash and important cards — credit, license, social security — and put the wallet back into his hip pocket. He slid the cash and cards into the very tight front pocket of his jeans making sure they were secure and couldn't be lifted without taking his pants off him. All of this activity brought about a small chuckle. *These people are homeless, without food, without a place to sleep, and I'm worried about thirty-five dollars and some plastic. What a loser.*

It was about half an hour or so after Rob had left when Mike returned to the dining area of the tent to find Paul sipping on a cup of coffee.

"Where's Rob?" Mike asked, looking around.

"He went back," Paul said without looking at the priest. He didn't want to see the expression that might be unwelcoming.

"And you?"

"I'm going to stay a few days."

"Good. Let's get lunch started. I thought we'd heat up some stew and corn bread. There's a bakery downtown that delivers day old bread every day, and they brought a whole batch of good looking cornbread this morning. Just before you guys got here as a matter of fact. The cans of stew are over there in that storage area. Here's the key to the padlock. If you can get about ten of those big cans out and dump them in the pots on the stove, I'll start unwrapping the cornbread and putting it in bags to warm in the oven. Ida and Irish should be by any minute to help out. They're the lunch crew. They're identical twins, so try not to get them mixed up. They get offended real easy. It's hard for these people to have much to be defensive about, so they protect their names. In some cases, that's all they've got. Ida is the one with the blue dress and Irish, of course, wears green."

"They always wear blue and green?" asked Paul innocently.

"What? You think they've got a wardrobe full of clothes in a penthouse somewhere? These people are homeless, Paul. They have nothing. What they are wearing is what they've got. That's it."

"I'm sorry. I guess I have a lot to learn about indigence. It's amazing how much we take things for granted. Doesn't a city this size have a shelter for these people?"

"Yeah, there are shelters, but they're always full. Some even charge people to stay, if you can believe that. Some are run by churches and other non-profit organizations, but they don't all have equal opportunity admittance."

"For instance ..."

"Okay, take Mick for example. He couldn't get into a shelter because he's an addict. Granted, he's homeless because of his addiction, but this had to start somewhere and someone needs to take responsibility. Mick isn't in any condition to do that. It's hard to imagine it now, but he was once a corporate executive pulling down six figures."

"What happened?"

"Drugs. He'd been an over-achiever all his life. His folks were hard on him, pushing him all the time to do more, do better, you know the type. Meanwhile, they were doing their socially acceptable drinking and dope smoking. They freaked when they caught Mick smoking dope and couldn't understand how he could get involved with drugs. They didn't think he knew about their social habits. So, Mick goes through college in a marijuana fog, makes great grades, goes for his MBA and CPA, gets on with a big corporation making the big bucks. He marries his college sweetheart and they have their two kids. One day he comes home and finds the wife has changed the locks and won't let him back in. He went off the deep end. The pressure had been building up for so many years he didn't know how to handle it. So he started doing heroine, coke, whatever he could get his hands on. The wife divorced him and took everything — the kids, the house, the cars — you name it. When Mick lost his job because he was stoned more often than he was sober and couldn't get to work more than two or three days a week, the money ran out. She wasn't getting her child support, so she had him thrown in jail. Meanwhile, she's married to some other guy and they're living together in the house Mick bought. What did he have left? His parents? The mom's gone and the dad's disowned him. He was an only child."

"How long has he been coming here?"

"A couple of months, I guess. He got out of jail the last time right after Halloween, and started coming around here. He and I had a few heart-to-heart talks and I told him I'd help him get off the stuff, but he'd have to go cold turkey and do it without medical help. It's been really rough, but he'll make it."

"Okay. I see Mick's plight, and it's really sad, but what about the others? Do all of these people have drug problems or something that keeps them out of shelters? Isn't the city providing for them in some way? I thought there was a ton of money coming out of Washington to help the poor and the homeless and the hungry. Where's all that money going?"

"I wish I could answer all your questions, but first you've got to start paying attention to that stew. If you don't stir it now and then, it's going burn to the bottom of the pan. Okay, that's better. Now, let me see if I can say this in a way that makes sense. Yes, there is money for the poor. And no, all of these people do not have problems that would keep them out of shelters. The problems are, one, the city doesn't like to recognize the fact that there is a homeless problem, and two, there aren't enough shelters for everyone. And three, families are often separated in shelters — men on one side, women on the other. How many mothers do you know who will let their six year old son go spend the night with a bunch of down and out strangers all sleeping on cots in the same room? This is really toughest on them, the single mothers. When I started in this job about two years ago, there were 1500 homeless people in the Twin

Cities metropolitan area. Since that time, the numbers have escalated at a rate of about 50 or so a month. Many of these people are like Mick. Once upon a time they had a real life. Once upon a time they had homes and cars and bank accounts. Many of them lost their jobs and couldn't find another one. In order to get the money from Washington you have to have people to write grants. Not enough people care enough to give up their time and talents to get involved. Grants are being written, but they take time. There's a Metro Cities Homeless Alliance, MCHA, which is made up of concerned citizens, local charities, and even a few formerly homeless people. They're doing everything they can to fix the problem, but it's like using your thumb to patch a dam. When you patch one hole, another one pops open. The toughest part about this whole thing is the kids. When they get here for lunch, look into their faces. Tell me what you see. If it doesn't tear your heart out, then you don't belong here. This isn't a place where one can be selfish, Paul. You've got to know that before you even begin. You come last, they all come first."

"How do you do this? I mean," stammered Paul, feeling the knot in his gut grow tighter remembering his own selfish thoughts, "how do you keep doing this day in and day out without going bonkers?"

Mike laughed out loud. "And where exactly did you get the impression I have not gone bonkers? You're almost as funny as I am. Oh yeah, the stress gets to you because there's only so much you can do. I pray a lot. I pray for strength. I pray for courage. I pray for wisdom. I pray for more money. I pray for people to donate food that didn't expire three years ago. I pray for people like you to come down here and help out, even if it's just for a few days at a time. Are you stirring that stew?"

"Yeah," smiled Paul getting comfortable in his new role and with his new acquaintance. "I'm stirring. I'm stirring. What do you do for Mike? I mean, when it all gets too much and you need some release, what do you do?"

"Was I not speaking out loud when I said I pray a lot? I could have sworn I spoke out loud. Maybe I *am* losing it. Maybe I just thought I said it. But you're right, there are times when I need to get away, let loose, relax. Once every six months or so, I do find myself needing to get away for a day or two. I have this obsession, you see. I am addicted to great homemade food. My family's all moved around the country and my mom's too crippled with arthritis to cook anymore, so I go to Lexington, ever hear of it?"

"Kentucky?"

"No. Minnesota."

"Okay. Don't think I've heard of that one. What's so great about Lexington?"

"How about homemade Amish chicken, made with fresh cream and seasonings and then baked? It's at a place called Carol's Calico Kitchen. That chicken and some mashed potatoes and some veggies, and to top it all off, homemade rhubarb cream pie that just melts in your mouth and ... mmmmm ... I'm going to have to stop now or we'll never get lunch done here. It's not like I can hang out a 'Closed — be-back-later' sign and take off for a few hours."

"So, who takes over when you go to Lexington for this meal you're swooning over?"

"I find someone to fill in for a day and just go. It's not always easy to line someone up, but I figure by Friday I should have you trained well enough where I can get away."

"I have to go back Thursday though."

"No problem. I'll take off Wednesday."

"You what?"

Just then the air was filled with a loud screech from the small room behind the stove. Mick had awakened from his short nap and was suffering from the withdrawal again. The screech was as close to blood curdling as Paul could imagine, and shot chills up and down his spine. He knew though, that he needed to get his feet wet if he was going to be any good around here, and cooking wasn't his only talent.

"Can I go talk to him?" he asked Mike.

"I don't know. It's your first day and all. I don't want you to say anything to upset him, and if you haven't lived this life ..."

"Mike," said Paul reassuringly, "I may not have lived this life, but I am a psychologist. Things like tact, diplomacy, counseling, all that, I learned in second grade. Trust me, I think I can handle one drug addict."

"Okay, but be careful, he can be a little, um, shall we say assertive, during these dryouts."

Paul walked behind the curtain slowly, not exactly sure what he would find there. The wild, anxiety driven Mick was tearing at his clothes, clawing at the air and looking around hysterically, eyes wide with fear. Paul approached cautiously and spoke very softly to the man, hoping to calm him down, to reassure him everything would be alright. When he reached the bedside, Mick realized for the first time someone else was in the room. He reached out and grabbed Paul by the hair and growled like a wild animal. Pulling Paul's head down to his own face, he sneered into it and spit, then he threw Paul aside as if he were a toy. Paul landed awkwardly on the tent floor beside the bed and tried to raise himself up. His wrist felt slightly bruised from trying to break his fall, but otherwise he was okay. The sole of Mick's shoe came up and caught Paul across the cheek, drawing blood and bruising a few bones as it passed. Turning to right himself again and attempting to regain his strength, Paul grabbed on to the edge of the cot. He was able to pull himself upright before Mick swung a right fist and hit him in the jaw. This time Paul shook his head to clear it and grabbed both of Mick's arms to subdue the wild beast in him. The man was strong. Paul looked directly into his eyes, mere inches from the frightened man's face and growled back with one word— Stop! Mick drew back and seemed to relax just slightly. Paul continued in a voice of authority.

"Stop this right now. You are no longer under the power of that insane drug. You are free, as of this very minute. Relax every muscle in your body and listen to what I have to say."

Paul felt the man's arms relax, so he let go of his grasp. Instinctively, he placed his left hand in his pocket and felt for the piece of the cross. It warmed his hand and he felt the strength run through him. For the next twenty minutes he talked calmly and rationally with a subdued Mick, holding tightly onto the man's hand. When Mick had relaxed as much as he could and had fallen back to sleep, Paul tiptoed out of the makeshift bedroom and back around to the kitchen where Mike was pulling the cornbread out of the oven. He glanced up at Paul and smiled.

"Well," said Paul patting his sore, bleeding cheek with the tail of his shirt. "I think that went well."

"I hope he looks better than you. You should put a piece of steak on the cheek or you'll be black and blue in a couple of hours."

"You're right. Where's the steak?"

"I'm sure it's probably in the walk-in next to the lobster tails and shrimp cocktails. But why don't you track down the chef or the maître d and ask one of them. They should know."

"I'm sorry," said Paul shaking his head, "I did it again. I'm not quite used to this yet. You got any ice maybe?"

"Right outside the door, sonny."

Paul walked outside the tent and grabbed a handful of snow, smacking it in all its damp coldness against his left cheek. It wasn't steak, but it was definitely cold. When he walked back into the tent he noticed people starting to arrive for lunch already. He wanted to stand there for a minute and just look at them, study their faces, their eyes, their expressions, their conversations. But, he knew Mike needed him inside and, quite frankly, he was getting hungry himself. It had been quite a few hours since that big breakfast at Al's Diner. He'd have to try and get Mike away from here one day, he decided, and treat him to breakfast at Al's.

"I'm gonna get fat," he said, not realizing he spoke out loud.

"Not here you won't," spoke one of the customers arriving for lunch. "The food's good but you work it off walkin' around tryin' to stay warm. Go ahead, get in line, I don't mind."

"Oh, thank you no. I'm actually here to help Father Mike for a few days. You go right ahead and I'll see you at the top."

The man smiled a semi-toothless grin, and for the first time Paul realized there was a small child beside the man. There was no way to tell if it was a boy or a girl, but the child held onto the man's hand tightly, and tried to hide behind his arm.

"Hey, there," said Paul squatting down to get on the child's level. "What's your name?"

The man spoke instead. "Name's Melissa, but she can't talk. She's deaf. She's my grandbaby. My daughter run off and leff her wit me to raise. What kinda dumb broad leaves a kid with a homeless guy? I may be her mama's daddy, but I sure as shootin' don't have to admit it to no one. I ain't proud of what I done with my life, but I think what she done's a might worse, don't you?"

"I can't say," said Paul straightening up while still smiling at the little girl Melissa. "I don't know all the circumstances surrounding the situation."

"Circumstances is like this. She got her a new man who don't like kids. He tells her it's him or the kid and so she, bein' the sorta woman she is, she takes the guy and leaves the kid. What kinda woman would do somethin' like that? By the way, my name's Augie. What's yer's?"

Paul stuck out his hand and received the outstretched hand of this strange little man. "Nice to meet you, Augie. My name's Paul, Paul Grant. I better get up there now, though, and help Father Mike. He looks a bit overwhelmed."

"You tell Father Mike I said to treat ya right, y'hear?" yelled Augie as Paul retreated to the front of the tent.

"I'll do that," Paul yelled back smiling. "And I'll save some extra dessert for you and Melissa."

"That should be fun to watch," said Mike as Paul approached. "What's for dessert?"

"You don't have anything for dessert for these people?"

"Not unless you plan on snapping your fingers and whipping up some éclairs or something. How about some wine to go with that, or maybe a light cordial. Paul, my son, you're in the real world now. This isn't uptown. This is as far downtown as you'll ever get."

"I'm not your son," Paul snapped, embarrassed at his own incredible insensitivity.

"Sorry. Habit I guess. Got any cash on you?"

"Yeah, a little, why?"

"There's a grocery store just a couple of blocks that way." Mike pointed towards the back of the tent. "Here, I'll add twenty to whatever you've got. Maybe you can find some cupcakes or cookies or something to give out. That'd make this crowd very happy, and you'd look like a real hero."

Paul turned on his heel and started out of the tent, leaving Mike with the twenty dollar bill still in his hand. At the door he turned back in the direction of the store, and jogged the two blocks to the small mom and pop grocery. He found seven dozen moon pies on sale for twenty five cents apiece, and one frozen chocolate éclair for a dollar. He'd take the moon pies back to hand out to everyone, but the éclair he'd save for Melissa. As he was about to walk out the door with his purchases, he saw a small stuffed animal, a little gray kitten with a pink bow, sitting on a shelf by the door.

"Hey, how much for the kitten?" he yelled back to the proprietor.

"Twenty-two dollars, plus tax. You want it?"

"Do you take American Express?"

"Oh sure," retorted the clerk sarcastically. "We take American Express, Mastercharge, Visa, gold, rubles, even pesos if you got em. Want we should wrap that up for you too? Maybe we could deliver it later as a big surprise for your girlfriend. What you think this is? FAO Schwarz or something?"

"Hush your mouth," snapped his wife coming into the store from the backroom. "What's he trying to do, get you to pay ten times more for something than it's worth?"

"I don't know," smiled Paul. "I was asking about this kitten. How much is it?"

"Two fifty," smiled the woman kindly. She was heavy set with short gray hair. The bib apron she wore around her neck was being used as a towel on which to dry her hands, while her gray and white dress stayed clean as a whistle. Her cheeks were rosy and there was a definite twinkle in her soft brown eyes. Paul liked her at once. She reminded him somewhat of his grandmother, but this woman was probably no more than sixty-five or so. It was apparent life had not been easy on either her or her husband, but her eyes reflected a happy spirit.

"You look like a nice man to me," she said softly, coming nearer to Paul and the kitten he was now holding in his hand. I saw you at the mission this morning. You're over there helping Father Mike, aren't you? If you don't have the cash for the kitten now, you can come back later and pay. It's okay. We don't have any way of running credit cards and Saul, well, he's just a horse's patoot, but he's my horse's patoot, okay? So if you forgive him, we got a deal."

Paul took five dollars out of his pocket and handed it to the lady. "Here," he said. "Keep the change. It's for a very special little girl. And thank you so very much for your kindness. Saul is just a man being a man, right Saul?"

"Yeah, whatever," grunted Saul from behind the counter.

Paul headed back to the tent with his purchases. The packages were too bulky for him to run, but he walked as quickly as he could. When he was within a half block of the tent, he heard the commotion. The first thought going through his head was that he had actually burned the stew and the guests were complaining. Then he realized these were not angry voices, they were excited, jubilant. He quickened his step to get there fast and find out what was going on. Entering the tent, he saw the whole group crowded around Mike and someone else, but he couldn't see who it was. Mike's face was white, as white as if he'd seen the ghost of his own mother, yet he was smiling and patting whoever was seated by him on the back. Paul jumped up in an effort to see better, but the crowd was too dense and the person in the middle was sitting down. As a last resort, he stood up on the bench beside one of the tables near him. Placing his packages on the table, he hoisted his bruised, sore body up onto the bench and looked into the crowd. Mike caught his eye, stared at him for a moment, and then waved him over to the side. Mike made his way out of the crowd and pulled Paul back a short distance from the backs of those craning to see whoever it was in the center.

In a very hushed voice, Mike spoke to Paul. "What did you do back there?"

"Back where? At the store? I got ..."

"No, back there. In the back room with Mick."

"Why? Is something wrong?"

"Not at all," smiled Mike. "Go see for yourself. In fact, I think Mick is waiting for you." Mike smiled a strange, mysterious smile. "Go ahead," he said as he gently pushed Paul towards the group gathered around Mick.

Slowly he made his way through with a 'pardon me' here and an 'excuse me, please' there. When he was just two people back from Mick, he saw him. The man's face was glowing with sobriety and sanity. The smile was radiant, the eyes bright and alert, and the general demeanor that of what Paul imagined Mick had once been before the drugs had dragged him to the bottom. It was a moment or two before Mick spotted Paul, and when he did he went to him, arms outstretched.

"I've never hugged a man before," said Mick heavy with emotion, "but you did something back there that changed me. It was a miracle, a true miracle. Look, I'm not shaking, I'm lucid again. I can even imagine myself making a comeback. I haven't imagined myself doing anything but getting stoned for so long—I can't remember when I felt like this!" With that he put his arms around Paul and pulled him into a big, masculine hug.

"I ... I don't ... I don't understand," stammered Paul trying to pull out of the hug which made him feel very uncomfortable. "What exactly happened?"

"You tell me! I remember you coming in there when I was in real bad shape, and we wrestled. Hey, sorry about that cheek, man, I wasn't myself. After you left, I slept and I dreamed and in my dream there was this angel and he touched me. It was like this white heat going through my entire body. When I woke up just a little bit ago, all the drugs were gone out of my system. I knew it. I don't know how I knew, but I knew. And I knew it was something you did. Are you the second Christ?"

"Oh," said Paul, "Oh no. This can't be happening." He turned back to Mike who had moved in closer and was standing just a couple of rows of people behind Paul. "I came here for answers, not more questions. I've got to go. I've got to get out of here." His heart was racing and he felt panicky. It was getting hard to breathe. His first thought was that he was having a heart attack, that he was going to die. But he knew it was just another panic attack. He needed air, cold air, and to get out of this mob.

"Why?" yelled Mike as Paul tried frantically to step backward. "Why do you want to run away when you're the big hero here? You want to know if that was a true piece of the cross? You tell me." There was a bit of an edge to Mike's voice.

"But," yelled Paul as the crowd started clamoring to get nearer to him and touch him, "He thinks I'm the Christ. This is wrong. I have to get out of here." He saw the mocking look on Mike's face and knew that Mike thought he was a charlatan, a phony.

Paul turned and ran around the table, pushing people aside in an effort to get out of the tent. Sitting beside the bundles he had left on a table in the back was Melissa. She couldn't hear, so had no idea what was going on. She looked up at him with a frightened expression in her small, oval face. As he reached the table, Paul pulled the little gray kitten out of the bag and held it out to Melissa. She looked up at him questioningly, and he motioned for her to take it, that it was for her. Her tiny, dirty hands reached out and embraced the small gray kitten. Love filled her baby blue eyes as she hugged her kitten and rocked it back and forth. Paul leaned down and kissed her forehead, reached into his bag and pulled out the éclair, placing it next to her on the bench. Then he left the tent and ran back to the store where he had met Saul and his wife. He knew of no other place to go.

Chance might be God's pseudonym
when He does not want to sign his name.

Anatole France
French novelist

Chapter 13

aul was nowhere in sight when Paul returned, and the woman who had been
so kind was casually dusting the shelves
behind the cash register counter, humming softly to herself. She didn't turn immediately when
Paul entered, but when she did, she had a radiant
smile on her face.

"Back so soon? You must be looking for a place
to stay for a few days. Am I right? Did Father Mike
tell you about our spare room?"

"Actually, uh, no. I was just running away, I
think." Paul stammered, not knowing how to explain what had happened at the shelter. It was
obvious Saul and his wife were Jewish and would
find it difficult to understand about the relic and
the dream.

"That life and the people you meet can be a bit
overwhelming at first," she said. "By the way, my
name's Ruth," she offered, holding out her dainty,
pudgy little hand, "I don't believe we properly introduced ourselves earlier. I was just about to lock
up for a couple of hours while Saul rests. He's not
well you know. Why don't you come in back with
me and I'll make you a cup of tea. Help settle your

nerves and then you can decide if you want to go back and help at the mission or not."

Ruth, humming to herself as if Paul wasn't even there, closed the front door of the shop and bolted it. She turned over the sign which read "Closed." and pulled down the old-fashioned shade. After that, she turned out the lights and motioned for him to follow her into the back of the store. Their home was the back of the store and the upstairs portion of this building, so the place to which she took Paul was her own fully-furnished kitchen. It was bright with yellow and green everywhere. The counter tops and walls were both yellow. Curtains at the window above the kitchen sink were a gingham check with yellow and white and green ivy running through. The same pattern was used for the curtains that covered the window of the back door. Along the wooden floor, molding had been painted a pale green, and the pantry door molding was done in the same color. At the table, a Formica-topped square piece with iron legs dating back to the late fifties, were four chairs with green and yellow vinyl padding on the seats. In some ways it reminded Paul of the table at the Landers' home. The table sat to the left side of the room, across from the back door, while the remainder of the room was reserved for cooking and storage. A doorway, opposite the other end of the table and to the right led to a hall with a stairway under which was a small half bath. On the wall before the doorway was a built-in desk, a wall-mounted telephone, and shelves with far too many pictures of children and grandchildren to begin to count. This was a warm, inviting room, the kitchen of a grandmother, reminding Paul of his own Nana and the summers on her farm. Whenever he thought of Nana, he thought of the dream.

"There now," said Ruth as she placed a tea pot on the stove. "Why don't you just have a seat

125

there at the table and I'll see what I can throw to-gether. I know you haven't had time for lunch. Do you like lasagna? I have some left over from last night. I could heat it up in a jiffy and throw some garlic bread in the oven. Yes, I think that'd make a fine lunch." She continued without waiting for his answer. "Do you take your tea with lemon, cream, or straight?"

Paul began to feel mothered, something he hadn't enjoyed in years, "A little cream and artifi-cial sweetener if you have it." He sat down at the bright little table and made himself at home, lean-ing forward with his elbows on the table.

After putting the leftover lasagna in the oven and putting the tea in the pot to steep, Ruth sat down opposite Paul. "So tell me, Dr. Paul Grant, what exactly brought you to the shelter to help Mikey?"

Paul thought for a minute, trying to come up with a story that would quench her curiosity with-out offending her own religious beliefs. "I guess I just needed to get away from myself for awhile. A good friend of mine went to school with Mike's older brother Patrick, so he suggested I come down here for a few days to help out."

Paul noticed a slight wince briefly cross Ruth's face when he mentioned Patrick.

"Well, if you're trying to get away from your-self, this is certainly the place to do it. Mikey's a good boy, isn't he? He works so hard for those people and gets no reward or recognition from the Catholic Church. They just don't treat him right. We do what we can to help out down there, but we have a pretty big family of our own, as you can see." She turned and pointed to all the pictures on the wall. "Plus Saul's health isn't what it was and he kind of resents the fact that all the services down there are Christian. But I don't mind. As far as I'm concerned, we're all going to end up dead anyway and then we'll find out the truth. Don't you think?"

Obviously, and much to Paul's relief, this was a rhetorical question. Ruth just kept on talking. "So, dear, how long do you plan to stay? Are you from around here? Do you need a room for a few nights?"

"As a matter of fact, I don't know, no, and yes, in that order. I had hoped to stay until Wednesday evening, but haven't decided for sure. I live in Duluth, work in a clinic there. And, yes, as a matter of fact, I do need a place to stay. You mentioned you had a spare room to rent. How much is it?"

"Oh dear, there's no charge. No charge at all. There's an outside entrance that goes straight up those stairs once you get inside the door. I'll give you a key to that. The room is at the top of the stairs and you make a complete u-turn, it's right there at the end of the hall. The bathroom is right there on the right as you come up the stairs. I'm afraid we only have the one bathroom up there, but we keep it clean and I'll have clean towels for you in the morning."

Ruth got up and washed her hands in the sink, drying them on her apron. She pulled two pot holders out of a drawer next to the stove, and opened the oven door. The smell of the lasagna greeted Paul and he suddenly was ravenously hungry. She laid out his lunch for him, poured his tea, and then sat across and smiled as she watched him eat.

"Oh yes," she said dreamily. "It will be so nice to have a young man around again. I miss my children and grandchildren, but they live so far away. Maybe you could stay longer if you like it here."

> Dreamer of dreams, born out of my due time,
> why should I strive to set the crooked straight?
>
> ───────────
>
> William Morrison
> English poet

Chapter 14

After lunch, Paul thanked Ruth, got the key, and was shown the outside entrance door which was the next door down from the front entrance of the store. Then he headed back to the shelter, renewed in his quest to find answers and get on with his life. When he arrived, every indication of lunch had been removed and Mike was sitting alone sipping on a cup of coffee, reading a book. A few of the homeless patrons had made pallets on the floor and were napping. Paul noticed a Hispanic woman and baby on one side, Augie and Melissa a little further along, and several others laced in and out between the tables. Melissa was cuddling her kitten close to her chest and had a peaceful smile on her tiny, dirty face. The last remnants of stew and chocolate éclair remained around her small mouth. Paul felt a stab in his heart for the children. He and Sarah had talked about having children, but had agreed not to bring any into this unstable world. He regretted that decision now and wished they had children of their own.

"I'm glad you decided to come back," said Mike as Paul approached the picnic-style table where he was seated. "I was afraid you might have been scared off by what happened. Why don't you grab a cup of mud and sit down? Maybe I can help you through this."

Paul strolled over to the large coffee pot and poured himself a cup of very strong, sludge-like liquid. The powdered creamer can was nearly empty, so the result was a gray mess that looked barely palatable. Heat, however, was an objective and Paul took the stained cup of coffee-like substance to the table and sat down on the bench opposite Mike.

"So," said Mike without looking up, "what's all this about a dream?"

"It started when I was really just a kid, maybe five or six. I was staying at my Nana's house on the farm for the summer and it was hot outside. She was going to bake cinnamon rolls. You know the kind, with raisins in them? But, before I could have a roll, I had to take a nap."

Paul stared off into space, remembering every moment of that day...

Nana Grant was making me take a nap while she baked cinnamon rolls in the kitchen. At least this time she let me nap on the couch instead of that big old, stinky bed in Uncle Charlie's room. Uncle Charlie smoked cigarettes and his whole room smelled like stale tobacco. Nana's cinnamon rolls with raisins and powdered sugar icing were my favorite treat. Impatiently, I tossed and turned on the worn old couch. The doilies Nana had crocheted covered the thin spots on the arms. My pillow, the one I'd had since I was probably two, cooled my cheek. An afghan from the couch back had been draped over my small body. I was a scrawny kid back then. It was summer and warm outside, yet Nana believed one couldn't sleep without a cover. There was a box fan across the room which helped keep the flies off even though Nana left all the windows wide open hoping for a breeze.

I remember I was thirsty, but if I dared to ask for another drink Nana would scold me and I'd run the risk of missing out on the cinnamon rolls. I can still see butter dripping down the soft, puffy-doughy, cinnamon and raisin-lined layers. That's how I went to sleep, just thinking about the heaven that waited when I awoke. So, pretty soon I was drifting into that weird, unexplainable land of dreams.

I remember waking up with a start that humid, sunny afternoon. My pillow was soaked with sweat. The afghan had fallen onto the floor. In spite of the summer heat, I was shivering. It took a moment, lying very, very still, and listening to my heart pound, before I could piece together the segments of the dream that had frightened me.

There was a sword, a sword raised. A big man, big and solid as a rock, swung his sword and cut off my ear. I raised my hand to where my ear had been and the blood was running down the side of my face, through my fingers. The pain was unbearable. I cringed in fear because I had led the Roman soldiers to arrest this man's leader, Jeshua, the one who claimed to be a king of my people. We didn't have kings anymore. My ear had been severed and I was in pain, but this man, the one who was supposed to be arrested, put a hand on the place where my ear had been, and it was whole again. I put my own hand up to the side of my face and felt the spot. The pain was gone. The bleeding had stopped. It was as if the incident had never happened. The priests had said this man was a criminal, but what criminal would, or could, heal a severed ear? The man behind me called me Malchus and asked what had happened. He saw it all. The next thing I remember, the man who had healed my ear was being taken away to be tried before the Sanhedrin for blasphemy.

Next I see the final stages of a trial before Pilate. Jeshua of Nazareth, the man who had healed my ear, was condemned to die by crucifixion, the most horrible way to die. The scourging he suffered was far more brutal than the soldiers usually gave, and the man, Jeshua, was nearly dead already. He died before sundown which made me glad because they didn't have to break his legs or anything. When they took him down from the cross, I was there. I waited until everyone else was gone, and I chipped off a small piece of wood from the cross and stuffed it into my pouch. His blood had stained that wood. If that man could heal a severed ear with just a touch, who was he? Could His blood from the cross heal my father? My father was so sick and I didn't want him to die. I wish I could have known Jeshua before and let my father meet him. I didn't think anyone saw me take the piece of wood, but when I turned around one of the Roman soldiers was standing there, watching me. He had his sword in his hand and was beginning to raise it over his head. I don't remember him talking or saying anything, but I knew he thought I was one of the followers of Jeshua and he wanted to kill me too. I tried to hide my souvenir. He had already seen it and was wondering why I had taken it and was trying to hide it. I tried to explain that I wasn't a follower, but this was an unusual execution and I wanted a souvenir to show my family, my friends. He didn't seem to believe me. That's when I woke up.

131

If you bear the cross willingly,
It will bear you.

———————

Thomas à Kempis
German mystic

Chapter 15

hen Paul had completed his story, both he and Mike were still sitting at the picnic table. Paul felt a certain sense of relief at having been able to unload the burden of that dream after so many years. Mike looked self-satisfied, which puzzled Paul.

"It's not as big a mystery as you might have thought after all," Mike stated flatly, looking directly into Paul's eyes. "I would venture to guess you had heard the story in Sunday School, it stuck in your mind, your imagination added the soldier with the sword part."

"But what about this?" Paul asked, taking out the piece of stone-wood from his pocket. "How do you explain this and the things that have been happening? How do you explain Mick?"

"You're a psychologist, Paul," Mike said smugly. "You know all about mind over matter, the power of suggestion, positive thinking, all that bull that people lap up with their tongues hanging out. That's all this is. You believe it can work miracles, so you're seeing miracles in the things that are happening naturally. Take Mick, for example. He's been going through this withdrawal thing for a couple of weeks or more. It was his time. When all the drugs and alcohol are out of the system the body craves the sugar that it is now being denied. That shot of orange juice I gave him probably did as much good as your little chat. You're seeing what you want to see, Paul. Your wife left you. You need to be a hero to someone, somewhere, and this little joke someone played on you," he took the relic from Paul's hand, "just happened to fall into your hands at the right time."

"Maybe you're right," said Paul thoughtfully. Mike's explanation was so anticlimactic, so clinical. It felt wrong, but yet it made sense.

"Well," said Mike more cheerfully, "now that we've got that settled, how about helping me set up for bingo? We don't have to cook tonight because it's outreach night for Bart Braddock's group of followers. They bring the dinner, serve it, even clean up afterwards. Plus, they bring the prizes for bingo." He stood up, a big smile on his face, and nonchalantly slipped the relic into his pocket.

133

"Um, I know it may not be worth anything, but, um, could I have that back?" stammered a stunned Paul.

"Oh, sure," said Mike, laughing, trying to look embarrassed. "You have to be careful around me. Never loan me a pen. It's a bad habit of mine and most of the time I don't even know I'm doing it. Sorry about that."

Paul retrieved the piece, but he could see in Mike's eyes he wasn't sorry at all. He had meant to keep the wood splinter. Something just didn't feel right about all this, but then again, maybe he was just paranoid and needing some attention after losing his wife, as Mike had said.

While the two men set up for the bingo games, Paul asked Mike what the story was on Augie and Melissa. He'd felt an instant bonding with the child and wanted to find out how he could help her and her grandfather.

"That's sad," said Paul. "Such a pretty little girl, afflicted with hearing and speech loss, and homeless, too."

"Except," said Mike, putting the wire bingo drum into the stand, "she's not deaf or a mute. She can talk, but she won't. Augie's daughter dropped her off with him when she ran off with some guy she'd met in a bar. The child cried for days after her mom left, and then she just quit talking. Augie tells people she's deaf and dumb because he's embarrassed by the whole matter. Truth is, he'd die for that little girl."

"How'd she learn to sign?"

"That's another interesting story. Augie was a teacher back in his day. His wife was also a teacher and she worked with deaf mutes, teaching them to sign. Augie and Rose just had the two children. Their son, Augie Junior, was born with a lot of defects and didn't live to be two. Rachel, their daughter, on the other hand was everything a mother and father could want. Life was perfect for them. Rachel married a fine man and they had Melissa. Augie and Rose were as proud as any parents and grandparents could be. Then Rose got hurt. She was shopping for groceries one day and as she pushed her cart in the parking lot, some kids backed out of a parking space too fast without looking. Rose was behind the car. It didn't kill her, but it changed her personality drastically. She became mean and abusive toward Augie, Rachel, and even Melissa. They kept her on all kinds of medications trying to get her straightened out, but she just got worse and worse. Rachel stayed with her a lot because she couldn't be left alone. One day Rachel found her mother dead — suicide. It tore Rachel up and she started taking some of her mother's pills just to get through it all, trying to cope with the pain. Well, she got hooked. August and Gary, Rachel's husband, tried everything they could to get her off the prescription meds, but it didn't do any good. She was addicted. When the meds ran out, she started in on heroine. Gary left her and tried to take Melissa, but the courts gave custody to Rachel. Shortly after that, Gary took a job in Europe and quit sending child support because he knew it was just going to buy the drugs. Well, you know the rest of the story. Rachel slid further and further down, met another junkie, tossed her child aside with Augie and took off. Augie had spent everything he had trying to get his wife well and then trying to get Rachel straightened out. When everyone else was gone, he had nothing left. That's how he got here. No one wants to hire a down and out history teacher. All he had left was Melissa, and though he talks like she's a burden some times, that child is the only thing keeping him alive. Without her he would have taken his own life long ago. He misses his Rose, the one she was before she got hurt. I never met her but he talks about her like she was the most wonderful woman in the world. If you ever get him to talk about it, you'll see what I mean. You'll feel like you know her by the time he's through. And Melissa? Well, you look into her eyes and tell me."

"You were right about the faces of the kids. It's hard to look into them and not feel like there's got to be a better way, more that can be done. If Augie was a teacher, why does he talk like he does. Y'know, poor grammar and all?

"It's easier to get by on the streets when you fit in. If Augie used his intellect and talked the way he had as a teacher, he wouldn't have a friend in the homeless world,"

"How old do you think Augie is?"

"Why do you ask that?"

"I'm just thinking. There are jobs at the hospital sometimes, you know, for maintenance and stuff like that. Melissa deserves better than what she's had and so does Augie. If I could get him a job and help them find a place, maybe Melissa could get into school and start talking again."

"Are you serious? You're willing to take on the responsibility of an old man who probably has some serious health issues, and a child who most certainly has some psychological issues? Maybe you are a saint."

"Do I have to keep reminding you I'm a psychologist? I really think I could help Melissa. And, if Augie has health problems, working at the hospital would be perfect. He'd get medical coverage and could see doctors whenever he needed. I have a few connections at the city and I bet they'd help me find out how to get Augie into one of those government subsidized apartment complexes and get them food stamps and stuff. And he could get Medicaid for Melissa."

"And exactly where is Melissa going to be when Augie's working? Hanging out at a homeless camp in Duluth without her grandpa?"

"You really do think I'm heartless, don't you. I have friends who don't work and would be glad to watch her. It's worth a try, don't you think?"

"Anything's worth a try. I hope this works out for them. Augie's a really good guy and that child is a little doll. I'd like to see them get a break. We'd better get busy. That church group will be here any minute and they like things ready to go when they arrive. Tonight I think they're going to be setting up grills and serving hamburgers and hot dogs. I suppose they'll have chips and sodas too, along with some homemade bars for dessert."

"How late do you stay around here at night?" Paul asked.

"I don't know, eleven or so. A lot of the group will make pallets on the floor and sleep in here to stay out of the cold. We lock up the tent and some of the guys take turns guarding the perimeter so the women and children can feel safe. You have a curfew or something?"

"No, but I did find a place to stay."

"Good. I was wondering where you went. Didn't realize you'd gone apartment hunting in the middle of the lunch rush and a miracle cure. Now I don't have to worry about finding an extra pillow and blanket at my place. Where you going to be staying, with Saul and Ruth?"

"How'd you know?"

"Lucky guess. You're not the first. They're really good people. Stayed with them myself for a couple of weeks when I first started down here. One piece of advice. Saul's not well and they keep that upstairs apartment way too hot, so open the window just a tiny bit at night before you go to bed. It'll save you a lot of sinus pain if you do. The first night I was there I woke up with bleeding sinuses and a headache I thought would kill me. I don't know how Ruth stands it. And by the way, if she gives you advice, you won't understand it completely, but listen to her."

> I ... chose my wife as she did her wedding gown,
> not for a fine glossy surface,
> but for qualities as would wear well.

Oliver Goldsmith
Irish dramatist

Chapter 16

Angelina Scott sat in her small apartment looking out the second story window at the dreary streets of Duluth. This was not how she had anticipated her life being when she was in her mid thirties. Her dream had been far removed from this lonely life of service to others and no life of her own. She loved her job, felt genuine compassion for the families to whom she was assigned, and enjoyed a good rapport with her fellow workers. Still, her heart was empty wanting a family of her own. Pride kept her from taking the chance of calling her husband, the one who had left her on their wedding night fifteen years ago. Robert Scott, the only man she could ever love.

After the huge, joyful reception, the bride and groom had left the country club in a white limo. Angie's heart was beating with joy, with all the beauty of being a bride, and with fear for what was yet to come. Growing up in a very strict Catholic home, she knew that God had an extraordinary plan for her life and she must never break her vows to Him, no matter what. It had been the teachings of her mother and her grandmother that let her know how special she was, that God had chosen her and her alone for some remarkable place in His service. They didn't know what, but Angel knew. She had dreamed of it for years and now the final preparations were being made. All of her dreams, her vows, and her mission from God could come to fruition now, after this one night.

Robert was so handsome in his tuxedo. All the trepidation he had shared with her about his family had dissolved and they had welcomed her and loved her immediately, as she had them. She hoped that now Rob and his family could begin a new life of sharing and communicating, something they had not done for many, many years. The family he had run away from had changed and grown just as much as he had. Understanding his mother's love for his father, and now his father's disease, had softened him up a lot. Although it was a very difficult decision to make, she and Robert together had gone to visit his father. Their reunion was the most touching, spiritual event of the entire week. The elder Scott had held her hand in his own very frail older hand and told her what a beautiful bride she would be. He asked her to call him Dad and she responded by telling him she considered it an honor. It had shaken Rob to see his father so small and fragile. The skin on his hands and face was like onion skin that could tear at the touch. Their visit had been short as the older man's strength didn't last long. Angel saw the red rings around his eyes when Robert leaned down and kissed his forehead and said 'I love you dad' before leaving. She was quite sure it was the first time those words had been spoken and the response was from the heart when the father spoke with weakened breath, "I love you too son." Three months later, Angie heard, Robert's father passed away. She didn't know if he had, but she hoped Robert had gone home for the funeral. She also hoped he'd been kind when speaking of her.

Robert's big surprise for their honeymoon had been more than she expected. Neither of them was able to take a lot of time off, nor did they have a whole lot of money to spend, but Rob had saved up for many months to pay for a bridal suite at the Mansion on Turtle Creek in Dallas. It was the most exclusive place in the city and it was to be theirs and theirs alone for one night. After changing into what they considered normal dress clothes, they enjoyed a delicious dinner in the Antares Restaurant at the top of Reunion Tower. The lights of the city twinkled like baby stars winking at the newlyweds as if to say 'we're twinkling just for you.' The restaurant within the huge ball that could be seen from many miles away, slowly turned, giving them a provocative view of the city from every angle. Ribbons of car head lamps reflecting off the pavement of the myriad roads, highways, and freeways twisted, turned, and draped to wrap this gift of beauty in a golden, often shimmering light.

With dinner complete, a last limo ride around the city, and then back to their bridal suite for the moment of truth. Once inside their room, Robert popped the cork on a chilled bottle of champagne and poured a glass for each of them. Handing one to his bride, he held his own glass up and toasted the most beautiful, most wonderful, most precious gift he had ever received, his wife Angelina Scott. Seconds later he was taking off his jacket and tie, and pulling her into his arms, all at the same time. His physical need was evident, as evident as her reluctance. The further he progressed in his romantic overtures, the further she withdrew. At last, in total exasperation, he had asked her what was wrong. Was she afraid? Did she not love him? It was time. Time to tell him about God's mission for her, the vow she had made to the Father and the Blessed Virgin.

Some moments later Robert sat staring at her in total disbelief. Gradually, as if his mind could not grasp what he had just heard or what he was supposed to do next, he turned his eyes away from her and slowly put on his clothes once more. Without a look back, he walked out of the room and left his bride of seven hours sitting alone in the bridal suite of the most extravagant lodging place in Dallas, Texas.

Fifteen years had passed since that night. Fifteen years of regretting, of loving, of being alone, of wishing and hoping and never really daring to dream or believe. How could she have been so naïve and foolish? How could she have misunderstood her mission from God? Upon her return to Duluth, she sought counseling from Father Frank at the Cathedral of Our Lady of the Rosary. He had been able to enlighten her, to show her that the Son of God would return in the skies and all her fears for His safe return had been fruitless. Father had encouraged her to seek out her husband and ask for forgiveness, but her pride would not let her face him, not after what she had said.

Hundreds of times she had picked up the phone and attempted to dial his number, only to put the phone back and not be able to go through with it. Each time her hands shook, her mouth went dry, and she knew she would not be able to say the words she needed to say, nor would she be able to stand the humiliation when he laughed at her, which he surely would do. So many nights throughout these long years she had waited for the phone to ring and it to be him and his voice on the other end of the line. Unfortunately, whenever her phone rang at night it was for work related emergencies, like the Landers' family and the death of that precious little boy.

Why had she not done more? Why had she not gotten the children away from that man? Why hadn't she checked up on them more closely after Ralph was allowed to move back home? Why? Why was a child's life lost because she hadn't done enough?

In the middle of her self-criticism the phone began to ring. Once again her heart began to pound. What was it this time? Another child murdered because of her? Was it a mother beaten to a pulp by an alcoholic father? Or maybe for once, it was just someone wanting to let her know she was appreciated for all she tried to do. She nearly laughed at the cruel joke she had just made. Ralph Landers was in jail, Mary Esther in the hospital after suffering an emotional breakdown, little Billy was cold in his casket lying in the mortuary waiting for the summer thaw that would allow him to be buried, and Bobby, the only other child was in foster care and frightened. Grandma was in a nursing home, and there was no one left in that family to call her. This must be a new one. She finally reached for the phone on the fourth ring and offered a sleepy sounding hello.

"Angel?"

The pace of her heart beat was racing out of control. This couldn't be happening. "Yes, this is Angel."

"This is Robert."

"Yes, I know."

"Can we talk?"

His voice was so soft, so frightened, so unsure. She wanted to cry, for him, for her, for whatever this meant. And she did.

A single moment of reconciliation is worth an entire life of friendship.

Gabriel Garcia Márquez
Colombian Novelist

Chapter 17

When Paul was finally able to leave the shelter and drag his tired body to the small upstairs apartment, he was dog tired and fell asleep as soon as his head hit the pillow. He had made a call on his cell phone earlier and asked Kim Frazier if she would dog-sit Sheba for a couple of days. She'd agreed to go by the house, find the spare key, and take Sheba home with her. She seemed awfully concerned about when Paul would be returning and he hoped she wasn't getting any ideas about their relationship actually being a relationship. Rather than encourage her, he asked how her husband was doing, things of that nature, to keep the conversation less personal. And then there was the excuse of having to prepare lunch which gave him a reason to get off the phone quickly.

At some point during the night, Paul awoke feeling like he was suffocating. In his exhaustion, he had forgotten to open the window, and just as Mike had predicted, his sinuses were drier than the Sahara in a sand storm. He padded in his bare feet over to the window and opened it just about three inches. Not enough to allow too much freezing air into the room, but just enough to cool things off a bit. He thought too about getting a bowl of water to add some moisture to the air in the room, but as he was pondering this and taking in a few deep breaths of frigid air, he heard voices arguing. Looking out the window, he could see no one anywhere near the building. The voices were loud enough to be heard, but not quite loud enough to be understood. He was pretty sure there was a man's and a woman's voice. The voices seemed to be coming from the kitchen. Why? At last Paul heard a door slam, and all was quiet. He waited a few more minutes to see what would happen, but all was silent once again. Finding his way back to the bed, he lay down and was asleep again in minutes. In the morning, the angry voices were all but forgotten. He showered, dressed quickly in the same clothes he'd worn the day before and left through the exterior door down the stairs. There were no sounds of stirring from the other bedroom when he stepped out onto the street at 6 a.m. The two-block walk to the mission site was refreshingly cold and he was ready for that first cup of coffee, even if it looked like river silt.

The days until Wednesday pretty much flew by, one fading into the other. Each day was the same. Breakfast at seven, lunch at twelve, dinner at six, entertainment and/or sermons until ten. Paul was able to spend a little extra time with Augie and Melissa each night after dinner and mentioned his plans for relocating them to Duluth. Augie didn't appear as enthusiastic about the idea as Paul had thought he would be. Melissa, on the other hand, stared into Paul's face as if he was a saint. He learned from Augie that she was seven years old and had never been to school. Augie kept trying to hide because the local child protection agency was trying to find them so they could take Melissa away from him. Paul assured him that coming back to Duluth would be the best thing. They could stay with him until they found a place of their own. He'd pull some strings to get Augie a job at the hospital and he had connections in child welfare that could help with Melissa. Still Augie balked and said he had to think it over before he made any rash decisions. Not understanding the reasoning, Paul agreed to let it ride until the next time he came down for a few days, which would be after the holidays. In the meantime, he left his phone number and said they could call collect any time they needed him.

Shortly after lunch had been served on Wednesday afternoon, but not before the clean-up was done, Rob arrived in his beat up old Volvo.

"Hey, big guy," Paul smiled at this friend when he entered the tent. "What're you doing here in the middle of the day? Don't you work either?"

"Paul," Rob retorted, obviously glad to see his friend, "it's Christmas Eve, or have you forgotten?"

"Yeah, I guess I did. How's Sheba? Have you heard from Officer Frazier? Is she okay?"

"Who?" laughed Rob. "The officer or the dog?"

"The dog, of course. Why? Is something wrong with Frazier?" Paul's brow creased in a line of worry remembering what Kim had said the last time he saw her. He hoped she was alright, but right now, he really missed his dog.

Goodbyes were quickly said, hands shaken, and a few minutes spent with Augie and Melissa before Rob and Paul took to the road back to Duluth. Augie still would not consent to moving north with Paul, but agreed to think about it over the holidays and they could talk the next time Paul came down. Once in the car, things settled into the comfortable routine of two old friends. Paul was more tired than he had believed, and longed to see his own home, his bed — at least the one in the guest room — and his dog.

"So," smiled Rob, "what do you think of Father Mike?"

"I don't know," mused Paul thoughtfully. "His perspicacity is amazing. I think he knows more about me than I do, but I still have trouble seeing him as a Catholic priest. Are you sure he's for real?"

"He is, as far as I know. Why? Did something happen?"

"Well, not exactly. The first night I was there, I heard voices, angry voices arguing, downstairs in Ruth's kitchen. I could have sworn it sounded like Mike."

"Who's Ruth?"

"Oh yeah, I forgot you weren't here." Paul sighed as he lay his head back against the head-rest on the car seat. "Ruth and Saul are this really old Jewish couple that run a little mom-and-pop grocery store just a couple of blocks from the mission. She let me stay there for a few nights, without pay I might add. Really nice old lady, but her old man's got a chip on his shoulder the size of Babe the Blue Ox. At first I thought the arguing was outside, but when I opened the window I realized it was in the building. The only place it could be would be in the downstairs kitchen or the store. Then I heard the back door slam. I can't imagine what Mike and Ruth could be arguing about."

"Maybe," laughed Rob, "just maybe he thought she should be charging you rent."

"And he decided to confront her on this at two-thirty in the morning? Interesting time to discuss fiscal responsibility with your neighbors, don't you think?"

"Whatever," smiled Rob. "Not to change the subject, but I have some news of my own."

"Oh yeah? What?"

"I have a date with my wife tonight!" The smile on Rob's face was as wide and bright as a toothpaste commercial. Without turning his head more than just a skosh, he glanced sideways to catch Paul's reactive expression. He was not to be disappointed. Paul's look of surprise and matching smile were all Rob needed to see.

"You old dog, you. When'd you two hook up again?"

"I called her. When I heard all the details of that Landers kid's murder and found out she was the social worker, well ... I just knew it had to be real hard for her to go through stuff like that alone. At first it was kind of awkward, but then we just started talking. It was just like old times. Then we decided to have dinner together to catch up, you know. By the way, she wants you to call her as soon as you get back. I told her you'd be back Thursday."

"But today's Wednesday," argued Paul. "What if it's really important?"

"I guess you didn't hear me the first time. I am having dinner with my wife tonight ... and guess who's not invited? You. You can talk to her tomorrow."

"You're right. Besides, I got my own gal waiting on me and I can't wait to see her."

"Sarah's back?"

"No, Sheba. I miss her."

"You're starting to worry me buddy. You need to find a new woman, the kind that walks on two legs. Speaking of Sarah, any word yet?"

"No. Tina came by to let me know she's okay, but that's it."

"Who's Tina?"

"Heck if I know, says she's some old family friend. She said some weird things, so she definitely has to be one of Sarah's friends from weird-a-fornia. "

"Well, what kind of weird things did she say?"

"Oh, it was stuff like 'Sarah's fine but needs some healing in her soul,' and stuff like that. I'm thinking she's some kook who thinks she's being a Good Samaritan when she's not really telling me anything. She's probably never even met Sarah and made it all up. Weird chick."

The remainder of the trip was spent in silence, each man inside his own thoughts. Paul wondered more about the mysterious Tina, he wondered if Augie would take him up on his offer, he worried about those voices in the night, and he couldn't wait to take Sheba for a walk. Rob, on the other hand wondered what he should wear to dinner, what time he should really pick her up, and what was wrong with his good friend, Paul, who seemed to be losing it, one step at a time.

Expect poison from standing water.

William Blake
English romantic poet

Chapter 18

Officer Kim Frazier answered her phone on the first ring. She was glad to hear Paul was back in town and invited him to come over right away for Sheba, plus she had some exciting news for him.

Paul drove the five miles to Kim's house and parked in the driveway. It looked like no one was home, but her car may have been parked in the garage. The house in which she lived was rather large and rambling, a ranch style. Paul was impressed with the richness of it all ... the landscaping which would be positively enchanting in summer, the white vinyl siding accented with a rock chimney, and the double doors at the top of four wide steps. Before he had a chance to ring the doorbell, he heard Sheba's bark and Kim was pulling the door open.

"Come on in here," she smiled, genuinely glad to see him. "This lady's been waiting all day for you. I told her this morning you'd be coming home today and she hasn't stopped pacing since."

Paul knelt down beside his beloved dog and allowed her to lick his face all over. The smell of her breath made him want to gag, but he was so glad to be with her again, he didn't even comment, as he normally would have. Kim invited him to have a chair, so he seated himself in a large recliner where Sheba took up her post at his feet, tail slapping the floor.

"You look great," he smiled at Kim. "Something's different. You said you had a surprise, so ... what is it? No ... let me guess. You're pregnant, right? You've got that glow about you. That's gotta be it."

"Nope. Not even close," smiled Kim. "The truth is, your miracle touch has done it again. This time, for me."

Paul's face went white. He had nearly forgotten about the cures that seemingly were related to the piece of wood in his pocket. He liked Kim and didn't want something like this to interfere with their friendship. "What exactly happened?" He asked, hoping it was something he could explain away excluding the relic.

"My doctor found a lump in my breast. He took X-rays and they confirmed there was a small mass in my left breast, so he was ready to schedule surgery. Do you remember me asking you for a hug just before you left? Well, that was the day before I went to see my doctor to get the results of the X-rays. So, after he gave me the bad news, I insisted he take the X-rays again. He did a breast exam and found no lump. Then he ordered new X-rays and there is absolutely, positively, a one hundred percent certainty that I do not have any kind of mass in my left breast, my right breast, or anywhere else on my body." Kim's face was gleaming and she expected Paul to be as excited as she was, but the joy wasn't there for him and she couldn't figure out why.

"I thought you'd be excited for me," she said softly. "I thought you'd be happy to know you'd done good for someone again. Why are you acting like you're ticked off?"

"This thing isn't real, Kim. I've spent the last few days with a priest in the Cities. We talked, we argued, we discussed, we looked at it every which way you can, and there is no way this thing can be real. It's all coincidence, and nothing more. You probably never really had a lump or mass in the first place or maybe it was one of those self-dissolving cysts or something."

"Sure, and Billy Landers had a self-dissolving scar, and that kid in the snow had cuts that healed themselves ... and ... and ... oh, just take your dog and go home." She hurried out of the room and locked herself in a room across the hall.

Paul gathered Sheba's things, left a note with a check on the table for Kim's trouble, and let himself out. He was as low as he felt he had ever been. Too many things were out of sync in his life and he couldn't fit the pieces back together. Standing on the doorstep with Sheba, the thought came to him that he should at least stay and calm Kim down. He knocked on the door again and found it hadn't locked, but pushed right in. Across the hall from the living room was the room into which Kim had disappeared. Paul knocked softly, waiting for some response from within before barging into a lady's bedroom. At least, he thought to himself, I'm still a gentleman, if not totally sane. He could hear voices whispering inside and felt very foolish standing in the hall. Just as he was about to turn and leave again, the door opened a little way and Kim stuck her face into the opening.

"What!" she snarled at him.

"Hey, I just wanted to say I'm sorry. Wishing doesn't make it any ..."

"Who's out there?" barked a gravely, masculine voice from somewhere inside the room. "Let me see who your lover is this week, tramp."

Tears were welling up in Kim's eyes. "Please go," she whispered to Paul. "He's not himself anymore."

Paul gently pushed on the door and forced it open. Kim stood back, her head hung down to avoid seeing his face or that of the other person in the room. Paul gasped. The grotesque figure of a man lay on the bed with tubes, wires, and braces everywhere.

"Well? Who is this?" the man snarled at Kim. "If you're going to bring your johns home, at least be polite and introduce them to your ugly invalid husband."

Paul broke the silence. "I'm not her john, as you suspect sir," he said very softly. "Mrs. Frazier was kind enough to take care of my dog while I was away on vacation and I have come to pick up my dog and pay her. Ours is a business relationship, but certainly not the kind you are imagining. Your own mind is crippled in more ways than your physical body. You have a kind wife who speaks admirably of you at every occasion. I do believe sir, you owe her at least the same respect. If you ever wish to talk to another man, Mr. Frazier, I am Dr. Paul Grant, psychologist and man. Please feel free to give me a call."

"I don't need no shrink you pansy quack, and if I did, how exactly do you expect me to give you a call? Just dial you up on my cell phone?"

"If the desire is there, you'll find a way to humble yourself enough to ask for help in calling. Good evening, sir."

Paul walked back out into the living room and waited for Kim to join him. He heard her tell the man in the bed she would be back in just a moment, and she purposely left the bedroom door wide open so he could see there was nothing going on.

"I'm really sorry," Kim said softly. "He used to be a wonderful man, but a drunk driver hit him head-on and he's bitter about the results of the accident. Carson was one of the best lawyers in the state before the accident." Tears were brimming over in her eyes again. "After I got the news from the doctor about the lump in my breast, I was sure you would be able to help Carson, too. I know that's a lot to ask or even think about, but if you could have met him before, if you could have seen what a great guy he was, you'd know how desperate I am to find a miracle. I want my husband back, Paul. I need something to believe in and maybe I was wrong, but I started believing in you." She turned around to look at her husband. "I look at that person in there every day and every night and think about the children we'll never have, the trips we'll never take, the ... you get the picture. I'm sorry. I really am." She turned then and walked back into the bedroom, closing the door softly behind her.

Paul stood for a moment wishing for the first time that what people thought he could do was true. Finally, he walked to the front door, made sure the handle was locked before he stepped outside with his dog, and pulled the door closed behind him.

*I have more memories than if I had lived
for a thousand years.*

<hr/>

Charles Baudelaire
French lyric poet

Chapter 19

odney Michael "Mick" Tandeski looked into the yellow, veined mirror of the flop house in which he had spent the night. A clean suit of clothes, a shave and hair cut, and a toothbrush could make him look somewhat like the man he used to be. Peering past his own image in the mirror, he saw the reflection of the telephone beside the bed. It had been years since he had seen an actual circular dial phone, but this was the real thing. And in black. The hot shower had been heavenly, and he wanted so very badly to pick up the phone and make that one call, but it wasn't time yet. There were a few more things he had to do.

Digging into his pocket, he found exactly thirty-seven cents in change. Not quite enough for a cup of coffee or any of the other things he needed. Now that his mind was sharp once again, he was able to focus on what needed to be done and have a one-man brainstorm on how to accomplish each task. He sat down on the chair next to the desk and pulled out paper and pen bearing the motel's logo. The list was short, but he spent time outlining each detail to an exact degree. Not just a haircut, a specific style of haircut. Not just a set of clothes, a particular style, design, maker, and color. This time he had something to prove and there could not be *one* flaw in his armor when he presented himself for their approval. The lives of many people depended on how well he was able to pull this off, so at the top of the page he wrote, in large block letters, MISSION CRITICAL. Below that, each task was titled and meticulously detailed, leaving no room for error. At the bottom, when he completed his list, he wrote, again in large letters, ZERO MARGIN FOR ERROR. He knew the list would be revised several times before he was through, but the feeling of accomplishment at having begun flooded through him and empowered him. It was time now to take the first step. This, the first, would probably be the most difficult of them all, because it was personal.

Maxine Jenson smiled at her children playing cards in the family room of their home. They were only five and nine years of age, but they played so well together and were so very close. A boy and a girl. Exactly as she had always planned. It would be months yet before they could play outside in the swimming pool her husband, Oliver, had had installed last fall. She couldn't wait and wondered who would enjoy the pool more, the children or her. Glancing quickly around the room she had only recently completed re-furnishing, she was quite pleased with what she saw. The big rock fireplace was the focal point, surrounded by dark wood built-in book shelves, a forest green paint on the walls, and pictures of fox hunts and equestrian feats brought to mind an English gentleman's club. Oliver loved this room and she was glad to be able to make him happy. He had done so much for her and her children after the divorce from her first husband. In spite of the raw bitterness remaining from that dreadful experience, it was a pleasure to see the children, bright, happy, and well adjusted, had come through it all unscathed. She hoped they had been too young to remember their biological father, or sperm donor as she and Ollie called him behind closed doors. Katie had only been two, and Morgan six at the time.

Max frowned at her own thoughts of the man to whom she had once been married, and with whom she had borne two children. His handsome face still haunted her. For the past several days the song they had both loved when they were dating had been running through her mind, non-stop. Whenever she thought about someone she hadn't seen in a long while, within days that person would call or write or appear. She hoped that would not be the case this time. There was no doubt in her mind that hearing from him again would disrupt everything in their lives. And Ollie, how would he react? Through all his bravado, she could see the insecurity behind his eyes, his fear that she would never love him as much as she had loved ...

"I'll get it!" yelled little Katie running for the phone that had begun to ring. "I'll get it!" she sang out again making sure everyone heard her and didn't object. Even before the child picked up the phone, however, Max knew who it was and her stomach produced the proverbial butterflies while her hand shook and forced her to place her cup of tea on the saucer and put both on the table next to the love seat on which she had been seated, feet curled under her as she watched her children.

After a few short moments, Katie brought the cordless phone to her mom and handed it to her, with a questioning look on her little face. "It's a man," she said, "and he said he needs to talk to you about a weather port in Suffern, California?

He said it don't rain there. But you gotta go to Suffern, California 'cause that's where it don't rain. Never. Can we go there? I don't like rain."

"Hand Mama the phone, Katie, and go play your game. We'll talk later, okay?" Katie skipped away, back to the game of chutes and ladders she'd been playing with her brother. Max held the phone for a second, staring at it, her heart pounding, before she took one last deep breath, put the phone to her ear and said, "Hello, Mick. What do you want?"

The voice that came through the phone lines still had the power to seduce her, and for this she was ashamed. "I need some money, Max, but before you say no, please let me explain."

Maxine stood up and walked into the kitchen with the phone and her tea cup. The children would think nothing was amiss if all she was doing was getting another cup of tea.

"I believe," said Max, "your opening line should have been 'I have some back child support money to give you, Max.' What is it this time? More drugs? A flop house for a couple days? Maybe a hooker to relieve some of the stress in your non-existent life. I'll bet panhandling for drug money all day can get pretty rough on the nerves at times, huh, Mick? I mean, what if you don't make enough and can't buy that fix? Good gawd, what do you do then? I guess you'd have to steal from, say, your best friend or your wife's brother just to make it through to the next day. Added to all the stress of finding money for your next fix, you now have legal problems for stealing. It must be a very, very stressful life, Mick, and I'm sure you could use a good massage, maybe a week in a spa, but hey, I'm out of pity and now I'm going to hang up."

"Max. Please don't do that. This is different … I …"

"Mick, it's always different. How many times have you done this in the past four years? How many times have you needed …"

"Max, listen. Please. Just listen. You don't have to believe me, but at least listen just this once. I don't need money for drugs. I'm clean and sober."

"Oh yeah! That's a new song and dance. I'll just pretend I haven't heard it before."

"Max, please? This is important, far more important than you can possibly understand right now, but I really need your help. Just give me a few minutes to explain what I can and then you can hang up, think about it, talk to Oliver Twist or whatever his name is, and make your decision. That's all I ask."

158

"I'm setting the timer, Mick. When the tea kettle starts to whistle it will be exactly three and five-eighths minutes. At that time, I hang up."

"Thank you, Max, you won't regret this. I am a new man, Max, and it's all because of one man who gave me a miracle. God used this man to help me get sober and the only way I can give back all that I owe to so many people is to get some decent clothes, get a haircut and shave, a place to stay for a little while, and a chance to find a job."

"Mick, when did you start believing in God?" The tea kettle started a low whistle. Maxine reached over and removed it from the stove, turning off the power to that burner. Something in Mick's voice reminded her of the man she had married, and yet, this one was even better. He sounded sober. He sounded lucid. He made sense, but she wasn't sure what he made sense about.

"I met a man who had the gift of healing and he healed me. He's just an ordinary man, not a preacher or priest or whatever you'd expect, but he changed my life with a few words and his touch. I went from the homeless shelter where I'd been staying, trying to go through withdrawal, straight to a church. I didn't particularly trust the priest at the shelter, so I went to a church to talk to a pastor. I felt like one of those lepers in the Bible that had been cleansed and was told to go show himself to the priest. That's pretty much what I did. We talked, this pastor and I, for hours and hours. It changed my life, Max. There really is a God who gave His Son for us. Each of us, individually, can have a personal relationship with that Son, Jesus, and He will provide all the answers. I don't know much yet, but I'm learning and ... well, I don't know what else to say. I know I don't deserve another chance from anyone, but if God's willing to give me one, I'm hoping you will too."

159

Maxine sat in total silence for a moment, not knowing how to respond to this new approach, one Mick hadn't used before. Finally, she found her voice again. "I don't know, Mick. It's never going to be easy to trust you. You put us through so much." The tears had begun pouring down her face. "I can't go through any of that again and I will not put my children through it."

"Our children, Max. I was there, too. I owe them a life. I owe you everything. I owe, I owe, I owe, but without one last chance to start all over, it can't happen. Max, I have never begged you to help me stay sober and do the right thing. I've always used excuses and begged for help staying sick. It's not easy for me to beg at all, but this time I'm on my hands and knees and I am begging for a chance to save my own life and give back to everyone I owe and many I don't owe."

Max sat in her kitchen staring at a snowman the children had built. His eyes were drooping, the right-side button having slid down his cheek. The scarf, she realized with a giggle, was the one Ollie had given her for Christmas, cashmere, expensive, unimaginative, green. Her home was cozy, it was clean, it was free of drugs and the hell that accompanied substance abuse. Ollie wouldn't even allow them to consume alcohol in front of the children. All of it, even his personal favorite, Chivas Regal, was locked away in a cabinet. She wondered if the slimy wimp Ollie became when drinking was any better than the man Mick had become. Ollie was a good provider, a great provider, but he wasn't the exciting man she had married the first time. Maybe she was the addict, addicted to danger, to excitement, to Mick Tandeski.

"I'm a little teapot, short and stout ... here is my handle ..." Mick had begun to sing into the phone. "Max, are you still there?"

"Yeah, Mick, I'm here. Can you give me a little time to think this over? I don't know what to say or do at this point. I'm confused and talking with you, hearing your voice, doesn't make it any easier. How can I reach you?"

"I'm not sure. I had enough cash for this run down motel for one night and I'm going to have to get out of here by three, so I won't have a phone. Can I call you? When? Just tell me when and I'll find a way to call you."

"Give me twenty-four hours. That should give me enough time to sort through this and ..."

"And talk to Oliver Twist?" Mick said sardonically. He despised the man who had taken his place in Max's life and was raising his children.

"Mick, his name isn't Ol ..."

"I know what his name is, Max. I just don't like the guy, okay? I just have this thing about someone else sleeping with my wife and raising my kids."

"You gave them away, Mick. For a dime bag you gave away your wife and your kids."

"I'll call you in twenty-four hours. And Max? Katie sounds like the angel I knew she would be. You don't have to tell the kids why, but if you could slip in an extra hug and kiss from me sometime today, I'd appreciate it. And, while you're at it, give yourself one, too. You're still my One Max-in-a-million!"

Max held the phone to her ear long after the connection had been terminated. Hearing Mick's voice, sounding sober and alive again brought back so many memories, and, yes, hopes.

"Hey mom, Katie said we're going to California. That true?" Morgan had come into the kitchen and was peering into the refrigerator for a snack. The child never seemed to get full, and yet he was as slender as a reed. "I've never been to California. It sounds like fun. Katie said it never rains there. So, when're we going?"

Maxine had to chuckle at the innocence of her beautiful children. Morgan so studious and smart, a little on the shy side, and Katie the little butterfly flitting here and there, afraid of no one and hard to pin down. "No Morgan, we're not going to California. That was an oldies radio station with one of those on air contests about songs from the seventies. If I could identify all seven songs, I could have won a trip for two, just two, to California for three days. But alas, I missed most of them so none of us are going to California."

"If you had won, who would you take, me or Katie?"

"I don't know." Max turned on her most serious, thoughtful look. "Maybe I should take King Solomon's advice and cut you both in half, take half of each of you. What do you think?"

"I think you and this Solomon dude are nuts! Take all of Katie, all of me can stay here. Someone's gotta make sure Ollie gets his fiber every morning. You know how cranky he gets without his fiber."

"Morgan, where on earth did you learn to talk like that? You sound like an old man, not a nine-year-old."

"You grow up fast when you gotta," said Morgan seriously. "I don't have no dad, I got an Ollie, so I hafta be the man around here."

One more time, Max had to turn her head away and look out the window at the snowman as tears brimmed over the lower lids of her eyes. "Damn," she thought. "Why do I have to be such an emotional fool? Why do I have to love them all so much, Mick, Morgan and Katie, my Tandeski Trio?"

Mick placed the receiver back in its cradle and breathed a sigh of relief. The call had gone far better than he'd dared hope. Max sounded good. No, she sounded great. He knew he would never love anyone the way he had Max. They had been soul mates, best friends, lovers, and adventurers sharing everything. They could read each other's minds and finish each other's sentences. He could still see her in his mind, short red hair, scrawny little legs and arms, freckles everywhere, and the biggest, bluest eyes he'd ever seen. She never looked like a mom, she always looked like a little girl. When she drank her tea, he'd always thought of her as a little girl playing tea party with a teddy bear and a doll. There was a frailty, a fragility about Max when you looked at her, but once she spoke that illusion was quickly erased. Maxine the Mini Warrior he had called her. And then they'd had Morgan, followed in four years by Katie. Morgan, the very image of himself, and strawberry blond, bubbly Katie, her mother's clone. How could he have allowed drugs to take all that away from him? Mick Tandeski was not the crying type, but for now, a few tears were allowed, shed for what he had had and lost.

It was time to make his second phone call. This one wouldn't be as easy. He picked up the receiver one more time and dialed the number he had written on the single sheet of cheap motel stationery. He could hear the ringing ... one ring, two rings, and just as he was about to lose his nerve, a pleasant female voice spoke into his ear ...

"Thank you for calling the Drug Enforcement Agency. How may I assist you?"

O father forsaken, forgive your son!

James Joyce
Irish novelist

Chapter 20

The taxi cab in which Mick was a passenger allowed him a moving picture show of the city and its suburbs, places he had not seen in nearly three years. It surprised him how much each area had changed in such a short amount of time. Strip shopping centers sat vacant while new ones were built within blocks. Malls and mega-malls were springing up every which way, each one with bigger, more extravagant signage seducing shoppers to the many pleasures hidden behind the fortress built of brick and mortar.

Although it was only the first part of February, early signs of spring were peeking out on lawns and roadsides. Lakes had begun the slow decline into fluidity once more as river banks held their breath to hold back the ebbing waters of melting snows. Tracks from various winter toys criss-crossed the banks along roadways, the flat terrain of parks, and even some front yards. Snowmobiles towing skiers or kids on a toboggan were frequent sights. Mick wondered why the red-cheeked children weren't in school until he remembered it was a school holiday in honor of President's Day.

Inside, the taxi was too warm and in spite of repeated efforts to request a reprieve, his pleas were ineffective on his foreign-speaking cab driver. The seat on which he sat was stained and dirty from too many people shuttling in and out of the wind, the rain, the snow, sleet, and humid heat of summer. There was a strong smell of incense in the vehicle which tended to nauseate Mick, as if he needed another reason to feel ill at ease. At last the car turned off the road and they began the long, tree lined drive up to the main building of the areas most elegant and expensive retirement community. Mick looked down at his dingy, shapeless slacks. He had tried to wash them and lay them flat so they would look presentable for this audience, but his attempts seemed to have failed. The same was true of his shirt and jacket. He looked as he was—a homeless bum. When the taxi came to a stop in front of the main door under the canopy, the driver sat in his place, making no attempt to open the door for his passenger. He turned to Mick only to explain in his broken English the amount of the fare. Mick paid the man out of money he'd made shoveling a few sidewalks the day before, and gave him no tip, even though the man's hand remained out as if begging for alms. As Mick let himself out of the car, he could hear mutterings from the driver which sounded vaguely similar to "filthy American jackass." The car pulled away, leaving Mick facing the door he wished he didn't have to walk through, not this way, not now.

At the front desk, he asked where he might find Stefan Tandeski and was pointed in the right direction by a middle aged, rather plump, woman in a gray business suit. The halls were spotlessly clean with floors gleaming to a high shine. Mick felt so terribly out of place, but he had received his message and was about to pay his dues. Knocking on the door of suite number 65, he was softly greeted by an attractive young lady in a French maid's uniform. Some people never change, Mick thought to himself with a chuckle. Stefan Tandeski would surely be one of them.

"Come in here and let me see what you look like," barked Stefan from behind the door. Mick walked in and was surprised to see his father looking frail and shrunken, seated in a wheelchair. An even greater surprise was Max sitting on a love seat to the old man's left, nearly behind the door.

"So, you think you've finally kicked it, do you?" snarled Stefan. "How long you been clean this time?"

As much as he hated the "domineering father, obedient little boy" routine, he went along with it. "Just over two weeks," he said not daring to remove his eyes from those of his father.

"Just over two weeks, what!" barked his dad.

"Just over two weeks, sir."

"That's better. You sure as hell don't look clean and sober. Maybe sober, but I'll be damned if I'd call you clean. What do you want from me?"

"I, uh, I don't think ..." At a loss for words, Mick glanced quickly at Max who sat up and leaned toward Stefan.

"Stefan," she said softly, "Mick wants to borrow money to get back on his feet. He and I have had a long talk and I truly believe it's a good gamble this time. I asked him to come here today to see you. I'd like to take ten grand out of Morgan's college fund to help Mick, but I need your signature."

"Damn you, woman, don't you ever learn? He's done nothing to help you and those grandkids of mine for years and now you want to take my only grandson's college money to help him? What makes you so damned sure it's a good risk this time? What's so different?"

"He found God," whispered Max softly.

"Well, I'm glad somebody did!" snorted Stefan. "I didn't even know He was lost!" With that, Stefan fell into peels of laughter at his own joke, collapsing into a coughing fit in just seconds. His wrinkled, reed-thin old hand with skin as sheer as an onion peel waved for the French Maid/ Nurse to come to his aide. She slapped him on the back a few times very gently, then began to rub his back and shoulders, all the time chanting softly in French. The coughing spell passed and he straightened up once again.

"Okay," he said, returning to his ornery demeanor, "I'll sign for it this time on one condition. If he falls back off the wagon or whatever it is you dopeheads fall off of, he has to pay back every single stinking cent to Morgan personally. You got that, boy?"

"Yes, sir," demurred Mick, feeling ill on the inside for having to go through this humiliating ritual. "I will pay it all back, with interest, and that's a promise to you and to my son."

"Good, now you get out of here while I get the money and give it to Max. I trust her but I sure as hell don't trust you, my own flesh and blood. So you get yourself out of here while I try and remember where I hid the safe in this damnable place."

"Thank you sir," said Mick..

"Don't thank me, you sorry no good ... Thank this woman who was too good for you in the first place, and thank your son who'll probably have to work his way through school thanks to a father who'd rather do drugs than support his own kids."

"I promise, I won't disappoint any of you, sir," Mick tried again.

"You already have. Don't insult me with your worthless promises, Rodney. I've heard them all before. If it was up to me, I'd kick your ass clear to the Canadian border before I'd give you another damned dime. Now get out."

"I'll leave," said Mick, "but I'd hope that in the future you'd consider using fewer cuss words around ladies like Max and your nurse. Again, I thank you for your help, and good day."

Mick sat on a bench outside the ranch style building waiting for Max. The air was fresh, crisp, but not so cold as to be uncomfortable. He didn't have to wait long.

"Here you go," Max smiled handing over ten thousand dollars in cash. "I still can't believe he keeps that much cash on hand. Maybe he had his maid get cash just for this. It still surprises me. And you! I can't believe you dared speak to him like that. What were you thinking?"

"I was thinking you deserve better than me, and better than him too. You're a lady Max, and no one should speak like that around any lady. He's not perfect either, just rich and angry. The rich always think they're better, but they don't realize it isn't money that makes the soul. Maybe I can ..." His voice trailed off as he squinted his eyes and look out across the sculptured lawns peeking ever so daintily through the snow on rare occasions. He turned once again to look at Max. "Can we just ... I don't know ... just talk for a little while? I don't have any friends since I got sober, and talk is nice."

"Sure," said Max without hesitation, "I think it would do us both good." They both sat down on the bench Mick had occupied before she came out of the building. "How are you doing?"

"I'm good, really. With this I can get myself some decent clothes, a small apartment, and some food. It's so hard to find a homeless shelter with really good food these days, you know? Tell me about you, though, and the kids. Tell me about the kids. Did you bring pictures?"

Max reached into her handbag and pulled out an envelope of pictures she had taken recently of the children. "Wow," said Mick, "Katie is the spittin' image of you, isn't she? And Morgan, I can't believe he's so tall and handsome. How are they doing? I want to know everything."

"There's not a lot to tell. They're normal kids, I guess. They don't care much for Oliver, but that's because Morgan still remembers you and still blames me for running you off. Katie doesn't like anything Morgan doesn't like. He's her big brother-slash-hero."

"Is Oliver that bad?"

"No. He's really not. After you called that day, I started fantasizing about how great things had been with you, how exciting, how romantic. It's not like that with Ollie, but it's good. He's a good man, he's honest, he loves me and the kids, and he has to put up with a lot competing with your memory. I love him, Mick. He's given me and the kids a lot and I really do love him."

"I guess I'm glad. Maybe I'll be so lucky some day. Find me a nice girl, settle down, you know, all that normal stuff. You're going to be a tough act to follow, though."

Max tried to change the subject. Even though she knew she would never go back to Mick, the thought of him loving someone else made her jealous. "Mick? You said you were going to church. Did you mean it?"

"Yeah, I did. It's the only thing keeping me clean. What about you and he kids?"

"We've never gone. My family force-fed church down our throats as kids and I saw what hypocrites they were, so I never thought about it as being beneficial. Do you think it's too late to start taking Morgan and Katie?"

"Let's see, Morgan's nine right? Yeah, it's too late. God cuts the entrance age off at seven."

"Are you serious?"

"What do you think?"

"You're right, that was a dumb question. I just don't know where to begin. Morgan isn't going to want to go someplace where he doesn't know anybody. He's so reserved and uncomfortable in new places. He likes to be where he knows people and knows what's expected of him, how he's supposed to act. And I'm not sure about Ollie. I don't even know what church we would go to if we did go."

"How about Morgan's friends? Does he have any that go to a church near you? Maybe he could visit with a friend a few times, get involved a little. Let him make the choice. I can't answer for Ollie since I've never met the man. And as far as which church you go to, well, you might need to visit several before you find one that feels like home. It's not like God's at some and not others. He's pretty much non-denominational. I hope you can find a place that fits all of you. It doesn't sound like Katie will be a problem as long as Morgan's happy. I wish I had known God a lot sooner in my own life. That old man in there, I don't think he's ever set foot inside a church in his whole life other than to attend a funeral. Today's not the day for me to bring the good news to him, but you can bet I will before he's a goner. I wonder how different my life would have been if he and Mom had been churchgoers instead of country club members. There's nothing wrong with the country club, but God deserves at least equal time. I really wish you could meet the man who turned my life around. It was a real miracle, Max. One minute I was delirious going through withdrawal, and the next minute I was completely clean and lucid. I can't begin to describe it."

"Where's his church?"

"I think I told you on the phone, he's not a preacher, he's a psychologist up in Duluth. He was visiting the shelter, seeking some kind of answers for himself from Father Mike."

"Are you sure you're off the drugs? This story doesn't make a lot of sense."

"Miracles don't make sense. That's why they're called miracles. They're unexplainable except for divine intervention. If I told you I felt spiritually clean, would you understand what I meant?"

"No. I don't think I understand. Have you been baptized by one of those churches that dunks you all the way under?'

"That's symbolic of death and rebirth. What I'm feeling is a one-ness, a clean, spiritual connection with God. It comes from communing with God through meditation and believing, having faith. It comes from knowing that you are a part of God, just like Morgan and Katie are a part of you and me. It's hard to explain, but it has nothing to do with the body, it's all about the spirit, the soul."

Max stood up. Mick could sense how uncomfortable she was listening to his story, but he'd found that many times since his conversion. She'd have to find out for herself.

"I need to get back home, Mick. It's been good talking to you. I'm glad things are going well."

"When can I see the kids?" he asked with true confidence.

"I think it's a bit too soon yet, don't you? Besides, you're way behind in child support."

Mick held out the ten thousand dollars, but Max shook her head. "That won't work. It has to be money you've earned, not money you got from your dad. It has to be honest money. Besides, you need that to set yourself up again. Give me some time, Mick. It's been enough of a shock for me, I'm not ready to share that with the kids just yet."

"And Ollie?"

"He knows. He doesn't approve, but he loves me and trusts my judgment. Call me when you get settled in and we'll talk."

Max turned and walked away. Mick stood staring at her, admiring the way she carried herself, the same way she had when he first met her. She wasn't a strikingly beautiful woman, but to Mick she was gorgeous. He loved her and ached to be near her again. The car she got into was new, expensive, and shiny. It felt good to know someone was taking good care of her, even if it wasn't him. When she was far enough down the road where he could no longer see her tail lights, he walked back into the building and asked the young lady at the front desk to call a cab, and asked that someone come and get him from Mr. Tandeski's suite when the car arrived.

When he reached his father's rooms again, his knock on the door was once more answered by the pretty young maid.

"Did you forget something, Mr. Tandeski?" she asked sweetly, her big mascara-laden eyes batting coquetishly.

"Yes, I did. I'd like to see my father again for just a moment."

She opened the door to allow his entrance. Stefan Tandeski was sitting in his wheelchair, staring out the window.

"You're back," He snorted without turning around as Mick entered the room. "Not enough money?"

"Oh, the money's plenty good. And I'll pay it back. I just stopped back to tell you I'll be picking you up for church at 9:30 Sunday morning, so be ready and waiting. Oh, and Dad—I love you."

Mick walked out of the room once more, closing the door softly behind him. He didn't turn around to see the tears filling up the eyes of seventy-four year old Stefan Tandeski, Man of Steel.

"Moral indignation is jealousy with a halo."

H. G. Wells
English novelist

Chapter 21

Spring came early to Minnesota for a
change. The tiny green buds on trees
peeped out to see if it was warm enough
to pop out and play, each one as innocent and as
soft as a newborn babe. One could almost hear
their giggles as they waited for the chance to grow
into big leaves and shade the world. It was an
awesome responsibility for a tiny leaf bud.

Paul Grant sat in his therapy room wondering
how much longer Sylvia Tomlinson was going to
drone on and on and on about her problems. She
had gone over the same scenario every week for
the past three months and made no progress towards resolving her issues. Paul was pretty sure
she just liked to hear herself talk about the sexual
functions of her marriage. He called it voyeurism
into your own bedroom via psychotherapy. He decided to submit a new diagnosis for the DSM, au-
dio auto voyeur erotica ... talking about your own
sex life as if seen through someone else's eyes.
The budding trees outside captured more of his
attention than Mrs. Tomlinson and her husband
Don, or "Don, the Human Dynamo" as she called
him. At long last he was able to interrupt and
state their time was up. When she had gone, he

wandered into Rob's office to see if he was planning anything for lunch.

"What's on the menu for lunch?" Paul muttered nonchalantly as he stepped into the office. Things had been somewhat different between the two men since Rob had begun dating his estranged wife again, and Paul was now the lone ranger. It had been four months since Sarah had left and all the April showers in the world wouldn't wash away the pain and wondering Paul still had.

"Having lunch with my Angel," smiled Rob. "I'd ask you to join us, but we're meeting the Father for lunch at the church. We're going to renew our vows and start over ... *and*, Angel wants to start a family."

"Rob, that's great man, that's the best news I've heard in I don't know how long. I'm really happy for you. Give Angel a big kiss from me and congratulate her too, will you?"

"We're going to the Surly Cow to celebrate for dinner. That's where we got engaged. Want to join us?" The invitation was made with the hopes Paul would decline. This night was too special. Rob planned to ask Angel to marry him once again.

"Thanks, but I can think of things I'd rather do than hear you and Angel discuss how you plan to start this family. I'm sure my sock drawer needs rearranging and I really have to give Sheba a bath. Thanks for thinking of me, though." Paul turned to walk out of the office, feeling the pangs of jealousy and hating himself for them.

He had been avoiding contact with everyone else for the past few months, trying to get his head re-wired and trying to figure out what to do with his life. Sometimes he felt like the relic was a real gift that had given him the power to heal and he should go on TV and become one of those rich and famous televangelists. Somehow his ego wasn't big enough or his slime-ball factor low enough. He thought about giving the piece away, but knew he couldn't do that until he found out where it came from and why. He no longer carried it with him. It lay on top of the night stand in the guest bedroom where he still slept.

There had been no word on the Landers family, although he had noticed in the morning paper the trial was scheduled to begin next week. Bobby would be in need of someone to turn to at this time, and Paul hoped there was a strong male role model in the family who would be there for him. His doubts were high, but there was a chance. Kim Frazier had taken a leave of absence from the police department to spend more time with her husband. No one had heard anything at all from Sarah. With the weather warming up, maybe it

was time to make another visit to the homeless shelter and Father Mike. He could leave tomorrow after work, and spend the weekend. There it was ... a real plan. But, who would watch Sheba? Dare he call on the Fraziers? No. He decided it would be better to ask Elmer if he'd take her for the weekend. She could visit all her old pals and he could pay Elmer a few bucks for watching her. Now he really had a plan. And with the success of that plan, one of the few he had worked through in the past four months, he decided to treat himself to a burger and fries at the Burger Barn for lunch. There was only one more plan to make and that was to call Ruth and see if he could stay there. Something was amiss in that household and as much as he didn't want to stay with them, his curiosity got the better of him and he decided to call Ruth from home after work. After consuming a double cheeseburger, French fries, a large Bubble Up, and a huge piece of fresh blueberry pie ala mode, he drove by Elmer's place and made arrangements for Sheba before returning to work. For the first time in several months, his head felt clear and he felt a sense of accomplishment. They were small steps, but they were definitely steps.

Back in the office, neither Rob nor Paul had any appointments until two or two-thirty, so they spent a few minutes discussing their respective lunch events.

"You look like a man about to be married again," Paul smiled and shook Rob's hand. "When's the big day?"

"We're planning to redo our vows the last week in May, and then take a week of vacation to, um, get to know one another. We've decided to sell my house and move into a larger one because we'll need more than two bedrooms, I hope. Believe it or not, Angel still wants to wait until we renew our vows. I just hope it's not another ... you know."

"You never did tell me exactly what it was she said to you on your wedding night. I know it was something weird, but what? Can't you tell me?"

"Paul that would be like gossiping about my own wife. If that story ever gets told, it'll have to come from Angie. I couldn't do that to her."

"You're a good man, Robert, and I hope she's worth what you've gone through for her, not to mention what you've done without because of her. I hope everything works out this time. I really mean that. I, on the other hand, didn't talk to any of my wives over lunch, but I did talk to Elmer, the guy I got Sheba from, and ... "

A look of shock ran across Rob's face. "You're not giving Sheba back are you?"

"Oh, no, no, nothing like that. What I started to say before your anxiety attack, was that Elmer has agreed to watch her for a couple of days. I thought I'd go down to the Cities and visit with the old gang at the shelter, help Mike out a little. You know, just get away for a couple of days. I'll drive down after work tomorrow and come back Sunday night."

"Yeah, sure. The last time you said that, you stayed a week. Be sure to keep your cell phone in your motel room or wherever you're staying so you can call me when you decide not to come back right away."

"I'll be back Monday. There's really no reason to stay. I just want to spend some time away from me and my own pity party. Besides, Sheba needs to be around other dogs now and then."

"Does Mike know you're coming?"

"He will. I'm going to call Ruth tonight to see if I can stay there again. She'll run over to the shelter and tell Mike."

Rob had a frown on his face. "Are you sure you should be staying there, with her and that old man?"

"No, I'm not sure at all, but I've got to find out what all that was about. It may sound egotistical, but I have the strongest feeling it was about me and that Ruth and Mike were arguing ... about me. I probably should have gone back before now to find out, but I needed to get my own head together first."

"And have you?" Rob sat back in the big leather executive chair behind his desk, pulled his glasses down on his nose, and gave Paul his now famous 'I'm the analyst, you're the patient' look.

Paul turned sideways in his chair, lifting his right leg over his left, hooking his left arm around the chair back. The window behind Rob's desk framed a young Maple tree struggling to get its babies out onto each limb. Paul stared at it for a moment, wondering what it would be like to have children of his own. "No," he finally said sadly, "I haven't. I know how you hurt when Angel jilted you on your wedding night, but at least she gave you some kind of explanation. I have nothing. I don't know where she is, who she's with. I don't even know why she left. I tell my patients they need to find closure on lost relationships, but I can't tell myself the same thing. I don't want closure. I want some answers and I want my wife back."

"Paul, this is going to sound rather odd coming from me, but, have you thought about seeing other women?"

"How many women did you date during the fifteen years you and Angel were apart?"

"Maybe I was wrong. Right now I don't think so, though."

"Of course not. Right now you're planning your future with your wife. A couple of years ago you weren't planning anything. Ten years ago you weren't planning anything. So, what were your thoughts about seeing other women during all that time? You know as well as I do, once you find your soul mate, no one else matters."

"Maybe if I had gotten past waiting and started seeing other women I wouldn't have wasted fifteen years of not knowing anything for sure. Maybe I'd have found someone else and had five or six kids by now. I've always loved Angel, and I know I always will, but that doesn't mean I couldn't have loved someone else just as much. I just never gave myself a chance to try. To be perfectly honest with you, Paul, until I change the diaper on my first-born child delivered through Angel, I won't be absolutely sure of her. If Sarah did come back, could you be absolutely, positively sure she wouldn't leave again? Could you ever leave the house and trust her to be home when you got back? Trust is a pretty big issue in any relationship, Paul. If you can't trust your mate, you have no future together."

"Spoken like a true hypocrite who's making plans to procreate with the only 36 year old virgin in the western hemisphere. I can't say what I'd do or how I'd feel, but I don't want to be in bed with another ..."

Paul's words were interrupted by the ringing of his cell phone. Pulling the device off his belt he saw the caller's identification as 'private.' "Hello?" he said into the phone, wary of what was going on.

"Paul, oh Paul," cried a woman's voice. "You must come today please. My Saul, he's dying. He needs you Paul, he wants to see you. Please come. Please, tell me you will come."

"Ruth, calm down," said Paul with some frustration, looking at Rob and rolling his eyes to show he couldn't understand what was going on. "Slow down and tell me what's going on."

"It's Saul," she said again, only marginally slower, and still with sobs choking her voice. "It's my beloved Saul. He is dying. The doctors say he has no more time. He wants you to come. He says he must talk to you before his time is up. Can you come today, please?"

Paul closed his phone and put it back on his belt. "Well, I guess I'll be going to the Cities after work today instead of tomorrow. I'll call my patients and reschedule so you won't have to do that. I'd best get started on that and then call Elmer, too. It's weird how she called today when I was going to call her tonight. She sounded strange too ... almost like it wasn't her. But, I guess if Saul's dying ... ?"

"What exactly happened?" asked Rob, still not clear on what had been said.

"She said Saul's dying and he wants to talk to me before he dies."

"I thought Saul didn't like you."

"He doesn't, but I guess when you're dying, you're willing to talk to a man who can work miracles with a little old piece of nearly petrified wood."

"I thought he was Jewish."

"Maybe religious sectarianism goes out the window when you're on your way out the door."

"Do me a favor, okay? Call me tomorrow night and let me know what's going on. I'll be at my place or Angel's but I'll have my cell with me."

"Okay. If you don't hear from me, why don't you call the cops and have them frisk poor old Ruth, slam her up against the wall and make her spread 'em, then place her hands on her head so she can be cuffed."

"You watch too much TV," laughed Rob.

"And you, Doc, worry like an old lady. I'll call you tomorrow night. I promise."

Often you just have to rely on your intuition.

Bill Gates
Microsoft

Chapter 22

Friday evening Rob enjoyed a nice home-cooked meal with his wife at her place, after which they looked at some of the homes in the area that were listed for sale. Around eleven-thirty when he was about to head home, Rob realized he had not yet heard from Paul. He tried to reach Paul's cell phone number several times, but got the recorded message each time, so he was sure Paul had turned the phone off. Maybe, he thought, the old man had died and everyone was milling around the place, the priest, the rabbi, the family, and, of course, Paul. Certainly he'd call when things settled down.

Once settled into his own living room again, Rob sat in the dark, reminiscing about the past seventeen years of their friendship. He'd been a fresh-out-of-school doctor of psychology waiting to defend his thesis when he was hired by Paul and Dr. Bell who ran the Superior Clinic. It had been on a whim that he'd taken a week off to get away from the Cities and all the headaches of completing his thesis and decided to visit Duluth. Instantly he had fallen in love with the city. Lake Superior was like having the ocean in your back yard. The hills around the lake reminded him of the San Francisco movies he'd seen where cars flew down one level to the next. During this one week visit, he'd also visited the public library to find out some of the history surrounding the enchanting land.

Duluth, he found, was named after a French Marine Captain in New France, or what is now known as Canada. The French Captain's name was Sieur du Lhut. This captain was also an explorer moving into the uncharted waters of Lake Superior. In the late 1600s, du Lhut and his men held a meeting to try and resolve issues between the warring Sioux and Chippewa Indian tribes. The meeting was held at the "Head of the Lakes" on or near the site of the city now bearing his name, Duluth. Rob read on and on about the fur trade, the Chippewa, the copper mining and much more. He went on to read about the building of the St. Lawrence Seaway and the passage from the Atlantic Ocean through all of the Great Lakes, to here, Lake Superior, by way of the St. Lawrence River. He was enchanted by the pictures of dog sleds delivering the mail from the first Post Office, and huts being built along the lake shore. Everything about Duluth and Northeastern Minnesota spelled home to the young Doctor of Psychology. If there was such a thing as reincarnation, he was certain he had lived here before.

The night was glistening with stars visible through the large pane of glass at the front of his small house. Rob sat back in his big leather recliner fully at peace with his life. So far away from where he'd been raised, he'd found his home and the woman of his dreams, then his nightmares, and now again his dreams. And the funny part was, they'd been raised just miles apart in a Dallas suburb only to meet and fall in love way up north in Duluth. "When it's meant to be," he said aloud to himself, "God makes it happen. And, as long as we're on the subject, God, what's going on with Sarah Grant? I don't understand this part of your plan and what it's doing to Paul. It's almost like he and I aren't allowed to be happy at the same time. If Sarah comes back do I lose Angel again?"

By Monday morning, Rob had still not heard from Paul and he was a no-show in the office. Repeated calls to his cell phone were exercises in futility. The day came and went without a word or message of any kind. That evening, Rob decided to make a quick trip to the mission to talk with Paul and find out was going on. Angel was going to spend a part of the evening with the Landers family, so he was free from obligation in her regard. The drive was quick, frequently exceeding the posted speed limit.

Lights were visible under the tent flaps at the shelter. The voice of a preacher, not that of Father Mike, could be heard sermonizing somewhere within the enclosure. Rob locked his car and walked to the back door flap of the tent. Peering inside he saw thirty to forty of the regular patrons sitting at the tables listening. At the front was a tall man with thick gray hair, a Bible open in one hand, the other arm and hand gesturing emphatically, calling these sinners to come to the Lord and be saved or face the hell fires of eternal damnation.

"Personally, I think these people have already experienced hell."

The voice behind him startled Rob. He turned and found himself looking into the laughing eyes of Father Mike. "I believe you're right," he said when he'd regained his composure. "Isn't there some kind of Catholic law against priests scaring the bejeezes out of a person in the middle of the night?"

"Yeah, it's the commandment right after 'thou shalt not peer into the mission tent and scare the guests'." Mike smiled and held out his hand. "Good to see you again, Rob. It's not like you to drop in on a Monday night. What's up? You alone or did you bring Paul with you?"

"Actually," said Rob, looking at the priest quizzically, "I was expecting to find Paul here with you."

"Why? Did he say he was coming by here today?"

"No. He said he was coming down here Thursday evening. Ruth what's-her-name called and said her husband was dying and wanted to talk to Paul right away."

"That's interesting," said Mike, lifting the tent flap slightly and taking a peek inside, "Saul passed away two months ago. Do you suppose Paul's using Ruth and Saul as an excuse to get away for a little free hanky panky time?"

"If that was the case, he'd be bragging about it and he would have shown up for work today. When he left Thursday, he promised to call that night and said he'd be back for sure by Monday. I haven't heard from him. Why would Ruth call and say that about Saul if it wasn't true?"

"I wish I could answer your questions," said Mike, turning back to face Rob, "but right now I've got a room full of sinners going to hell in a hand basket if I don't get in there. Brother Braddock can get a bit carried away. Keep me posted, okay?"

The priest started to duck under the tent flap when Rob grabbed his left arm to stop him. "Where does this Ruth lady live?" he asked. "I can't just turn around and go home without finding out what's going on."

Father Mike told him how to get to Ruth's store and apartment and then let himself into the shelter with a smile, a wave, and another reminder to keep him posted.

Rob didn't like the feel of the knot growing inside his gut. But he got back into his car and found his way to the little store owned by the Goldstein's. There was light coming from an upstairs window. He parked his car and stood by the front door of the store wondering how to get someone's attention upstairs. He paced a short ways up the street and found another door which apparently opened onto the stairway which led to the apartment. He knocked on the door several times, finally resorting to a heavy banging, before an older woman opened a window above and asked what all the commotion was about.

"My name is Dr. Rob Scott," he yelled up to the woman. "Are you Ruth?"

"What do you want?" came the abrupt reply.

"I'm looking for Paul Grant. He's a friend of mine. I was with him when you called the other day and asked him to come down because your husband was dying. Is he still here?"

Rob couldn't measure the expression on Ruth's face from this distance in the dark, but it took her a moment to answer. "I did not call your friend," she said. "My Saul, he died two months ago. Why would I call Paul now?"

"Did he call you last week and ask to stay here over the weekend so he could work with Father Mike?"

Again, the hesitation before answering, "No. He did not call me and I have not seen him for many months. Please now you go away."

"May I come up, please? I need to see for myself that he's not here. He's my friend and I'm worried about him."

"No. You go away. I don't know you and I'm not inviting you into my apartment in the dark of night. Paul is not here. Go away or I call the police." With that she closed the window and disappeared. Rob felt like calling the police himself, but everything was so uncertain, and he had no proof of anything. He had heard only Paul's side of the conversation when Ruth had supposedly called him. There was really nothing else he could do but go home and wait, unless he waited around and asked some of the people at the mission. Maybe one of them had seen Paul.

Somehow it seemed pointless to drive his car back for only two blocks, so he decided to leave the car where it was and walk back to the mission. Along the way he looked for signs of Paul, but found nothing. He had hoped to see Paul's car parked in an alley, or something to give him hope.

At the mission, things had quieted down considerably. Many of the residents were laying out bedrolls on the floor to sleep on for the night. Father Mike was shaking hands with the guest preacher who was preparing to leave. Some of the faces of the people in the tent looked familiar, others not. One little girl sat up and stared directly at Rob as he came into the tent. Her eyes were intent on his face, and she placed her arm protectively around a scruffy gray stuffed kitten. Rob smiled at her, but she refused to smile back. Her stare followed him all the way up to the front of the room where he stood aside waiting to speak with Father

Mike again. Each time he looked back, the little girl was staring, clutching her kitten. The elderly man next to her chided her into laying down, but still she refused to take her eyes off Rob.

"Well," said Mike, finally escaping from his guest speaker, "What did you find out? Anything?"

"No. She said she never called Paul and knew nothing. She acted weird though, like she had to think about it before she answered."

"I can understand that. You probably told her Paul came because her husband was dying. That's just what she needed to set her off balance, a reminder of her grief. I wouldn't worry about it too much, I mean about her. I am curious about what your friend is up to, though. Got any more ideas?"

"I'd like to talk to some of the guests here if I may. Maybe some of them have seen him. He mentioned a guy named Augie once or twice. Is Augie here?"

"Yeah, he's right over there," said Mike pointing to where the little girl was still staring at Rob. "You can ask him, but I doubt if he's seen him if no one else has."

Rob stepped around the several sleeping and nearly sleeping bodies. He was surprised to see some reading classic literature in the form of old, discarded books, a few working crossword puzzles from the newspaper, and others reading Bibles. Nowhere did he smell any hint of alcohol or drugs, which was what he had expected. On their last visit, he hadn't had a chance to mingle with the guests, and hadn't paid much attention to them as people. When he finally made it to where the child and the man were lying, the man sat up as if expecting him.

"Are you Augie?" asked Rob.

"Yes. That's me. Who're you?"

"I'm Rob Scott, Paul Grant's friend. I understand he's your friend, too. Paul's been missing since last Thursday when he told me he was coming down here. I was wondering if you've seen him or talked to him."

Augie looked at Rob who had knelt down to look into the old man's face. College courses in facial expression and body language served him well only when he was able to observe. There was fear in the man's eyes. He glanced at the child beside him who was still clutching the kitten. She shook her head no, ever so slightly, her eyes reflecting the old man's fear.

"I'm sorry," he said, turning away from Rob and pulling the little girl into a hug. "We haven't seen him. He ain't been here."

189

"What are you afraid of, Augie?" Rob asked with genuine concern. "If you know something about Paul, you don't have to be afraid to tell me. I'm his friend."

"The county wants to come and take away my granddaughter. We are both afraid. I don't know anything about Paul. He hasn't been here. If the police get involved, we know nothing."

Even as he was speaking, Rob caught Augie glancing past his shoulder to the priest who stood nearby. Could they be afraid of Father Mike? Not possible. He was a priest.

"That's an awfully cute kitten you have there, young lady. Mind if I hold him?" Rob had hoped for a friendlier response from the little girl, but she clutched the stuffed animal tighter and turned away from him, looking to her grandfather for support. She was a pretty child with huge, round, blue eyes, naturally long lashes, dark blonde hair that hung in natural ringlets down her back, and a tiny, freckled turned up nose, and two of the cutest dimples he'd ever seen in a child.

"That kitten was a gift from Paul," Augie interrupted. "It means more to her than her life. She won't let anyone touch it. It is her miracle kitten, the one that gives her hope and the assurance that Paul will return to help her as he promised. She knows I'm old and she waits for him, watches for him every day."

"But you say she hasn't seen him. Would she tell you if she did?"

"Melissa can't talk." Augie turned away from Rob and pulled the child to him on their makeshift beds. Together they lay their heads down in an attempt to sleep in this room filled with men and women of all ages and sizes.

Rob looked back at Father Mike, waved once and then left through the tent flap. Something in Melissa's eyes, something Augie had said, nagged at him, biting away at the knot in his stomach hoping to untie one little piece. They knew where Paul was, he was sure. At the very least, they had seen him when he came down to visit. But where was he, and why? There was only one other person he could turn to for help. And even that would be a long shot.

"You prepare by getting older than God himself
and keeping every dime you can
just in case they change the rules and
decide you can take it with you."

Stefan Tandeski
fictional character in "Relic"

Chapter 23

The late-breaking news interruption to the local evening newscast brought a smile to Mick's face. Lying back on his garage sale double bed, watching his thrift shop television, he was proud of the work he had accomplished in such a short time. The best part was, no one would suspect him because he was just another addict feinin' for a fix, or so they all thought. He grabbed the oversized, ancient remote control to increase the volume ...

191

"A drug bust initiated by an unnamed informant, led police and ATF personnel to the offices of Hammerle and Hammerle, Attorneys at Law, where fifty-one people were arrested and charged with everything from possession to trafficking of several illegal substances, including heroine, crack cocaine, and methamphetamines. The drugs, along with a vast assortment of drug paraphernalia were seized. Hammerle and Hammerle, one of the largest and most prestigious law firms in the Twin Cities, was started over sixty years ago by Gunter Hammerle. The Senior Hammerle passed away in 1986, leaving the bulk of his estate to his wife, Regina, and their son, Glen. The younger Hammerle has been serving as President, CEO, and Senior Partner since taking the reigns upon his father's death. Regina Hammerle, known for her society dinners and civic involvements, is currently vacationing in Europe and was advised of the situation by Interpol there. Glen Hammerle has been taken into custody along with fifty of his employees and is expected to be released on bond within the next few hours. The cache of drugs and drug-related products is estimated to have a street value in excess of forty-five million dollars."

Mick turned off the TV and jumped off his bed with a new spring in his step. "Forty-five million dollars saved from killing hundreds of kids. Wow! This is a great feeling!" He dressed quickly in a button-down sport shirt, slacks, loafers, and clean socks. This was his Saturday night date and he wasn't about to be a minute late. The car he'd purchased, a run-down, two-tone rust-and-primer gray Ford Escort would get him where ever he needed to go, as long as he didn't need to go very far. With a splash of expensive cologne, the only luxury he'd allowed himself, he hopped into his low-class limo and headed for the retirement community. The drive was short, just about ten minutes. He'd purposely chosen a cheap apartment near his dad hoping to make amends to the old man for all his years of neglect and drug induced anger. Every Saturday night at six-thirty, he drove to the community and spent at least two hours with his dad, playing chess, arguing about the weather and sports, even taking in a movie on occasion. This Saturday would be different. He had new plans to spring on Dad.

"Evening, Mr. Tandeski," smiled the pretty young lady at the front desk. "I believe he's ready and waiting for you. He's called up here three times in the last five minutes asking if you were here yet."

"Thanks, Brittany. I'll go put him out of his misery." Mick continued to walk at a brisk pace down the hallway to his father's apartment, inhaling the fresh scent of pine cleaner. Each chandelier along the way was made of sparkling crystal which obviously was cleaned on a regular basis. There was nothing but the best for those who could afford it. At last he reached the dark wood door to the senior Tandeski's apartment and rapped lightly only once before the nurse in French Maid uniform answered the door, her smile as gloriously bright as the dollar signs in her eyes.

"Please come in, Mr. Tandeski. Your father's been waiting. It seems he heard some rather troubling news on the television this evening."

Elocution lessons, thought Mick. She's been taking lessons to appear smarter. Maybe she and dear old dad are planning my next marriage arrangement. Better yet, maybe she's going to be my new mom! Wouldn't that be a hoot! "Evening, Dad. What's all the excitement about?"

"You didn't see it? It's all over the news. Your old employer's been taken down for pushing drugs all over the place. Took 'em all. At least fifty of them. Did you know they were doing drugs over there?"

"Of course I knew, Dad. Where do you think I got into it so deep? Boy Scouts?"

"So what can you tell me about this whistle blower who turned them in?"

"I doubt if I can tell you anything about him you don't already know, Dad. So, what're we going to do tonight?"

"We're going to talk about what your plans are. You haven't told me a single thing since I loaned you that money. I like to know where my investments are going."

"Your investment, as you so eloquently put it, has provided your son with a cheap room, a cheap car, and some cheap furniture until his ship comes in."

"I don't want to hear any crap about ships coming in. You work hard and make your own way in this world. No one's gonna do it for you. Have you even tried to look for a job?"

"No. Actually I thought I'd wait around until you kick the bucket and grab up what I can here. Sound like a fair enough deal."

"Over my dead body!" screeched the older Tandeski in a breathless and angry voice.

"That's what I said," laughed Mick.

"You haven't changed a bit. What if I don't leave you anything and give it all away to charity? How'd you like that?"

"Actually, that's exactly what I want you to do." Mick couldn't contain his excitement any longer. "Dad, with your help, I want to open a rehab center for kids on the street. Not a fancy Betty Ford kind of place, but a real place where kids can get help for their drug problems, counseling for their personal problems, play some basketball, get tutoring, that kind of stuff."

"Who's going to run this place? Not you, I hope?" His dad laughed and spittle sprayed from his livered lips.

"Why not me? Who has more experience in the problems that arise from drug use?"

"Yeah, you got that. But what about the counseling, the other stuff? How you plan to counsel one kid, play basketball with yet another, and let a third one cry on your shoulder all at the same time?"

"Well, first I need to incorporate and apply for the non-profit thing through the government to become a 501(c)(3). Then I'm going back to school mornings to get some more education in counseling and psychology, and third, I'm leaving Monday on a recruiting mission in Duluth. The psychologist who got me out of the drugs works in a clinic up there. I'm going to see if I can't get him involved in this project."

"So, what do you want from me, money?"

"Of course I want money, but I also want you to be a part of this project. It'll give you a whole new perspective on the life these kids lead, the kind of life I was leading. I don't want you to accept it or condone it. I want you to see it first hand, make it personal, and get involved."

"Don't you think I'm a little old to start shooting hoops down at the Y?" smirked the elderly man sitting in his wheelchair, his nurse never far from his side.

"No. I don't," replied Mick, fully serious. "You're limited by your own mind, not mine. You're still my old man, the hero I always looked up to and adored. The one person I could never please, no matter how hard I tried, and the harder I tried, the worse I got at it. I want you to be my partner in this one last venture together. Sure, I need your money, but I could get it other ways if you didn't have it or refused to help. It's not the money that is important to me any more. It's my dad." Mick looked deeply into the watery blue eyes of his father, and wiped his own tear away at the same time. He reached out to take the old man's fragile hand and felt a strong squeeze in return. "I'm going to go now so you can think about this. I'll be here at 9:30 in the morning to pick you up for church, so be ready."

"I'll be ready, but I won't like it," the elder Tandeski croaked through his tears. "I don't like preachers telling me how to die. I got that part figured out already. You prepare by getting older than God himself and keeping every dime you can just in case they change the rules and decide you *can* take it with you."

"Yeah, yeah," laughed Mick, pulling open the front door to the apartment. "Nine-thirty. Be ready. If you're late we'll have to sit down front and I know you won't like that."

———

196   At 9:30 the next morning when Mick pulled up to the retirement community, Stefan Tandeski and the nurse were waiting impatiently on the sidewalk at the circle drive.

"I'm only going so I can see what you plan to buy me for lunch," screeched Stefan as Mick got out of the car, a big smile on his face. "We're not going in this piece of mechanical excrement are we?"

"Sure are! Would you prefer front seat or back seat?" asked Mick as he deftly lifted his father from the wheelchair.

"Rumble seat if you've got one. If not, I'll ride in the trunk. That way no one's going to see me."

"People would see you in a rumble seat," argued Mick.

"Sure they would, but they'd think I was an eccentric old man in an antique car."

"Well, they're going to have to settle for eccentric old man in a Ford," laughed Mick as he placed his father's fragile body in the front passenger seat. He was amazed at how little his father weighed. The skin was like the very finest silk, so thin, so translucent. If he should accidentally brush his watch against it, he was sure the skin would tear. The thought of his father being this old, this weakened, and this helpless brought a lump to his throat once again. Why had he let so many angry words, lost hours, days, and years pass by? How little time did they have left? Would they ever have enough?

Swallowing hard to hide his moment of melancholy, Mick turned to the nurse. "Will you be joining us, Miss ..."

"No, she won't," barked Stefan from the front seat. "I gave her the day off and if I can't have any fun, at least let her have some. Now get your body in this bucket of rusty bolts so we're not late. I won't be hauled up to the front row by a bunch of hyprocritic oafs. And take me someplace nice for lunch. Someplace they don't know me ... or you. I'm not going to some dive where every junkie in the place knows my son, not to mention all the hookers. By the way, you been tested for AIDS? How about standards? You been tested for them?"

Mick looked at his father, completely puzzled. "Yes, I've been tested for AIDS because of my drug use and no, I don't have it. What are standards?"

"It figures you'd have to ask. Standards, STDs. Have you been tested or not?"

"Yes," laughed Mick with a light heart knowing his father really cared. "I've been tested for standards and I have none. I ranked high on the list for scruples and ethics though."

"Yeah, I'll bet. Tell me, son. What's it like with a hooker? They any good at what they do?"

"I don't know, Dad. I was just about to ask you the same question!" Mick laughed out loud at the look he got from his father. The blubbering and sputtering from the passenger seat continued all the way to the church.

He thought he saw a buffalo
Upon the chimney piece
He looked again and found it was
His sister's husband's niece
Unless you leave this house, he said
I'll send for the police.

Lewis Carroll
English mathematician

Chapter 24

The slow change from winter to spring comes grudgingly to northern Minnesota. Mounds of snow melt at alarming rates as the sun turns up its atmospheric thermostat for the first time in several months. Winter's blanket slithers through muddy hillsides and roadsides to flood into rivers, lakes, and roadside ditches. Children play gleefully in high boots, building rafts and floating down the spectacular waterways created along farm roads. Visions of faraway places and worldly adventures tumble through imaginations as the wind paints their cheeks and ears. Tom Sawyer rides again. Meanwhile, farmers pray the rain will hold off until the ground is dry and the crops are in. Home owners along the thousands of miles of lakes and rivers are joined by neighbors, friends, and total strangers in sandbagging efforts to ward off ruination of their home in the rising waters, cresting higher than the year before, and flowing more ferociously. Late into the night and early dawn hours, men

and women, the young and the old, labor tireless-
ly, all prejudices set aside, to help families hold
onto their precious belongings. An elderly neighbor brings coffee and passes it around. Peals of
laughter fill the crisp night air. Just before dawn,
as the waters appear to have crested or even begin to abate, aching shoulders and backs clothed
in red plaid flannel shirts with sleeves rolled up to
the elbows, slosh through the mud in thigh high
rubber boots to find their cars. Arms are raised
in farewell, backs patted in unspoken gratitude,
and the chill suddenly realized as comrades in the
effort board motor vehicles to return to their own
world until next year ... or sooner.

Rob sat glumly in the front room of his small
home. The day was dreary with a high prospect
of unnecessary rain. It was the first of May, a
time for celebration, for singing and rejoicing,
May Poles and May basket. His first call of the
morning had been to Angel, letting her know of
his unsuccessful attempts to find Paul the previous evening. She had serious concerns about
the Landers family and their future as the father
faced charges in the death of their youngest son,
Billy. The trial was about to begin. The second
call went to Paul's home with low hopes that he
had miraculously returned during the night. No
answer. Maybe it was time to contact the police,
put in a missing persons report. Paul had left
Thursday, was expected back Monday, it was now
dawn on Wednesday. He wished he could remember the name of that lady cop Paul had gotten to
know ... Fisher, Forest ... something ... it had to
be something like that. Elmer would know, and
Rob knew exactly where to find Elmer. That lady
police officer was his last hope. She knew Paul,

and surely she cared enough not to leave him as just a poster on the telephone pole.

Rushing through his morning routine of emptying his second cup of coffee, scarfing down a piece of dry toast, a thorough, hot shower, and pulling on his uniform of the day, consisting of shirt, tie, slacks, belt, socks, shoes, and jacket, Rob was on his way to Elmer's domain in less than an hour. The streets were still fairly bare and most of the sludgy gray remains of winter had slid into the great lake. As expected, lights were on at Elmer's house. Rob parked his car at the curb and walked toward the door, glancing around the side to see if Elmer and the dogs were out already. There was no doorbell, so he knocked five times on the rim of the storm door. The thought skimmed across his mind that everyone seemed to knock five times. Why? Was there a code, a rule of some sort written down before ...

"Who the blazes is it at this time of day?" yelled Elmer from inside the house. As his last words fell on expectant ears, he opened his front door to look out at what appeared to be a white black man, or a black white man. He couldn't tell. "Who're you?" he scowled, making no move toward the latch on the storm door. "I ain't buying nothing." His movements indicated his plans were to slam the wooden door shut and terminate the encounter at once.

"Wait," Rob pleaded, putting his hand out as if to stop the door. "I'm a friend of Paul, Sheba's owner."

Elmer hesitated with the door half closed. "Yeah? You come to pay for her care since he didn't show up on Sunday like he promised? I asked if he was giving her back. He shoulda told me the truth insteada walkin' out on her like that. Dogs got feelings y'know and that one's been mopin' round the house ever since he dropped her off. That ain't right and it ain't responsible. I sure hope he don't have no kids. Poor younguns is probably makin' their own breakfast right now, pourin' sour milk over stale cereal and wonderin' where the old man is this time. A man has to take responsibility. Y'know, when I was a kid ..."

"Elmer, trust me, Paul has no kids. Tell me what he owes for Sheba and I'll pay it right now, but I need your help, too."

"He don't owe me nothin'. He owes Miss Sheba an apology, though. What you need from me? I ain't givin' no dogs to the likes of you if you're gonna treat her like he done. If Miss Kim hadn't brought him over herself, I wouldn'ta let him have Sheba. You a black man or a white man?"

"I'm a married man. Miss Kim. Elmer, I need to know her last name. Please, it's important."

202

"And she's a married woman. Don't go gettin' no fancy ideas about Miss Kim. She ain't that type."

"Elmer. She's a cop. I need to find her. Paul Grant is missing. Please, what's her last name?"

"I just call 9-1-1 and ask for Kim. They all know her y'know. Don't you got a phone?"

Rob could feel the heat rising in his cheeks. Why hadn't he thought of that? "Elmer, would you ..."

"Yeah, yeah. C'mon inside here and we'll get her on the line."

Rob was surprised at how clean and orderly Elmer's small home was. Along the wall in the hallway were fourteen dog beds of different sizes and shapes. In the large kitchen, fourteen bowls of dog food and fourteen bowls of water, each with a dog name painted on it, were lined up against the cabinets. The countertops were spotless, and there were no signs of dog hair, or smells of dog urine or feces anywhere. In one corner nearest the stove, a tiny Chihuahua lay shivering in a small dog bed under a blanket. The big brown eyes pleaded for love and attention, so Rob knelt down to pet the little creature. His hand was quickly retracted when the animal let out a vicious growl and yap.

"That one there don't like strangers," said Elmer, phone receiver held up to his ear, the spiral cord trailing down to the rotary dial yellow phone on the wall. Suddenly he turned his head as if needing privacy to concentrate on the business at hand. "Yeah, ain't no 'mergency yet. I need Miss Kim. This here's Elmer," he barked into the phone. "Send her over." With that he placed the receiver back on its base and poured two cups of coffee. "Might as well relax whilst we wait on her. She won't be long, though. Cream and sugar?"

"No, sir, black is fine. Thank you."

"So, you never did answer my question. You black or you white?"

Rob had to chuckle. Elmer wasn't one to beat around any bush. "I'm both," he replied with a polite smile. "My mother is black and my father is white."

"Oh," was all Elmer said in response. They waited in silence for the next seven minutes until Kim showed up. When she did, Elmer opened the door and invited her right in. Rob was amazed at how tiny and petite she was. Even with all her police gear on she couldn't weigh more than a bowling ball. "This here's Rob. Says he's a friend of Paul and he's missing."

Kim reached out her hand to shake Rob's. "Kim Frazier," she said. "What's this about Paul?"

Rob repeated the whole story to Kim and Elmer, ending with his call to Paul's house earlier.

"So," said Kim very seriously, "do you want me to write up a missing persons report and put out a call with his description?"

"I'm not sure what I want to do. I'm just worried."

"'Scuse me for buttin' in," said Elmer, "but didn't you say you were suspicious of some of those people in Minneapolis?"

"I don't know if I'd say I was suspicious," countered Rob. "I just don't feel like they were telling the whole truth."

"I bet Sheba'd find him in a minute if ya let her," replied Elmer.

"That's a thought to keep in mind if we get some idea of where to start looking. Officer Frazier, would you go ahead with that missing person's report? I'm going to get a picture of him from our files at the office and make up some fliers. I'll post them around town, but I want to go back down to the Cities and post some around that shelter, too."

"Sounds like a plan," said Kim rising to her feet. "By the way, I understand congratulations are in order. Aren't you the lucky man who's going to renew marriage vows with our very own Angel Scott next month? I'm really happy for both of you. I'll stop by your office later today with the paperwork on Grant and we'll go from there. I'm sure he's just fine ... we'll find him." Turning away from Rob, she addressed Elmer. "Thanks for calling, Elmer. Got any new babies to show me?"

The two of them were off to the kitchen corner to check out the feral beast reclining under a tartan blanket in a bed by the stove. Rob let himself out the front door and drove quickly to his office.

In spite of the early hour, there was already one car in the parking lot when he arrived. It appeared to be a banged up, rust and primer colored Ford of some kind. A man was sitting inside, apparently dozing. When Rob shut his own car door, however, the man came awake and got out of his vehicle.

"Can I help you?" asked Rob.

"I hope so," said the man dressed in neat slacks, shirt, and jacket. "I'm looking for Paul Grant. I guess it's kind of early yet though, huh."

"Who're you?"

The man approached Rob quickly with outstretched hand. "Mick Tandeski," he replied. "We met at Father Mike's mission in the Cities. He helped me get clean and sober. It was the most amazing thing that's ever happened to me, and now I want to talk to him about helping me help others. When do you expect him?"

Rob unlocked the office doors, and opened one, motioning for Mick to come inside. As Rob went around turning on the lights, Mick looked around in the reception area.

"Come on back here," yelled Rob from his office. "I'll put some coffee on and we can talk in my office. It's the second one on your left. Go ahead and make yourself comfortable — this'll just take a minute."

Mick made his way down the hallway towards Rob's office, adjacent to a consultation room. It was still a bit cool in the building with the heat having been turned off all night. Rob had turned up the thermostat, but time was needed to feel its affect. Even though spring was well on its way, the outside temperatures barely peaked at fifty degrees most days.

"Well now," said Rob, settling into the executive chair behind his desk. "You're looking for Paul, right? I don't suppose you've seen him in the past week or so, have you?"

"As a matter of fact, I haven't seen him since I left the shelter and that's been, gosh, four or five months. It was right around Christmas time."

"And you just happened to remember where he worked and all this other stuff?" asked Rob as he dialed 9-1-1 on his phone.

"Yeah," said Mick, becoming concerned at the direction these questions were taking. "Is there something wrong?"

"I don't know ... Kim Frazier, please, Rob Scott calling. Yes, this is an emergency." Rob held up his index finger to indicate to Mick he'd be a minute. "Officer Frazier, hello, this is Rob Scott. I have a gentleman in my office who is looking for Paul even though he only met him one time during a rehab stint at the shelter in Minneapolis five months ago. Yeah, sure. We'll be here."

"Officer Frazier? You want to explain what's going on? Is there a law against looking up someone who helped you or remembering his name?"

"Why don't we wait for Officer Frazier to get here and let her ask the questions?"

The two men sat in silence as they waited for Kim to arrive. Rob occasionally glanced suspiciously in Mick's direction, and Mick just looked around the room trying to figure out what kind of mess he'd stepped into. It was a good ten minutes before Kim pushed her way through the front doors and into Rob's office.

"Hello there," she said, putting her hand out to Mick. "I'm Officer Kim Frazier, Duluth's finest. What seems to be going on here?"

Rob filled her in about Mick sleeping in the trashed out car in the parking lot when he arrived. Mick countered with his own explanation of his miraculous healing from Paul and his desire to see Paul and invite him to join him in a drug rehab program for kids.

"So," said Kim, "after nearly five months you remember the full name and place of employment of a man you met while you were experiencing withdrawal from coke, right?"

"Yes, sort of. The cure was instant, I mean instant, miraculous, as you say. But Paul took off right away after it happened, like it freaked him out or something. We were introduced, but that's about all. Father Mike filled me in later on who Paul was and where he worked. I wrote it down in my connections book. It was the last entry I made."

"What's a connections book?" asked Kim.

"In my case, after I lost my job, I kept a list of guy's names and numbers, the ones who'd give me drugs to sell on the street and in return, they'd make sure I got my daily fixes. They were my connections."

"So you wrote Paul Grant's name in your connections book. Was he supplying you with drugs?"

"No!"

"Then why would you write his name and work address in the same book with those who were providing you with drugs, to sell and to use?"

"You're making this into some kind of crime. I told you, Paul got me through it, got me off the drugs. His is the last name ever written in that book because I wanted to remember him, pay him back in some way for helping me. I never met the man before that day and I haven't seen him since. If he's into drugs, which I doubt seriously, I have no knowledge of it. I figured he was one of those healing evangelists until Father Mike told me he was a psychologist. It didn't mesh at the time, but I was so grateful to be out of the pain, out of the agony of withdrawal, I wouldn't care of he was a ditch digger. The man saved my life. Now, I want to find him to ask him to help me save other lives. Is that so impossible to understand?"

"And you're sure you haven't seen him in the past week?"

"Lady, I haven't seen him since Christmas week in December. Are you hard of hearing?"

"It's officer, if you don't mind. Not lady ..."

"I'm beginning to understand why!" snorted Mick sardonically.

"And, it just so happens, Paul Grant has been missing for the past few days. You can imagine how suspicious it appears with you sleeping in a ratty old dump of a car outside his office in the early morning hours less than a week after his disappearance. Do the Minneapolis police know about your connections book?"

"Oh yeah, they've got it, along with a lot of other names. I'm sure you've heard about the big bust at Hammerle and Hammerle, Attorneys at Law."

"You did that? Why?"

"I used to work there. They got me started on the hard drugs way back when I was a snot-nosed kid fresh out of college. I felt like I owed them something for all that time and money they invested in me."

"You're a lawyer?" asked Rob.

"No, actually, I was the accounting manager for the firm. CPA. It's a wonder their books ever balanced as high as I was all the time. But, everyone else was high too, so I guess no one noticed. We all made a lot of money, had a lot of fun, spent a lot of money, and lost a lot of ourselves in the process. In my case, I lost my job, my wife, my kids, my home, my sanity. When I tried to kick the habit, they let me go. Most companies make you take a drug test when you apply for a job. Generally they're hoping for a negative result. At Hammerle and Hammerle, if you tested positive for drugs you got to keep your job. I should have re-applied after I got canned because I went right back to the hard stuff."

"So who else was on your list?" Kim asked.

"You'll have to talk to the police in Minneapolis. The only page I tore out before turning in that book was the last one, the one with Paul's name and work place on it. My own name's pretty much mud in the Cities right now, at least around dealers and junkies."

"Aren't you afraid of repercussions?" asked Rob, "I mean, isn't your life in danger at this point?"

"I suppose it pretty much is, yeah. But, if God saw fit to give me one big miracle, I'm counting on Him keeping me alive long enough to pay back my debt. I'm not going to cower in corners and keep looking over my shoulder, if that's what you mean."

"So why are you driving that car, why not something a little more presentable?" Kim was staring out the window to the parking lot, writing down the license plate number.

"I said I was sober. I didn't say I had a job or money. I had to get my ex-wife to ask my dad for money. Can you believe that? She didn't like it, and he sure didn't like it, but he loaned me a few thousand to get off the streets and find a job. I didn't want to blow a lot on a car or anything else, so I got just what I needed and put the rest in the bank. Jobs aren't easy to come by once you've been a homeless addict. That three-year employment gap usually requires an explanation and honesty isn't necessarily the best policy. I bought that baby out there for four hundred and seventy five bucks."

"You still haven't explained why you were sleeping in the parking lot," said Kim.

"It's not easy to keep a schedule when you're not working. I sleep a lot during the day and then can't sleep at night." Looking at Rob, he continued, "You psychologists probably call it depression. Anyway, last night I couldn't sleep, as usual, so about four thirty I got dressed and started driving. I decided it was time to see if I could locate Paul Grant and at least shake his hand and say thanks. I got here earlier than I expected, and by that time I was tired so I napped in my car waiting for the office to open. That's where you found me. I have nothing to hide, but I would like to know more about Paul's disappearance. I may be able to help, who knows."

Rob stood up and invited Kim and Mick into his therapy room so they could have more privacy. The office staff would be arriving soon, and they didn't care to be interrupted. He hung an "In Session" sign on the hallway door to avoid disturbances. He poured a carafe of coffee and brought it into the room. Once they were all settled into comfortable chairs and had full cups of coffee, Rob began again relating the events of the past few months. Mick and Kim would interrupt occasionally to ask questions. Two hours later, they both knew all about the relic, the healings, the missing wife, and everything in between. Kim was able to add her own story about the healing of the breast lump. Just as they were about to end their meeting, having made plans to get together and strategize more after work, the intercom buzzed.

"Dr. Scott?" the high pitched voice of the receptionist intoned. "I know you didn't want to be disturbed, but the lady on line one claims she's Sarah Grant."

No pain, no palm; no thorns, no throne;
no gall, no glory; no cross, no crown.

William Penn
English Quaker

Chapter 25

Another wave of nausea swept through Paul's body. He leaned over the side of the small single bed, and waited for the retching to begin again. There was nothing left in him to come up except perhaps his intestines and testicles. He wasn't sure they, too, had not already been eliminated in the previous day's storms. Too weak to care, he lay back once again, covered in perspiration. The vision of Sarah remained and in his own hallucinatory state, he attempted feeble conversation, his voice so weak he could barely hear himself speak.

"Sarah? Why?" he whispered.

"Oh, but I'm not Sarah. I'm Tina, remember me?"

All of his strength expended in that short conversation, Paul rolled back onto the bed and succumbed to his weariness. "Please, don't leave," he breathed. "I don't want to die alone."

"You're not going to die," soothed the image of Sarah claiming to be Tina. "I'll be here with you and this will all be over soon. Just don't drink the tea."

"The tea, why not? I'm already dehydrated from this blasted virus. The tea helps me keep my strength up."

"It's not a virus, but you will recover soon if you just listen to me. Don't drink the tea. Pour it into the bucket. Ask for water."

Paul felt a minute surge of strength and raised himself just enough to lean on one elbow. "She won't let me. She stands here and spoons it into my mouth if I don't drink it. She says it has medicinal herbs that will cure me. Can you go away, I need to rest. I want Sarah."

"You can't rest. Not now. Sarah will be fine, but she needs you. That's why you've got to get better. You also have other obligations to take care of, but we can talk about all that later. Paul, where's your souvenir? The one I sent you from Italy. Is it in a safe place?"

"You sent it? Why? Who are you?"

"You'll understand the whole reason later, just trust me. I'm here for just a little while and then you're on your own, so you have to listen to me and trust me. Is the piece safely hidden?"

"The safest," he murmured softly, reclining on his back, his strength once again waning. "Why is everyone so interested in it?"

"False hopes. People who have known about it have come to believe it is a power in itself. The things that happened when it was in your possession were not done by you or the wood. They were all manifestations of what God can do."

"Tell me about God, Tina. What's it all about really?" Paul groaned again as dry heaves wracked his frail body.

Tina moved gracefully from her perch on a chair by the dresser to his bedside. Her soft, gentle touch on his forehead was cool and reassuring.

"God is very real," she said softly. "He created men and women to be perfect, like He is, and to live carefree lives in this beautiful world of His. But alas, there came sin and life became a struggle, not just for you, but for everyone. Those televangelists who get up and preach about God wanting you to be prosperous and God wanting you to be this or that are only there to make themselves rich. Their riches are measured in earthly lusts of wealth, homes, cars, and jewels. And the wigs, mercy, where do those women find those wigs and mascara? I'm surprised they can walk and hold their heads up at the same time. God never promised anyone an easy ride. He wants you to prosper, yes, but not just or always in material possessions. Prosperity comes from giving of yourself to others, taking care of your neighbor's needs, putting yourself last and others first. That kind of life makes you prosperous in spiritual gifts, the kind of prosperity you *can* take with you when you leave this earth. Those wigs just won't fit through the gates of Heaven. Those people tell you God wants you to be wealthy, and then ask you to send your money to them. How could that make you wealthy? He really wants you to face hardships and struggles, to learn the real lessons of life and come back to Him a changed soul, a wiser soul. Jesus didn't have an easy time here on earth. Job sure didn't. Abraham, rough all the way. Jacob, same thing. Moses ... you guessed it, one thing after another. So what makes people of this century think they should have it all so easy?"

Paul groaned and looked at her through foggy eyes. "Sure, Jesus died a horrible death, but, other than that, what was so terrible about his life? He had great folks. From what I hear, his Dad's the best. And his mom, people still pray to her, too. Not everyone grows up with the perfect home life, you know. And besides, he chose to die that way. He didn't have to. I thought His death was for our sins so we didn't have to go through all this pain and misery."

The caretaker walked in with the usual gelatin and hot tea. She looked older today, more worn and stressed. The same purple gingham bib apron hung over her blue and white flowered dress. The same orthopedic hosiery rolled down below the knee on each leg, extending into swollen ankles over black oxford shoes. Stray strands of gray hair flew into her eyes, to be tossed back by a shake of her head and a blow through an extended lower lip. Her cheeks bore red blotches from the exertion of carrying the tray, laden with a watery broth, gelatin, and tea. She was too old to be tending to him like he was her own son, but she adoringly bathed him, fed him, read to him, and prayed for him each and every day. He tried to offer her a weak smile, but his face felt rubbery and uncooperative. Maybe, he hoped, his eyes showed his gratitude and when he was strong again, he would find a way to repay her for all she'd done. His life was in her hands and he owed her so much.

"May I have a glass of water, please?" Paul whispered softly. "My throat feels parched."

Her smile was sweet and sincere. "Of course, my dear. I'll get the water while you drink your tea. The herbs will help to make you stronger. Go ahead, drink it, and I'll be right back."

Tina spoke in a voice of normal volume. "Now dump the tea in your slop bucket there and let her believe you drank it. When she returns, ask for more. She won't give it to you."

Paul did as he was told, then tried to give a shhh signal to Tina, afraid the caretaker would hear.

"It's okay," smiled Tina brightly, standing beside his bed. "She can't see me and she can't hear me. I am here for you only. Here she comes. Remember, ask for more tea."

"May I," Paul croaked through his dry, cracked lips and swollen throat, "may I please have some more tea?"

The cheerful caretaker smiled. "I'm afraid the herbs are helpful in small doses but can be too much in larger doses. Now, drink your water, dear. Sip your broth and eat your gelatin. I made the green kind you like best. And then you get some rest." She tidied the coverings on his bed, tucking the sheets in tightly around the side. She peered into the slop bucket, but made no effort to empty it or remove it, in spite of the horrible smell. Straightening her apron and smoothing her hair back, she turned to leave. "By the way, my dear, have you given any more thought to where you might have misplaced your lucky charm? I do believe it would help you get better faster if you could remember. The mind is such a powerful, powerful thing. I'm not the superstitious type, but if you are, then I believe that charm could help you."

"Not yet," groaned Paul, tired of the daily questions about his lucky charm. He had no idea why she was asking and cared less at this point. Death would be a welcome relief to this agony. He'd lost track of time and had no idea how long he had been here, how he got here, or what had made him ill.

The caretaker left, quietly closing and locking the door behind her.

"Now," said Tina, perching her small frame on the foot end of his bed. Let's talk about Jesus. You seem to think He had a great life. Wrong again. He was born an illegitimate child. Bad start."

"I thought He was God's son," said Paul, feeling strangely stronger for a few moments.

"He was, and is," smiled Tina, "but that story didn't fly in Nazareth. You see, Mary was engaged to Joseph when she told him she was pregnant. And, of course Joseph, he says 'Mary, I think you got some 'splaining to do!' So, bad start for poor little Jesus. Then, He's ostracized His whole life because of this stigma of being a bastard. That meant, too, that he couldn't go into the temple or take instruction like other Jewish kids His age. He was considered unclean."

"Bummer," smiled Paul weakly, wanting to laugh at her Desi Arnaz impersonation. "He could have had some awesome show and tell days, and meet the parents' night would have been a trip. I can just about see Him in His little robe, 'this is my Dad, He created the Universe. And this is my mom, she's a virgin.' I've known kids who had it a lot worse."

"Those kids weren't born two thousand years ago in a Jewish country where the priests made the rules and their rules were strict. Have you ever read the Old Testament?"

"Can't say that I have," admitted Paul, feeling even stronger than before, taking a sip of cool water.

"You should read it sometime and tell me if you could follow all those rules they had. The priests were the ultimate authority on everything you did in life, and if you did something another way, you were unclean and not allowed into the temple."

"So, being conceived out of wedlock was a real bummer for Jesus, huh?"

"Big time. The priests never believed Mary's story. Who would? So, not being able to give a name to the father of her child, Mary produced a child of unclean birth. Then, too, He didn't come into the world kicking and screaming, declaring himself the son of God and able to work miracles. He had to learn the same way you and every other person has to learn."

"How did He learn? What did He do differently?"

"That's enough for today," soothed Tina. "I can see your strength returning, but you need rest. Don't worry. I'm not going anywhere. I'll be here when you wake up."

"Thank you," said Paul through a muffled yawn. "I really am tired. I'm glad you're not leaving. I don't want to be alone any more."

What is drama but life with the dull bits cut out?

Alfred Hitchcock

Chapter 26

Rob picked up the phone, staring wide-eyed at Kim and Mick. "Dr. Scott here," he said into the receiver.

"Rob," said a frantic voice on the other end of the line. "Where is Paul? I need to talk to him."

"Sarah, where are you?"

"I'm in a sort of hospital, but don't say anything until I talk to Paul. Please get Paul on the line. I really need to talk to him, explain everything to him." She was crying.

"Sarah, honey," said Rob in his best therapist's voice, "I'm going to put you on speaker phone. There are some people here with me who need to hear this, okay? Hold on just a second." He pressed the hands-free button on the phone and replaced the receiver in the cradle.

"First of all, Sarah, are you alright?"

"Yes," she replied anxiously. "I'm going to be fine, but I have to explain things to Paul. Who's there with you?"

Kim scratched a note on paper and handed it to Rob. He read it quickly and nodded. "Sarah, Paul's not in right now. He's taken a few days off to rest and get out of town. He's been terribly worried about you. Can you tell us what happened?"

"First tell me who's there with you. Do I know them?"

"Actually, no," said Rob. "They're friends of Paul's who stopped by the office for a visit, not knowing he was away. One is Kim Frazier, a police officer who was trying to help him find you, and the other is a guy named Mick. Paul met him when he did some volunteer work at a homeless shelter in the Cities."

"Is this Kim his girlfriend?"

"Whose girlfriend? Paul's? Of course not. It's *Mrs.* Kim Frazier and she just happened to be on patrol in the area this morning. So, she stopped in for a cup of coffee and to see if Paul had made any progress on his search for you. Trust me, Sarah, Paul hasn't even looked at another woman. Now, will you please, please tell us what happened?"

"Rob, I can't. These are things I need to tell Paul first. This is between him and me and I don't want to share it with his friends before I get a chance to talk with him. Can you understand? Just tell me where I can reach him, or when he'll be back so I can call him."

"I fully understand," said Rob, taking another quickly scribbled note from Kim. "You said you were in a hospital, Sarah. Can you at least let us know why? Assure us you're okay?"

"Oh Rob, you're always so sweet. I had an accident and have some physical challenges, you might say. Don't tell Paul that, though. He'll go berserk if he thinks I've been hurt. I'm really okay, just ...um ... just different. When's he going to be back, Rob?"

"I can't honestly say, but I'm expecting him in the office in about a week or so. Can I have him call you?"

"No. I want to call him, and don't tell him I called, okay? Now, one more question. When are you and Angel going to put your childishness behind you and get back together?"

Rob laughed out loud. "Sarah, my dear, you're timing is perfect. We're going to renew our vows the end of this month and we're both ready to start a family. You need to be here to be Matron of Honor again, so why don't you let us come and get you?"

"Not 'til I talk to Paul. I'm really happy for you and Angel. I knew it would happen one day. I hope I can be there for both of you. Goodbye, Rob. Give my love to Angel and give yourself a great big hug."

221

The line went dead.

"That was great," said Kim. "Now we know she's alive and okay, and it won't be hard to find her. Your Caller ID showed Fergus Falls Rehab Center. That can't be too hard to find. There's a state hospital there, but then there's Lake Region Hospital, too. The rehab center may be associated with one of them. Or, it might be a separate facility for rehabilitation only. I'll track her down and maybe we can make a trip to see her."

"I think tracking her down is good," said Mick, "but I don't think a visit is wise. Like she said, this is between her and Paul and he needs to be the one to go see her. The good news is, when we find him we can tell him his wife is okay and looking for him. Then we'll be able to give him the information on where she is and how she is by talking with her doctors, so he can be prepared before he goes to see her. Is this starting to sound like a fairy tale to anyone besides me?"

They all laughed. "I don't know as I'd call it a fairy tale," said Kim, "but it sure has the makings for an interesting story. Wife leaves. Husband goes into depression. Husband starts to work miracles. Husband disappears. Wife returns. I can't wait until we get to the happily ever after part."

"You know," Mick tapped his lips with his right index finger, deep in thought. "Something you just said is probably the key to Paul's disappearance. He starts working miracles and then disappears. I'd be willing to bet someone is keeping Paul to get the relic. It's the only thing that makes sense, right?"

"I don't understand why you think it's the only thing," said Rob with a frown. "The man's been desperately lonely for months worrying about a wife who took off and never looked back, or so he thought. He's been a classic example of depression. Depressed people do funny things sometimes, even run away thinking they can hide from their problems. Some go into seclusion, not wanting to be around people. Others aren't able to function at all so they just sleep and, occasionally, eat."

"But," said Mick, "you said you were right here with him when Ruth called."

"Correction," said Rob, "I was right here with him when he got a phone call and he claimed it was Ruth. I've talked to Ruth and Father Mike and neither one of them saw him, heard from him, or called him. He may have set up the phone call to provide a smokescreen before he took off to who knows where."

"I don't particularly trust Father Mike," said Mick thoughtfully. "There's something not quite right there."

"Hey, I've known Father Mike since he was a kid in high school. I went to college with his older brother, Patrick. Mike's always been a prankster, but I'd vouch for him any day."

"What's this brother of his do?" asked Kim. "If Mick's got questions, maybe we should talk to the brother."

"What possible good would that do?" asked Rob. "They're brothers. Patrick's not going to tell us Mike's a crook. He's a priest, for crying out loud."

"I'm with Kim on this," said Mick. "I'd like to talk to the brother. Any way you can get in touch with him?"

"Sure," shrugged Rob, "but what should I say? A cop, an ex junkie and I want to talk to you about your brother the priest? That should get us an automatic invitation to lunch at one of those exclusive lawyerly clubs in Minneapolis."

"He's a lawyer?" asked Mick. "What's his name? I know most of the lawyers in that town."

"Patrick O'Shea. Know him?"

"Could he go by Donovan?"

"He could go by Mildred, for all I know. I've always known him as Patrick, didn't ask about his middle name."

"Well, I've heard of a Donovan O'Shea who works with one of the big, big law firms, but it's not in Minneapolis. He used to be with West, Walker, Smith, and Speegle, but last I heard he'd left the Cities and moved to Dallas. Got licensed to practice in Texas and is with some big corporate firm. I don't know the name of it, though."

Rob looked at Mick for a long minute, studying the man's face. He was far younger than Rob had first believed. There was a gentleness in his eyes surrounded by a hardened crust of facial skin. Times had been tough on this man. Rob guessed him to be in his late thirties, early forties. He wondered if the man had a family, how he had gotten to the point of needing Father Mike's help. There was something else in those eyes, intelligence. The mind was still sharp even as the body was mending from the ravages of long-term sustained drug abuse. Mick was dressed in nice, though not necessarily expensive clothes. All of a sudden it dawned on Rob, he didn't know this man at all. It was possible Mick was involved in Paul's disappearance and was trying to steer suspicion in another direction. Okay, he thought, I'll prove him wrong.

Out loud he said to Mick and Kim, "How about if I called his mom and ask her how I can get in touch with him? I spent a lot of weekends at their place so she knows me pretty well."

"That sounds good," said Mick and Kim in unison.

Rob looked up the phone number on his rolodex, and dialed carefully. "Mother O'Shea? Rob Scott here. How are you?" His shy, little-boy-smile lit up the room. "Yes ma'am. No ma'am. Yes ma'am."

The conversation went on for several seconds with Rob being talked to like the prodigal son. After Mother O'Shea had taken her turn, Rob was able to get to the point.

"I was hoping to get in touch with Patrick, but I've lost his phone number. No ma'am, I wouldn't dare lose yours. Yes ma'am, I will. I'll write it down right now. Okay, two one four …"

When Rob finally put the phone down, he was blushing. "She kind of adopted me because I grew up so far away and didn't have any family here," He said by way of explanation, though none was needed.

Mick smiled. "You should call your Mother O'Shea more often. Don't you know she worries about you?"

Rob blushed redder. "You could hear her all away across the room, huh?"

"Didn't have to. She's no different than any other mom who hasn't heard from her son in awhile, birth or adopted. So, where is your dear brother, Patrick, these days?"

"You were right. He's going by Donovan, or Don O'Shea and he's in Dallas. She gave me his office number. Maybe I should give him a call."

Lawyers are the only persons in whom
ignorance of the law is not punished.

Jeremy Bentham
English writer on jurisprudence

Chapter 27

The American Airlines flight from Min-
neapolis/St. Paul to Dallas/Fort Worth
was smooth and uneventful. Mick and
Rob enjoyed getting to know one another better,
and Rob had the pleasure of filling Mick in on life
in Texas. It was Mick's first trip to the area. After
bragging about the beautiful women, the balmy
temperatures, and the beautiful Dallas skyline,
they disembarked at DFW International Airport.
The temperature was in the nineties, the first
woman they saw had hair bigger than her behind,
and the Dallas skyline was not visible through the
haze of another ozone alert day.

Rob tried to salvage his home state's reputation by pointing out grand sites along the route
from the airport all the way down Interstate 635
to the Dallas North Tollway. Along the tollway
were more exciting buildings to see which were of
no consequence to Mick who was hot, tired, and
hungry. The saving grace for Rob was restaurant
row in Addison. Rob was disappointed to find that
Copeland's, his favorite Cajun restaurant, had
closed, but there was still a wide range of great
restaurants from which to choose. They settled
on Houston's for dinner and each ordered huge

steaks with baked potatoes and asparagus. The food, as Mick admitted, was divine. He was promised some great Tex-Mex the next day.

By the time they reached their rooms at the Hotel Intercontinental, they were too tired to do more than take showers and go to bed. Rob thought about calling his mother, but knew she'd demand to see him the next day and he wasn't quite sure he wanted to take Mick there. Then he considered calling his mother-in-law, but they hadn't spoken since his wedding day. No telling what Angel had told her about their relationship. He didn't want to mess it up. He settled for a long, hot shower and the late news on a local TV station. From his room on the tenth floor, he could see across the tollway, and off to his right, the skyline of Dallas. It had been fifteen years since he'd been in this town. No nostalgic memories lingered. Nothing tugged at his heart strings when he thought about growing up here or getting married here. He wanted to get this business over and done with, prove Father Mike was just a great priest, and get home to Duluth, Angel, and his job.

Early in the morning, Mick and Rob sped south on the tollway towards Dallas. A quick jog on the LBJ Freeway to Central Expressway, and then south again on Central to the Elm Street exit, brought them to the underground parking area of a high rise building which housed the law offices of Brown, Bailey, and Lynch, LLP, seventeenth floor. Rob had called and made an appointment to visit with Patrick, or Don as he now preferred to be called, but hadn't mentioned the accompaniment of Mick. Their appointment wasn't until 10:30, which Don had felt would give them time for a quick tour of the office followed by a long lunch at his personal favorite Mexican restaurant, Luna de Noche in North Dallas. Their early arrival gave them an opportunity to grab a cup of coffee and a bagel at the coffee shop on the first floor and discuss the strategy of how they would bring up Mick's suspicions of Father Mike. Rob felt like a traitor making a trip to see an old friend for the sole purpose of possibly slandering his brother.

At 9:45, Mick and Rob stepped into the elevator which took them to the seventeenth floor, and opened directly on to the reception area for Brown, Bailey, and Lynch. A statuesque, elegant African American woman greeted them with a smile.

"Good morning, gentlemen," she said, completely without saccharine, "Welcome to Brown, Bailey, and Lynch. How may I assist you?"

"We have an appointment with Pat ... excuse me, Don O'Shea at 10:30. I believe we're a little early, but we don't mind waiting."

"That's quite alright. Mr. O'Shea is expecting you. You must be Mr. Scott," she extended her hand to Rob who shook it as she introduced herself as Denitra Johnson. Turning to Mick, she said, "And you are?" again, extending a hand, giving Mick an opportunity to introduce himself. "Welcome to Dallas. Can I get either of you a soft drink, coffee, latte, espresso, or spring water?"

Each said water would be nice and, at her invitation, they followed her down a rather lengthy hall to Don's office. While Rob and Don were shaking hands and patting one another on the back in the macho-mock-hug style of most men, Denitra slipped out silently and reappeared with a tray containing two bottles of chilled spring water, two crystal glasses with clear cubes of ice, and a cup and saucer of espresso for Don. When all the introductions had been made, the three men sat around a coffee table in large leather chairs in a corner of Don's office.

"Pretty sweet set-up you've got here," said Rob, glancing around the huge office. "Do you live here or just work here?"

"That's a good one," said Don. "I think a little of both. My work is so time consuming, I don't have much time for a home life. Guess that's why I've been able to stay single so long. What about you? How's your old lady doing? How many kids? I haven't heard a word from you since you got married. How's that guy you worked with, what's his name?"

"Paul?"

"Yeah, that's the one. How are he and his wife doing? They sure were nice people."

"Well," said Rob, hesitating and chancing a quick look in Mick's direction, "that's part of the reason we're here. Paul's missing."

Don looked from Rob to Mick and back. "I'm sorry, guys, we don't do private investigations here, and even if we did, we're not licensed to work in Minnesota."

"Actually," interrupted Mick, "this has more to do with your brother Michael."

"Michael? What's he got to do with this? Don't tell me he's in trouble again."

"Again?" asked Mick.

"I'll tell you what, why don't we head over to Luna and talk about this over lunch. I don't think it's something I want to discuss in the office. You never know who might be listening, and I certainly don't want my bosses to judge me by my little brother." He stood up and went to his desk to call someone named Vivien and let her know he was leaving for a few hours. Then he got his suit coat out of a closet and grabbed his wallet and car keys from a desk drawer. Mick and Rob followed him down the hall and out into the lobby where they said goodbye to Denitra and thanked her for her hospitality. In the elevator, no mention was made of Michael. Don spent the time all the way to his car, bragging about the wonderful Tex-Mex food they were about to enjoy at Luna de Noche. His car, a brand new black Mercedes SUV was loaded with every possible luxury option which he enjoyed showing off for his two guests. The speed of his entry onto the freeway caused Mick to hold his breath and Rob to grab the handle above the car door. In and out of traffic he swerved, barely missing one car after another, and waving back at those who took the time to salute with a single digit. After what felt like an eternity, they arrived at the restaurant and fell out of the car on shaky legs.

"Well," said Mick holding on to the door handle to get his bearings, "I wasn't sure we'd get here in time, but I see there's plenty of parking spaces left."

A young Mexican man wearing black pants and white shirt escorted the three men to a table. Don ordered a margarita, while Rob and Mick opted for the iced tea. After perusing the menu and ordering two servings of Rudy's Request and one Chili Relleno, Don dug into the chips and hot sauce on the table. With his mouth full of chips, he reopened the conversation which had begun in is office.

"So, what makes you think Mikey has something to do with your friend disappearing?"

Mick and Rob took turns explaining the sequence of events over the past few months, leaving out the part about the relic and the miracle cure Mick had received. It was apparent Don didn't remember Mick from his association with Hammerle and Hammerle which made it easier for them all. Had he connected the two, he might have been less than eager to share any information.

When their lunch arrived, Don looked down at his plate and then across at his two guests. "I'm about to tell you some things you have to promise me you will never tell my mother. If Mom knew I'd broken her trust and revealed a family secret, she'd disown me. So, before I begin, I've got to have a solemn oath from each of you that this information does not get back to Mom."

Rob and Mick turned to look at each other and then back at Don, both agreeing with a solemn oath to never reveal any information from this conversation to Don's mom.

"When I was six, Mom brought Mikey home from the hospital. She wasn't even pregnant, so we were all kind of wondering how we could have a new baby brother so fast. To make a very long story short, Ruth and Saul Goldstein had no kids. Saul went off to war and while he was gone, Ruth had an affair with another man, a non-Jew, and she got pregnant. When it came time for Ruth to deliver her baby, she knew she couldn't keep it or she'd lose Saul. The other guy ran out when he found out she was knocked up. As far as I know, she never heard from him again. Anyway, my Mom's a nurse at St. Michael's right, so she's there when Ruth comes in to have her baby. Mom's the labor room nurse and they get to talking. Ruth spills her guts and begs Mom to take the baby and raise him as her own so Saul will never know about her affair. My Mom, with a heart bigger than Texas itself, said yes. They signed all the adoption papers right there, with my dad included, and Mom brought Mikey home when he was four days old."

231

"That explains the relationship with Ruth," said Mick. "Was Mike told he was adopted and Ruth was his real mother?"

"Not exactly. He knew he was different because you take one look at him and you see Jew all over the place. You just don't see red headed Irish Catholic like the rest of us. Mom named him Francis Michael, but that didn't give him freckles and red hair. Anyway, when he was old enough to understand and started asking questions about why he was so different, Mom gave him that usual 'we chose you because you were special' speech all parents of adopted kids give. Mike wasn't buying it. He didn't feel special or chosen, he felt different. And then there was Ruth. She just couldn't leave well enough alone. Every year on his birthday, she'd come around and bring a present and claim she was an old friend of the family. Mike started asking her why she didn't show up on my birthday or Sean's birthday, or Kathleen's birthday, or Colleen's birthday. So the old biddy blurted out that she was his real mother and she loved him so much she couldn't stand to be away from him."

"Wow," said Rob. "How old was Mike when that happened?"

"Oh, he was probably about ten or so, I don't remember exactly. I know it ticked Mom off big time and she told Ruth to go away and never come back. From then on there was no living with Mike. He was angry, he felt sorry for himself, he hated the rest of us, said he was a Jew and we all hated him, and on and on and on. He started getting into trouble with the law when he was about twelve or thirteen. Just petty stuff, y'know? A little petty theft here, some joy riding there, nothing to get all excited about. Most boys go through a stage where they try stuff. But with Mikey, it was different. He was so hell bent on getting even with the world that he kept on getting in trouble. Finally, Mom and Dad sent him off to a Catholic school, hoping that would straighten him out."

"And did it?" asked Mick, totally engrossed in this unusual story. "Something must have stuck if he became a priest."

"That's what we thought," continued Don. "For awhile everything went great. He was so smart he was jumping ahead in classes. His favorite subject was history, especially Biblical history. It was like he became obsessed with finding out the truth between his birth and his adopted faiths. Even to this day you ask him anything about the history of nearly any religion, any Biblical fact, anything, and he'll regale you with stories for hours on end."

"I know that for a fact," said Rob. "When Paul and I first went to see him, Paul had some, uh, theological questions he was seeking answers to and that's why I introduced him to Mike. That guy knows his stuff. We spent a good two hours listening to him talk about the history of the cross and crucifixions. It was amazing."

The waiter cleared their plates and asked if anyone wanted dessert. Don ordered flan all around and made sure the waiter knew he was to get the check. Mick and Rob had to loosen their belts after the scrumptious meal of Tex-Mex they had just experienced. They shot each other a wary glance wondering where they would find room for dessert, but the flan proved as creamy and delicious as any custard either had ever tasted. In spite of their over-sated conditions, they did all but lick the burnt sugar caramel off the plates. Don, his suit jacket open, leaned back with his arm over the back of the chair next to him, enjoying the pleasure he saw on his companion's faces.

"Pretty darn good food, huh!" he said without pre-amble. "I can't eat here more than once a month or I'll get as fat as a pig. But, boy howdy, I love the food here."

Rob laughed. "You sure sound like a Texan. I never thought I'd hear you say things like 'boy howdy'. If it wasn't for the slight Midwestern ac-cent, I'd think you were born here."

"Hey," smiled Don, "a man's gotta get along, so when in Rome, yadda, yadda, yadda, right? Now, where were we on my little brother? Oh yeah, he was away at school and making everyone so proud of his intelligence. Then one day he comes home and tells the folks he wants to become a priest. You can imagine how that went over. By this time we all knew all about Mikey, so Mom and Dad were saying things like ... "we had four kids of our own, and the only one who loves us enough to become a priest is our adopted son who's Jewish." I think we were supposed to feel guilty or something, you know how Catholic mothers can be, but instead we all felt a little suspicious. Sean, Colleen, Kath, and I could see through Mike where our parents couldn't. He said he wanted to be a priest, but all the time we were wondering what his real agenda was."

"How did Ruth take this news about him want-ing to be a priest?" asked Mick.

"As far as we knew, she didn't know. After she spilled the beans to Mike about his birth, Mom and Dad told her to stay away and leave us alone."

"And did she?"

"We thought she did, but it seems Mike was keeping in touch with her on the sly. He went to seminary and all that, but he stayed in so much trouble with the church that he was never or-dained and never actually became a priest. I know, I know, he's pretending to be a priest at some homeless shelter or something in the Cities. The folks don't know he's not a real priest. I don't know what Ruth knows or thinks and I don't care. I gave up on Mikey years ago, right after he got caught stealing really valuable stuff from the church, like a gold chalice, stuff like that. My question is, what's all this got to do with your friend, Paul? You don't think Mike had anything to do with his disappearance do you?"

"That's what we don't understand either. I guess you know Mike's shelter's just down the street from Ruth's store and apartment. Her husband, Saul, passed away a couple of months ago. When Paul stayed in the Cities to work with Mike the first time, he rented a room from Ruth and Saul. That was back last Christmas, right after his wife left."

"So Ruth is involved too, huh? I'm not surprised. The only way Mike could have anything to do with this whole thing is if Ruth was in on it too and your friend had something they wanted. It has to be something of really great value for them to go that far. Unless Paul's carrying the Hope Diamond, I'd say Mike and Ruth have nothing to do with this. Paul's probably just gone off for some rest and to get over the wife thing. I just don't see kidnapping, not even for Mike. He's a real turkey, but even he wouldn't go that far."

"An even bigger question," said Mick, "is why he continues to pose as a priest and really helps homeless people when someone with his intelligence could make a fortune in the business world."

"I wish I could answer that for you, Mick, but I don't honestly know the answer. In my opinion, I think he's still trying to save himself. He's a pretty confused man. Do you mind if I ask how

you fit into all this, Mick? You haven't said anything about your background and how you know
Mike."

Rob and Mick shared a look, trying to decide
how much they should tell Don.

"I was once a homeless drug addict," started
Mick cautiously. "The shelter was my base, a
place where I could get a hot meal and a place to
sleep. It's just a tent with some cooking stuff and
a bunch of tables, but we all made our pallets and
slept there, even through the winter. Father Mike
took great care of all of us. He never preached, he
taught. It was while he was helping me go through
withdrawal the last time that Paul showed up.
Paul has a, um, well, sort of a gift, and ... well, he,
um ... he was able to heal me. Instantly."

"Okay, you lost me. What kind of gift? Are you
trying to say he was like those guys who claim to
heal people? We all know that's fake. Don't tell me
you fell for it?"

"No. I didn't. But it happened."

"You just said you were going through withdrawal and Mike was helping you, so what makes
you think this guy Paul healed you?"

"Because Mike didn't have the ... um ... the uh ...
the gift."

"What gift?"

"Something more valuable than the Hope Diamond, I assure you."

> No problem is so large it cannot
> be run away from.

Charles M. Schultz
(Peanuts)

Chapter 28

Kim enjoyed getting away from Duluth occasionally. Whenever she was in town, Carson would have the nurse calling to check up on her at least ten times a day. Leaving this morning she'd told the nurse her cell phone would be off because she would be visiting a hospital in Fergus Falls regarding a missing woman. She drove in her own vehicle, in civilian clothes, with no radio or phones to disturb her. It was the most relaxing day she had enjoyed in a long time. Carson was in good hands, she was about to meet, hopefully, the missing Sarah Grant, and spring was in full bloom. She took highway 35 south as far as State Road 23 which cut across to St. Cloud. From there she drove north and west on Highway 94 to Fergus Falls, over three-fourths of the way across the state.

Because of the distance and not knowing how much of her time would be needed in Fergus, Kim had made arrangements for twenty-four hour nursing care while she spent the night away. Knowing Carson's jealousy, she reserved a single room at the Holiday Inn and left the number with the nurse so she could be checked up on any time during the night. Guilt crept through her as once again she wished Carson had died in that accident instead of being left an invalid dependent on her for everything, and trusting her with nothing and no one. She was imprisoned by a quadriplegic with an acerbic tongue and poisoned mind.

Turning on the radio to some soft classical music, she tried to tune out her thoughts of Carson and tried to concentrate on what she would find in Fergus. Sarah's words on the phone had given her reason to believe the woman was no longer the way she had been. Soon, she hoped she would know a lot more about the elusive Sarah. Turning off Highway 94, she pulled into the Holiday Inn and registered. After a very light lunch she found directions to the Fergus Falls Rehabilitation Center and drove there directly. The building was much smaller than she had imagined, and appeared more like a nursing home for the aged than a rehab hospital. Parking her car, she looked around the area before walking to the front doors of the building. Spring was being kinder to Fergus Falls than it was to the folks in Duluth. The leaves were green on most every tree. The fragrance of lilacs perfumed the soft tepid breeze. Large bushes of the purple spring flowers lined each side of the center, blossoms hanging down like heavy clusters of grapes. A robin chirped from a cottonwood tree where its nest was snuggled in the joint of a limb. Swallows batted one another for space in the four-story bird hotel someone had carefully erected upon the verdant lawns sloping back from the one story building down to a small lake of ice blue water.

Kim walked through the doors and up to the reception desk without hesitation. "I'd like to speak with the director, please," she said, displaying her police badge. "I'm officer Kim Frazier with the Duluth Police Department."

"I'm the director," a sharp voice spoke from behind her. Kim turned to look into the face of a middle aged, large boned, thin woman with short dirty blonde hair and a dress that made her look ten years older than she probably was. "What can I do for you?"

"I'd like to speak with you in private, if I may," said Kim. She put her hand out and introduced herself, but the hand was ignored.

"This way," said the lady who had yet to give her own name. Kim followed her to a short hallway just to the left of the reception counter, and to a cubby hole of an office directly behind.

When they had both entered the room, the woman closed the door and told Kim to have a chair while she seated herself behind the desk. The name plate facing Kim read Constance Reed, Director.

"Are you Mrs. Reed?" Kim asked as pleasantly as she could.

"Miss Reed. Yes. What is it you want?"

"I'm here to inquire about Sarah Grant. Maybe you can tell me something about her before I meet her."

"Who is Sarah Grant?"

"Well," said Kim, somewhat taken aback by this answer, "I believe she's a patient of yours here. This is the Fergus Falls Rehabilitation Center, isn't it?"

"Yes it is, but I have no one here by the name of Sarah Grant." Miss Reed pulled out a clip board which apparently held the names of all the current patients. She began going down the list as if double checking her own memory. "I have one Jane Doe, could be your Sarah Grant."

"I don't know. Do you have a picture of her?"

"Of course not. This is a rehab center, not a spa or photo studio. What makes you think this Grant person is here anyway?"

"She called her husband's office a couple of days ago. She's been missing since just before Christmas."

"So why didn't her husband come and get her if she called him?"

"Well, because now he's missing, too." Kim knew as soon as she said it that her whole story sounded fishy. "That's why I came. They were having some problems, and she left him just before the holidays. No one has heard from her since. He took it pretty hard and last week he, too, disappeared. Then, I was visiting his office trying to get some details on his disappearance when she called asking for him. She claimed she was different, that she didn't look the same, and caller ID told us she was here. We didn't tell her the husband is missing because she was so adamant that she talk to him and explain everything before she told anyone where she was. What can you tell me about this Jane Doe you have?"

The lines in Constance Reed's face softened a bit. "I apologize for being somewhat cold to you when you first arrived, Officer Frazier, but many of our patients are here because of spousal abuse. This is actually more of a shelter than a rehab center, but the disguise works well and keeps the unwanted spouses at bay. Our Jane Doe arrived here about a week before Christmas. She was found in a car that had run off the road over a rather large hill. The poor thing was unconscious and frostbitten. We weren't sure she would survive. We have a very fine medical staff here in town, and Dr. Vandermere felt this place would be better for her just in case she was running from something."

"What's her condition Miss Reed?"

"Please, call me Connie. I hope you can understand my first concern is always for our patients and their privacy. Jane has had two of her toes amputated, and has several scars on her face from the broken glass of the windshield. She wouldn't speak to anyone for several months, even after she recovered from her surgeries. We've had a psychiatrist in several times to talk with her, but she never opened up to him or anyone else. Then, about a week ago she started talking, asking for her clothes, where she was, why she was being held here, when she could go home. Stuff like that. We didn't know what to think. She still wouldn't tell us her name, but she did ask to use the phone a few times. Each time she was given permission to use this phone right here in my office with complete privacy. The first few times were in the evening and she came away more depressed than when she came in here. Then, a couple of days ago she again asked to use the phone, this time it was about 9:30 in the morning. When she came out of my office she had tears in her eyes, but she was smiling too. She even said 'thank you' before she went back to her room."

"That was the time we received the call in her husband's office. How has she been since then?"

"Different. She's polite to the staff, spends time with some of the other clients playing games and talking. No one has ever learned her name though. We all just call her Janie."

"This may sound like an odd request," said Kim, "but I'd like to meet her, talk with her, without her knowing who I am. Can that be arranged? We promised her, or actually, her friend Rob, promised her we wouldn't do anything until she was able to talk with her husband. We want to make sure she's okay and then we'll have to decide if we should let Rob tell her about Paul or what. We'd like to get her back home as soon as possible. She might even be able to help us find Paul."

Connie stood up and walked around her desk. Opening a wardrobe on the opposite wall, she pulled out a uniform. "This looks like it's about your size. How'd you like to take Jane some lunch and clean her room? Maybe you'll be able to chat with her a bit. If she thinks you're new here, she'll probably be willing to answer some questions. Most of the residents and their families eat in the dining room. Janie doesn't seem to want to join in, though, so we take her meals to her each day. Residents are also required to do their own cleaning, but again Janie's kind of a special case."

"Sounds like a plan to me!" said Kim eyeing the blue striped uniform. "Where can I change?"

Less than an hour later Kim was pushing a cart with a covered tray on top, fresh linens on the second shelf, and cleaning solutions on the bottom. She knocked on the door of room two fourteen and waited for the voice from inside to invite her in. The lady sitting at the desk was very thin with silky blonde hair and round blue eyes. The left side of her face bore a bright red scar from her nose down to the bottom of her ear. The tip of her nose had been removed because of frost bite, as had the lobe of her right ear. It was obvious to Kim the lady had once been extraordinarily beautiful and she could understand why Paul had fallen in love with her.

"Hi," said Kim sweetly. "I'm Kim Johnson. This is my first day so I hope you'll bear with me if I mess up. And you are ...?"

"They just call me Janie around here," the voice whispered so very, very softly. Kim couldn't tell if it was the same voice she'd heard on the phone or not. This one seemed frightened, more so than the caller had been.

"Did I come at a bad time?" asked Kim. "I could leave your lunch and come back to clean later if you like."

"No," Janie said softly. "I'm just having a bad day. Please come in and do whatever you need to do. I'm not really hungry, though."

"You need to eat, sweetie, you're much too thin. Today we have some delicious baked potato soup with grilled cheese and, wow, would you look at that, cheesecake for dessert!"

Kim's exuberance brought a slight smile to Jane's face. "You're new, huh," she said. "What'd you do before you came here?"

"I was a nursing student in Fargo at St. Luke's. Then when my folks ran out of money I had to find a job, so I started sending out resumés. It's not easy to find a job when your claim to fame is 'started nursing school, degree pending.' So, here I am a nurse's aide in good old Fergus Falls. Are you from around here?"

"I can't tell you that. We're supposed to have complete anonymity here."

"Oh yeah, I forgot. I'm sorry, I didn't mean to pry. There's so much I have to learn about all this. I've never been in that sort of relationship, y'know, where some guy beats the daylights out of you for kicks. It's kind of hard to understand what you must have been through."

"Oh, no. You've got it wrong. My husband didn't abuse me. I just got all ... well ... I got all confused about some things and I left for awhile."

"I'm sorry. I didn't mean to assume things. See how klutzy I am? I can't even carry on a conversation without messing up. How can I ever be a nurse?"

"You'll learn. It just takes time and listening. That's the most important part, listening."

"This probably isn't any of my business, but, you said you got confused about some things and left for awhile. How long have you been here? Are you planning on going back to your husband?"

"You're right," said Jane, the smile vanishing, "It is none of your business. You didn't hear a word I said about listening, did you?" With that she turned away from Kim and began to pick at the grilled cheese sandwich on her plate.

Kim finished cleaning up the room, changing the linens, and left quietly, feeling as if she had failed completely in her attempt to draw Jane or Sarah into admitting who she was for sure. This could mean another couple of days here before she would be able to go home. Back in Connie's office she made a quick call to her husband's nurse and explained that she would be a couple of days longer, and left the phone number at the center making sure they insisted on asking for Constance Reed. Connie was the only one who knew the facts and Kim was afraid Janie/Sarah might overhear someone call her by her real last name which would blow everything wide open. The receptionist had been warned not to tell anyone who Kim was or what she did. Any loss of confidentiality on her part would result in immediate dismissal. The message was well understood.

That evening she tried to call Rob's cell phone and got no answer. She left a message and asked him to call her either at her hotel or, again, at Connie's number. After a quick call to her husband, allowing him to once again berate and accuse, she wondered if her own situation would qualify her for sanctuary at the Fergus Rehab Center. A hot shower did little to revive her spirits. Thoughts kept going back to the days when Carson was whole, a handsome, exciting young attorney ... the big fish in the small pond of Duluth, Minnesota. None had been better at defending the innocent, the almost innocent, and those who were in the wrong place at the wrong time. Carson believed in his work and believed in the innocence, near innocence, or rehabilitative probabilities of every one of his clients. If they were guilty, he didn't want to hear it. If they said they were innocent, he believed them and fought with all his might to get them acquitted. Cutting deals was never a part of his game plan because that would assume culpable responsibility on the part of not only his client, but him personally. If a client was guilty, then Carson was guilty for trying to defend a guilty man or woman. As long as he believed in their innocence, everything was fine.

Stiff, clean sheets lined the cozy cocoon Kim wrapped herself into for the night. Her body ached for the feel of a man, for Carson to touch her and make love to her the way he once had, back when he was a man. The thought of Paul Grant seeking a God that didn't exist made her shiver. Still, the cure had happened. Hadn't it? There really had been a lump. What kind of God would heal a little lump in her breast but take away the body and spirit of a man?

As she had done every night for the past three years since Carson's accident, she allowed the tears of self pity to slide down the sides of her face as she stared straight upward in the dark. Life, she thought, was the real hell and when it was over, when the lights went out, that was it. There was nothing more. A dark box and nothing. And if there *was* a God, He was somewhere in His heaven looking down and laughing at the pitifully weak creatures who swarmed this earth, bowing down and saying their prayers as if they could change the course of hell. In return, they got hit by drunk drivers and were paralyzed for life, or ran off the road and lost toes but gained ugly red facial scars. Or, like Paul, just disappeared from the face of the earth. Why did Sarah run off the road? Was it slippery or had she been frightened? Kim made a mental note to make inquiries into the status of the weather and roads on the date she was found, the exact place she was found, and most importantly, where her belongings were which would have identified her. When she left Paul, she had supposedly taken more than one suitcase full of clothing and personal items, and certainly carried a purse with several forms of identification. Where were these? Who found her? What exactly did she remember of her accident? Too many questions, too little time to find all the answers. As these thoughts swirled through her head, she began to doze off on the too-firm mattress with the stiff, cold sheets and lightweight bedspread. At the point where she was no longer sure what was real and what was dream, she could hear the ringing of a phone. Three rings had successfully been completed before she awakened enough to answer the black phone at her bedside.

246

"Mrs. Frazier?" the voice on the other end asked. "We have an emergency call from Duluth. Please hold to be connected."

Optimistic lies have such immense therapeutic value that a doctor who cannot tell them convincingly has mistaken his profession.

George Bernard Shaw
Irish Novelist

Chapter 29

Paul slept. The haziness was dissipating and his mind and body felt at peace. The cool hand of Tina pressed softly against his forehead. Clear, fresh water flowed through his veins and washed away the toxic herbs which had been poisoning his system. He had believed in his caretaker and still felt sure she meant him no harm.

At dawn, he awoke to the rays of a spring sun peeking through the window under the shade. Tina was once again perched on a stool beside the dresser, watching him as he roused from a restful sleep. The door to his room opened and the care-taker came in with his breakfast tray. He sat up, much to her amazement, and greeted her with a smile. The tray nearly toppled from her hands as she stared at him.

Regaining her composure, she set the tray on the stand beside his bed. "You are so much better, my dear. See? Didn't I tell you these herbs would make you well? Now, drink your tea so you can get even stronger."

"No, thank you," smiled Paul in return. "This morning I think I would like to go to the kitchen with you and make myself a pot of coffee and perhaps a couple of eggs. How does that sound?" As he spoke, he pushed the stand holding the tray aside and moved his legs out from under the covers to set his feet on the floor.

From her position, Tina smiled mischievously, looking back and forth between Paul and the caregiver.

"Oh, no, no, you mustn't push yourself too soon. Lie back and drink your herb tea and I'll make you some coffee and some eggs." The old lady tried to lift his legs back up onto the bed and force the covers over him again. It was apparent she was unnerved by this new development of a healthier patient.

"Okay," laughed Paul, his eyes twinkling up at the elderly woman, "I'll drink the tea if you promise to make me some strong coffee and four scrambled eggs."

"That's a good boy. Now here, drink your tea." She held the cup to his lips as if to force him to drink.

"First," said Paul, "You'll have to leave the room so I can relieve some bladder pressure. I'll drink the tea. You just go ahead and make my breakfast."

"But, but ... I need that cup for your coffee. I only have two and the other has my own tea in it. So drink quickly then I can leave to make what you need."

Paul wanted to laugh. Her excuses were becoming ridiculously thin, if not quite sad. "I can't drink the tea," he said with some authority, "until I have more room in my bladder for the liquid.

Now please step out of the room for a moment while I relieve the pressure that is building at an alarming rate."

There was nothing she could do. The gray wisps of hair hung in her eyes as they darted back and forth as if this would help conjure up a more reasonable excuse not to leave him alone until he had drunk the tea. At last, a light went on and a smile lit her face. "I'll just turn around here so you can do your business, and then we can sit and chat while you drink your tea."

"My business, as you call it, ma'am, could take more than a moment and might certainly cause some olfactory distress. I highly recommend departure of your person as I perform my ritual of elimination."

"Why are you talking so funny?" she asked. "You sound like Shakespeare or something. Maybe you're not as well as you believe you are. I'll just turn around while you do whatever it is you need to do and then we'll chat."

"Get out!" Paul demanded with unquestionable authority. "I do not wish to share this moment with you at this time or any other. Now go."

The caretaker left.

"Well," smiled Tina, "that's one way to handle it. How do you feel?"

"Great!" laughed Paul. "Who is she anyway?"

"Not time for you to know yet."

Paul walked over to the single window in the room, lifted the old pull-string shade and looked out into the spring morning. Infrequent, gray pillows of slushy snow remained along curbsides of a narrow street. A short stretch of yard peeked through between where he stood and the street.

Tufts of green grass were peeking through the muddy surface. The window through which he peered was sealed shut with heavy coats of flat enamel paint. He tried, unsuccessfully, to raise it enough to breathe the crisp spring air he knew his lungs would invite eagerly. He was in a second story room with no ledge or other appurtenance on which to gain access to the ground without injury. His plight seemed hopeless, for now.

Turning back into his prison, he noticed it was an attractively neat room with few accessories. The wood dresser near which Tina normally sat was old, but well cared for and free of dust. A chair and small table were positioned just inside the door. A rather large braided rug covered a good portion of the wood flooring which Paul recognized as both quite old and quite authentic. Other than the narrow bed on which he had been lying, and the small stand beside it, there were no other furnishings to the room. A hand crocheted doily, starched and pressed, sat upon the dresser and one on the table by the door. The lilac and cream curtains were hand sewn and pressed to perfection, not a wrinkle in sight. Whoever lived in this home was poor but tidy. There were no decorations on the walls save a small seascape above the dresser. A rectangle of lighter paint stretched beyond the framed picture to indicate something larger had recently been replaced by it. Perhaps a mirror, he thought. It surprised him that no pictures of Jesus or The Last Supper hung on the walls as did in so many elderly people's residences.

Warm air rose from a vent in the floor. Paul knelt down to peer into the vent, hoping to see more of the house and the floor beneath him. Nothing. Next he tried the door to the room and found it locked from the outside. He was, indeed, being held prisoner, but for what reason? He didn't even know this lady, and the street outside this room, outside this house, held no familiarity for him. Even Tina had disappeared. It dawned on him, as he continued to investigate the room, that there was not even a closet. The room was longer than it was wide. Perhaps it had never been meant to serve as a bedroom, or, it may have been built without closets and once held a standalone wardrobe. That would have left very little room for mobility. One light bulb behind a frosted globe provided light for the room, turned on and off by the electrical switch just inside the door. The switch plate was very low on the wall compared to most light switches, giving Paul reason to believe this may have been meant as a child's room or a playroom.

When he turned back into the room, Tina was sitting delicately atop the short dresser, her dainty legs hanging down the side.

"Like that spot do you?" asked Paul.

"Since I'm so much shorter than you, when you're standing I can look into your eyes, and when you're lying in bed you can look up at me more easily. There's a reason for everything."

"You know," he said looking at her as if to pronounce his pet peeve, "everyone keeps saying that. What does that have to do with everything we talked about yesterday?"

"Oh, a great deal. As I told you, people weren't created and put on this earth so every time they wanted something they could ask God and get it. Most people don't understand the concept of prayer. It's meant to be a time of communion with God, not a time to read your wish list. Some so-called preachers have even devised formulas for getting exactly what you want from God when you pray. Every living creature was put on this earth to face challenges. How you meet those challenges is your test. You can whine about the challenge. You can blame others for your problems and lots of people tend to blame their own parents. Freud had a field day with that idea. I think he invented it and everyone was and is so anxious to blame someone else, they gobbled up Freud's philosophy like candy. The Bible says 'honor' your parents and Freud says 'blame' your parents.

"You can meet each challenge head on and accept it graciously. Or, you can ignore it and move around it. Study your Bible, Paul. Think about the talents you were given at birth, and then think about the situations you've had to face. If you look closely, you'll realize that your personal challenges are in some way directly proportionate to your talents and assets. You have been given the resources with which to meet these challenges and learn whatever you are required to learn from them. No life is without pain. If anyone tells you they don't have any problems in their life, that they turn everything over to God, they're probably lying. God wants you to look to him for guidance and support through this journey, but He's not going to do it all for you, and He's not Santa Claus. All too often, when things go a little bit awry, people crumble and grumble about 'poor, poor pitiful me.' Pity parties are pretty popular on earth."

"So, exactly what is the main theme in all this?"

"It's so simple I can't believe people don't catch on. Put others first. Listen to the words of that old song ... *Walk a Mile in My Shoes*. Try to see things from the perspective of the other person and stop judging. Do for others exactly what you would want them to be doing for you if you were in their situation or one similar. When adversity hits you, take a look around and you'll see someone, many people with even greater challenges than your own. Get your eyes off your own ego and go help that person."

"Okay. I understand that, how about this scenario: I know a lady whose husband works two jobs. She stays home, pays for a fitness trainer, has her nails done every week, and loves to shop. Whenever they don't have enough money to pay their bills or go out to eat, she says she believes God will provide, then she calls her mother-in-law and asks for money. Is she meeting her challenge?"

"Yes, actually she is. She's meeting it her way, though, not God's way. She's using her talents to get by rather than learn the lessons God meant for her to learn. Her eye isn't on God, it's on the mirror, on herself. Her challenges could become greater and greater, or, they may never increase. But, if she slides through life in this manner, believing that she has put all her trust in God and He's going to grant her every wish like a Fairy God Father, her rewards will not be so great at the end of the line. Just like any good parent, God wants you to be happy, but He also wants you to learn how to earn that happiness. You work for a pay check. No one hands you money to do nothing, right? Why would God, your one true parent, give you everything you want without asking you to do something to earn it?"

"So, does that mean you have challenges, too?"

"Of course. Every living creature faces challenges. The challenges are designed in direct proportion to your talents and your ability to face and overcome the challenges. Sometimes, overcoming means accepting. Your friend, Rob, is challenged by his race, but he's accepted it and isn't whining

253

about being discriminated against because he's bi-racial. He's moved on to the next challenge."

"Is that piece of wood supposed to be one of my challenges?"

"It's not a test when you know the answers. It's time for you to rest. I have work to do and she's about to take some drastic action. Be prepared. Bye."

Paul turned over on this bed and fell instantly asleep. Less than an hour had gone by when he awoke again, wondering if his encounters with Tina were real, or a dream. The knocking on the door was just a way of covering the turning of the key in the lock. His caretaker didn't wait for an invitation to enter the room, but came on in followed by an elderly gentleman dressed in a white shirt, tie, slacks and knee-length lab coat. The caretaker stood back as the man approached. He bore a strong odor of cigarette smoke which Paul found rather disturbing if this man was supposed to be a doctor.

The doctor pulled the chair up beside Paul's bed, sat down, and leaned towards the bed with his hands on his knees. From this close angle, Paul could see the man was not elderly at all, but had colored his hair to make it appear gray, wore a false mustache, and round spectacles with wire rims.

"Hello there, young man," he said, trying to make his voice sound older, too. "I'm Doctor Metcalf. I've been a family friend of your aunt Hazel for many years. I'm retired now, but when Hazel called and told me you were back home again and not well, I just had to come by. The last time I saw you, you were knee high to a grasshopper."

The doctor leaned back in his chair, laughing at his own stupid joke, and looked up at the caretaker who was nodding her head in approval. Paul began coughing from the acrid smell of stale smoke on the man's clothing.

"How long have you had that cough?" asked the doctor.

The caretaker, whose name must be Hazel, answered for Paul saying he'd been ill for several days and the cough was a new development which had come on only since Paul quit taking his herb tea."

"Oh, dear," said the doctor rubbing his chin. "You must take the herbs or you will not get well."

"I want Father Mike," Paul interrupted. "If I am going to die, I want my own priest here." His mind was whirling. Getting Mike here, he was sure, was the only way he was going to get out of this. Hazel and the doctor exchanged looks, not of surprise, but of alarm. The doctor turned back to Paul, trying very hard to look confused.

"Who? Who is Father Mike? Where can we find him? Ah, but you're not going to die. I have been a doctor for over fifty years and these herbs will help you, I promise, unless you have a talisman of some kind representing your faith which you can use in your prayer time. Do you have maybe a rosary or missal or ... what? Perhaps some symbol of your faith which can help you through this rough time."

"I have," said Paul pretending weakness again, "a piece of the true cross."

"Yes, yes," shouted the doctor turning to Hazel who made no attempt to mask her excitement. "Tell me where that is and we will help you get well very, very fast." Sobering once again to a more pseudo-professional level, he added, "Of course, the icon itself will not heal you, but as long as you believe it can, that is all that matters."

"It can," whispered Paul. "I have healed a lot of people with it."

"Then I must insist you tell us where to find it so we can get you well, or you may get much, much worse, maybe even die."

Cough, cough. "I thought you said I wouldn't die," said Paul.

"I did not want to frighten you, but now that we know there is a way, the truth can't hurt you. Where is your piece of the cross?"

"I can't tell you until I see Father Mike. Please, get Father Mike for me. Please!"

Death be not proud, though some have called thee
Mighty and dreadful, for thou art not so
For those whom thou think'st thou dost overthrow,
Die not, poor death, not yet canst thou kill me.
For rest and sleep, which but thy pictures be,
Must pleasure, then from thee much more must flow,
And soonest our best men with thee do go,
Rest of their bones and soul's delivery ...

John Donne
English metaphysical poet

Chapter 30

Rob and Mick caught the first plane out of Dallas early the next morning. There was no reason for them to stay around when there was so much to do back home. Running into some turbulence half way through the flight, Rob found himself wanting to order a drink while Mick slept soundly as if rocked to sleep in the big steel cradle with wings. When they finally landed in the Cities, Mick was ready for lunch and Rob ready to lose his breakfast. They compromised by drive-through burgers for Mick and a soft drink for Rob. Taking their lunch to Mick's apartment, they sat down to discuss their next strategy. Rob pulled his cell phone out of his pocket and checked his messages. There were several from Kim and a couple from Angel. He checked Angel's text messages first and there were no alarming reports from her end. The first message from Kim was a voice message saying she had located Sarah who was listed as a Jane Doe in a battered women's shelter posing as a rehab clinic. The next one gave details of her encounter with Jane Doe and her confidence that this was Sarah. The third message was shorter, saying only, "My husband has gone into a coma. I'm heading back to Duluth."

While Rob was checking his messages, Mick made a call to his father to check in and see how things were going. Mick knew Stefan was glad to hear from him, but he had to endure the usual tirade about how Stefan had figured he'd gone back to the drugs and was in that shelter again since he hadn't heard from him for a couple of days, and yes, he knew he'd said he was going to Dallas, but that could have been just an excuse to get high. And, why did they call it high when it just brought a man as low as he could go? The lecture lasted about ten minutes and then Stefan reminded him he had better not be late for dinner Saturday night or for church on Sunday morning. This Saturday night was going to be special. It was movie night for the seniors at the church and Stefan had his eye on a pretty little thing named Iris. She might be too young for him, she was only sixty eight, but he'd give it a try and see if she was interested. Mick hung up the phone with a promise and a chuckle.

When each had finished with the messages and calls, they sat in silence wondering where to go from here. The information on Mike hadn't been good, but it really hadn't given them any reason to think he could be involved with Paul. Same for Ruth, nothing concrete to implicate her either. Kim's situation warranted a trip to Duluth on both of their parts, and Rob felt he'd best get back to work after having missed Tuesday and Wednesday of the week already. Mick was deep in thought as Rob stood up to leave.

"Wait a minute," he said to Rob. "My dad just said something that might be useful. He knows I'm clean, but he's gotta rub it in, you know how folks are. So, what if I faked it. I could go back to the shelter and beg Mike to find Paul for me again. If Mike's involved in any way, or knows anything at all about this, I think I can crack him."

"You really think something's happened and Paul didn't just walk away from everything because of the pressure?" asked Rob.

"Yeah, I do. Don't ask me why because I can't answer that, and you surely know him a lot better than I do. What do you think? Is he a man who could just walk away from everything?"

"No, I really don't think he is. Do you want to know what I think?"

"Sure." Mick leaned forward, elbows on his knees, hands clasped in front of his wide spread legs. His body language told Rob he was really into listening to what was about to be said. And for the first time, Rob understood how important his sobriety was and how much he was willing to risk to find Paul.

"Paul's a decent man. He's never been religious, but he's not a flake. Being a psychologist doesn't make you naturally immune to things like depression, but Paul is different. He has a great sense of humor which carries him through a lot of tough spots. Two things have really gotten to him these past several months: Sarah leaving without giving him a reason, and that piece of the cross that was sent to him from Italy. He had dreams about Malchus when he was a kid and actually thought he had been there and was the reincarnation of Malchus for awhile. Then he read about how cells can carry memories from generation to generation, just like transplant recipients can re-

259

ceive memories of their donor in the cells of the transplanted organ. It all sounds kind of weird to me, but Paul now thinks he is a descendent somehow of this guy Malchus and that the memory cells are still being passed down in the DNA from generation to generation. But, that's a whole other subject. Do I think Paul would just walk away? As long as there's a chance Sarah will return home, no. He wouldn't leave on his own. I believe someone wants that relic believing it can produce miracles. Someone who feels he's always gotten the short end of the stick, or maybe someone who thinks her kid has always gotten the short end of the stick and wants to help him become a hero."

"I'm with you one hundred percent. I think it's time for me to buy a bottle of booze. Not to drink, just to rinse out my mouth and spill on my clothes. I've spent so many years stoned I should be able to fake it with no problem. I hear practice makes perfect."

The two men spent another hour formulating their plans. Mick would have to go see his father and explain what was going on. Rob would go back to Duluth to check up on Kim, work two days and then he and Angel would take Stefan to church Saturday night and Sunday, if necessary. Mick wouldn't be able to take his cell phone in with him, nor his car keys, so he'd take a bus as close as he could to the shelter, and then walk the remainder of the way. His plan was to start the next afternoon after spending time with Stefan. Because he would be without phone, money, or means to contact anyone, Rob would have to wait to hear from him.

Once they had agreed on everything, Rob took his leave and drove back to Duluth, arriving just before dinner time. He called Angel from his cell phone and asked her to be ready when he stopped by, he needed her to go somewhere with him. She agreed and was prepared when he arrived. While driving to the hospital, he explained very briefly about Carson Frazier and his condition. Carson would be in ICU, Rob explained, and they were going to provide support and comfort for Kim. Paul had been missing a week and a half now, and Kim was crucial to their investigation, but she had also become a friend and someone Rob, Paul, and Mick all cared about. Angel agreed that Kim was a very special person who had endured a great deal at such a young age. It was hard to imagine having her husband be so drastically impaired for so long, and now this. She and Kim had worked together on several cases involving family issues, and she had the utmost respect for the Micro-Mini-Cop as the other officers called her.

The halls of the hospital were shiny from high gloss waxing and buffing. This did not temper the combined scents of antiseptic and illness. Their shoes tended to squeak just slightly on the highly polished floors and they spoke only in whispers as though someone could hear and misconstrue their meaning. It was a long walk to the ICU and there were only two people in the waiting room. Neither of these was Kim. Rob and Angel waited for awhile thinking she may be in with her husband since only short visits were permitted. Angel leafed through a *National Geographic* magazine, while Rob sat impatiently, one leg pumping up and down in a rapid tempo.

"The men's room is that way, I believe," smiled Angel.

Rob shot her a look of irritation. "I don't think she's here. They don't let you visit very long, do they? I'm going to go ask a nurse, if I can find one. Stay here." His nervousness showed. Apparently Rob didn't like hospitals.

When he was finally able to find a nurse, Rob asked where he might find Kim Frazier, wife of patient, Carson Frazier. After a rather lengthy hesitation, the nurse looked at him as if she was providing information which was top secret and it was making her very uncomfortable. "You might want to try the chapel," she said softly, and then looked into Rob's eyes as if she had just imparted the most profound information and was expecting a reaction. It was only then that Rob realized Carson had not survived. He went back to the waiting area to get Angel, and together they found their way to the chapel.

The chapel doors opened into a beautiful chamber lit only by stained glass windows on three sides, and one in the ceiling. Six rows of short pews lined each side, and the floor was carpeted in a soft gray. Sitting alone in the front pew, staring straight ahead at the barren altar, sat Kim. Looking around, Angel realized there were no religious symbols. All the windows were made up of nature pictures, sunrises and sun sets, trees and lambs, children and pets. Without turning around, Kim sensed the questions and responded without request. "It's a non-denominational chapel so everyone can feel welcome and worship whomever they wish in their own way. Pretty sad, isn't it? We can't even all agree on a god."

Rob and Angel went forward and sat down beside her. "He had a will," she said calmly without looking at them. "He left everything to me, of course, but he also had what's called a living will. How can it be a living will when it gives them permission to let him die? Do not resuscitate. What a stupid, stupid will. If you're wondering, I'm not here praying for him. It's for me because I'm glad he's gone. To me he died three years ago, and both of our lives have been living hell since. I'm glad, really, really glad he's gone, finally." At that, the tears burst forth in convulsive sobs. Rob placed his arms around Kim and let her use a shoulder to lean on while she exhausted herself in grief. Angel patted him on the other arm and nodded in the direction of the door. She stood to leave them alone for a few minutes. Her heart swelled with pride. She didn't remember a time when she had loved Rob more. She wondered who she could call to help Kim through this time, but she had never heard Rob mention any family outside of Carson. And now he was gone.

"Hey, you there," a rough voice called at her from a short ways down the hall. "You work here? I'm looking for Officer Frazier. I'm her friend and friends come when ya need 'em. Where kin I find 'er?"

"May I ask who you are, sir? Are you family?"

"Did I say I was family? I said I was a friend. They's spelled different and friends is always more dependable than family. My name's Elmer. Who're you? You gonna tell me where I can find Miss Kim or not?"

Angel put her hand out graciously, if not hesitantly, to shake the hand of Elmer, the dog man. He was wearing an insulated gray jacket, bib overalls on top of a red checkered shirt, work shoes with rubbers over them, and held a grimy baseball cap in his hand respectfully. "I'm Angel Scott," she said in response to his question as he pumped her hand up and down like a water pump. "I'm sure Kim will be glad to see you, Elmer. She's in the chapel with my husband right now. Her husband, Carson, passed away this afternoon."

"I heard. That's why I'm here. Gonna take that little missy home with me so's she don't hafta go home and face that there empty house alone. Be right nice if you could fix us a nice meal though and let us keep the leftovers. That's what people done when my wife passed. All kinds a people brought food. You talk to folks, tell 'em to bring it to my house. Okay? I'll take good care of Miss Kim, don't you worry. Now where is that chapel?" Elmer self consciously swiped at the hair on his head, trying to make it lay down in preparation for his entrance into the mysterious world of the Holy.

Just as Angel was about to direct him to where the chapel was, Kim and Rob emerged, his arm around her shoulder protectively, she looking drawn and red faced. "Hi, Angel," she said first. "Thanks for sharing this guy with me. Hello, Elmer," she said softly. "Thank you for coming."

"I come to take you home with me, Missy. You don't need to be in that big house all by yerself right now. You just stay with me and I'll take care of everthing. This lady here's gonna fix us some food and maybe find us some more. That's what folks do for friends at a time like this."

Kim smiled weakly and put her arms around Elmer to give him a grateful hug. "You're so sweet, Elmer, and I really appreciate the offer, but I've already agreed to spend a couple of days with Angel. At a time like this I don't want anyone ruining your reputation by thinking the new widow is taking advantage of your charm. But thank you for thinking of me first. You're a true, true friend."

Elmer blushed and put his head down. "Ain't nothin' Miss Kim. But you're right. There's bound to be talk what with me bein' the most eligible bachelor in these parts and you the newest widder." He looked expectantly in Angel's direction, "Maybe I could join you for a meal, just all us friends together in your time a need for comfort."

Angel smiled at him with her heart bursting for love towards this strange man, her own eyes brimming with tears, and said she would be honored to have him as a guest in their home for dinner this evening and tomorrow evening as well, if he was available. She had never doubted Rob would ask Kim to stay with her for a few days and she knew there was no need to remind him. They, she and Rob, were truly becoming one in so many ways. Her heart went out to Kim thinking about the man she had lost, not the one who'd passed away today, but the one who'd been taken from her three years ago. Had they experienced the joy of unity that she and Rob had been building together? Were they best friends? What secrets had they shared that no one else could know? There were so many things for Kim to remember over the next years. Hopefully, with time, she'd find someone else with whom to share her life. She was such a young and beautiful lady. From what she had learned from Rob, Angel believed Kim was a truly good person who cared about people. Thus far, their acquaintance had been merely working in the social service community, but she felt a new era beginning, one of close friendship.

"Are there any further arrangements you need to make from here?" Rob asked Kim.

"No," she said softly. "He didn't have any personal effects for me to pick up, so I just have to call the funeral home tomorrow to make arrangement for his cremation, another part of his will. I'd really like to get out of here, if it's okay."

"Sure," said Angel. "I haven't had the pleasure of getting to know you outside of work, Kim, but I'm glad you've agreed to stay with me. Paul and Rob think so very highly of you. You've been invaluable to Rob in helping locate our missing couple."

265

"Oh," Kim stopped short in the hallway, "we need to decide what to do about Sarah. The sooner I get back on that project, the better I'll feel. Maybe we can go over some ideas tonight, Rob, what do you think? Any chance Mick's in town?" She turned back down the hallway in the direction they had come from and noticed Elmer standing back, left out. "Elmer, come on, I think I have some undercover work for you to do."

The man's face lit up. "Really? Hey, count me in. I'm your man."

"Great," said Rob, glad to be through the comforting role and on more solid ground. Carson was gone, but Paul and Sarah were still alive and needed them. At least he hoped Paul was still alive. "Angel, you think you can whip up some supper for this hungry group of super sleuths?"

"I think I can manage something," smiled Angel, glad to be included in Rob's work. She slipped her arm through Elmer's and smiled up at him. "So, you're going under cover, huh? I can see why you're the most eligible bachelor in Duluth. Unfortunately, I'm already married to that mad man up there, but if I was single, a man of your charm and mystique would be a hard one to refuse."

Elmer glowed. "I thank you for the compliment, ma'am, but I gots a girlfriend. Her name's Shania. Lives out there on the reservation. I sneak in sometimes on Saturday night and ..." His voice trailed off as the blush rose like the red line in a thermometer up from his neck to his face.

The four new friends sat around Angel's dining table and enjoyed a wonderful dinner of homemade spaghetti from a recipe Angel had been sent from a friend in California. The intoxicating aroma of the sauce lured the whole clan into the kitchen as Angel warmed it up. It had taken her eight hours over the weekend to prepare the sauce, and now it would be put to excellent use. A tossed salad, garlic toast and a light spumoni ice cream topped off the wonderful meal.

Adjourning to the den when the meal was finished, leaving the dishes for later, the group was ready to get down to business. They quickly filled in the gaps for Elmer, and then Kim reported on Sarah in Fergus Falls. Rob told them all about the visit to Dallas and Mick's plan to go back to the mission pretending to be on the booze again.

"Has he gone yet?" asked Kim. "I was wanting to use Elmer for a similar idea, but he won't have to use alcohol, and this Mike guy doesn't know him. Don't you think he'll get a little suspicious if Mick shows up after his miracle cure and shortly after you've been down asking questions about Paul? Elmer's face is fresh and new."

"Well, thank you, Miss Kim." Elmer glowed with pride. "I'd love to help out with this. What can I do?"

"You may have a point there, Kim," said Rob. "Let's get Mick on the line and see what he thinks. He can always be nearby to rescue Elmer, plus, there won't be any suspicion of Elmer so we could actually wire him, couldn't we?"

"I don't see why not," said Kim. "That is if Elmer's willing."

"I ain't afraid of no danger, Miss Kim. I fought in Vietnam with the Marines. Nothin' ain't gonna scare me mor'n that did."

"What about me?" whined Angel, "I want something to do, too."

"Oh, you'll have a big part, honey," smiled Rob taking her hand. "You get to keep me from falling apart until we find Paul and get both him and

Sarah home safely. Now, let's see if we can reach Mick and get his view on all this. By the way, Kim, can you get a few days off from work? Do you really think you're ready to get into this so deep right now?"

"First of all, I get four days bereavement leave with pay, so I'm all yours until Wednesday morning next week. And secondly, there's not going to be a religious service for Carson. His body will be cremated tomorrow. His ashes aren't him so I don't want them. We haven't had a marriage in so long I'm not feeling anything right now. It'll hit me later and I'll miss him terribly when I can remember the times before the accident, but for now, I want to work and keep my mind going. I don't want time to think. Get Mick on the horn and let's get this project under way."

Mick was in his apartment when they called. He said he was just about to go visit his dad and explain his plan to return to the world of intoxication. Rob put him on speaker phone so everyone could listen and speak. He told Mick about Carson, introduced Elmer and Angel, and then gave him a rundown on their new plan. Mick offered his condolences to Kim and then agreed the plan was better than his, and offered to stay with Kim in the van where they could monitor the wire Elmer would be wearing. Rob would also make another call on Mike to see what reaction he could get, and they all agreed that maybe Angel should take a couple of day's vacation and see about talking to Sarah. Kim would call Connie Reed to prepare her for Angel's visit. The plan was in place. Mick asked if they could pray together before they hung up, which made Kim somewhat uncomfortable, but all agreed and the prayer led by Mick was short but included each of them and their challenges for the next few days.

> Don't turn down the light
> I'm afraid to go home in the dark
>
> ———
>
> O. Henry
> American short story writer

Chapter 31

Angel was delighted to be included in the plans to find Paul and bring Sarah home. She and Sarah had become very close friends while she was dating Rob, and remained close throughout all the years. It had not surprised her then when Sarah had shared her secret with her. Angel had tried to get Sarah to tell Paul and convince her things would work out, that everything would be okay, but Sarah was adamant and had taken off without warning. Many times over the past few months since Sarah disappeared, Angel had been tempted to tell Paul or Rob what Sarah had told her in confidence, but she felt certain Sarah was alive and well somewhere and would never forgive her for breaking that confidence.

269

The long drive to Fergus Falls gave her plenty of time to think and plan what she would say to Sarah when she saw her. It also gave her the opportunity to reflect on the years since she first met and fell in love with Rob. How could she have been so naïve, so full of herself as to think God would chose her for such an important mission? The years had been difficult after the catastrophic wedding night, but she had done her best to move on and put it all past her. She was married and that's all that mattered, except to her heart.

———

"Rob, darling. Please try to understand. I love you so much more than you can possibly believe and being your wife is the most wonderful thing in the world. But, I have to stay a virgin until He returns."

"Until who returns, Angel? You're talking crazy. What's this all about?"

"Rob, our Lord and Savior suffered so much as a child because He was born of unclean birth. His mother wasn't married when she conceived. One day soon He's going to return and this time I believe God has chosen me as the vessel for His return. So you see, I have to be married so He's not illegitimate again, but I also have to be a virgin. That's the only way to prove He is who He is."

"Angel, this is crazy. I thought He was supposed to return in the clouds. I don't mind waiting until tomorrow, but ... "

"No Rob. Not tomorrow. Until He returns."

"That could be a hundred years from now, Angie."

"Then I'll wait a hundred years."

"I won't. You need to make up your mind right now. Either you're my wife or you're waiting for a fairy tale to come true. Pick me or pick Him. You can't have it both ways."

"I'm sorry Rob ..."

The door to the bridal suite slammed shut as Rob left ... and never came back.

———

After graduation from the university, she had taken a job with the child social service agency serving St. Louis County. The children and families she worked with left her drained at the end of each day. It was hard to fathom the depths of depravity to which so many parents had sunk, the looks of despair on the faces of the children. The senseless murder of Billy Landers had nearly crushed her spirit to the point where she was ready to give it up. Seeing Paul the next day, knowing Rob was well and still alone, gave her hope. The hope she had never dared to believe in, the hope that kept her alive and breathing each day, was in her marriage to Rob Scott. She had seen him from a distance on several occasions for the first few years after the wedding, and each time it had turned her legs to rubber. She wanted to run to him and say she was sorry, maybe she was wrong, but her legs wouldn't move. After awhile the sightings became fewer and fewer, probably because she became more involved in her work and had less time to loiter in areas where she was most apt to see him. Her counseling with the priest had helped her realize how silly her fantasy had been, but she still didn't have the nerve to call Rob. The humiliation of what she had done didn't allow her to face him.

Now, everything was contingent upon Sarah recognizing her. From what Kim had said, there was no real assurance that Sarah had regained all of her memory. Soft classical music played on the radio and soothed her nervousness. She was excited to see her friend and at the same time afraid of what she would find. Kim had not been encouraging. At last she reached the outskirts of the city and checked her instructions on how to get to the center where Sarah was staying. Feeling a bit weak, she stopped for a bite of lunch first, and then at 1:30 pulled into the Rehab Center parking lot. Lunch may have been a mistake as it now appeared ready to return to the world, undigested.

Walking briskly to the front door, taking no more time to think, Angel pulled the door open and entered the lobby, which by all appearances, was a real hospital. This would fool anyone, she thought. At the desk, she asked for Connie Reed and waited for the director to come out, introduce herself, and invite her back to the office. Their conversation was very short and then Connie led Angel to the room. Connie entered first, leaving Angel in the hall, the door open so she could hear.

"Janie, how are you doing today?" asked Connie. Without waiting for an answer, she continued, "I've brought a visitor to see you. I hope you're up to receiving callers."

"Who is it?" Sarah's voice trembled with fear. "I don't want to see anyone. No one knows I'm here."

"Well, I think you're going to want to see this lady. She drove a long, long way to see you and she says she knows you very well." Turning to the hallway through the open door, Connie gestured towards Angel. "Why don't you come in and say hello."

Angel hesitated just a second and then walked into the room. "Hello, Sarah," she said very softly. Sarah stared at her with wide eyes, not moving, trembling from head to toe. At last, she stepped into Angel's arms and sobbed.

"I'll leave you two alone to talk," said Connie and she left the room, closing the door quietly behind her.

"I lost it," sobbed Sarah. "I lost it and then I couldn't go home because I'm so ugly now."

"You're not ugly, Sarah. You're still the most beautiful girl in the world to Paul. You always will be."

"Does he know about the baby? I couldn't tell him. We had agreed we didn't want children and then when I got pregnant after he had a vasectomy, I knew he'd think I was cheating on him. I just couldn't face him. Angel, please believe me. I would never cheat on Paul. I love him too much."

"He doesn't know anything about the baby, but I truly believe if you had told him the truth he would have believed you and been as excited as you were. No vasectomy comes with a one hundred percent guarantee."

The two friends sat, holding hands, and talking for a long time. Sarah said she had never lost her memory, but didn't want to be found, so she faked it. She had hit an icy patch in the road and lost control of the car. When she hit the ditch, she was going very fast, and the car slammed into a large boulder, causing her to bounce forward into the windshield. She had not been wearing a seatbelt and the airbag never inflated. She didn't know how long she had lain there unconscious, but the men who found her took all of her things before coming back and calling for help. The police had brought her here thinking she may have been running from something. She talked about the pain of the frostbite and surgeries, and the hideous scar on her cheek and how ugly she felt. Finally she admitted she had been lonely for her friends and home the past few weeks, and that was when she started talking. Before that, she had refused to talk with anyone, so they had kept her confined as a patient rather than allowing her to move about the center as other residents would do. A psychiatrist came by every week to talk with her, accomplishing nothing. Her physician had been wonderful, as had the nurses, and she had received excellent care, but the loss of her baby was a pain she had to keep inside. She'd had several surgeries over the past few months, so she had been sedated or medicated most of the time. There were still hopes that plastic surgery could help with the scar on her face and to fix her nose and ear.

It was time for Angel to break the news to Sarah about Paul. She didn't know how to begin, but said a silent prayer asking for the right words to flow through her mouth.

"Sarah," she began, looking down at her hands, unable to face Sarah with this news. "Paul needs your help. He's been missing for a couple of weeks and we're afraid someone is trying to harm him because of a birthday gift he received. Did he ever tell you about his childhood recurring dream about Malchus, the Jewish servant whose ear was cut off by Peter in the Garden of Gethsemane?"

Sarah's face was white. "What are you saying? None of this makes sense. I know about the dream, but he didn't tell me. His Nana Grant told me about it. I don't think he even knew that she knew. She figured it was because of the Easter story he had heard in church and then some reading he had done about Malchus. He was so fascinated with that part of the Easter thing. But, what kind of birthday gift would have anything to do with his dream and then get him in danger? This is all my fault, isn't it!" She was on the verge of hysteria.

"I don't think so," said Angel calmly. "I think God has been trying to get a message through to Paul and had to take some drastic measures to get his attention. Unfortunately, someone else seems to have taken some drastic measures to get his attention, too. Rob and a guy named Mick, plus a cop named Kim and her friend Elmer are all working on this."

"I talked to them, Rob and this guy Mick and the cop. They were all in Rob's office when I called. Why didn't they tell me then?"

"Is that really something you'd want to hear over the phone when you're away from the people who love you and can support you through all this?"

"You're right, that was stupid of me. You said I could help. Tell me what I need to do. I'll do anything. My life is nothing without Paul."

"The first thing we've got to do is get you home," said Angel. "As soon as we get back, we'll meet with Rob and go from there. Elmer has gone undercover at a homeless shelter, and Mick and Kim are monitoring him there. Let's get everything together and get you out of here right away. Do you have to check with any of your doctors?"

"I don't think so. I'll leave instructions with Ms. Reed where I can be reached if there's anything I need to do. Let's go. I've got to find Paul."

The two ladies talked for a few minutes with Connie Reed and then got back into Angel's car for the trip home. It was already pretty late in the afternoon, but neither one wanted to spend another night away from Duluth and family. Angel called Rob on her cell to let him know she was bringing Sarah home and that she would be staying with her and Kim at her place until things were a little more settled. Rob agreed and begged her to drive safely, telling her how much he loved her before he hung up.

"You sound like a girl about to be married," smiled Sarah. "I am so happy for you and Rob. What changed?"

"We grew up, I guess. Of course, most of it was my fault. I had a very Catholic upbringing and some of the stricter rules of the Catholic Church can cause a great deal of guilt. I felt like I had to be perfect and had this fantasy even from childhood that I could be chosen as the mother of Christ when he returned. It was silly, really. If God had chosen me, I think He would have brought it to my attention before I got married to Rob, or at least stopped the wedding or something. Poor Rob, he's been faithful all these years and is willing to take me back. I couldn't ask for more than that. We're getting re-married in a few weeks, so we have got to find that best man of ours, now that we have our matron of honor back!" She reached over and squeezed Sarah's hand. "I am so glad you're coming home. I know things are going to be fine now, just fine."

The rest of the trip was spent chatting about everything and everyone they knew. Angel filled Sarah in on everything she had missed since she left, including the Landers case and Kim's husband, and Paul at the shelter, Father Mike, Mick, Kim's visit to Fergus Falls masquerading as a nurse's aide, and whatever else she knew. When they arrived home, very late, Rob was at Angel's apartment where he had fixed a nice meal for them to enjoy before retiring. They were both exhausted, but both very, very glad to see Rob. Hugging them both, one at a time, Rob felt a catch in his throat. The only thing missing from this happy reunion was Paul ... and maybe Sheba.

Sarah was very tired after the big day, so she fell asleep quickly in the guest room. Kim was staying in the Cities to help monitor Elmer, so

276

there was plenty of room for the two of them. After a hot shower, borrowing a night gown from Angel, she went straight to bed. Angel stayed up and talked with Rob, telling him everything Sarah had shared with her about the accident and why she had left.

"You knew about the baby and didn't tell me?" asked Rob.

"If I recall, we weren't communicating at that time," Angel shot back, recognizing the edge in his voice. "What was I supposed to do? Sarah said she would handle everything. I didn't know she was planning to run away and have the baby."

Rob started laughing, not hysterical laughing, or even comedy laughing, it was more like a chuckle when one realizes the irony of things. "Paul," he said, "never got a vasectomy. He thought Sarah didn't want kids, so he told her he would get one, but he couldn't go through with it because he was hoping she'd change her mind."

"You're kidding!" Angel looked at him in total shock. "This whole six months has been for nothing? If Sarah had stayed, Paul would not have gone to Father Mike and none of this would have happened."

"We don't know that, Angel. There is supposed to be a reason for everything. He might still have gotten that piece of the cross, still been haunted by his dream, still have sought answers through Father Mike. And besides, you're assuming Mike has something to do with this whole matter. We have no reason to believe that's true at all. Mike hasn't led the perfect life, but neither have I. He may be totally innocent."

"Do you really believe that?" Rob shook his head slowly. "Neither do I," said Angel, putting her head down on his shoulder and pulling her feet up under her as they sat together on the sofa. "I'll be glad when this is all over," she whispered, half asleep. "I want everyone home and safe, even Kim and Mick and Elmer. Speaking of Kim and Mick," she sat up to look into his face, "what do you think about that?"

"About what?"

"You know? Kim and Mick? What do you think?" Angel looked at him as if he should easily understand what she was talking about.

"I don't think anything," he said with one of those looks that meant he thought she was meddling where she didn't belong. "Her husband just died yesterday, for crying out loud. And here you're trying to get her married off again already. Let his ashes chill a bit, okay?"

"Oh, Rob, you know she hasn't been married, like in 'married'-married, for three years. She needs a man to take care of her. And you have to admit, she's a cute little thing. I think she and Mick make a darling pair." She put her head back on his shoulder and closed her eyes dreamily. "I think we make a pretty cute pair, too."

"I agree with that one. When are we having the wedding night rehearsal?"

She punched his side gently, "Not until after the wedding."

"Which one, the one fifteen years ago or the one this month?"

Much to his surprise, she stood up, grabbed his hand to pull him up and led him to the bedroom. "The one first one," she said softly and closed the bedroom door behind him.

title of novel by ...
John LeCarrè
English novelist

Chapter 32

Mick, Kim, Elmer, and Sheba, Paul's faithful dog, spent three hours gathering all the things they would need. Kim and Carson had been technology nuts, so had the very latest, most compact listening equipment available. No strings attached. A device that looked like a regular hearing aide was placed in Elmer's ear. No one would question a man's loss of hearing, and it would also serve as an excuse to have Sheba along to be his ears. Thick glasses rounded out the disguise, as a second reason to not worry about a man who can't see well, and again provided a reason for Sheba to be present. The earpiece served not only as a great camouflage, but worked well when Kim or Mick wanted to communicate to Elmer. It had a mini-microphone which allowed them to not only hear his voice, but the voices of those within three feet around him. The highly sensitive device was not available to most police departments, but was mainly for agencies higher up in the food chain. This was not a concern for Kim since the operation was somewhere outside the definition of authorized police procedure anyway. The glasses served the additional purpose of containing a small video camera in the right

279

screw that held the earpiece to the front. No one would ever recognize it, and it gave Mick and Kim an opportunity to see to whom Elmer was talking. Having Sheba added a third benefit. Elmer could lie down at night and talk to his dog, no one being the wiser that he was really talking to Kim and Mick. The plan was foolproof, perfect. At last, they were ready to go. The van, one which Carson and Kim had bought five years earlier, looked like a VW wagon from the sixties with painted flowers all over the olive drab exterior. It had been re-equipped with the video receivers and listening devices needed to monitor Elmer. Mick toyed with the idea of inviting his father along for the stake out, so excited was he about their covert operation. Kim laughed and made the comment that he should have been a cop.

"What about me?" asked Elmer. "I think me 'n Sheba here make a pretty good undercover team, too."

"Yes, you most certainly do!" replied Kim as they headed out into the evening traffic along Interstate 35 to Minneapolis. "I think the four of us will do just fine. By the way, Elmer," she asked turning in the seat to look back at him and the dog, "who's watching your family while you're away?"

"My brother, Roy, come up from Moose Lake to spend a few days. He was due for a vacation anyways and wanted to get away from the humdrum of the country and back into the excitement of big city life. You know how it is when country comes to town. He'll be good with the animals though, jist as long as he don't try and get eggs out from under 'em or milk 'em in the morning. His wife'll be happy to see him go, too. She kin take care of her cows and chickens and get a chance to sleep in the house."

"Where does she normally sleep?" asked Mick.

"In the barn. Tried to make Roy sleep out there 'cuz he snores so bad, but that only lasted one night. Kept the cows so upset there weren't no milk the next mornin'. So Ruby sleeps in the barn and Roy sleeps in the house."

"Elmer, is that a true story?" Kim smiled looking back into the rear seat at him and Sheba.

"Naw, but I thought it'd help pass the time. I don't like long car rides."

"Well," said Mick, "what can we do to entertain you?"

"You can fill me in more on the details of this Paul character who done got Sheba then run off and got hisself in trouble, and his wife who done the same, and then this preacher guy. I got some of the facts, but there's a lot of fill-in I could use."

The rest of the journey was spent with Mick and Kim bringing Elmer up to speed on the whole situation, everything they could think of. Kim was the only one of the three to have met Sarah and she knew scant little about why she had left Paul. She did know that Angel had been sent to bring Sarah home and hoped that part of the operation had been successful. She would try and give Angel a call in the morning and check up on them. In the meantime, they had their own plans to follow in an attempt to at least find out what happened to Paul. Dusk was just beginning to fall when they neared the area where the shelter was situated. With final instructions and hugs for good luck from Kim, Elmer and Sheba got out of the van about four blocks from the site. Sheba had an old collar and a rope for a leash. Elmer was attired in his normal clothing, which was as close to vagrant chic as anyone could get, plus he carried an old military duffel bag with his few belongings in it. The glasses made it hard for him to see, so he looked over the top a great deal. Several times along his route to the shelter, he did air checks with Kim to make sure they were in communication. She would also describe what she was able to see through the camera in the glasses. At one point Elmer pulled off the glasses and held them up so they were facing him. He made a funny face and then put them back on. He enjoyed the sound of Kim's laughter and Mick's remarks. Finally, he reached the door of the shelter.

Elmer poked his head through the entryway and looked around. No one seemed to notice him at first. He stood in the doorway and waited, looking around as much as he could so Kim and Mick could take in the sights of the interior.

"Alright," said Mick in a whisper, "that man sitting on the table on the far right up front is Father Mike. He's not wearing a clerical collar, but has on a check shirt and nice slacks. See him?"

Elmer made his way around the many tables and people who were just sitting around as if waiting for something. Some were deep into conversation, most were just there. He approached Mike somewhat cautiously.

"You the head man 'round here?" he asked. "Had a friend tole me 'bout this place. Okay I crash here? Brought my own bed roll, if ya wanna call it that."

"Father Mike," said Mike, stretching out his hand and smiling. "You're welcome to stay, but we don't allow pets. Who's your friend that told you about us?"

"Sergio. A Mescan dude, old guy with long gray hair," replied Elmer.

"Sergio passed away about a week and a half ago." Mike looked at Elmer suspiciously.

"Didn't say he tole me today, did I? And this here mutt ain't no pet. I ain't got good eyes and can't hear too well neither, so she comes along to keep people outta jail."

"I don't think I understand."

"Well, some driver hits a homeless guy, he's goin' to jail, right? Don't wanna be 'sponsible for no upright citizen goin' to jail, so I keeps my dog here with me to be my eyes and ears."

"In that case, I guess she can stay, as long as she doesn't bark all night and doesn't bite anyone. What's her name? What do you feed her?"

"She don't bark. She don't bite. I call her Dog, and she eats what I eats. I hear you serves three meals a day here, right? Don't cost nothin?"

"Tell him you'll be glad to help out around the place to earn your keep," whispered Kim into the microphone.

"Okay, I'll just do that."

"I beg your pardon?" said Mike looking at Elmer curiously.

"What'd ya do?" said Elmer, serious as he could.

"Um, nothing. You just said something and I didn't know if you were talking to me or ... or maybe someone else."

"Oh, don't mind me. Mind wanders now and then. I was jist thinkin' I could help out 'round here some to pay for my meals and stuff. I know it's kind of a burden to bring a dog in an' all, but she's all I got leff, me and Dog."

"You never did say what your name is," said Mike.

"Elmer. Like Elmer Fudd, ever heard a him?"

"Do you have a last name, Elmer?"

"Do I need one? Don't have no social security card and no driver's license either. Your first name's Father and your last name's Mike. My first name's El and my last name's Mer. So be it."

"Great job, Elmer," came a whisper over the microphone.

"I know," smiled Elmer.

"You know what?" Father Mike was becoming a bit exasperated with this new guest. "Never mind, don't answer that. Why don't you find a place to spread your bedroll for the night. Have you had supper yet? I could find you a sandwich and some coffee if you like. What about Dog? Is she hungry?"

Elmer took the offer for a sandwich and coffee. He had not been allowed to eat dinner because he had to fit into the part one hundred percent. Being ravenously hungry when he arrived would be a good start. The cold Spam sandwich and lukewarm coffee weren't what he was hoping for, but they were what was offered. Dog got a slice of Spam and an old bone, along with a bowl of water which she lapped up quickly. She sniffed at the Spam and looked up at Elmer as if to ask permission or ask if that was the best he could provide. He nodded his head and she ate it.

After his supper, he started looking around for a place to make his bed. Here again he relied on the guidance of the microphone and camera. Mick could tell him who had been there the longest, who looked familiar and would probably remember Paul. He spotted Augie and Melissa in the center aisle between the tables, near the front of the tent and directed Elmer in their direction.

"Hey you," said Elmer in a friendly manner, "My name's Elmer. Mind if my dog and I bed down close to ya?"

Augie appeared as if he was about to tell Elmer to move on, but already Melissa was petting Sheba while looking up at her grandfather as if to ask if she could keep her.

"That there dog bite?" asked Augie.

"Never bit nobody. Just a good ole dog keeps me from walkin' into the street and gettin' myself kilt. I don't see so good and don't hear so good, neither. Got this here hearing aide turned all the way up and still can't hear so much. That your little boy there?"

"That's my granddaughter," said Augie. "You can bed down here, but you don't touch the kid, okay?"

"I like my wimin a bit older and plumper, if ya don't mind," laughed Elmer. "Ain't never been into that kiddy stuff. Them's sick people do that. Now, if it's all the same to you, I'll park myself right over here and if we keep my dog between me and the little girl, and then you on the other side, no one's gonna mess with her for no reason. Dog don't bark much, but she's a good guard dog when it comes to protectin' kids. My name's Elmer. What's yers?"

"You already told me you were Elmer. I'm Augie and this here's Melissa. Don't that dog have a name besides Dog?"

"I asked her once, but she won't tell me."

Melissa smiled and snuggled onto her pallet, close as she could get to Sheba, who in turn lay down as if her only reason for existing was to protect that little girl.

"I'm going to cry," said Kim over the microphone. "You're so sweet, Elmer, and Sheba obviously loves that little girl. I think that's the one Paul talked about. But Elmer, please don't answer us when we talk to you. They'll think you're crazy and send you away. Before you go to sleep, set your glasses on your bag so that the camera is facing the doorway. That way we can see if anyone comes and goes throughout the night. I wouldn't say anything more to Augie tonight. Let them all get used to you for a day, and then start talking to Sheba tomorrow night. We'll meet up at that place we talked about and figure out how to proceed. Augie and Melissa are the best catch of the day. Paul got very attached to them. Good night, Elmer. Sleep tight. Mick and I'll take turns sleeping and keeping an eye on things, so you have nothing to worry about. Good night Sheba."

"Woof!" the dog barked.

"Thought you said she'd didn't bark," said Augie.

"She was just tellin' me goodnight," answered Elmer. "Good night, Dog. Sleep tight."

Be not forgetful to entertain strangers:
for thereby some have entertained
Angels unawares.

Bible
Hebrews 13:2

Chapter 33

After Hazel and the phony doctor had left the room, locking the door behind them, Paul lay on his back hoping Tina would reappear. She did. He looked up at her and began to cry.

"I'm not sick, am I, Tina." It was a statement, not a question.

"No," she responded very softly.

"Why are they doing this? Who are they? They're after the relic, I know that much, but I don't understand why they had to make me sick and kidnap me. It's just a piece of wood, and no one even knows for sure that it's real. The only way they could know about it is through Mike or maybe Mick, but I don't think they would do this to me. From what I can see out the window, I'm not in Duluth, so I must be nearer the Cities."

"I can't answer all the questions yet, Paul. You have to get through this to know the answers."

"Then talk to me some more about challenges. I like that. It makes sense, a lot more sense than what some preachers pass off as the Word of God as if they really understood it. Most of them either try to scare you into religion, or act like they've got a direct line to God and keep saying things like, ' I got a word from God for you.' That sounds stupid to me. Then they go on and tell you what God told them to tell you. If God has something to say to me, I'll bet he doesn't need a total stranger to tell me. Or does He?"

Tina smiled a beautiful, bright smile. She still looked so much like Sarah it made Paul's heart ache. "He has already told you everything you need to know to make it through life facing each challenge as it comes along. He still answers prayers, but not the gimme kind. You want to know about challenges? I'll give you a few examples, and see if you can't relate, okay?"

"Sounds like a test, but I'm up to it. Go right ahead, angel lady."

Tina laughed a hearty laugh, throwing her head back and shaking her long blonde hair. "You are too much, Paul Grant. Okay, here's your test. You're stopped at a red light and there's one car in front of you. The light turns green but the car in front does not instantly move into the intersection. What do you do? Honk and make an enemy? Let it pass knowing that if it were you, you'd be irritated by a honk? Or, let it pass because that person may have something very important on his or her mind."

Paul looked at as if she was out of her mind. "That's a challenge? That one's easy. The last two make sense. I don't like being honked at, that's for sure, and that person might be upset about something."

"But you honk."

"I just said I wouldn't," argued Paul.

"You said you wouldn't, but if you think back, you frequently do. And, you've been known to make an un-gentlemanly-like gesture at a few people who have honked when you were the lead car. Answering questions correctly is easy. Thinking before you act and react all through the day every day, is the real challenge. Are you starting to get it?"

"Let's say a situation comes up where I don't know how to act or react. What do I do then?"

"Rely on God to provide the answer. Keep that line of communication open, so on a moment's notice you can say, Okay God, what should I do here? He'll provide the answer, sometimes before you ask it. Have you ever been at an intersection and the light turns green, but you don't go and you don't know why? Then, out of nowhere a speeding truck runs the red light. If you had been in the middle of that intersection, you'd be dead. That was answering your question before you asked. In fact, you never even thought to ask because you didn't know there was a need. You just found yourself unable to act."

"Hey, yeah, I've had that happen. Tell me more. This is interesting."

"I can't tell you much more. My time is almost up. So, let me summarize. Challenges are there every minute of every day. How you choose to meet them is up to you. The best way is to keep a smile on your face and in your eyes. Treat everyone with kindness and consideration no matter who it is, homeless person, clerk in the store, bus driver, auto mechanic, school crossing guard, members of your family, everyone you encounter during your lifetime. Always act and speak out of courtesy, kindness and consideration. Put yourself last and others first. Keep your line of communication with God open at all times. Accept your challenges without complaining, even if it means suffering painfully with cancer or AIDS, and when this life is over, be prepared to accept your rewards for having met your challenges God's way. No life is without challenges. Now, go to sleep. It's time for me to leave and for you to face the rest of your challenges without me."

"But I need you," Paul cried as he sat up in the bed. When he turned his head back toward the dresser, Tina was gone. The door to the room opened quickly and Hazel and the doctor came in. They looked at him and shook their heads as if to say he was delirious.

"He's hearing voices and answering them. This is not a good sign," the doctor said to Hazel, speaking as if Paul was not even in the room. "We must make an effort to find his priest and his religious symbol. If not, I'm afraid he will not make it much longer. The fever is destroying his brain. Do you know who this priest is? Where we can find him?"

Paul looked at them through eyes that were bright and clear of any sickness. "I know where he is," said Paul, "and so do you. If you find him, you'll find the relic. Then you can have it and you can let me go home. By the way, doc, you make a lousy Freud and that get up doesn't make you look older, just more stupid. I'm tired of playing this game for you. Get Father Mike. Let me talk to him about the relic. And then get out of my life."

The doctor shook his head, but Hazel's eyes had gone wide. She was not nearly as good an actor as he. Her hands twisted her apron front as she waited for the next clue from the doctor person. He looked back over his shoulder at her and winked, then gave a little smile.

"I think we should leave our young patient alone while we go and hunt for this priest of his. Surely someone will know of him. Come my dear, your nephew is very, very ill. Maybe a priest is exactly what he needs. I hear they do something called last rites. That should be fun to watch." The two of them left the room, doctor pushing Hazel who could not figure out what was going on. They were sure to lock the door behind them.

Paul stood up and paced the room wondering what would happen next. He would refuse any more tea and that would help him gain strength, unless they withheld food and water. He could break out the window, but would have no way of getting down to the ground without injuring himself. He walked over and looked out the window again, trying to judge the distance, just in case. The doctor was walking out of the front door, his disguise half removed, and he was laughing. Paul wished he could hear what was being said. Hazel was standing in the yard with the doc, still wringing her hands on her apron, and looking anxious. As Paul watched, the doctor continued to remove his disguise. He happened to glance up at the window where Paul stood watching. When he did, Paul knew he'd seen that face before. Where? When? Who was that man?

Handing the disguise and his black bag to Hazel, the doctor impersonator, still looking up at Paul, saluted once with a smile on his face, then turned and walked across the street and between the houses, out of sight.

Even a paranoid can have enemies.

Henry Kissinger
German-born American diplomat

Chapter 34

Kim and Mick took turns monitoring Elmer's activity in the camp. Frequently
they would drive around for awhile and
find a new place to park. Occasionally they'd tell
Elmer they were breaking for lunch and go to
some diner for a quick bite to eat. Neither of them
wanted to be away from the monitoring system
too long, just in case. So far very little of interest had caught their attention. They spent a lot of
time smiling at Elmer's way of putting things into
words and the way he talked to Sheba like a mad
man might. It wasn't easy finding places to move
the van to every few hours to avoid suspicion.
However, they found that a spot just down the
street from a very active beer joint seemed quite
safe, at least from detection. Several drunks had
walked by and pounded on the side of the van,
making comments about having owned one just
like it way back when.

The inside of the van, behind the bucket seats,
was insulated with a thick, heavy foam rubber all
around. Remnants of old carpeting with half inch
foam padding made the floor more comfortable
than the metal would have been. A bench seat, retrieved from Carson's old Oldsmobile, circa 1970,
covered three fourths of the width in the back, leav-

ing just enough room on one side to get around to the back doors. The bench served as an excellent bed for the person not on duty. Two bucket seats from an older model Mustang had been bolted to the floor on one side of the van's cavernous back area and served as the hot seats directly in front of the monitoring station. The station itself took up only about three feet along the wall opposite the driver's side of the vehicle, and protruded just about eight inches from the wall. It was perfect. A small screen for watching what Elmer could pick up with the camera glasses, some controls for adjusting the monitor as well as others for adjusting the sound. A set of headphones for each of them was available to be plugged into the console, and each headset had a mouthpiece through which they would communicate with Rescue One, the code name Elmer had selected for himself and the project. He called them the Mother Ship which guaranteed his solitude within the shelter.

The first night had passed without incident and in the morning, Elmer, like everyone else, packed up his bag and, after breakfast, headed for the door. Throughout breakfast he spoke to them as if talking to himself. When people looked at him strangely, he just smiled and tried to introduce himself with an outstretched hand and a mouth full of Cheerios. That usually cut any budding friendships rather short. Even Mick and Kim had to turn down the volume while Elmer ate, smacking loudly with each mouthful.

After lunch, things began to appear a little more exciting. Everyone stayed around to take a nap after the noon meal, including Elmer who once again positioned himself and Sheba by Augie and Melissa. Melissa had grown quite attached to the dog and the dog seemed to be enjoying the child's attention.

"Incoming," said Elmer, looking around the interior of the tent. "White male, Caucasian, dressed in nice slacks and shirt, neat haircut and horn rimmed glasses. 'Bout forty years old. Looks shifty eyed. Will monitor closely."

"Who are you talking to?" asked Augie a bit irritated. "You sound like someone from the looney bin."

"I bin alone so long, I pretend I got friends in the Mother Ship waiting to come git me when the trouble starts. Ain't nothin to worry about. I'm just entertainin' me. Dog's a good ole dog, but she don't talk much. Who's that feller over there? He don't look homeless, but I guess looks can be deceivin'."

"That's the Right Reverend Braddock, also known as Brother Brimstone. He comes in here 'bout once a month and preaches all hell fire and brimstone and tells us all about when we get saved Jesus is gonna give us new homes and fancy cars and all that crap. Not my kinda preacher at all. He keeps talkin' to Father Mike about going on television and spreading the gospel to the world. I ain't sure how the good Father feels about him, but he doesn't seem too interested."

"Think I'll get me another cup of that coffee over there. Is that okay?" asked Elmer. "Little girl, you watch Dog here for me, will ya?"

Melissa's gratitude was in her eyes and in her smile. "Okay," she said, as she hugged Sheba around the neck and pulled her down next to her on the pallet.

Augie and Elmer shared a look of extreme surprise. "Thought you said she couldn't hear and couldn't talk," said Elmer.

"I ... I ... go get your coffee," sputtered Augie. "We'll talk later."

The two little ladies, Melissa and Sheba, stayed cuddled together while Melissa closed her eyes to rest, the smile still on her lips. Once Sheba leaned over and licked her face, and Melissa giggled and scrunched up her nose, keeping her eyes tightly shut.

"Good afternoon Brother Braddock," said Father Mike glancing up from the newspaper he was reading. "What brings you out this way on a Thursday afternoon? Is everyone in your congregation healthy and happy? Or are you just slummin' a bit?"

Brother Braddock looked suspiciously at Elmer who was helping himself to a cup of coffee, his back to the two clerics. "New one?" asked the Brother.

"Yeah, just came in a day ago. Poor guy's got real bad eye sight and wears a hearing aid. Don't worry, he can't hear you if you've come for confession." The Father laughed at his own joke.

"So why's he just standing there? Why doesn't he go lay down like the rest?"

"Well," said Father Mike, still smiling, "Looks to me like he's enjoying a cup of coffee. With his eyesight, if he tried to walk back to his pallet he'd probably spill it on several people before he got there. Then, he'd have to come back and fill it up again and walk back through the same people, spill some more, come back up and fill it ..."

"Okay! I get the picture," snarled Brother Braddock. He put his legs over the bench seat of the picnic table where Mike was sitting, and sat himself down, looking around the entire shelter as if looking for someone in particular.

"Something I can help you with, Brother?" asked Mike. "You seem a bit on edge today. Confession really is good for the soul, you know."

"Yeah, yeah, whatever," Braddock turned back to face Mike with a serious expression on his face. "What do you hear from your friend the miracle worker with the piece of the cross? Does he ever come around anymore?"

"Now that you mention it, seems he's disappeared. Some friends of his came asking about him a couple of weeks ago. He'd told them he was on his way here, but he never showed up. They said Ruth had also called him, asking him to come down because Saul was dying, but Saul died a couple of months ago. So, it's kind of strange. I should get in touch with his friends and see if they've got anything new on him or if he came back."

"They didn't have any idea what happened to him? Did he have that piece with him? Maybe he got robbed or something. That's too bad. He could have made a fortune with that thing."

Kim and Mick's ears perked up. Why was this preacher guy so interested in the relic and where did money come into play here? Didn't Augie say this guy was wanting to get into television? What was that he said about preaching wealth and prosperity?

"Don't suppose he left that thing with you, did he?" continued Braddock. "I mean, didn't you tell me he was pretty upset about all the stuff that was happening when he had it?"

"He may have been upset, but he never asked me to take it and I wouldn't have done it anyway. It was sent to him for a reason, not to me."

"But a man like him doesn't know the value of such a piece. He doesn't realize the good he could do for all the people in the world if he's able to work miracles with it. That relic belongs in the hands of a man of God, one who knows how to reach out and touch the lives of millions of people and bring souls to God through the miracles performed through his hands."

"Whose hands, God's or the man who has the relic?"

"Why, God's of course," sputtered Braddock.

"I wasn't sure there the way you were talking. Are you still looking for a chance to get on TV and be one of those rich and famous televangelists?"

"Now Father Mike, you know I'm not in it for the money. I want to touch as many lives as I can before the Lord calls me home. I'm just a lowly servant like you, spreading the Gospel and bring- ing souls to Jesus."

Slowly Elmer turned around and faced the two men at the picnic bench. Approaching Brother Braddock, he put out his hand. "You are truly a man of God, ain't you, brother. I ain't had good hearin' since I was in the war, but God spoke to me through you today and I can feel the power of the Holy Spirit in your hands. Take me with you, Brother. Let me be your disciple. I want to learn from you all there is to know about Jesus." Elmer went down on his knees, crying as he looked up at Brother Braddock, both of his hands clasping the preacher's one hand. The Brother looked down at him in shock and disgust.

"I'm here on personal business today, but why don't you come to my church next Sunday? Here, take my card."

"But I know where the relic is," said Elmer very softly so only the preacher could hear. "I know where it is and how you can get it. You're right. It belongs in the hands of a man of God."

"You're talking nonsense," Braddock smiled a humiliated smile. "I don't know what you're talking about."

"Yes you do," urged Elmer. "You know about the relic and the man who was here. I know where he is. I can take you to him."

"Now I know you're insane," said the preacher loudly as he stood up. "I don't know who you are or what you're trying to pull, but I think you'd better move along."

Brother Braddock said his goodbyes to Father Mike and then turned to walk through the chorus of bodies lying hither and yon taking siesta. As he neared where Augie and Melissa were lying, a deep growl started in Sheba's throat. When Braddock was abreast of them, Sheba stood up and barked at him, growling more as if she were about to attack. Elmer came running over and calmed her down. "Sorry, Brother," he said. "Dog's a little nervous today. She gets like that when I have one of my spells. Didn't mean nothin' by what I said. No hard feelings, okay? Just trying to make a friend."

Braddock snarled and walked away, out of the tent.

"Rescue One to Mother Ship." Elmer said softly, standing up watching the fleeing preacher. "Hot shot preacher gots itchy fingers. Over and out." He turned and smiled at Melissa. "It's okay little one," he said, "Dog's just trying to protect you and that man got a little pushy. Nothin' to worry about. Take your nap now. Dog'll watch over you. And don't forget to say your prayers."

Elmer noticed that Melissa slept with one arm hugging her tattered gray stuffed kitten, and the other arm around Sheba. It would have made a really cute picture if it hadn't been in this place. "A little girl needs a home, and a mom and dad, and a dog all her own," He whispered. A tear rolled down his cheek as he looked at the angelic face of little eight-year-old Melissa sleeping on a pallet in a homeless shelter in Minneapolis, Minnesota. "What a challenge for such a sweet little girl," he said.

Back in the van, Mick couldn't look at Kim. His own eyes were tearing up as he looked into the face the camera was catching. The child was beautiful, in spite of the dirty hair and smudges on her cheeks. He thought about his own daughter and how much she had compared to this child. He vowed in his heart that when this was over, when they found Paul, he would get Augie and Melissa out of there. "Don't worry, Rescue One, we won't leave them behind. When the Mother Ship leaves, they'll be on board, I promise."

'Thanks," said Elmer softly, and then he too reclined to take a rest, placing his glasses and camera in a position that would catch anyone coming through the front of the tent.

Kim was having a hard time getting rid of the lump in her throat. She and Carson had never had the chance to have children. They had decided to wait until their careers were well established before ... and then it was all over in the blink of an eye. If that drunk hadn't been out driving, if he hadn't hit Carson, if Carson hadn't been paralyzed, if Carson hadn't died, she could be a mom right now. Her sobs finally broke through, the grief for all of it gushing forth like a flash flood of emotion. Her body crumbled onto the bench seat. Mick pulled her over to the bucket seat where he

299

was sitting, monitoring the shelter, and rocked her in his arms like a child. She was light as a child as he lifted her onto his lap, his arms were strong and reassuring. His cheek pressed against the top of her shoulder gave her the assurance that she was safe here, with him. She didn't have to be the big bad cop. Today she could be a child, she could be a widow, she could be a woman and cry for all the things she needed to cry for. Too much had been bottled up for too long and the release was cleansing and exhausting. It was some twenty minutes of rocking her before Mick realized she had fallen asleep in his arms. As gently as he could, he lifted her while he stood up and placed her on the bench seat they used for a bed, placed her weary head on the pillow and covered her small body with an army blanket. Then he sat back in the monitoring seat and watched her sleep. Long black lashes splayed against soft white cheeks with blotches of pink from crying. Her short dark hair framed that innocent face and her beauty captured his heart. It was hard for him to think of her as a widow, a widow of just a few days at that. Looking at her now he wanted to protect her forever, and yet he had no job, no income, nothing to offer a lady who'd been newly widowed. Insanity must be caused by small closed-in spaces, he mused. Kim sniffled and turned over to face the back of her bed. So much for daydreams, he thought and settled back into watching and listening.

Nothing was going on inside the tent. Everything seemed very quiet. Mick started to stand up and reach around the driver's seat for a can of pop in the small cooler, when he noticed some activity outside the van's front window at the door of the bar. It was Brother Braddock and he was speaking to another man who looked to be on the sleazy side. Braddock was talking feverishly and pointing towards the shelter as he pulled two bills out of his pocket and handed them to the man. He pointed his finger in the man's face as if threatening him, then gestured towards the shelter again. At last he made movements with his hands indicating glasses and something lower ... like a dog.

Mick was sure the man was being instructed to keep an eye on Elmer and Sheba. He didn't want to wake Kim, and he certainly didn't want to alarm Elmer just yet, but he had no choice. He spoke softly into the headpiece, hoping Elmer hadn't fallen asleep for real, and made him aware of what he had just seen. Elmer listened and grunted, eyes closed in case anyone was watching him, while Mick described the man in detail and warned Elmer to keep a lookout for him. "Oh yeah," said Elmer as if talking in his sleep, then he turned over. Mick was confident his message had gotten through.

Moments later, the man appeared on the monitor screen as he entered the shelter tent. Mick's heart beat in his chest. "Kim," he reached over and shook her with his right hand while keeping his eyes on the screen. "Kim, wake up. I think we've got something going on."

Kim shook herself awake and sat up. Her eyes felt swollen from the hearty cry she had enjoyed. "What's going on?" she asked as she moved over closer to Mick to see the screen.

"That man," said Mick, "was sent in there by Brother Braddock. I'm sure he's after ..."

He stopped in mid sentence, looking at Kim's face which had gone white. "What is it?" he asked. "What's wrong?"

"I know him," she said, still staring with eyes wide at the figure on the screen. "That's Ralph Landers, the man who killed his kid, Billy. But it can't be. He's in jail.

"Could he have a brother?" asked Mick, not knowing what she was talking about.

"If he does, Paul's in big trouble. We've got to get Elmer out of there. That man is dangerous."

"Before we jump to conclusions, get on your cell phone and see what you can find out about this guy, Landers, and any living male relatives of his. I'll keep an eye on Elmer for now. Keep your mic off, we don't want to panic Elmer. I hope Sheba's got good teeth and bad breath. Elmer may need them."

After about ten minutes, Kim closed her cell phone and looked at Mick, real fear in her eyes. "He's got a twin brother named Waylon Landers with a rap sheet as long as your arm. Mick, if he's involved with Paul's disappearance, this is for revenge and Paul won't be coming out alive."

Kim spent the next few minutes filling Mick in on the situation that had sent Ralph to jail and gotten him convicted for murdering his youngest son, Billy. She explained about the scar and Paul's involvement.

"So, what you're telling me is if Paul hadn't healed that kid, that guy wouldn't have beaten him to death, at least not on that day, and Ralph wouldn't be in jail for murder. Right?"

"That's it in a nutshell."

"Then you're right. We've got to get Elmer out of there. I wonder how this preacher guy figures into the whole matter? Uh oh, we may be too late. Waylon's got Elmer and Sheba's staying with the kid. The glasses, son of a ...he left the glasses on the duffel bag, We won't be able to see where he's going. Elmer. If you can hear me, Elmer, tell that dufus you need your glasses."

There was no answer.

I would walk miles for a bacon sandwich.

Diana
Princess of Wales

Chapter 35

There was silence in the house, a stillness that felt like death. Somewhere, in another room, in another vacuum, Paul could feel Hazel breathing. Why hadn't she brought him anything to eat or drink? His watch was gone and there was no clock in the room. He felt as if he couldn't breathe and he knew another anxiety attack was coming on. Air, he had to have cold air or he would die. The pounding of his heart pushed him to the point of panic and he began to bang loudly on the door.

"Hazel! I need help. Please. I'm sick, I need help!" His pleas seemed to go unanswered as he bent at the waist gasping for air. "Please God, don't let me die here, not this way," he pleaded in his mind. He gasped again, still nothing. The burning in his eyes was fierce, and the cold sweat ran down his body inside his shirt. Both hands shook, and once again he bent over, gasping for air, but nothing. After what seemed like an eternity, he could hear somewhere in the distance, a turning of the key in the lock, the door opening. Hazel stared at him, eyes wide with fear. His face was ashen as again he bent at the waist gasping for air. In his panic, he rushed, pushed her aside and stepped outside the room where the air was cooler. One more time, gasping, and at last a breath, a deep, clean breath. His pulse began to slow and the relief brought him to tears. It had been months since his last attack and this time he had no medication with him. Without thinking about the opportunity presented to him, Paul walked back into the room and lay down on the bed. He was too weak to escape.

"Are ... you ... are you alright?" asked Hazel, fear quivering her lips as she spoke. Her eyes were as large as his must have been when she entered the room. "Can I get you something?"

"I need water and sugar, orange juice if you have it."

She left the room and Paul lay on the bed regaining his composure, his strength. When he realized what had happened, he stood up and tried the door. It was locked. Hazel had been frightened by his episode, but not too frightened to remember he was her prisoner. When she returned, the tray on which she had placed a glass of juice and a glass of water, nearly fell off her hand as she opened the door. She placed the tray on the side table and Paul gratefully drank the orange juice in one long drink. The fructose would get into his system quickly and bring his blood sugar level back up.

"Hazel, sit down. Please. Let's just talk. I'm tired of being up here all by myself. I just want someone to talk to, someone to listen to. I'm sorry I frightened you. That was an anxiety attack. I get those sometimes when my blood sugar drops drastically. I'm okay. You can relax. Tell me about yourself, just talk to me."

The woman sat on the chair by the door and looked down. "I don't have anything to tell and

I'm not supposed to talk to you. I might say too much."

"Is that what he said? Has he convinced you that he knows everything and you know nothing?"

Hazel's face turned crimson with anger and she nodded ever so slightly. Still she didn't say anything, just sat on the chair, eyes downcast, fingers twisting the hem of her apron.

Paul cleared his throat and tried again. "Hazel, do you know what challenges are? They're things we encounter every day on our road through life. Take you and me for example, we can accept each other as equals, look each other in the eye and see the humanity. Or, we can keep on being silent strangers. We're both in this world. We both feel the same things. We each have different challenges to face, but facing them together is so much easier. Life is sort of like a game. You have obstacles set in your way that you have to find a way around or through or over or under. You can choose to face each obstacle alone, or you can turn to others for help and help them in return. We're all so busy either judging each other or wanting what someone else has that we totally forget that other person has feelings, too. We yell and scream when someone steals something that belongs to us, but we don't care how much a person is hurt when we steal from him. And stealing isn't always just stuff. Sometimes it's a parking place or a frown instead of a smile that's really needed. Have you ever thought about that? I mean that your smile can make the difference for a whole day to a total stranger. And, it didn't cost you anything. It's the same with courtesy. How much time does it take to let someone ahead of you in line at the store, or on the street? How much time are you losing if you let someone else have that close up parking space or get waited on in a restaurant before you? Is your life over if the mailman is having a bad day and brings your mail late? When's the last time you said good morning and gave a bright smile to every stranger you met as you walked along the street? It's fun and it's contagious. I saw this lady one time. She loved music and when a good song came on while she was washing the windows on her car at a gas station, she started dancing. Then she yelled at the people around her to join in and some did. Most of us thought she was crazy and didn't want to make fools of ourselves, but those who joined in and danced, I'll bet they felt great all day. I was one of those who drove away, embarrassed. Next time I'll dance, no matter how funny I look. And I'll sing, too. There are enough serious moments in life as it is. We don't need to create more by being selfish and angry."

Hazel looked at him through droopy eyes. She was not able to comprehend what he was saying. "Why are you telling me all this?" she asked.

"Because these are the little challenges we face in life each day and I believe each time we give someone else a break, offer an unexpected smile and wave, and enjoy exactly where we are every second, it's a little miracle."

"What you're saying is God doesn't work big miracles, just little ones?"

"Not at all, big miracles happen everyday. We just don't look at them as miracles because we're too busy expecting God to cure us of cancer to bother thanking him for the breath we're still able to take. God does cure cancer, but I don't think He cures all cancer for His own reasons."

"I've got faith. My brother's a preacher. I know all about ..."

"Brother Bartholomew Braddock. I know all about him."

Hazel sat up straight and stared at him, eyes wide with horror. Paul suddenly realized his mistake. Not only could he identify his captor, in spite of the disguises, he knew his name. There was no way he was going to get out of this room alive. He wasn't afraid of dying, but he believed he'd found a message worth sharing, and he wanted more than anything to see Sarah again, if she was alive. Tears began welling up in Hazel's eyes and Paul realized how scared she was. Being a party to her brother's scheme was one matter, accessory to murder was another. Paul wondered how a man who claimed to be a man of God could do this to him, and even more, how could he do it to Hazel, his own sister.

Hazel stood up and slowly wiped her eyes with the bottom of her apron. She looked at Paul sadly, hung her head, and left the room, leaving him alone behind the locked door once again. His heart sank for just a moment, and then he realized what Tina had been telling him. God does work miracles and he could talk to God. For the first time in his entire life, Paul Grant got down on his knees, clasped his hands in front of him, put his head down on the edge of his mattress, and prayed. The prayer was short, asking for direction, strength, and release to spread the news of challenges, small and large, daily challenges. For the next hour he remained in the same position meditating and communing with God. His heart swelled and his whole body shook with the emotion of being accepted by God.

"It took you long enough," said a soft voice from somewhere behind him. Paul, still on his knees, turned to see Tina sitting in the chair by the door. "You just found the key to it all. Ask believing and you'll receive. Unfortunately, most people just hear the part about ask and receive. Believing is the hard part. You have to commit one hundred percent of your life to that one request and know that you know that you know God will answer your prayer. People just can't seem to get to that part. Another one they have trouble with is the part about God granting the desires of their heart. They get that one all wrapped up with the desires of the ego. If you read in your Bible how God provides for the birds of the air and everything else, surely He's going to provide for man even more. Well, man doesn't understand this one at all. How many sparrows have you seen with a three bedroom, two bath, two car garage, plus swimming pool? People don't buy houses for themselves they buy them to impress other people. The same with clothes and make-up and cars. God provides needs, not ego trips, and when we accept the needs as enough, He allows us to build on that for ourselves and produce more using the talents He gave us. No one seems to want to accept the fact that their actual needs are very few. I liked what you said about making every moment a special experience, though. That was great, and true. I hope you do dance next time, and sing, too. I've heard you sing and it's nothing to write home about, but it's definitely in the category of joyful noise."

"Well, Miss Tina, I thought you were gone. You've just interrupted my first prayer session and insulted my singing. Now, tell me how I'm going to get out of here alive. I slipped and let Hazel know I knew her brother by name, so he's not about to let me go."

"How much faith do you have?" asked Tina.

"Right now, I have nothing else."

"Then why are you asking me how you're going to get out of here? Remember, the desires of your heart, not your ego; and whatever you ask in His name, believing. So, start believing with all your heart, with your whole soul, with every molecule of your entire being until you are so consumed with God's confidence. Then you'll know that you know that you know. It's not easy, but it's the only way."

She was gone again. Paul returned to his knees and opened a Bible that Tina had left lying on his bed. He read, he prayed, he suffered and strained to clear his mind of every doubt. He sweated and cried, read more and dozed. Hours later he looked up and it was dark outside the window. Hazel had been there and left his dinner, but he hadn't noticed. There was a note on a piece of paper on his tray, it read simply ... *pray for me. H.*

Dinner was cold broth, a small cheese sandwich with mayonnaise, a glass of ice water, and a small cookie. Without even considering it may be polluted, he drank the broth with gusto. The soup had probably been warm when it was delivered, and the sandwich not quite so dry, but it was the most delicious meal Paul had tasted in days and he rejoiced in every bite, thanking God constantly for not only the food, but for the adventure upon which he was about to embark, and the challenges he had yet to face, every minute of every day. After he had finished eating, he rapped on the door and called to Hazel. When she came up, he stood back by the window so she wouldn't be afraid he would try to overpower her. She took the tray, never taking her eyes off him, and he asked her for a pen and some writing paper. Again she started to weep, believing he was about to make out his last will and testament, but he assured her he was not going to die, not yet, and he needed a Challenge Journal. His first challenge was to smile and say thank you to her for the kindness she had shown in providing him a meal fit for a king. She blushed and felt like he was mocking her, but he assured her the meal was the best he had tasted since he had been here and it was truly and sincerely appreciated. More tears from Hazel.

When she had left, he waited a few minutes longer and then noticed a thin tablet and a pen being pushed under the door. He was eager to get started. He labeled the first page Challenges for Today and left a space for the date. He wasn't sure what it was. Below that he listed the things he had faced and how he had reacted to each. By late into the night, he was exhausted but felt a glowing excitement build within his whole being. He knew then, without a doubt, God was answering his prayer and the adventure was to see how it would be carried out. Just as he was dozing off, Paul looked out the window one last time, at the stars in the Minnesota sky, and said 'thank you,' knowing the One to whom he was speaking would get the message.

If we don't succeed, we run the risk of failure.

————————

Dan Quayle
Former Vice President of the United States

Chapter 36

Mick started the van and circled around
to the front of the tent, hoping to spot
Elmer and Waylon Landers. Kim was
on her cell phone trying to get through to a police detective friend of hers in Minneapolis by
the name of Cadence McShane. Cady was not
answering her cell phone, so Kim had to leave a
voice mail. The thought of calling 9-1-1 crossed
her mind, but she didn't want to get a scene going
just yet until she could explain everything to Cady
and make sure they had some cooperation that
was discreet enough to pull this whole thing off.
If, as both Mick and Kim believed, Waylon was going to lead them to Braddock who was eventually
going to lead them to Paul, they would probably
need Sheba. At the front of the tent, Mick stopped
and let Kim out. Pulling her badge out of her bag
as she exited the van, she walked with authority
into the shelter, and straight over to Augie, Melissa, and Sheba. Sheba recognized her immediately
and was wagging her tail in excitement. Bending
down and showing her badge to Augie, she did her
best not to frighten him and the child.

"Hey, Augie, Melissa, my name's Kim, I'm a cop
and a friend of Paul's. You're not in any trouble,

and I'm not taking Melissa away from you Augie, but I want you to pick up your things and come with me. Dog is coming too. If anyone asks any questions ..."

Before Kim had a chance to finish what she was hoping to say, Father Mike was at her elbow. "Is there something wrong here, young lady?" he asked. "I'm Father Mike and I run this shelter. I don't particularly care for people walking in and harassing my guests."

"I'm here to help them," said Kim with a big smile. "Name's Kim Frazier of the Duluth Police Department." Again she flipped out her badge to show Mike.

Mike took the badge and looked at it very, very carefully. "These can be faked," he said. "Do you have a picture ID on you, like a driver's license or something like that?"

312

Kim pulled out her wallet and gave him everything he wanted. Once he was satisfied, he insisted on some time with Augie and Melissa to say goodbye and to pray with them. Kim was getting antsy knowing each moment they waited meant Waylon was getting farther and farther away with Elmer. Finally, she had waited long enough, "Father, if you don't mind terribly, I've had to rent a van to come down here to get them and I have to be back on duty in a couple of hours, so we really need to be running along now. Thanks for everything." She helped pick up the belongings of the two and hurried them into the van. Mick told her to take the driver's seat and follow him. He was going to use Sheba to trail Elmer on foot. The second ear piece had been planted in his ear so he could communicate with Kim from outside the van. Augie and Melissa sat on the bench seat in the far back, totally confused and somewhat frightened. Melissa clung to her grandfather trying to hold him together. He was shaking from fear and anxiety. Whenever Mick wasn't talking, Kim did her best to piece together some of the puzzles for Augie without being too explicit for the sake of Melissa.

The trek, lead by Sheba, took them down narrow streets, garbage can-filled alleys, and through a park. Kim was forced to drive around the park, receiving her instructions from Mick. At one point, Mick relayed the message that he thought he'd spotted them, but came back with the discouraging news that he was mistaken. After several minutes, Augie had relaxed enough to sit alone by himself. Melissa joined Kim up in the front to watch the action. Augie protested, for her safety, but Kim reassured both of them that the van was as secure as a tank with reinforced steel walls and bulletproof glass. Melissa asked what would happen if they shot out the tires and Kim had to laugh. "Guess we'll be sitting here like a can of tuna," she said and both of them laughed. Kim liked having the little girl beside her in the front, even more so when Melissa admitted she hoped to grow up to be a cop just like Kim.

After more than an hour, Mick told Kim she might as well pick him up, he'd lost the trail. She drove to where he was sitting on a bench along a street and pulled over for him to take the driver's seat while Melissa eagerly greeted Sheba and placed herself in the bucket seat with the dog at her feet.

"What's next?" asked Kim.

"I don't know," said Mick with the sound of failure in his voice. "Maybe I was wrong to try and use Sheba."

"Who's Sheba?" asked Melissa, an eager expression on her face.

"You know her as Dog, honey," said Kim.

"You mean that's Sheba? That's Uncle Paul's dog? He told me to watch for her and to give her ... um ... where's my kitten, grandpa?"

Mick and Kim looked at one another trying to understand what the child was attempting to tell them. She anxiously rummaged around the back of the van through the belongings of her grandfather and herself. She became frantic when she couldn't find whatever it was she was looking for. "We've got to go back," she screamed. "I've got to have Fluffy, my kitten, I've got to." By now she was in tears and the sheer fright on her face was painful for Kim to see.

"We'll buy you another kitten, sweetie," said Kim. "We've got to keep trying to find Elmer and Paul. We don't have time to go back now."

314

"But Uncle Paul gave me something and said to keep it until someone came to help him. I put it in Fluffy where no one would find it. I promised him I'd never let it out of my sight. We have to go back."

"What exactly did he give you?" asked Mick. "Was it a note or his watch or something that would identify him?"

"I don't know," said Melissa, shaking her hands wishing they would hurry and get started back to the shelter. "It was just some dumb piece of wood."

Kim and Mick stared at one another for a fraction of a second before he put the van in gear and squealed a u-turn in the middle of the street. Unbeknownst to him and the rest, Kim had come prepared with portable red light for the van roof, and a built-in siren, both of which she put into play to give them quicker, easier access through traffic on the way back to the shelter. When they arrived, Father Mike was sitting in his usual spot at the picnic table. The stuffed kitten was in front of him, and he held something in his hand. The piece of the cross.

"Well," whispered Mick, "If he's in on this, we may have some trouble here. Let's see what happens. C'mon, Kim, Melissa, Augie. We need to all go in there."

Father Mike looked up with tears in his eyes. "Melissa, Augie," he choked, "how did you get this? Did you steal it from Paul?"

"No, Father," Melissa spoke up bravely. "Uncle Paul gave it to me and asked me to keep it for him when the bad guys came for him. I need it back, Father, so we can find my Uncle Paul."

"You know he's not your uncle," said the sad priest.

"Yes, he is. In my heart he is. May I have my kitten back, please?"

Mike looked up at Kim and Mick, Augie and Sheba. "Mick," he said at last, "I wouldn't have known you. You look great. I never would have dreamed he would go this far, honestly, I didn't know.'

"Who?" asked Mick softly.

"Braddock. He filled in for me for a few days while I was away, took a couple of days off. That must have been when Paul called. I never spoke to Paul. Braddock knew about this and what had been happening in Paul's life. I was excited because it was another example of the Paul of Tarsus story all over again. God was taking drastic action to get Paul on His side. Somehow Braddock's got this lust for money more than God and believes he can make it as a televangelist, but he needs a gimmick. I really think he saw this relic as his gimmick and set out to get it away from Paul. I am so sorry, I don't know what to say. I should never have ..." Mike broke down and covered his eyes with his hands. His shame and the burden of responsibility were weighing him down. He looked up again for just a moment. "You thought it was me, didn't you? A few years ago it might have been, but God's taken me down my own road and shown me my challenges. This piece isn't part of them and doesn't belong to me. Go find Paul and tell him I'm praying for him every second."

"Father," Kim quickly began questioning, hoping to get more information from the distraught Priest, "do you know anyone named Waylon Landers? How he might be associated with Braddock?"

"Oh, yeah, Waylon the Wayward, we used to call him. Has a twin brother up in Duluth who I hear killed his own kid. Waylon's not beyond doing that himself. The Landers' and the Braddocks are cousins, mothers are sisters from what I understand."

"Well," responded Mick, "that certainly answers a few of our questions. What about Braddock? Where would he take Paul if he had him?"

"Oh, that could be anywhere. His mom died several years ago, and she was a widow. I think they sold her house, or no ..." He stopped, deep in thought. "Maybe not. He has four sisters, Hester, Hazel, Helen, and Harriet. All of them are married and have husbands and families, except Hazel. She stayed home and nursed the mother through her last few years with Alzheimers and, if I'm not mistaken, she stayed on in the house after the mother died. She must be in her fifties by now. Bart was the youngest in the family, and he's in his mid forties, so I'd say Hazel's probably early fifties. There're two girls between them, Helen and Harriet, and then Hester is quite a bit older. I think. I may have it all wrong with all those H's in a row, but it sounds close to right."

"Do you think Braddock would take Paul to his sister's house to hide him out?" Mick looked at Father Mike.

"Anything's possible with that guy. I should never have told him about what happened, but he preached here that night after you received your miracle cure and I was too excited to keep it to myself. Give me a second and I'll see if I can find an address on Hazel or whoever is left over at that house. I know she lives outside the city, one of the suburbs, I think." He went into his space behind the kitchen area and came back moments later with a small black book out of which he took a newspaper clipping which appeared to be an obituary notice. "Yeah, this could be it. Ophelia Granger Braddock, mother of Bartholomew , and his sisters, etcetera. Here, here it is. 19971 Shiloh Circle Lane. That's where the mom lived, so it might be where Hazel is now. It's not in the best part of town, but it's not the worst either."

"Thanks, Mike," said Mick hurriedly taking the kitten and relic, and corralling his small group, heading for the van."

"Wait," called Mike. "Can I do anything? Can I go with you?"

Mick stopped for a second. "Yes, as a matter of fact, there are two things you can do. First, pray. Second, if you've got a cell phone number for Braddock, see if you can get him over here."

"Once you know he's on the way, interrupted Kim, "I want you to call this number and insist they page Cadence McShane. Tell her Kim Frazier asked you to call and you need her here, at this shelter, immediately. You'll know how to handle it from there. And here, this is my cell phone number. If Braddock shows up and you're able to get anything out of him that we don't have, give me a call. We're going to get Paul ... today! Thanks, Father."

When they had left, Father Mike O'Shea took out his own cell phone and dialed a number. Waiting for the fourth ring, and then the fifth, he wasn't sure how he was going to do what he had to do, but he felt certain God would put the words in his mouth. On the sixth ring, the phone was answered.

"Brother Braddock here," said the voice. "Father Mike? Is that you?"

"Yeah," said Mike. "I need to see you Bart. It's pretty important."

"Sure. Is tomorrow too late? I'm kind of busy right now."

Father Mike looked down at the picnic table and tried to think, fast. "No." he said. "I think we should talk right away. I have what you're looking for. They were here. I know everything."

There was silence at the other end of the line for a few minutes, and then he could hear voices talking hurriedly in the background. After some long seconds, Bart's voice came back. "I don't understand what you're saying, Mike. Who's been there? What do you have? You're going to have to be much more specific."

"Okay," said Mike, realizing how this had to be handled. "I'll tell you everything, but I want a cut. I want my share of whatever you make. Got that? That Paul guy, he left the relic with the little girl and she hid it in her stuffed cat. Some of his friends got worried about her, so they came and got her and she left the toy behind. I picked it up and started pressing around on it for no particular reason, and then I felt it. The piece of wood that Paul had, the one that works miracles for whoever has it, I have it here."

"What makes you think that has anything to do with me?" Mike could hear the pressure building up in Bart's voice, like he was salivating, holding himself back as much as he could while his body was screaming to get his hands on the relic.

"Let's just say I have a diabolical mind, sort of like yours. Everything points to you. Of course, if I'm wrong, I'll keep it for myself. I could use a good gig on cable TV after working in this dump. Suit yourself. Goodbye."

"Wait! Don't hang up! I'll be there in half an hour. Mike? Mike, are you still there?"

"Yeah, I'm still here," said Mike. "Half hour. 319 One minute longer and I'm gone. You can run this place. Oh, and bring back that old man. He's got nothing to do with this. He's just a crazy old man. When I saw him leaving with Waylon I knew you were involved. Waylon's not smart enough to figure all this out on his own. Why'd you pick on that guy, anyway?"

"He just seemed suspicious the way he was hanging around when we were talking. I'll get Waylon to bring him back."

"No. You bring him back. I don't want Waylon around here. This deal's between you and me. No old man, no deal. Got it?" Before Bart could answer, Mike terminated the call. His palms were sweating, his heart was racing. "God, please forgive me," he whispered.

Each morning sees some task begin
Each evening sees it close
Something attempted, something done,
Has earned a night's repose ...

Henry Wadsworth Longfellow
American Poet

Chapter 37

320

Mick drove to the nearest gas station and asked for a map so they could find the address on Shiloh Circle Lane. It appeared to be about twenty minutes away if traffic wasn't too heavy, and at this hour it shouldn't be a problem. Back in the van, he and Kim discussed what they should do once they arrived, and it was agreed that the two of them plus Sheba should go to the door. Augie and Melissa needed to stay in the van and out of sight with the doors locked. If anything happened, no one wanted them to be hurt.

The tension in the air inside the van could have been sliced with a dull knife. Kim looked over at Mick and saw him sweating bullets. She reached out her hand and placed it on his arm. "Hey," she said reassuringly, "I'm a cop, remember? I'm trained to handle stuff like this. It's going to be okay. You, me, and that dog are going up against one little old lady. How bad can it get?"

"What if she's a descendant of Bonnie Parker of the infamous Bonnie and Clyde gang? She could rip us apart with an Uzi before we get to the door. Ever thought of that?"

"No. I can honestly say I have never thought of that. In fact, I can't recall ever running into an Uzi while on duty," smiled Kim.

"But," continued Mick enjoying the relief of a little comedy, "you're not in Duluth now and you're definitely not on duty. So, anything can happen. How many weapons do you have with you?"

"Let's see," she purred as she opened the glove compartment, "we have a stale donut, three firecrackers from July Fourth four years ago, a can of pepper spray that's probably empty, and, oh yeah, here we go ... an ink pen that leaks."

"I said weapons. You don't think we'll need a show of force to get in?"

"And what, have tea with a middle aged spinster at gun point? Take a left up at the next light." She was holding the written instructions in her hand while he drove. "Maybe we should stop and pick up some crumpets or something."

"Now you're getting ridiculous. I just don't want to be surprised by anything. What if Waylon's there? What if Father Mike doesn't reach Braddock and he's there, too?"

"If it makes you feel any better, I have a small gun on my person. But just one, and I'm the only one licensed to carry it so don't go getting any macho ideas."

"Who me? I'm scared of guns. I always try to find me some hunky police woman to hang with so I don't mess up this pretty face."

"Hunky, you're calling me hunky? And what pretty face are you referring to? Surely not the one you're wearing today." When Mick nodded,

Kim looked to the back at Melissa and Augie. "Okay, everybody, we need to take a vote here. Who thinks Mick has a pretty face?"

"I think I'll abstain from voting," said Augie. "It's tough enough being homeless without people thinking I have other issues to deal with. I'm sure the right gal, or guy, will find him very attractive provided it's very dim lighting and he's wearing a hood."

"Augie, that's not funny," said Mick pretending to have his feelings hurt.

"I think he's gorgeous," swooned Melissa which got the whole group laughing out loud. Even Sheba howled a bit.

Shortly, however, the laughter died down. They were driving on Shiloh Circle Lane and looking for 19971. It was at the far end of the block, on the left side, between a corner house set catty corner on the lot, and an abandoned frame house on the other side. No cars were in front, and a drive around the alley way didn't give any indication of activity either. Everyone in the van held their breath. This was it.

Pulling up directly in front of the house on the corner, Mick put the van in park. "Okay, everyone, let's say a quick prayer before we proceed." They all bowed their heads. Even Sheba covered her eyes with her big paws while Mick prayed out loud. When everyone had said amen, Mick continued with the instructions. "Sheba, Kim, and I are going out the back. Augie, I want you to get up here in the driver's seat and if anything starts going wrong, you put this baby in gear and get out of here. Make sure you and Melissa are safe. This is my cell phone. Get Melissa to dial 9-1-1 and tell the police where we are only if you have to. Remember the address, 19971 Shiloh Circle Lane.

Got that? Okay. Anyone have any questions? Well, then, this is it. Kim, Sheba, out the back door. Let's go get Paul."

They waited a few seconds outside of the van, looking at the house and listening for anything that could mean danger. Nothing was going on. Slowly they proceeded down the sidewalk to the house at 19971. It looked quiet and undisturbed. Sheba's tail was wagging and she seemed anxious. When they reached the walkway to the Braddock house, Mick went up to the door, leaving Kim and Sheba at the sidewalk. He knocked once, twice, a third time. No one answered. He stepped back to look at the windows on both the downstairs floor and the upper floor. To his amazement, he saw Paul standing in the upstairs window waving down at them, a huge smile on his face. By gestures, he indicated they should keep knocking, someone was home.

Once more, Mick knocked. One time. Two times. He stopped and yelled out, "Hazel, are you in there? I need to talk to you." The mention of her name must have gotten the better part of her curiosity. Hazel opened the door ever so slightly and peeked out.

"Who're you?" she asked. "What do you want?"

"I'm a friend of Bart's," he said.

"Bart's not here right now. He had to go, but he'll be back later. Why don't you come back when he gets here." It was not a question, but a command. The shakiness of her voice indicated she was trying to act braver and stronger than she felt.

Mick opened his mouth to say something that would convince her to let them in when Sheba tore past him, knocked the door open and nearly knocked Hazel down as she sped up the steps inside the door. Mick ran in after her, following her up the stairs and around to the door where Sheba was barking and jumping up, scratching, trying to get in. Paul's voice could be heard through the door and Sheba was going nuts trying to get to him.

"Open this door, immediately!" Mick barked the order down the stairs at Hazel.

"I can't do that," said Hazel trembling.

"Oh, I think you can," smiled Kim who had entered behind an unknowing Hazel. She had her badge out and her gun in her hand. "I'm with the police, ma'am. If you don't unlock that door, we're going to break it down and you can pay to have it fixed. Then we're going to take you into custody and charge you with kidnapping and much, much more. Now, would you please unlock that door?"

Hazel walked on unsteady legs up the stairs and down the hallway to the door behind which Paul was waiting. She was sobbing as she stuck the key in the door, turned it and the knob, and released her prisoner. Sheba danced and jumped up on Paul with glee. Paul hugged his dog in return, and then went to Kim and Mick each to hug them. Sheba's tail all but knocked everyone over in her excitement. Before anyone had realized it, Hazel had gone back down the stairs and was on the phone to Bart.

"Put the phone down, Hazel," barked Mick again. "Don't make it any harder on yourself than it already is." She did as she was instructed, leaving Bart in mid-sentence. "Now," said Mick more softly, "I want you to dial 9-1-1 and tell them there is an emergency at this address. When they arrive, you will tell them everything. Do you understand?"

Hazel blinked and sobbed acknowledgement of the instructions, and did exactly as she was told.

Mick continued, "I want you to tell me where Bart is and where Waylon is."

"Bart's gone back to the mission to see the Father. Waylon's just gone off somewhere. I don't expect him back. Bart paid him so he's probably in the bar by now."

"What about Elmer?" asked Kim. "Is he still with Waylon?"

"That the old man? No, he went with Bart. Said something about getting the wrong guy and took the old man with him."

"How much were you able to tell Bart just now?"

"Not much."

"Let's get a little more specific, okay? Exactly what did you tell Bart just now. Remember, your life depends on you telling us the truth." Kim held the gun steadily on a very nervous, scared Hazel.

"I just told him you were here. I didn't have a chance to tell him who you were or nothing. He said it was okay, he was on his way to get what he wanted. He told me I should drink the rest of the tea so y'all couldn't get any information out of me."

"What tea? Where is it? Who makes it?"

"Herb tea. It's what we've been giving Paul to keep him sick. It's just some herbs to make you sick, they don't really hurt you. There's a jar of it in the kitchen with a label on it telling me how much to use. I haven't taken any of it, yet."

Kim walked into the kitchen and looked around on the counter for a jar of loose tea leaves.

There was nothing immediately in sight. Finally she spotted the jar in the window sill. It was a small jar, about a half pint size, and it was over half empty. She found the label and read it. Place one teaspoonful in a pot of boiling water. Contains black tea ... and then there was a list of herbs. "Oh ... my ... gawd," she breathed out loud. Still holding the jar, she walked back into the hallway and up the stairs to where Mick, Paul, and Hazel were standing.

"Hazel, did you say Bart told you to take the rest of the tea?"

"That's right. He said to make myself a pot of strong tea using the rest of the special herbs. That way I'd get sick, but it wouldn't really hurt me none. But I wouldn't be able to answer any of your questions, either. He said I should try and drink the whole pot to be sure."

"Hazel. Do you have any idea what's in here?" Kim was shaking.

"No, not really, just black tea and herbs. Bart promised me it wouldn't hurt no one. He's a good man, a man of God, he wouldn't lie to me."

"Hazel, if you had made yourself only one cup of strong tea using more than a teaspoon of these herbs in one cup, you would be dead now."

Hazel crumbled to the floor in shock. Her sobs were convulsive, uncontrollable. Her own brother had tried to kill her to keep her from talking and convicting him.

"What's in there?" asked Paul and Mick together. "I've been taking this stuff for a couple of weeks now," Paul said. "Am I going to die?"

"If you haven't already, I doubt if you will, but we'll get you to the hospital as soon as we can. What's in here? Oh, let me see, we have black tea, chamomile, rose petals, a few other herbs, and just a touch of White Oleander, enough to make you very, very sick."

Within minutes the sirens could be heard outside the house. Kim ran out and showed her badge to the officers who'd arrived and asked them to send for two ambulances, one for Paul who'd been ingesting poisonous herbs for two weeks, and one for Hazel who was now babbling like a child while sitting on the floor and picking at the carpet. It was a sad sight to see. Following closely behind the police were Augie and Melissa. Melissa ran and threw her arms around Paul and hugged him tight.

"I did like you said, Uncle Paul. I never let no one take the kitten you gave me, 'cept Father Mike, but he gave it back. Did I do okay? Are you really gonna buy me ice cream now, way up in Duluth like you promised?"

Paul could barely speak through his tears. "You bet I am," he hugged the child back. "You and your grandpa are coming back to Duluth and we're going to be a family, just the three of us."

"Um," said Kim with a big smile on her face, "you might want to make that the four of you."

"Of course," said Paul. "How could I forget Sheba. She saved my life."

"Okay. That would make five," said Mick.

"Five?" Paul looked between Mick and Kim wondering what they were talking about. "Did Sheba have a puppy? Hey, old girl, you been out playing while I've been in here? Did you get yourself ..."

"No," said Kim with a huge smile towards Mick, "Sarah's home. She's waiting for you."

The color drained from Paul's face and he collapsed to his knees bawling like a baby. Melissa put her small arm around his shoulders and patted him on the back. "It's okay, Uncle Paul. It's okay. Don't cry, please. Don't be sad. If you don't have room for us, me and grandpa can go back with Father Mike. We don't mind."

"Oh, but I would," said a voice coming up the stairs. Everyone turned to see Elmer taking one step at a time followed by Detective Cadence McShane of the Minneapolis Police Department.

"I've already had a chat with Augie and he's agreed to move in with me and help me with the dogs. Now you, young lady, you're going to a proper school and you're gonna have a proper home for you right there with us. You can have all the dogs you want."

"Really?" said Melissa. "Oh, is that okay, Uncle Paul. You won't be lonely without us?"

"My wife is back, honey. I'll be just fine as long as I know you're okay and you'll be more than okay with Elmer. Plus, we live nearby. You can visit us anytime you want."

"What do I call you?" she asked Elmer who had moved up onto the landing while Kim moved down the steps to talk with her old friend, Detective McShane.

"You can call me Great Uncle Elmer, I guess. Is that okay?"

"Wow," said Melissa. "I gots a whole family, two uncles and a grandpa. I'm the luckiest girl in the whole world. Grandpa, are we really gonna go there and live? Are we? Please?"

"I don't see why not," said Augie, wiping a few tears of his own away. "I ain't had a good friend in a long time and I think Elmer's about as good a friend as any man could find. We thank you, Elmer, and we'll do our share of keeping the place up and helping out. Paul said he would try and get me a part time job and if he's still willing to do that, I can buy some of the groceries, too. And I'm old enough for Social Security, so I'll apply for that right away since I'll have a permanent address where checks can be sent."

Paul looked around at everyone, his face wet from sobbing. "I want to go home now," he said softly. "I want to see my wife."

"Hospital first, then we'll take you home. Don't worry. She's not going anywhere. She's staying with Angel right now and they're having a slumber party every night. Here, use my cell phone and call her. Let her know you're okay. She's waiting to hear."

Paul looked into Kim's eyes. "I don't know the number," he said softly. "Dial for me, please?"

Kim dialed and when it began to ring on the other end, she handed it to Paul. Everyone else began to move down the stairs.

"Sarah? Is that really you? I'm coming home, honey. I love you so much. Please don't leave, I need you. I'm coming home, Sarah. I'm comin' home."

> The art of creation is older than the art of killing.

———

Andrei Voznesenky
Russian avant-garde poet

Chapter 38

Dear Daddy,

Please don't be upset with me for not writing more this year. It's been a bit of a hectic year for all of us here, as you can well imagine. Paul and I are doing fine now and the pregnancy is moving along normally. I think I'm due March twenty-eighth, which I happen to know is your birthday, so I'm hoping. If it's a girl, we're going to name her Tina Angelika which means tiny angel, and if it's a boy we're thinking maybe Billy after that little boy who died last year just before Christmas. We're into simple names as you know. I don't know where Tina comes from but Paul's promised to explain it some day.

We moved into the new house the first week of October and just love it. Can you imagine two stories and four bedrooms? I don't know how many children Paul wants, but we'll see. No, grandfathers do not get to vote! Where shall I begin? Let's see, Rob and Angel are due with twins in February, which means they started before the second wedding. That's okay, they were married for fifteen years before that!

Oh, and guess what, Mick finally convinced Kim to marry him and move to the Cities to help with the Tandeski Foundation. Stefan and Iris, his girlfriend, are going steady, she's in her early 70's or late 60's, and he's in his 80's. They say they're too young to jump into anything. Stefan says they definitely don't plan on having a family, so what's the rush! He's such a funny, funny man and so much fun to be around since he met Iris and got involved in the church.

Elmer and Augie get along like brothers, but better, and Melissa, is as happy as any child could be with her grandfather and Uncle Elmer at home, plus a dozen or more dogs. Then she calls the rest of us uncle and aunt too, so she's got a really big family now. She's ready to start babysitting for Angel and me anytime we're ready to pop these babies out, she says. The school system placed her in third grade because she hadn't had much schooling, if any, before we got everything legalized with the custody thing, but she did so well, they moved her up into fourth grade within two months. Now she's with kids her own age and is doing very well. I think she has a boyfriend, but she won't say anything. She did ask if she could invite a guest to Thanksgiving Dinner, so later today we'll find out.

For now, I have to run. Everyone is coming here for Thanksgiving, so I have a lot of last minute preparations to make. Luckily everyone is bringing something. Hope this is the first Christmas card of the season for you, and that you and Crystal are doing well and will think about coming up north for the Christmas holidays. We'd love to have you.

Love, Sarah

The meeting of the Board of Directors for the Challenge and Development Center commenced one hour before dinner was to be served on Thanksgiving Day at the home of Paul and Sarah Grant. As President of the Board, Mick opened the meeting with a prayer and a call to order. Those in attendance were, Foundation President Stefan Tandeski, Board President Mick Tandeski, Board Vice President Paul Grant, Board Treasurer Angel

Scott, and Board Secretary Sarah Grant. Executive Director Mike O'Shea was unable to attend because of the Thanksgiving festivities at the center. Others in attendance were Iris Jurecki, Stefan's girlfriend, Kim Frazier, Elmer Johnson, Augie Russo, and Melissa Russo. Oh, and of course, the Official Mascot, Sheba.

After the prayer, the meeting was called to order and business matters were discussed. Mick was glad to recap the success of the past several months since the return of Paul and Sarah, and his own return to sobriety. Stefan had set up the Tandeski Foundation which granted money to the Challenge and Development Center. The center, once a tent on the outskirts of downtown Minneapolis, was now a three story building housing the homeless who were serious about changing their lives. Other services offered through the CDC were substance abuse counseling and support groups, career and financial counseling, parenting classes, a free clinic, and a food pantry.

Mike O'Shea finally decided to admit he isn't a priest, will never be allowed to take vows as a priest, and is content to be the Executive Director of the CDC. He may not have been a perfect kid growing up, but he's doing a fabulous job with the clients who are seeking help from the center. Rumor has it, he is dating one of the volunteers who comes in each week to help with counseling battered and abused women. The center has over two hundred volunteers working different shifts, and of course the full time night staff and day staff. It's just too awesome! Even Ruth and Hazel come in every day to help cook. Hazel, of course, is working off her community service, but it's so good for her to be around people and get her mind off the incarcerated Rev. Bart Braddock.

"Before we close this meeting and dig into some turkey, is there any new business we need to discuss?" asked Mick.

"I have one question about Mike," said Rob, looking at Paul. "Remember that first night you stayed with Ruth and Saul? You said you heard voices arguing and you thought it was Mike and Ruth, and that you thought they were arguing about you. Did you ever find out what that was all about?"

"Not too much. I asked Ruth and she said they were arguing, but it was more about Mike being afraid she'd tell me he was her son. He was afraid it would get back to you, Rob, and all that stupid stuff. I blew it all out of proportion, and look where it got me."

"Very good," said Mick. "Another mystery cleared up nicely. Anyone else have any questions or other business? I'm getting hungry."

Melissa raised her hand and was given the floor. "I need to earn some money for Christmas because this is the first year I've got a real big family. Can I work at the center on weekends and get paid for it? I could stay right there and it wouldn't cost anything. I won't eat much and I'll work real hard."

"Hmmm," said Augie thoughtfully, "who's going to pay your fare to and from the Cities every weekend? That'd cost as much as you'd make. I'd be willing to pay you two dollars a day to scoop poop in the back yard. I hate that job."

"And I'd be willing to pay you two dollars a day to make sure all the dog bowls are filled with water and food," added Elmer.

Melissa's eyes lit up. Everyone could see her trying to add up all that money in her head.

"You know," said Angel, "being pregnant is one thing, but carrying twins, it's terribly difficult to get all the housework done on weekends. If you come over and help me Saturday mornings, after you finish your work at home, of course, I'd pay you five dollars a week just to help me do the laundry."

"Oh," said Sarah, "I didn't know you could do laundry. After you finish with Angel's laundry, I could use a little help over here too. I'll throw in another five dollars for a Saturday afternoon. Two hours, two fifty an hour. Does that sound fair?"

"Okay with me!" smiled Melissa. "Now let's move on to the next order of business."

Paul leaned over to Augie and whispered, "Are you sure this kid's only nine, she acts like she's twenty."

"She's a tough street kid. She's been around adults all her life until she started school. I wish she'd learn to be a kid."

"Hush, you two," said Melissa. "I have the floor, now back to business. Starting today, I'd like everyone to call me Missy, 'cause it sounds cooler. Next, I asked Aunt Sarah if it was okay for me to invite a guest to dinner. He's really cute and he goes to my school and he's so awesome and he doesn't treat me like a dumb kid and please don't embarrass me cause I really like him, okay?"

"That's more like it," said Paul, half in whisper. "When do we get to meet your young man?"

"You gotta promise first. Promise you won't make fun of him or me and embarrass me."

She looked around the room and made each person promise and then cross his or her heart before she continued.

"Okay. That's better. Before I introduce him there's something else I want to say. My mom left me with grandpa because she's got problems with drugs and sex."

A big gasp went through the room.

"I'm nine, okay? I know what sex is. Anyway, none of you judge me on who my mom is, right? You love me anyway. I want you to promise not to judge my friend on his family either. What grown ups do isn't his fault. He's a really cool guy and he's kinda scared to meet you, so please be nice, please?"

Once again they spoke individually around the room and promised, crossed their hearts, and smiled with great love at the little girl they'd taken in and made part of their unconventional family. Grandpa Augie, Uncle Paul, Aunt Sarah, Great Uncle Elmer, Uncle Rob, Aunt Angel, Uncle Mick, Aunt Kim, Grandpa Stefan, and Nana Iris. They all loved her and did everything they could to make up for her lost years. She was the best dressed girl in her class. She had the latest in everything stylish, and yet these were not the things that were important to her. Hugs, security, and a warm bed made all the difference in her little world. Paul and Sarah had wanted to adopt her, but Augie wanted her with him as long as he could. His will had been made out so that when he passed, custody of Melissa Cordell Russo would go to Paul and Sarah Grant. These arrangements had been discussed with Missy openly and she agreed to them wholeheartedly, but she wanted to stay with her grandpa as long as she could so she could take care of him. The bond between grandfather and granddaughter was amazingly strong.

After all the promises were made, Missy left the room to get her guest who had been sitting in the front hallway closet all this time, hidden from view. She proudly led him by the hand back into the living room where the meeting was taking place. Shyly, she looked up at her family and smiled. "This is my friend Bobby Landers. Bobby," she said shyly, looking up at him with the adoring eyes of puppy love, "this is my family."

Paul was the first to speak. He stood up from where he was sitting in the recliner, and put out his hand. "Bobby, it's great to see you again. Welcome to our home. Let me introduce you to everyone else. This is my very, very beautiful wife, Sarah."

Sarah smiled and offered her hand. "It's absolutely delightful to meet you, Bobby. I've heard many great things about you. Welcome to our home."

"This one," continued Paul, "you already know. Angelina Scott."

"Hi, Bob, "she smiled and gave him a big hug. "It's so good to see you again. And this is my husband, Rob."

Rob, too, shook hands with Bobby and said it was great to meet him. Next came Kim, who Bobby also knew and who introduced him to her new fiancé, Mick. After that, Mick introduced his dad, Stefan, and Stefan's girlfriend, Iris. At last, there were only two people left to introduce.

"This," said Missy, "is my great uncle Elmer. We live with him and we have a homeless shelter for dogs." After Bobby had shaken hands with Elmer, Missy continued, "And most important of all," she said with a huge smile on her face and a look of total adoration in her eyes, "this is my grandpa Augie Cordell Russo. I was named after him you know. Grandpa, this is my friend, Bobby."

Augie stood up to shake the young man's hand and smiled. "You're my baby girl's first boyfriend, my, my, my."

"Grandpa," squealed Missy. "You promised!"

"What? What'd I do?" said Augie, pretending complete innocence.

Bobby, however, smiled brightly and said, "It's an honor to meet you, sir. She's my first girlfriend, too."

Missy blushed but couldn't hide her big smile.

Dinner with twelve people around the table was festive, to say the least. The food was delicious and everyone ate until they were stuffed. Sarah, Angel, Kim, and Iris talked about having babies. Mick and Stefan talked about finances. Augie and Elmer had fun chatting with Missy and Bobby. Paul and Rob talked about the events of the past year.

"Bobby's little brother was the beginning, wasn't he?" said Rob very softly.

"Yeah, he was," said Paul. "I sometimes wish I'd never taken a walk that night."

"I know it's tough to look on the bright side in a situation like that," said Rob, "but have you ever thought that if you hadn't, Ralph Landers could eventually have killed both his boys and his wife? He had it in him. It's not easy knowing Billy was the sacrifice but look where it's led you, all of us, and Bobby. Angel tells me he's in foster care and doing really well. He sees a counselor every week and is allowed to visit his mom once or twice a month. She doesn't even recognize him most of the time. It was all too much for her. She calls him Billy and that upsets him even more, so they're trying to discourage the visits, but he's loyal."

"I'm glad for that. He's really a good boy and I know he tried real hard to take care of his little brother."

When the meal was through and most everyone was either in the kitchen doing clean up or in front of the TV watching the game, Rob pulled Paul into the garage for a talk. "Paul, you've never told me the whole story behind the Malchus dream and the piece of the cross. Was that piece for real? What happened to it?"

"Y'know, Rob," Paul lifted his right leg up so his foot was resting on the edge of a bench. "I started visiting a Christian counselor several months ago trying to get my head back on straight after all that happened. To the best of my knowledge, and with the guidance of the counselor, I think I started dreaming about Malchus after hearing the story in Nana Grant's church. She had a preacher that could scare you into just about anything. So, when I started having those dreams, I was only about six, and I put myself into the place of Malchus because the story had upset me so much. Nana had told my mom that part and Mom told me. Well, whenever I'd get upset about something in life, I'd go back to that same dream, and even began having earaches and bleeding from my ears whenever it happened. I'd sort of zone out, like in a fugue state, at the very mention of the name Malchus. That's what happened that night of my birthday last year. I didn't handle the thing with Sarah leaving real well."

"So, was the cross real?"

"I don't know that it wasn't, but I know that no piece of wood can work miracles. God alone can do that and it takes a lot of faith to believe in miracles. This last year has taught me a lot of things I never understood before. Take Jesus, for example. He was the son of God, but so are we. He had, for lack of a better word, 'evolved' to a higher level of spirituality so that he was able to rejoin the God entity and become one with God, just as we all strive to get to that level. I believe He was sent as an example of how we should live, how we should seek God in everything. When we're told He came to save us from our sins, that's just it. He came to save us from ourselves by providing the road map, the example for us to use to get to where He is. A lot of people may disagree with me, but we all came from God, from a part of God, and we are all striving to get back to God. Jesus wasn't the only one who had attained the deity level and reunited with God. He was the one, though, that God looked at and said, "Hey you. You're going down there to straighten this bunch out." And God was pretty pleased with the way this Son handled himself while here. Jesus wasn't thrilled about some of the stuff He had to endure, but he went through it to show us we all have challenges. How much plainer can it be? Jesus had a tough life, just like everyone else. Is Satan real? Darn tootin'! He'll take every opportunity we allow to steer us in the wrong direction. A lot of times you see him on TV with a Rolex watch, French cuffs, and diamond studs telling you God wants you to be wealthy, but gives his own address for you to send your money. It makes no sense, but people fall for it every day."

"This whole experience has charged me, changed me, invigorated me spiritually. I believed so strongly that the relic was a piece of the cross and that it could work miracles, even though I didn't want to openly admit it because I considered myself an agnostic. God pushed me to the ground and got my attention, big time. There were times throughout the year I didn't want to live. The only thing keeping me going was not knowing what happened to Sarah. I had to live to find her. God placed every one of these challenges in my way to bring me to this point, to bring all of us to this point. Look at the people we've met and all that's been accomplished to help people. God had a plan, but He had to get our attention to make it work. I don't know why He chose us, but I'm glad He did. Every minute of every day I'm looking at the challenges. I smile at people even though I don't know them because we really are all created equal. I am kinder and less judgmental. I take life less for granted and enjoy every breath more. I truly believe I'm a better therapist because of it, too. I even keep a journal of the challenges I face each day and how I handle them. I don't always do the right thing, but at least I can go back and see what I did and how I can do better next time. And, before you ask again, the relic is suspended in a block of acrylic and it's in the cornerstone of the CDC building. Now, do you have any more questions or can we go see who's winning the game?" 341

"Just one more," said Rob. "Who's Tina?"

Paul laughed. "I'm not sure, but I'm going to say she's my guardian angel. Whenever things got the worst, like when I was at Hazel's, she appeared and gave me advice. It's funny how she looked so much like Sarah in many ways, but then again, maybe not so funny. I've always considered Sarah my personal angel."

Just as Rob and Paul were about to go back into the house and join the TV watching crowd, Bobby came out to the garage. "May I have a moment alone with you, Dr. Grant?" he asked.

Rob nodded and excused himself. Paul invited Bobby to sit on the bench where he and Sarah sat to take off their snow boots. "What's on your mind Bobby? And please, call me Paul."

Bobby looked down for a second before responding. "I know," he said finally, "that what happened last year with Billy wasn't anyone's fault. And I know that if Billy was still here everything would be the same as it always was and I wouldn't have met all of you people. I just wanted to say thank you, but there are so many things to say thank you for I don't know what to say first." Tears were streaming down the child's face. He was ten years old and probably hadn't been allowed to cry like a child for many years. Paul was amazed at the innocence in this young man. His nose glowed, his eyes were rimmed with red, and his mouth was fighting against the urge to crinkle. The slight shoulders sagged inward towards the bony chest. The Thanksgiving sweater Angel had knit for him was a bit too big, but he was wearing it over his plaid shirt, the tails hanging down over new blue jeans. It was a comical scene of pure magic when a child first learns it's okay to cry with a trusted adult role model. Paul was struggling against his own tears as he reached for the lad. He wrapped the boy in his arms and allowed all of the pain to drain into his shirt through those tears. After awhile, Bobby pulled away and wiped at his eyes. "I'm sorry, sir," he said, "I ..."

"No, Bobby, never be sorry for showing your feelings. That's what makes you a man. I want you to know that you are just as much a part of this weird family as the rest of us, and you can come to me any time you need to talk, man to man. God planned all this for a reason, and you are part of that plan."

"Paul," said Bobby tentatively, testing the sound of the name on his tongue. "Could I go to church with you sometime? My foster family is really nice, but they don't go to church very often. I want to pray for my mom to get better and I want to learn about all the stuff that Missy's been telling me."

"Missy's talking to you about God?" said Paul, surprised and delighted at the same time.

"Yeah. She even gave me a Bible of my very own for my birthday. I turned ten last week."

"We'll pick you up at nine sharp on Sunday morning. But, you have to follow all the same rituals we do."

"Huh?" Bobby looked at Paul as if he was wishing he hadn't gotten himself into this situation.

"Okay. Here's how it is," Paul placed his hand on the boy's shoulder as they walked into the house. "First of all, we go to Sunday School. Then we stay for church. After church we all meet at a restaurant and have lunch together. Rob and Angel go to a different church than the rest of us. This week it's Uncle Rob's turn to buy, and by the way, you can call me Uncle Paul, I like that. Don't worry ... you have to be twenty-five, have a college degree, a good job, and a wife with a baby on the way before it's your turn to buy Sunday lunch. Now, let's talk about your intentions with regard to Missy. Are they honorable?"

"I don't think I understand?" said Bobby, relieved at the ritual part and wondering what Paul meant by intentions and honorable.

Making no attempt to hide his satisfied grin, Paul patted Bobby's shoulder as they walked through the house. "Good answer," He said. "Let's go watch that game."

And they lived happily ever after!

The Brothers Grimm
from Cinderella

The following pages contain
a preview of Kathleen R. West's
next book, *RSVP*

My eyes hurt.

It's hard to see. Everything is so blurry.

I hear voices. That one sounds like mom. Her voice is cracking. Either I'm in trouble or I've been hurt. My eyes hurt. Maybe I got hurt. Why can't I talk? Why can't I remember? My brain hurts. My jaw hurts. I'm trying to talk but there's something blocking my throat. It hurts to think. Back to sleep. Please, let me sleeeee................

✶✶✶✶✶✶

"Looks like she's gone again. That's good though, her body needs the rest. When she comes out of all this she's going to be just fine. Surgery went well. The heartbeat's strong. No signs of infection or rejection. She's a brave little girl."

"Thanks, Casey", the man patted the doctor's shoulder. "We're glad you're here. It's hard enough on Kris and me, and...well, you know." The voice was cracking, finding it hard to speak through the lump forming in the man's throat.

345

"I know if it was me in your shoes, you'd be right beside me, both of you," Dr. Casey Britain smiled back at his old friend. "I want you and Kris to get some rest now too, 'cause when our little Katie here gets going, she'll be making up for lost time."

Casey Britain walked out the door of the CCU and left the family alone once again. He and Karl Power had enjoyed a comfortable friendship for over twenty years. Just as he was nearing the corner of the hallway leading to the clinic and his office, he heard footsteps behind him. It was Karl again.

"Casey, I'm sorry I didn't even bother to ask how Martin and the kids are doing. Is Clarice ... ?"

Casey shook his head sadly. "She didn't make it. They said their goodbyes and we harvested her organs yesterday."

"Yesterday? The same day Katie ... ? Did she ... ?"

"You know I can't answer that question Karl," Casey soothed. "Donor names are kept private. Just be thankful Katie has a good, strong heart." The doctor walked away once again wondering if the Power family would accept this. Clarice and Martin Crocket had been neighbors and friends of the Power's for years. It was just fate that a car accident took the life of Clarice Crocket at the same time as a heart transplant became critical for Katie Power. Just fate.

Chapter 2

"Kate, would you hold still please!" Kris was getting frustrated with her daughter's constant motion while trying to pin up the hem on her wedding dress. She'd never dreamed making this dress for her own daughter would require twice as much work as any other she'd ever made. Sewing since she was a teenager, Kris Power had built up a decent home business making wedding gowns, bridesmaid dresses, and formal wear for over twenty years. Now her only child was getting married and creating this dress had become a nightmare. "Katie, I mean it! You are going to have to stand still or I'll never get this right. Hang up that damn phone and stand still!"

"Get a grip mom, it's just a dress! Eric'll probably rip it off the minute we get in the limo anyway," laughed the twenty-two year old bride-to-be, "you have no idea what an animal he can be."

"Nor do I want to," seethed Kris. "Some things don't need to be vocalized young lady. Now, put that phone down before I slap it out of your hand. This dress will be perfect if it kills me."

"Okay, sweetie, mom's havin' a cow so I have to go. Love you. See you tonight?" Katie pressed the off button of the cell phone and threw it across the room to a sofa. "How much longer?" she asked her mom. "I've gotta pee."

"Give me just a second more and I'll let you take a break. Please don't use that kind of language at the reception. Our guests would die if the bride announced she had to pee. There. Let's get this off you before you get it all wet."

The house phone rang just as Katie scampered from the room. Kris gently placed the gown across the back of the sofa and went to answer the ringing machine. At the same time, Cody, the family hound, came bounding through the room, nearly knocking her over. For some unfathomable reason, that dog got excited every time the house phone rang. Cell phones had never bothered him, but the house phone set him on a wild search for the offending culprit. Trying to maneuver her way around the canine tornado, she reached the phone just as the caller hung up. The old fashioned phone that Kris preferred in this room, her private space, didn't have caller ID. She placed the French styled receiver back on the cradle and sat down at her desk to go over the day's mail which had arrived shortly before the dress fitting had begun. Amongst the other RSVP envelopes from people invited to the wedding, was one from Abcde Brown. She smiled at the name, remembering how she had tried to talk Clarice out of naming her baby something that would beg questions every time it was written. Ab-si-dee, as it was pronounced, had indeed suffered her share of teasing over the unusual name and eventually asked to be called Abby, so Abby it was. The last time anyone from the Power family had seen Abby was the day of her mother's funeral. Katie, still in the hospital following heart transplant surgery had been unable to attend, but Karl and Kris had been there to support their neighbors and good friends. Martin and his family had turned a cold shoulder to their gestures and within weeks after the funeral had sold their home and moved.

When Katie returned to the sewing room, Kris handed her the stack of RSVP envelopes with Abby's on top.

"I can't believe she responded," said Katie excitedly as she jumped up and down. "Maybe she's missed me as much as I've missed her." Tearing open the envelope, Katie fumbled trying to get the card out. "Wow, it's been five years already... and ... oh ... no ... !" Katie sank into the sofa, right on top of her dress, with a face that had gone as white as the gown, her eyes wide continuing to stare at the card, her free hand covering her mouth.

"What is it?" said Kris. "What's wrong?"

Katie silently handed her the card, staring at her mother with a look of shock and disbelief. Kris took the card, her eyes not leaving the face of her daughter a full ten seconds before she dared look at the card. When she had read the short note scribbled over the printed lines which were to have been filled in by invitees to the wedding, her hand began to tremble.

"She can't be serious," Kris said with disgust. "Who does she think she is? She has no proof to back this up, no proof at all. She just, well, she just assumes things. You know how she is. She was always brash and, and, and ... she never thought things through. Just like her mother, she went off on wild tangents and, and ... what is she thinking?" Kris collapsed onto an ottoman in front of her daughter who still had not been able to regain her composure. "Don't worry honey, she's just jealous that you're getting married and she's not. You two were always competing like that."

At last Katie shook her head and looked at her mother. "You're blabbering mom. You don't even know what you're saying, and you're driving me nuts. I've got to think. Just shut up, okay?" With these last words, Katie placed her face in her hands and bent forward. Her head was spinning and she wanted to cry. Thoughts flew through her head so fast she couldn't grasp one before the next sliced through. *Is she just trying to stop my wedding? Is she serious about this? Can she do this? What's Eric gonna say? I should have told him the whole story. Why? It's not like it's important, is it? What if he calls off the wedding? He has 'opinions' and he won't stand for this. He'll leave me. He'd think our children ... no, she can't do this. I won't let her destroy me this way. I didn't do anything. I didn't have a choice.*

The ringing doorbell brought Katie out of her reverie. Kris got up to answer the door and Katie could hear Eric's voice in the front hall asking where she was. The strain on her face was brushed aside with a couple of hand swipes and a smile. She did her best to bounce out of the sewing room, closing the door behind her, and into Eric's arms.

"Hey beautiful," he smiled into her deep blue eyes, "where's the calf? I wasn't far away when you hung up, so thought I'd come by and take a look for myself." Turning his attention to Kris who stood back from her daughter, "I didn't really think you were having a cow, but with Kate you just never know. So, I came by to check. You okay Kristian? You look a little upset. "

Kris tried to smile but failed. "I'll leave you two alone," she said quickly backing into the sewing room and closing the door gently behind her.

350   "Hey, what's wrong with your mom? Wedding getting to her?" Eric Prince held Katie close and inhaled the sweet scent of her freshly shampooed hair. "What did you do to upset her this time?" he joked.

Katie pushed away angrily. "Why is it always me? Can't she just have a bad day without it being my fault? Not everything's about me, y'know!"

"What? You're admitting it? Not everything's about you? Wow, this is a big day. Now stop being such a twit and give me a kiss so I can go to work a happy man."

Katie quickly kissed her fiancé and mumbled a half-hearted apology, one she didn't feel. The red words written across the RSVP card were there before her eyes, in her mind. A headache was beginning to form behind her eyes, a migraine she was sure. As soon as Eric had closed the front door behind him, she walked slowly to the back of the house, to her own bedroom.

The Spanish style home her parents had built in Garland, Texas, a suburb of Dallas, was a sprawling labyrinth of corridors, rooms, patios, and airy spaces. The cool tile floors were heavenly to bare feet in the heat of Texas summers. The only carpeting in the entire house was in the media room. Karl Power had made his money in movies as an investor and he still enjoyed entertaining friends with the movies in which his money had been returned over and over. Locally, he made a good living at what he liked to call "wildcatting," although it had absolutely nothing to do with oil. A passionately spiritual man, Karl had only two loves outside of his God. One was his wife of twenty five years, the former Homecoming Queen of South Garland High, Kristian Leigh Taylor Power. The second was his daughter, Katie, born Katherine Taylor Power on a gusty October night three years after his marriage to Kris. He still chuckled at the memory of how it had taken Katie three years to show up when everyone was sure he and Kris "had to get married" as they used to say when a girl was pregnant. Headstrong, confident, and scrawny, nerdy Karl Power had marched from the back of the classroom to ask the very beautiful, very popular, and very wealthy Kristian Taylor to the senior prom. The room fell into complete silence as every head turned to see how Kris would tell this geek to move along. But she didn't. She said yes, she would be delighted. Karl wasn't surprised. He'd loved Kris for two years and dreamed of her during every waking moment. With the whole class staring at them, he could do no more than say, "Good. I'll call you then." Nearly three hours later he realized he didn't have her phone number.

Born to a middle class family with four younger siblings, Karl had learned to fend for himself at a young age. His first job was delivering the *Dallas Morning News* on his bicycle seven days a week. From there he graduated to courtesy clerk at a local supermarket, and from there to fry cook at a fast food joint. After high school he enrolled in junior college and married Kris. Their first date seemed to have never ended and everyone was sure the beautiful Kris Taylor was pregnant when they married October 7th, four months after graduation. The whole town held its breath for nine months waiting for signs of a child for the newly-weds, but it was three full years, to the day, before their pink bundle of joy entered the world.

When Kris became pregnant, Karl dropped out of college and made his own way with a sharp mind, a keen investment sense, and the conviction that he would one day gain the approval of his wealthy father-in-law. Robert Taylor dropped dead of a heart attack long before Karl made the kind of money that would have impressed him, never knowing that it wasn't money that impressed Rob Taylor. It took something deeper, something Karl had possessed all along.

Now it was Katie's turn to marry. Everything seemed like a fairy tale for the perfect family living the dream life in suburbia. Until today. Katie lay across her large bed in the cool darkness of her room. Crying would aggravate the headache, so she lay as still as she could to prevent the pain from consuming her. Her resolve went unheeded. Tears streamed down the sides of her cheeks, pooling in her ears and spilling over onto her satin pillow sham. "God, why are you letting this happen?" she sobbed. "Why is Abby doing this? Why now? Why?" She finally drifted off into an exhausted sleep, never hearing the doorbell announcing another unwanted arrival.

Look for RSVP in 2009
from Bottom-Up Media Publishing
www.bottomupmedia.com